# A TABLE FOR US

# A Table for Us

A NOVEL

Nuzhat Shahzadi

Book design: Sara DeHaan

Publisher's Cataloging-in-Publication Data

Names: Shahzadi, Nuzhat, author.
Title: A table for us : a novel / Nuzhat Shahzadi.
Description: Fairfax, VA: Nuzhat Shahzadi, 2021.
Identifiers: Library of Congress Control Number: 2021918364 |
ISBN: 978-1-7353520-1-5 (paperback) |
ISBN 978-1-7353520-2-2 (ebook)
Subjects: LCSH Bengali Americans—Fiction. | Women—Fiction. |
Emigration and immigration—Fiction. | Anthropologists—Fiction. |
Cooks—Fiction. | Love stories. | BISAC FICTION / Romance /
Contemporary | FICTION / Own Voices | FICTION / Cultural Heritage |
FICTION / Women
Classification: LCC PS3619.H3493 T33 2021 | DDC 813.6—dc23

*To Izara*

A third generation immigrant to America
and to many others like her...

# Contents


*Preface*  ix

PART I. WASHINGTON D.C., SPRING 2015
(AND THE PAST)                                      1

  1.  On That Fiery Morning                        3

  2.  Truths Don't Lie                             15

  3.  Falling For You                              25

  4.  Up Close and Personal                        39

PART II. FIJI, 1987–1990                           57

  5.  Carry My Dreams As Your Own                  59

  6.  Grains of Sand . . . and the Land of Hibiscus   73

  7.  Storm                                        85

  8.  Wheels of Change                             91

  9.  Many Shades of Grief                        103

  10.  Pale Incense, Faded Colors                 111

PART III. WASHINGTON D.C., SPRING 2015
(CONTINUED)                                        119

  11.  Coffee and Cupcakes, Dusts of Cinnamon . . .   121

  12.  Beginning of a Romance                     135

13. Caramel Canapés with Cognac—
A Recipe for Catastrophe 147

14. Realization . . . Taking Stock 161

15. One Slice of Onion, Two Drops of Lemon,
a Whisper of Tears 169

16. You Are the Butter on My Bread 179

17. Doubts 195

18. A Pinch of Tajin, a Shot of Tequila, Lime
Juice for a Good Margarita and for the Soul 203

19. Encounters—Strange and Surprising 217

20. The Book—and Untold Stories 231

21. Shadows Grow Darker in the Scent of Pines 239

22. In a Time of Countless Losses and Wins 253

PART IV. STONY BROOK, 2017 267

23. You Know How I Feel 269

24. On Home Grounds—Mist of Coffee on a
Sparkling Dawn! 285

PART V. PORT JEFFERSON, SUMMER 2018 301

25. One Spoon of Lemon Zest, Two Counts
of Laughter 303

ANTONIO'S DREAM DINNER RECIPES
FOR OPSHORA 317

Acknowledgments 324
About the Author 326

# Preface

I am fascinated by the stories of immigrants to the United States of America.

While writing this book, I spoke with South Asian immigrants (Bengalees and Indians). Some are descendants of second or third generation Americans. Some were born in the U.S., some came with their parents as toddlers while some others arrived as teenagers for educational pursuits and eventually became Americans.

I had some meaningful discussions with Kenyan, Nigerian, Somali, Ethiopian, Chinese and Latino Americans, as well as Caucasian Americans.

Some immigrants worked in restaurants, retail stores, drove cabs while some others were in white collared jobs—doctors, scientists, researchers, academics, corporate executives, humanitarian workers and IT geniuses.

All their stories were equally appealing.

I also had the opportunity to speak heart-to-heart with Italian Immigrants. In my younger years, I lived in "Little Italy" Baltimore-downtown, in a 150-year-old house for two years. My elderly landlord, a second generation Italian-American shared amazing life-stories. At the time I didn't know that I would be writing this book more than a decade later.

The enormous richness of the experiences of immigrants trying to craft a life in their new homeland is captivating—each storyteller became bigger than life as s/he narrated about her/his incredible journey . . . Being an immigrant myself I could inhale the flavors of their lives through the snippets they shared with me.

I feel privileged for being able to understand and appreciate the diverse cultures, faiths, food, colors and scents and laughter and tears and sweat and unique styles that the immigrants brought to the U.S. as their legacies. Without them the beauty of white, red and blue in America could have been colorless . . .

Though a fiction, this book tries to capture the pride and pains of immigrants in becoming Americans—and of course their patriotism . . . I have tried my best to weave facts and fiction together and present my readers with an honest narrative.

Nuzhat Shahzadi<br>October 2021

# Part I.
## Washington, D.C.,
## Spring 2015 (and the past)

# CHAPTER ONE

# On That Fiery Morning

Opshora Mirza steps onto the immaculate green of the Rock Creek Park in Washington, D.C., in mid-morning. She searches for the perfect grassy spot to sit down with her laptop. The large, colorful kiondo bag hanging from her shoulder holds in its womb a labyrinth of necessities—a large cotton scarf to be used as a mat on the ground, a novel she has been repeat reading (*Love in the Time of Cholera* by Gabriel Garcia Marquez, an all-time favorite), a packet of pita crackers and a small bottle of cold Fiji water. She likes this brand as the producers claim that the water is bottled directly from a spring somewhere on the Pacific island country of Fiji. She had been to Fiji decades ago and loved the endless sound of the ocean, every minuscule fragment of the air that circled around mixed with the heady scent of frangipani and hibiscus, water lilies, coconut blossoms and the incessant salty sprays stewed in decayed seaweeds, breaking on the beaches all day long. It seems like many "light years" ago, at the time of her impossible youth—bursting with curiosity, passion and immense joyful energy to toss out in the cosmos—that she truly fell in love for the first time, in the real sense, in Fiji. It was as incredible as the colors of the waves of the Pacific Ocean that changed with the time of the day, rejuvenated by the sun and the brilliant moon and the million stars at dusk . . . and the many hues that embraced the lush landscape—quaint towns, hill slopes and villages.

Fiji was an ecstasy, an incurable encounter that took her by surprise, awakened her spirit. It also brought immeasurable heartaches, mountains of tears that became her shadow . . . as the years passed she learned to manage those memories.

Even today if she closes her eyes—living in D.C. in 2015, when her thoughts float back to the time she was in Fiji she is able to pick up its incense . . . the distant humming of local tunes, the noise of cars honking on busy streets . . . and the ecstatic ocean. The colors of Fiji never left her soul.

After all these years, she still questions her decision for going to Fiji. Was she right or very wrong? She didn't know then. She doesn't know now, but allows the past to lie in silence.

On this sunny morning, Opshora brushes away all qualms and is geared up to spend the entire day in the open under the deep, plush trees lingering over emerald patches spread all over the park. So far she hasn't been able to find the impeccable spot. The feng shui has to be harmonized in the right proportions to give her the desired mood and energy to complete the writing assignment she has been working on for days but with little success. A very initial draft must be ready for the meeting scheduled for next week. She is not even sure how feng shui works outdoors. She recently learned about this method from her aunt Leila, a nurse by profession but a staunch believer of alternative approaches to emotional wellbeing.

When her mind inevitably gets stuck, burdened under the ardor of intellectual meandering, Opshora has a back-up plan—to read a few pages of Garcia's novel. She reads this book as a savory, a brain elixir. Usually such a break proves to be beneficial and forces a quick recharging. The sparkling green of the park is already having an effect on her, uplifting her spirit even amidst the strain of temporary creative paralysis.

It's only the end of May but the summer sun is already fiery. It's beating down hard, merciless. Spring had been much warmer this year. Thin beads of sweat trickle slowly downwards along her spine under the soft, thin black top she is wearing over a vibrant floral skirt that stops short of her ankles, baring her painted toes entrapped in leather strapped sandals.

She detects a near unspoiled area surrounded by lanky trees close to the creek. She can almost smell the freshness of the gurgling water. The only obstacle is a man reclining on a nearby wooden bench only a few feet away from her coveted site exhaling out smoke like a chimney in fire, of all things. The stench of his cigarette annoys her and invades the peaceful landscape. She involuntarily wrinkles her nose, moves away nearer to the water's edge. People who knowingly contribute so actively to their own gradual self-annihilation amaze her. They blow their chances to be healthy in meaningless smokes. But the man is an immediate reality now. In any case, she has to do the best under the circumstances and prays silently for his rapid departure. The sun is hitting him with sharp rays, and she hopes the heat may drive him away soon.

Opshora settles on the ground with her kiondo. Though the sudden meager breeze constantly threatens to take away the modest cover of the branches, she is resigned to the interruptions.

She sits comfortably, crossed-legged on the cloth spread on the grass. All set now. She hits the keyboard of her laptop. Ideas begin to cram into her brain as she labors away totally oblivious to her surroundings.

She isn't aware that the man has been watching her every move. She looks up at a slight sound, still lost in thought. She discovers him standing on her turf suddenly—towering over her but careful not to step on the scarf. A white male in his mid-forties possibly, standing tall—light stubble on his chin, thick eyebrows, mud-colored eyes, sandy hair, a sturdy body with a slightly protruding middle under his tucked grey-checked limp shirt worn over a pair of much-used blue faded denims. In the flash of a second her now-alert mind takes in the details, as much as possible. He definitely looks tired, perhaps somewhat jittery, she concludes, observing his rigid countenance and unsmiling eyes.

"I don't usually smoke. Only when I am sorting out the mess in my brain . . . I need a puff," he says, somewhat hesitant. He must have noticed her spontaneous reaction to his cigarette while in passing.

"It's not pot. I swear," he adds earnestly to reassure her. Opshora doesn't think she has betrayed any traces of fear. However, she is at a loss. Uncharacteristically, she struggles to find suitable words. The man waits, watching her and then throws the cigarette on the grass.

"See?" He crushes the cigarette with the heel of his right shoe. Is this a juvenile attempt to impress her?

"I feel nothing. I can do without it," he stands there in perplexed uncertainty mixed with a hint of a boast for aptly sacrificing his cigarette. Opshora doesn't take her eyes off him.

"I usually don't smoke. Gave up some years ago . . . only puff it when too much pressure. On and off... Something like... you... sometimes crawl back to your ex in low moments, in desperation," his voice trails off, smothered in hesitation.

Why is he so needy for her approval, she wonders and smiles involuntarily, not because she is amused but to impress she isn't affected. At the same time in quick seconds Opshora tries to calculate the immediate risks. She doesn't spot anyone nearby. The park is lonely in its own greenery. It's not certain he poses any kind of safety threat but it's indeed a strange encounter with a total stranger.

Surprisingly, he reciprocates and smiles back. A sudden

flash of his sparkling teeth transforms his face. The sternness vanishes. He looks friendlier.

"I see . . . thanks," she manages, finally.

"For what?" he asks, confused.

"For the explanation. Want to sit down?" She almost bites her tongue, as the words escape her—she doesn't know why she invited him into her private universe. Instantly he takes off his shoes and lands on the mark where the grass and the cloth meet, relieved.

"Antonio. Antonio Russo. Chef. Italian. Not a bad guy," he extends his right hand.

"Opshora Mirza. Anthropologist. Writer. One hundred percent a good girl, I believe," she says in an even tone matching his. Both laugh. And shake hands.

His grip is warm and firm as he takes her hand and bows his head in courtesy. The old smile returns, spreading up to his eyes this time. She likes it.

"Interesting name. Challenging—sort of," he muses.

"Op shora . . . begin with 'awe' the way you say it in awesome . . . that's how you have to say it."

"Op shora . . . awesome . . . hmmm . . ." he repeats after her. "Indian?"

"No. I am a Bengalee. But once upon a time my ancestors were known as Indians—not Native Americans, though. South Asian descent." Opshora adds, non-committal.

They begin with polite observations about not-so-important matters and successfully sabotage the possibility of any immediate awkward silence. They try out the names of the plants around them after the initial ice breaking. Antonio picks up an easy subject after that and tells her how his forefathers had migrated to the U.S., generations ago. He is quite pleasant to talk to, surprisingly.

"Being an Italian American hasn't been easy. Not for my folks initially," he affirms. "Not sure about you though . . . did you grow up here?"

"I've had my ups and downs . . . still do. Yes, I was born here," Opshora says.

"My great-grandparents came to this land for better opportunities. In the early 1880s, I am told. To be free."

"Are you?" she asks

"What?" He is puzzled but one look at her face and he understands what she means. "Hmm . . . interesting life here . . . for us like other immigrants. There have been many phases, many steps of becoming an American . . . integration, for sure!" he confesses, somewhat thoughtfully. "However, we maintain our own independence—the Italian kind. You know what I mean." His gaze doesn't waver from Opshora's face.

"I can understand . . . agonies of minorities," Opshora reaffirms.

"You are an anthropologist. You know the history of Italian migrants to this country. I grew up with my forefathers' stories . . . listening to the same ones over and over again. At every family gathering! Italians can't let go. Fifth generation—Italian-American," he continues much more at ease now.

"We are no different," Opshora agrees as flashes of similar scenes cross through her mind—endless story telling with many interruptions over countless large family meals. "Asians can't let go either."

The conversation becomes more comfortable. Antonio has Opshora's full attention as he elaborates on the historical background that propelled his ancestors to search for a new homeland. Though Opshora knows much of it, Antonio's personal touch makes the narrative much more appealing. He himself is somewhat astonished at his ability to open up to the woman he met only a few minutes ago. It is quite unusual for him, he is aware of that. With strangers he usually stammers or gaffes, often.

Opshora interjects politely as the discussion flows, but mostly enjoys his storytelling style, his perspectives. He is spontaneous though somewhat wrapped up in his own world-views—maybe a loner, probably hungry for a listener and he has captured her attention.

Antonio runs a restaurant in downtown D.C. on 23rd Street. "It is a family business. My younger brother, married sister with her husband and parents pitch in energy and finances."

He is proud of his expertise as a connoisseur of luscious Italian concoctions. He makes quite an impression on Opshora with his passion for culinary accomplishments. He doesn't talk particularly much about himself, per se.

"Columbus was an Italian," he adds proudly, at one point.

"History claims he didn't discover America, though," she puts in with a grin and they both laugh out aloud.

"He brought syphilis back home, I am told," he adds. "Italians are romantics."

She likes his slight accent, especially as he pronounces the 'r' with extra strength. It gives his words added character.

"You speak perfect English," Antonio looks at her with admiration.

"I was born here," she says.

"So was I. But my family speaks lots and lots of Italian. And eats bowls and bowls of pasta. We speak English in our own ways—mainly for business purposes . . . and when we discuss important issues. We love to swear in our native tongue, though." He somewhat comically makes a gesture of throwing his hands up in the air. They laugh again.

"At first glance, I actually thought you were a Latina," his eyes linger on her face.

"Some inter-marriages, possibly . . . untraceable . . . And my generation is the finished product, I guess."

"So, what do you do?" He is genuinely curious now.

"I write . . ."

"What kind of writing?" Antonio leans forward. He is curious to know more.

"Research Proposals. Report writing. Free-lance consultancies. I do creative writing as well." Opshora adds.

"You sound pretty talented!" Admiration is echoed in Antonio's voice. Opshora smiles.

"Not really," Opshora doesn't like to brag about herself. "And. . . I run a small boutique store on 17th Street in partnership with a friend. I also teach sometimes."

"Wow! Good mix." Antonio gives out a soft whistle now. "You are from this neighborhood?"

"I live in Arlington. Only fifteen minutes walk from the edge of Georgetown."

"You like living there?" he wants to know.

"It's kind of nice. Right kind of mix of the suburb and the city . . . I like the easy commute from my place to D.C.," she adds thoughtfully.

She doesn't mention that she has been living in the same house since birth when her parents had moved into that neighborhood. She lived away from them for some years but eventually returned. Lots happened in between . . .

"I enjoy living downtown as well. City life makes sense," he says in a matter of fact voice. "Any siblings?" His curiosity isn't yet satiated.

"One brother. Married. He has two lovely, annoyingly curious kids. Nine and eleven."

After thirty seconds of silence she suddenly says, "I also have my aunt. Her house is in Georgetown . . . And I have many more blood relatives spread all over America." She is not quite sure why she volunteered so much additional information.

"Are you married?" He is straightforward.

"Hey—you don't get to ask that! Impolite!" Her reaction is a mix of some seriousness and mock shock. Surprisingly, she isn't offended—she would have been under any other circumstances.

"I am Italian. We are famous for being direct." His gaze

is solemn and searches her face. "I am not married. Not any-more. See, no ring." He extends his left hand for her to see. "No harm in speaking the truth."

"You are so clueless . . . " She laughs in the strength of the unpretentious familiarity they have been sharing so far. They have been talking for almost thirty minutes in the comfort of the grassy spot.

"Italians do not want to lose time walking in a maze. They speak from the heart. No waltzing around when interest is stirred . . . " Antonio places both his hands on his heart, in ardent demonstration to match his words.

"Yeah?"

"Yeah. We have too much love in our hearts. Especially men," he adds sincerely, eyes filled with laughter. "It breaks easily, always. Hurts us . . . often beyond repair."

"Yours got broken?" she asks in jest.

"Yes. Many times. Each time worse than the other," he winks.

"You are not serious?" Surprisingly she finds it easy to tease him.

"You need to know me more to judge that," he teases back. "What about dinner tomorrow night?" His invitation sounds genuine.

"What? No! You hardly know me!" Opshora is totally unprepared for this.

"How can I know you unless you agree?" Antonio's voice sounds sincere.

"I don't have dinner with strangers. Rule number one for me," she stresses in a somewhat serious note.

"After dinner I won't be a stranger. That's a promise."

She is at a loss for words.

"What about lunch?" He is not yet ready to give up.

"I don't think it's a good idea." She still hesitates though somewhat flattered now.

"Coffee? Please?" he asks again. "It's 2015—what are you

afraid of? Coffee? Or me?" Some laughter is back in his tone now. "I don't bite . . . cross my heart. I may now look like the Trump of disaster land . . . but I swear I am far, far better, usually." They both laugh, again.

"Don't tell me...Donald Trump is running for presidency," Opshora can't help saying.

"You can never tell with that guy. Too much tan, too much wig or hair, too much theatrics . . . Let's not get distracted now . . . What about my petition? I am waiting for your vote for our coffee rendezvous." Antonio is almost comical. In a futile effort, Opshora mentally searches for a stronger plausible excuse but is unable to come up with something credible. She could refuse him, of course. Strangely, she doesn't want to.

"My free time is only tomorrow. Don't make me wait one week to ask you again," he pleads now—while she hesitates, still.

"Okay. Coffee," she agrees, finally, somewhat halfheartedly. Antonio looks quite decent and is amusing, no doubt. And a cup of coffee can't be risky. It may actually be fun to make a new friend, especially the sentimental kind. She toys with the idea.

He mentions that weekends are his busiest times. The restaurant is literally mobbed by customers. The waiting list of food lovers becomes a hazard from early evenings. His off days from work are only Tuesdays. That's tomorrow.

"Our place is called 'Pasta Paradiso.' We also make heavenly pizza. You must try our pizza. It's the best in America . . . The taste will travel from your stomach to the heart and reign there forever." Antonio offers in seriousness.

"Why is it the best?" Opshora isn't hundred percent sold on Antonio's proclamation.

"Because we use the original recipe from my great, great grandmother. She brought her secret recipe with her to this country when she migrated from Italy," he says with pride. With that he makes a dent in her doubts.

"Okay. Let's have coffee first."

"Don't like Starbucks. Too noisy! Let's meet at DuPont Circle Park at 5 pm . . . I will walk you to a tiny, cozy coffee joint. What do you say?" he suggests. She nods. No harm in trying out a new café.

He looks at his watch and jumps up. Quickly pushes his feet in his shoes, shakes the dead leaves and dry grass from his pants with one hand, and at the same time smooths his hair with the other hand.

"My extended lunch break and stress recovery time almost over. Got to go back now. So glad business is slower than usual today," he tosses his pleasant smile once more back at her. "Don't look at me like that! I will never be able to go."

"What look?" Opshora doesn't fall for it.

"Don't tell me this comes naturally to you," his teasing look lingers on her face. She shrugs it away. At the last minute they exchange phone numbers. Opshora is shocked at her own forwardness.

"I hardly pick up calls on my phone . . ." she tries to justify to herself with a shrug.

"You are going to pick up mine," he says with confidence. "Bye for now. Addio."

"Addio," she says after him. It sounds sweet.

He walks away. Before he gets swallowed in the bend among low lying branches, he looks back and presses his hands to his lips blowing a flying kiss towards her. She laughs at his gallantry and waves back. She is highly amused.

"Interesting fellow," she mumbles to herself, flattered, definitely.

# CHAPTER TWO

## *Truths Don't Lie*

Opshora's residence is on the top floor of her building, made up of two spacious rooms with large bay windows, a full bathroom, and a tiny kitchenette that serves as a sparse dining space, totally independent from her parents' abode below that has two levels—the first and the second floors. She uses the spiral stairs from outside to access her rooms without alerting them. There is a connecting door inside that joins her domain with her parents' but she keeps it firmly locked. It suits her to be close to them but also have separation from their well-meant, love-laden scrutiny, assistance and dictation. As teenagers, Opshora and her brother had used this separate space to study and hang out with friends without disturbing their parents. Though she offered to pay rent when she moved into the unit, her parents refused to accept. Culturally, it's improper—one can't accept rent-money from one's own children.

There is a story behind how she became who she is today. She had her share of ups and downs, struggles and rewards . . . she believes that though a person attempts to craft her or his own life, destiny commands the final shots, makes the ultimate call. In many ways, her life followed that same pattern.

Opshora Mirza was born to her parents Mohammed Akhlaq Mirza and Rubina Mirza—generally known as "Ruby." Both eventually became naturalized U.S. citizens. Mirza adopted the name MD Mirza because his first name gave him trouble from when he first arrived in the U.S. to study medicine in 1950 at the age of nineteen. Decades later this proved to be a smart strategy as hostility toward people of the Muslim faith escalated with the tragedy of 9/11. Even as American citizens, people of his faith were branded as "terrorists"—though they had no connection with the horrific tragedy that paralyzed the country and the world. MD Mirza and many like him who led honorable lives in the U.S., and contributed loyally in every possible way, who had nothing to do with the mindless violence of 9/11, found themselves on the wrong side of "patriotism." The tragedy tried to define them.

Back at home, he was known as "Akhlaq" as almost every Muslim male has "Mohammed" as the first name. He congratulated himself for shortening "Mohammed" into "MD" which people assumed to be a proclamation of his medical degree. It suited him and served his purpose. In line for coffee or a snack at the deli, his new name didn't turn heads when called out loudly by the store employee . . . He was always "MD" and almost invisible in the multi-cultural milieu.

His ancestors were originally from Lucknow, India. They were wealthy and belonged to nobility. Urdu was spoken at home but MD Mirza and his older brother were well versed in Bangla—they grew up with children from scholarly Hindu Bengalee families. The Mirza family moved to Dhaka during the partition of India and Pakistan in 1947 to escape communal riots. Geographical borders were drawn creating separate homelands for Hindus and Muslims. He and his brother both ended up in the U.S. to pursue higher education in the medical field. The brothers were born only a year apart. They got their medical degrees with flying colors as expected and stayed in the U.S. to advance their lives.

At eighteen, right after finishing her higher secondary education, equivalent to 12th grade, Ruby came to the U.S. on a visiting visa to see her sister Leila in Washington, D.C. Her family was from a small border town—sandwiched between India and east Bengal, known as East Pakistan at the time.

Leila, eight years older than Ruby, was working as a nurse in the U.S. and was married to the older Mirza brother, Dr. Mohammed Kahliq Mirza. The initial plan was for Ruby to help Leila with her three boys. The oldest was three, followed by the middle son who was two and the youngest barely ten months old.

On a cold, rainy, wind-swept day in 1962, Ruby landed at the Idlewild Airport in New York. It was a long journey but she was too excited to be tired. Leila was waiting for her right after Ruby came out of the exit door. The sisters hadn't seen each other for over two years. The last time Leila had visited with her family was after the birth of her first baby.

"D.C. weather is very much like ours. Rains a lot in summer . . . gets hot and humid. Thunderstorms are pretty regular. But winters can be real cold," Leila informed her as they walked to the parking lot. Everything was new for Ruby. She was overwhelmed, mesmerized. "We will drive to Dr. Mirza's friend's house and stay for the night to rest. Tomorrow morning, we drive to D.C."

"You learned to drive!" Ruby was charmed.

Leila nodded affectionately. "In this country, everyone drives. It's a necessity."

"Is this your car?" Surprise after surprise. Ruby was elated. What a beautiful car! Deep crimson. Suited her sister's vivacious personality. "Did *dulabhai* buy it for you?"

"I bought it with my own money. Dr. Mirza has his own car. Bought with his own money," Leila added with a smile, emphasizing the word "own." Ruby smiled back. She was learning a lot. Life was very different here. She felt so naïve. She knew her brother-in-law was wealthy. And that he was a doctor in America. But her sister seemed to be equally rich to have bought such a trendy red car with her earnings.

"So many foreigners here, apa!" she somehow managed to utter as she watched a stream of white people speeding past on the sidewalks.

"Where . . . ?" Leila followed her eyes as she efficiently maneuvered the car in traffic, and understood. "Oh, these are Americans . . . citizens of this country. About eighty percent of the population is white," she corrected her sister, laughing. Ruby blushed to the roots of her hair but heartily joined in the laughter. Back at home any white person was a foreigner. She had never met one. She watched them on television programs.

"*Kaala Manush* (black people) were slaves here, apa . . . I read about them." Ruby tried to rescue her tarnished lack of knowledge.

"Yes. Very sad stories about them in this country. They are still fighting for their rights . . . the civil rights movement is continuing. People like us also face many problems here," Leila kept orienting her sister.

"Why is that, apa?"

"Because we are not white. We are minorities. We go about minding our own business . . . some people don't like us. But don't be afraid. We live in a nice city. The capital. People are friendly. It's very safe," Leila added quickly, noticing the fear-filled frown on Ruby's face. "There are good people and bad ones in every society. Remember how the police killed the students in our language movement protests? Because they fought to protect our right to speak our mother tongue." Ruby nodded. Every Bengalee who grew up in East Bengal, or East Pakistan, learned about the "21 February martyrdom" of students.

"America fought the world wars to defend global democracy but so many problems here," Leila added to Ruby's amazement. Leila sounded almost like a pundit—her sister had acquired so much wisdom after coming to America!

When she landed, Ruby thought this country looked so right, so proper—clean, nice and friendly. She remembered the smiles she got from so many white folks while she passed through immigration and stepped inside the airport. She couldn't believe cruelty existed in such a heavenly place. With time, she learned more about inequality in America.

Leila and Dr. Mirza lived in Georgetown. Only a handful of non-white people owned properties in that beautiful town. It wasn't easy to buy the house. Georgetown was a black city within a white community. Segregation and zoning restrictions eventually saw the end of "Black Georgetown." A patient of Dr. Mirza, an elderly Irish-American real estate agent, helped him in purchasing the property. Dr. Mirza paid in full cash so his offer couldn't be thwarted. They were a wealthy young couple—Leila and Dr. Mirza, medical professionals and less "black." Both of them worked in a hospital in downtown D.C.—they liked Georgetown and the commute was easy from their new home.

Next day Ruby was only too happy to arrive in Georgetown and immediately fell in love with Leila's house, the beautiful town and her three nephews. Having met Dr. Mirza briefly only once in the past, she felt shy with him. Leila had taken the week off to help Ruby find her feet in a new place. She got a beautiful room with a great view. She could see the outline of narrow streets and the aristocratic houses of the quaint town. The bed was so soft, the sheets so smooth and silky that she was afraid of spoiling it. Very carefully she had climbed into bed and was lost for hours under the warmth of the comforter. She slept almost eighteen hours.

On the second evening, there was a guest for dinner.

"This is my brother-in-law. The younger brother . . . He is also a doctor," Leila introduced him. That was the first time Ruby met MD Mirza. Leila's marriage to the older Mirza brother was a scrambled event due to his parents' strong disapproval. The usual processes and rituals of a Bengalee wedding weren't followed. It was sort of a "shotgun" business that took place quickly in Dhaka at a relative's house, away from their hometown. So Ruby didn't get to meet MD Mirza in that chaos, though she attended the event with her family.

Thousands of miles away from home, Ruby embraced her new life. She adored her three nephews, loved Leila's house and the beautiful Georgetown. She was happy that she could help her sister in looking after her boys. Life couldn't be better for her at eighteen. Not a single friend she had back at home had travelled so far into a new universe!

After the first few days passed, the initial excitement of living in a foreign land began to sink in. Ruby felt isolated and overwhelmed in Leila's household looking after three babies with little skills as a caregiver. They were demanding and constantly needed to be watched or fed or cleaned. She was young and struggled with the uprooting from her known world, the comfort of her mother's loving arms in this new, strange place. Leila and Dr. Mirza kept extremely busy schedules in the hospital and slept most of the time when they were home, off duty. Leila was completely exhausted after the consequent births of three children and her workload. They had hired a cleaning lady who came twice a week and also did laundry. For meals they were mostly dependent on take-away menus from local restaurants. At least Ruby didn't have to do household chores.

But Ruby had no break. She was like a fish out of water, cooped up indoors with the pressures of caring for three babies. Leila and her husband were affectionate and tried to make things easy for her as much as they could. They bought a large television and stereo set, books and magazines so that she could be entertained at home but the babies never had a synchronized sleeping pattern. One or the other was always up. Whenever she could manage, Leila made efforts to take her sister to the local market or mall or to the park, but the three kids constantly tugged along. So it was never full respite from her chores.

Ruby was intensely fatigued, sleep-deprived, depressed and lonely. She missed her parents, her three brothers, their families and school friends. She was cautious not to show her distress as she genuinely loved her sister and understood her own role in Leila's household. Though Ruby wanted to escape from this adoring imprisonment, she did her best to spare Leila in every possible way from suspecting the truth. Her intention was to be a rock of support, as instructed by her parents when she was sent to the U.S.

"Sisters are like rivers . . . they separate after they are married. They flow in their own individual directions. You are lucky that Leila wants you to be near her. Make the best of it," were her mother's parting words.

In Bengal, women were not masters of their destiny. Their husbands and families decided when and where they should be, their roles and responsibilities. Seldom could they make their own choices. Meeting among sisters was a rarity, especially if they were married away in far flung places.

MD Mirza lived close by and it was customary for him to visit on weekends. Often he brought food and ice cream for everyone. Some days he helped with cooking and doing dishes with the women. He also volunteered to watch over his nephews while Ruby took a nap or went out for a walk in the park around the corner. If Leila was up to it, she joined her while the two brothers stayed home to talk and watch a game on TV over cold beer while monitoring the boys. They had no qualms about alcoholic drinks—as long as it didn't form into an addiction. That's how they interpreted the writings in the Holy Book—mixing of faith with alcohol.

MD Mirza liked to be around Ruby. It was gratifying when she smiled at him, thanked him for his assistance with the boys or took a second helping of the pistachio ice cream he had brought especially with her in mind. He made sure he never missed the flavors she loved. He felt a tug in his heart when he was with her and not with her. He soon started coming over on weekdays either during lunchtime or on his way home from the office, mostly when Ruby was by herself. She didn't mind. He had a good Chinese friend and co-worker who stood in for him on those extended hours of absences from the office.

With Ruby, MD Mirza had picnics in the backyard lawn or in the nearby park pushing the boys in the stroller on warm summer days. The children behaved very well as they were fond of the outings. She talked mostly while he listened. With him she found it easy to be herself. There were too many things that daily got stored up in her mind. She had no one to share them with. She never thought life could be so lonely, so friendless. MD Mirza was the only one within proximity in her new, isolated world. He was her only listener . . .

"You know . . . in my small town we have so many flowers. In America, flowers don't have much scent," Ruby remarked while she sniffed flowers randomly, blossoming in abundance in the park. MD Mirza agreed without any hesitancy. He immediately vowed silently to bring lilies for Ruby on his next visit, which he did. His heart hung on the smile that played on her lips as she inhaled the fragrance of the fresh lilies.

They ate hot dogs and potato chips under the trees while the three boys drowsed. The soft grass cradled Ruby's curvy body as she half reclined against a tree, her tiny toes sticking out. MD Mirza couldn't look away . . . his eyes feasted on every detail of beauty that this young woman unconsciously lavished him with. His heart obsessed with every trifle she uttered. He couldn't stay away from her. The thought of Ruby consumed him. He realized he had fallen in love. His methodical, scientific mind was swayed in absurd emotions he thought he wasn't capable of feeling.

Ruby also began to immensely enjoy her outings in the park. The void in her life was lessened, somehow. As the friendship began to mature, gradually her world of loneliness faded away. Her liking for him developed, crystalized firm. Ruby missed his absences, was animated and happy in his presence.

"Do you like cappuccino?" MD Mirza asked her while they pushed the stroller in the park as the whiff of freshly brewed coffee hit them from the near-by cafes. The three boys were peacefully asleep. The motion had helped.

"What is cappuccino?" Ruby never heard of it. She was getting introduced to so many new things in America.

"You must try cappuccino. We will make sure to take you to the best place for that—and soon!" MD Mirza promised.

The small town from where she came didn't have much modern amenities. "We don't have hot dogs, or pizza or sandwich sold anywhere in our town." Ruby smiled. "You know, pasta is called noodles back at home. I ate it only once. I liked it . . . I have tried so many different kinds of food here. My mother knows to cook only Bengalee food. We eat that without tiring—breakfast, lunch and dinner." She smiled again, her face stained with sudden sadness. "I miss her cooking."

In her hometown there weren't any proper eateries. Only a couple of small roadside restaurants with rickety chairs and tables that catered mainly to the men. Take away meals were for women who usually enjoyed the food at home. MD Mirza was very touched as Ruby described the life she had left behind. He understood the emotional ordeal of this young woman and tried to divert her thoughts. His heart was full of affection for Ruby.

# CHAPTER THREE

# Falling For You

MD Mirza planned a proper outing with Ruby. He requested to borrow Dr. Mirza's car, which had enough space to accommodate the babies. The boys would always accompany Ruby if she were to go out.

"So, what's happening, I wonder. They are going on an outing?" Leila was curious and somewhat amused as she asked her husband.

"Yeah . . . some pizza place downtown," Dr. Mirza continued to smoke his pipe as he browsed through a medical journal in bed, almost ready for the night. "He can show her around a bit. An outing would be good for Ruby. She has no friends, doesn't know anyone."

Leila left it at that but her feminine instincts picked up something. She brushed it aside—maybe she was seeing more than there was in their harmless association.

As the days progressed, Ruby discovered the decent, cultured mind of MD Mirza and appreciated his empathy. She had always dreamed of a prince, who would touch her life and make her fall in love. Someone in the image of the handsome Soumitra Chaterjee, the Bengalee film star of the time from Kolkata. Or Peter O'Toole, Cary Grant, and the Hollywood film icons from the movies she had watched on rare occasions back at home played in the one and only stuffy, humid cinema hall. Instead, it was the man with a medium height, small frame, intelligent deep-set eyes. The somewhat introverted MD Mirza with his disarming smile captivated her heart. She detected his sincerity and his massive love for her. A very great deviation indeed from the dreams she had in her girlish, young heart concerning her romantic heroes!

The baby-sitting arrangement worked quite well for the first six months, but after that Ruby and MD Mirza declared that they had fallen in love and wanted to marry. At the time he had joined a private practice with a group of fellow doctors and was ready to take a wife. It was pure destiny—that is what Ruby thought . . .

MD Mirza, at thirty-one, with a receding hairline and a muted, bulging tummy hidden with connoisseur tact under his tucked-in shirt, realized it was a stroke of good luck to be able to win Ruby's heart. The possibility of starting his own family with a woman from a similar culture and faith whom he had found in the U.S. at his own brother's doorstep so easily was beyond his expectation. In those days, not many people from his ethnic heritage resided in foreign countries. Age difference with Ruby wasn't a major hindrance, a fact to deter him. As a husband he considered this an advantage to getting the opportunity to influence and build up the still developing mind of a young spouse to his own dogma about life. Both he and his brother upheld progressive ideas that included recognition of women's rights and freedom of religion as well as equality for all races.

He liked Ruby the first day he met her—thirteen years younger than him, practical, pleasant, with large dark eyes set on a delightful face with a squarish sort of jawline. Her curly, unruly dense long hair gave her looks an extra edge. At eighteen, without even trying she stole his heart. Finding Ruby saved him the added irksome labor of searching for a bride, trying to appease an endless entourage of cousins, friends and parental well-wishers back in his home town. His prize was offered to him on a platter instead.

"Do you really want to marry him? Thought clearly about it? He is so much older, Ruby!" Leila wanted to be sure. She wasn't discouraging, but rather protective of her naïve younger sister.

"I know . . . But I want this, Leila *apa,*" Ruby had responded, her eyes fixed on the floor, voice firm. "He makes me happy." She was too shy to openly admit her love for MD Mirza to her sister, so much older than her and who was also her local guardian. Ruby was uncomfortable.

In those times in the Bengalee culture, a frank discussion on romantic associations with an older sibling was considered immodesty. But she had to speak out. Back at home she could have enlisted the assistance of a brother's wife or a friend to break the ice. In this distant land she had to stand up for herself. She knew Leila would give the news to their parents in a way that wouldn't paint her as shameless for having talked about her upcoming marriage so openly. Ruby knew her sister loved her and would try to shield her from harm. Leila's concerns came from a position of love.

Leila detected the brilliance in Ruby's eyes when she looked up, the blush that crept on her cheeks, waiting in anticipation for Leila's blessings.

"If you are happy, I am fine with it," Leila read the signs and gave her consent. She wanted the best for her little sister. She knew her brother-in-law very well; he was a decent, pleasant young man who would take good care of Ruby.

"Are you upset with me, *apa*?" Ruby wanted to make sure. She wasn't here to create trouble.

"No . . . no. I want the best for you . . . you are so young. But I am glad that we would be living near by." Leila didn't want to dampen Ruby's hopes. Her marriage with the older Mirza was a happy one. She was fond of the younger Mirza. He was a man of principles, enough to keep Ruby comfortable.

The blessings from Ruby's parents and good wishes from her three older brothers were instant. They considered Ruby fortunate to bag such a deserving husband at no effort and cost to them. He was a catch, no doubt. They couldn't attend the wedding but after six months were able to send her a gold necklace that once belonged to their paternal grandmother, and a newly bought diamond and emerald studded bracelet as wedding gifts.

For her husband they sent an expensive Rolex wristwatch that MD Mirza treasured and wore with pride for many years. He missed the bonding with Ruby's family. Except for Leila, he didn't get to know them at all.

Leila was also pleased to have found a good match for Ruby minus any hurdles. All her doubts were put to rest. The prospect of having her sister close by was a great comfort. Her own marriage to Kahliq Mirza was much opposed by his family, as she was a nursing student at the Dhaka medical college when they met while he was on vacation from the U.S. looking for a prospective bride. They fell in love instantly and after a hard battle with his family they were able to tie the knot. She followed him to the U.S. a few months later with her nursing degree completed. The parents-in-law, however, didn't object to Ruby, neither did they rejoice. They were resigned to their fate in stoic reserve based on their earlier experience—accepted that they wouldn't be given the scope to choose the wife of their younger son as well.

When Ruby agreed to marry MD, she did it because she genuinely wanted to be with him, not to escape from her existing situation. Throughout her life Ruby never regretted her decision. The gentle caring MD Mirza became bigger in real life—much more than all the film stars she fancied, combined.

Ruby's and MD Mirza's wedding was attended by a handful of co-workers and friends of the Mirza brothers and Leila. They had no relatives in the U.S. Ruby knew no one outside the family. She became a bride without any friends to share her joys and anxieties with . . . she needed moral courage, some tips about what to expect in married life. MD Mirza was the only man she knew in reality. She had never had a boyfriend, no boys as friends—it was unheard of in the conventional society she was born in. Leila tried her best to be of assistance but Ruby was shy about voicing her thoughts to a sister who was so much older.

A religious ceremony was hosted by Leila and Dr. Mirza at their home, presided over by an Ethiopian-American imam from a community mosque in downtown D.C. The same day after the ceremony, the couple had their civil marriage to conform with the law of the land. The next day Ruby applied to the immigration office for a spousal visa.

Initially, the newlyweds lived with Leila while they went house hunting. Ruby didn't want to be too far away as she still wanted to help with her nephews—till Leila could find a good alternative for the care of the boys. Eventually, the couple bought a house in Arlington, about five miles from Leila's, and moved out. By that time Ruby was already pregnant with their first born, Robin. Leila found a credible day care center close to her hospital for the boys, to the relief of everyone.

The house in Arlington was big, comfortable and just a few miles away from downtown. The neighbors were predominantly white. MD Mirza, as a wealthy man, could afford a house in that affluent neighborhood. Free of babysitting responsibilities, Ruby now had plenty of time to soak in her new life and craft it the way she wanted. It was the first time she was away from Leila's protective presence and of course from her family where she was always treated as the youngest and expected to be voiceless. Her role was to listen and follow the wisdom (or foolhardiness) passed on by the others older than her.

She watched her neighbors coming and going but no one knocked at her door with a welcoming gesture. She was very surprised. In her hometown it was a different story. People flocked to a new neighbor's house to make friends and to curb their curiosities about the new comers. It didn't happen here!

Language proved to be a big barrier for Ruby. She had started to learn English in earnest months before they moved. MD Mirza had bought a set of tapes. She listened and practiced as much as she could. She began walking to the nearby grocery stores at odd hours when there were fewer customers and struck up conversations with the staff in her broken English, usually inquiring about a product. They were friendly, mostly people of color like her. Ruby felt less inhibited.

One day while returning home with a bag of groceries, very pregnant, she bumped into Mrs. Linda Jones. The elderly woman and her husband lived in the picturesque house across the street that had a bright royal blue painted fence. Ruby had seen the couple sometimes in passing while they lazed in sun-chairs in their charming front lawn. Out of shyness, she avoided looking directly at them or greeting them. She wasn't sure whether it was okay to do so.

"Hello, I am Linda," Mrs. Jones extended her hand with a smile. Ruby had to put down her grocery bags in order to free her hands.

"There, there, let me help you first." Mrs. Jones assisted Ruby with the bags that she had clumsily dumped.

"Ruby . . . my name is Ruby," Ruby said with a shy smile as she shook hands with Mrs. Jones. Perspiration formed around her face. She was nervous, bashfully awkward. Ruby had never touched the hands of a white person before.

"I have watched you from my porch. Welcome to our neighborhood, Ruby. We wanted to meet you but Mark, my husband, was recovering from pneumonia. So we waited." She came inside the house following Ruby.

"What a beautiful home!" Ruby blushed at the compliment from Linda.

Ruby had taken pains to decorate the house with indoor plants and handicrafts she carefully picked from Georgetown boutique stores. MD Mirza just accompanied her and paid the bills. The picks were all hers. Leila had praised Ruby's artistic taste. Now a total stranger, a white woman, validated it!

Linda was the first white woman Ruby had ever talked to. In the stores she always chose non-white staff to practice her English. She didn't want to make a mistake with the language or mispronounce any words with a white person.

Ruby offered homemade lemonade and cookies to Linda, following the Asian custom to always offer some food and drink to visitors. Linda was the first visitor in their house apart from Leila and her family. MD Mirza was planning to invite some co-workers for a housewarming, which she thought was to bless their home, as was the tradition in her hometown. But because of Ruby's advanced pregnancy that hadn't happened.

The women sat down and talked a bit. Linda's kind smile reminded Ruby of her own mother whom she missed every moment, more so as she got pregnant. Linda understood Ruby's hesitation, bashfulness. So she asked questions to make her comfortable and continue the conversation. They were simple ones, easy for Ruby to answer with her fledgling language skills.

"I cannot call you by your name. I cannot! You are like my mother . . . in age . . . It is like insult to you," Ruby said at one point. She spoke slowly, somehow conveyed her dilemma.

"Okay. You can call me Mrs. Jones," Linda smiled gently. "Or you can call me aunty Linda if you want to. I would love that, Ruby."

Robin was born nine months after the marriage, a month after Ruby's nineteenth birthday. Opshora was born exactly a year after Robin. MD Mirza was keen to have a family without much delay. The same year, 1964, the Civil Rights Act was passed putting an end to the brutal Jim Crow laws. As the streets were breaking in protests, Ruby, like many immigrants living in the U.S., watched the bloodshed and brutality that owned the nation's landscape.

To Ruby's children, Robin and Opshora, Mrs. Jones was always "aunty Linda" as she was to Ruby from the day Linda stepped inside their house.

Ruby was always sharp with numbers, excelled in mathematics in school though she never studied beyond the 12th grade. She came to the U.S. after completing her higher secondary school exams.

"I want to work," one day she declared after Robin was born. "Everyone in this country works . . . most of our neighbors are doing something . . . I feel so useless." Her husband understood her feelings and agreed immediately. He never dissented from any of her wishes on any thing she ever voiced or wanted to pursue. By that time Ruby had made friends with some Bengalee and south Asian families through the mosque network and community mother's club formed by minorities. She had also learned to drive and MD Mirza bought her a small Toyota. She chose the color—crimson, very much like Leila's car.

Linda was always there with unconditional support, guidance and affection. Except for Linda, everyone Ruby knew worked. They were the reason she aspired to pursue a career— even if it meant starting at the bottom. She was aware that without any job experience, no college degree and some challenges with the English language and the color of her skin she couldn't expect a white-collar job. Fortunately, she wasn't the bread winner. She didn't have to pay any bills. That was MD Mirza's department.

Ruby began working at a convenience store, around the

corner from their home, owned by a Hispanic man, Mr. Santiago. Linda had introduced Ruby to Mr. Santiago. She and her husband Mark were frequent customers at his store. Ruby was hired immediately. A respectable white woman's reference worked like magic.

Linda guided Ruby through the basics—cultural contexts, how to speak to customers, proper attire. She also assisted Ruby with English. With her help Ruby picked out western outfits for the first time. Linda gave her opinions as Ruby tried different colors and designs. Finally, they picked a few pairs of trendy pants, some T-shirts with collars and semi-formal shirts with flowery motifs. Ruby liked colors and her clothes were upbeat. She looked different, much younger and confident in her new clothes. MD Mirza was amused at the transformation but liked it.

"It becomes you. You look amazing." His admiration made Ruby blush. She still had to learn to accept deserved compliments with confidence. Modesty was too overbearing—it was the expected behavior in her culture.

Ruby was quick with keeping the finance ledgers impeccable and her boss valued her services. He grew dependent on Ruby and left the calculations to her. She was elated that she could claim her worthiness as an individual—she was more than merely the wife of a doctor. She established her identity, became a person.

Initially Ruby used to work four days a week and only six hours a day—no over time. Mr. Santiago allowed Ruby to bring Robin to work. The store was in a small alley and the customers breezed in mainly from the neighborhood. Business flowed at an easy pace usually. The six month-old infant slept most of the time at the backroom of the store in one corner and didn't bother anyone. She breastfed him every few hours during her breaks.

She worked through her entire second pregnancy as Robin began to take his first steps. He ran among the aisles in his walker and happily spent his waking hours at the store. Sometimes Mr. Santiago kept an eye on the toddler when Ruby was busy with customers. Ruby took five months leave without pay when Opshora was born and was readily given her job back when she returned with both babies.

Robin was passive as an infant whereas Opshora would bring the store down with her loud wails should her mother be slightly delayed in feeding her or paying her attention when she woke up from naps. Sometimes, at critical busy hours, Ruby attended to customers at the check-out counter while Opshora suckled at her breast covered under a colorful scarf, making tiny cooing sounds but protesting loudly if she sensed negligence. This picture of motherhood was well accepted, not branded as a show of immodesty for publicly breastfeeding at work. Mr. Santiago didn't object. It was a different time. Even then women had to be careful about how they were perceived and defined by the patriarchal society they lived in. Ruby felt Mr. Santiago's presence like a parental protection.

One day a white man shouted at her at the store. His fat face got red in rage, "Woman, this is America! Take your kids and go home! What kind of nonsense is this?" He was almost her father's age. Ruby started to shake in fear and gathered Robin and the wailing Opshora in her arms. Opshora had just begun to crawl and both children stayed in the play area that Mr. Santiago had been kind enough to set up in one corner of the large store. Opshora's crying had disturbed the man. Ruby was in panic, fearful for her children's safety. It was the first time someone yelled at her face. Luckily, Mr. Santiago's nephew who also worked at the store heard the commotion and came to her aid. Very quickly, two more customers joined him. Amongst them they led the angry man away from Ruby. Though at the time the civil rights movement was rallying the nation, some folks were still prisoners of their prejudices.

Protesters were swarming in Washington D.C. The air around smelt of uncertainty, anxiety and anger. People of color and especially blacks faced extreme discrimination. For the first time since she came to America, Ruby realized she was very brown.

That night she narrated the story to Leila on the phone. She didn't want to alarm MD Mirza. She needed to unload her heart to someone.

"This man would have never yelled at a white woman, *apa*," Ruby added sadly.

"Things are turning grim, Ruby. Be careful. Last week one white woman refused my services. She wanted a white nurse. It was an elderly woman, possibly not used to a nurse like me. I forgave her." Leila had her burden to share as well. The sisters promised to be careful and decided not to discuss these incidents with their husbands. There was no need to worry them as well.

"*Apa*, sometimes some people don't talk to me nicely. They order me . . . I am not their servant. I work at the store," Ruby remembered the incidents she faced at the store when she couldn't understand what the customer was looking for or when she misunderstood the inquiry—how they looked down at her. Their rudeness was hurtful. She still struggled with the language sometimes and had difficulty with accents. They were impatient with her—reduced her to an incompetent "colored woman," into almost nothing!

"Ruby, we came to this country, made it our home. Our children are born here. So we have to learn to manage such unkind behavior . . . many are caring people. Decent folks like us. But let us be constantly on the alert." Those were Leila's words of caution that Ruby always remembered. Leila was right. Her co-workers were polite and nice. So was Aunty Linda. She was such a kind soul! They all made her belong to this country. On many occasions Linda and Mark had volunteered to look after Robin while Ruby took Opshora to work. In fact Robin enjoyed being with them. The elderly couple loved taking care of him.

Then there was the time when she had ventured out alone at the shopping mall since her husband was busy. It was easy to take the metro and walk a few blocks. It gave her a sense of independence and some exercise. She liked to walk around looking at stuff from one store to the other. It was fun! It was so different than the way they shopped back at home— very few choices and on the rare occasions when they went to the stores, her father always accompanied them and paid. He managed the money, even for regular household expenditures.

Ruby picked up a few things for the house, a woolen scarf for herself, a pair of leather gloves for Leila and some gifts for her nephews. She proceeded to pay with her credit card. The middle-aged white woman behind the counter looked at her and said, "ID please." Ruby didn't understand right away. She had given a legitimate credit card to pay!

"You have a driving license? What do you have?" The woman's voice was louder, deliberately berating Ruby as she fumbled in her bag to search for her ID.

"Honey . . . you are holding up the line . . ." The woman was patronizing then shrugged and said something in the intercom possibly calling for additional help. By that time Ruby found her photo ID and handed it over to the woman. She shrugged again and proceeded with the payment. To her surprise and dismay, the card went through without a hitch while Ruby waited anxiously. It was a joint account with MD Mirza. It always had more than enough money than many Americans could boast of. Ruby was nervous, embarrassed and sweating profusely by the time the entire saga played out. She was fifth in line and no one else was asked to prove their identity when they paid. The white woman behind the counter had picked Ruby possibly because she was a woman of color. The incident shook her so much that afterwards she didn't have the courage to stand in a line for a drink and snacks at the small bakery-cafe she liked so much.

Ruby decided that it was not wise to expose her babies to unkind behavior at the store. Shortly thereafter, she found a Nepali immigrant woman, Nisha, who looked after children in her own home. She lived only two blocks away. It was an informal, small-capacity day care center, as she didn't have a license. People she knew in her community kept her business alive. They dropped off their kids and she charged them by the hour. Ruby liked the place—she didn't care about Nisha's license to operate. She appeared to be kind and sincere. Ruby went back to her work free of worries after dropping her children there daily.

Even though she tried hard to be indifferent, it wasn't easy to get over the prejudiced way some customers treated her at the store. After every incident of unkindness she cried secretly in the restroom—her mind soured. Their heartlessness broke her heart; her self-esteem got damaged. Every morning before going to work she had to brace herself for the day. Fearing the worst, she would tremble inside each time a customer talked to her. It wasn't always bad and unkind behaviors weren't too frequent, but the trauma she faced even at isolated incidents left scars. She wished she could go back to her hometown with her family where her children could grow up in a loving environment instead of this alien, cold country. She felt alone, afraid and uncertain about a future in this new culture. She never shared her pain and humiliation with Leila again or ever with MD Mirza or any other living soul. She accepted that she was an immigrant and decided to cope and survive as best as she could in her adopted homeland, America—"the land of the free and the home of the brave . . ."

MD Mirza supported her decision to continue to work because Ruby wanted it so much. He kept busy hours, and she needed a break from motherhood, sometimes. Work was an escape to her; it kept her fully engrossed and gave her a feeling of being useful. Money was never the issue. He was earning more than enough. She never looked for better opportunities or a higher pay.

She remained loyal to Mr. Santiago till he decided to retire at the age of eighty-two. Ruby bought the store from him with some financial support from her husband and became the new owner. His three adult children didn't want anything to do with the store though it had been a family business. They were successful in their own professional careers.

Ruby employed more staff and expanded the store. But that was years later when Opshora and Robin were in high school. Ruby began to feel comfortable with her new life but never let her guard down.

# CHAPTER FOUR

# *Up Close and Personal*

In the 60s the world was different. Cross continental connectivity was limited, and expensive...

Photographs and phone calls were the only way Ruby's family had connected with her husband and children. She visited her parents with the entire family when Opshora turned two. That was the first and only time Robin and Opshora met their maternal grandparents.

"You work? In America?" Ruby's mom was surprised and proud of her daughter. "You can now speak English? When our headmaster's wife comes for tea in the evening you must speak to her in English," she said proudly. "I want her to see how smart my little girl has become. Works in America now!"

Her hometown hadn't changed much outwardly but it all seemed different to Ruby. She was away for only four years. The narrow, broken roads snaking through the lines of trees and bamboo bushes, the complacent green rice fields, the rain-dripped sky...all remained the same while she was gone. She couldn't pin down why everything felt so different. Her life had changed hugely, for sure. Her mom happily continued to welcome neighbors and well-wishers who poured into their courtyard frequently, interested to know about Ruby's life in America, and tasted the mouth-watering, delightful chocolates and cookies that she had brought packed in her suitcases. She had gifts for everyone—scented bathing soap in beautiful wrappings, made in England, cosmetics, trinkets, perfumes. She didn't forget to bring her mother's favorite— Yardley bathing soap in a packet of six. The British left the Indian sub-continent years ago but their products were still very popular in this region.

She overheard her mom's running commentary, proud of her youngest daughter's success in a foreign land.

"She drives as well! She has her own car, my Ruby!"

"Oh my God! I would die of fear if I touched the steering wheel. That's a man's job!" A very impressed young neighbor exclaimed while eating the chocolates. She couldn't think of such a brave deed. "These are so good! Ummm . . . so tasty! What we get in the market smells moistly . . ."

"How can you even compare, Moina! These are made in America! Very high quality! In our stores all are cheap stuff." Ruby's mom was flabbergasted almost to the point of indignation.

"Ruby has become very accomplished," Moina said trying to salvage her tarnished position—for making the absurd comparison, evoking Ruby's mother annoyance.

Leila graduated as a nurse before migrating to the U.S. so her success as a professional woman compared to Ruby's was considered a natural happening. It was an accepted fact that she would work in a hospital setting, contribute to her family's earning whereas Ruby left the country as a teenager with no experience to advance a career in a foreign land. So she surprised her family and her neighbors and relatives with her triumphs.

The southern wind blew in the smell of dampness and open toilets—a very familiar odor, an inherent component of Bengalee life that Ruby had almost forgotten. She inhaled hard.

The offensive whiff couldn't be stamped out. Sanitation wasn't the greatest priority here. Toilets were usually built further away from the residence quarters to keep away the odors oozing from human waste. However, her family had water-flushed toilets. In America it wasn't like this. But, she learned that certain locations in New York City were quite dirty, smelly and people in poorer neighborhoods survived under the burden of the minimum. Daunting conditions but humans found the strength to live. She had also heard about the hardships that undocumented immigrants endured in America. They came from disadvantaged societies and crammed at the shores of the U.S., living in sub-human conditions—under paid, afraid of being deported. Many from her country drove cabs and did lowly jobs they wouldn't have done otherwise in their own homeland.

Returning to her native town felt good despite its countless odds. When she lived here many of these conditions escaped her scrutiny. Ruby had accepted them as part of her existence, inevitable and real. Now she compared everything with her new life back in America. She understood she didn't belong here anymore—and she was so ready to claim her new identity that had begun to change her in a far away land. In the past when Leila visited, Ruby and the rest of the household actively cleaned the clutter, endlessly dusted furniture, washed linens and cutlery—contributed in creating a more comfortable condition for her sister and her family. Leila got a queen's reception, each time undoubtedly. This time Ruby took that place. Her parents, brothers and their families kept waiting on her, making her every wish realized.

Her mother's voice could be heard speaking with the barber whose services the men in the household used regularly. The man was thanking Ruby's mom for the chocolates he got.

"It was so good, Ama. My children have never tasted anything like this before." The man was full of gratitude. "I am a poor man. Getting rice and daal for the family is all I can do." The barber laughed good-naturedly. Appreciation from him was expected.

"These are from America. A very beautiful country . . . My both daughters live there now. It is so much better than our backward town . . . with so many problems . . . mosquitos, heat, rain . . . Have you heard of America?" Ruby's mom was gloating in the achievements of her daughters. Moving to a foreign land transformed them from "small town girls" to almost celestial beings.

MD Mirza returned back to the U.S. after ten days. He had too many professional engagements to be able to take a longer vacation. Ruby's brothers borrowed the mayor's Toyota car to take him to the airport in Dhaka to catch his flight—a ten-hour drive from their hometown. Everyone in town was ready to assist. MD Mirza was the *Jamai* or the son in law of this town, not only to Ruby's family. He deserved the highest attention otherwise the town's people would be embarrassed. Similar courtesy and kindness was extended to Dr. Mirza when he visited with Leila. The town felt like they owed them.

Ruby made sure to visit her family once every two or three years, but mostly on her own. The travel was too long, too expensive and her life was all set in America alongside that of her husband and children. But, she was glad that her parents got to know MD Mirza during that one brief visit. Her family loved him instantly—his humility and genuineness charmed them. They could see his love for Ruby and were reassured.

Meanwhile, the political turmoil in America kept boiling and boiling. The civil rights movement continued. It got stronger and stronger. The tension was tearing the country apart. Kennedy defined the civil rights crisis as "moral, legal and constitutional." April 14, 1968—the collapse came as the entire world and the country watched—Martin Luther King was assassinated. 1968 shattered America. It faced a grave crisis—a new history was being created. The protests against the

Vietnam War, racial violence against the blacks, police brutality against legitimate demonstrations for democracy shook the core of the nation . . . too many contradictions enveloped the lives of the people.

That's the America Opshora and many like her inherited.

Back in Ruby's hometown things changed as well. In 1971 after a nine-month-long bloody civil war East Pakistan (East Bengal) broke away from the dictatorship of Pakistan, became an independent sovereign nation and emerged as Bangladesh. By that time Ruby was already a U.S. citizen. Luckily, unlike many others, her extended family wasn't directly scarred by the war of independence.

Opshora never got the chance to meet her paternal grandparents as both passed away the year she was born. They never got to know Ruby and Robin, either. Their only connections were through photographs and some rare, awkward phone calls on faulty lines. The conversations verged on basic, formal, courteous talks about health, how their grandkids were growing, their house, life in general—not significant but necessary to fill up voids among strangers. They never inquired about Ruby's personal life; they didn't know she would have liked to meet them and make sure with every effort to win them over. That opportunity never came. It was not possible to bare her heart over the brief phone calls that connected them over thousands of miles. However, they died knowing both their sons, their only off spring, were prospering and were with loving families.

With the advancement of technology, communication became easier as the years progressed which helped Ruby to constantly keep in touch through long distance phone calls with her own parents till they passed away. She maintained her connection with her three brothers and their families. Leila lived close by and was a constant presence in her life. Their sisterly bond remained unbroken and grew stronger with the passing years, especially after the death of Dr.

Mirza, decades later. Even after he was gone, Leila continued to live in their house at the edge of Georgetown, much renovated gradually based on the needs of the three boys. In time, Leila's three sons, all doctors, settled down in San Francisco with their families. The large house quieted down. A smaller place would have been logical, definitely more manageable but Leila wouldn't hear of it. She always listened to her heart. To her that was common sense, though the empty house was a source of heartache sometimes.

As she stepped into her adolescence, Opshora realized she had inherited a mother who ran a convenience store in ardent zeal, a father extremely busy with a medical profession, and a brother who was an outdoor-loving maniac. She was aware Robin loved her as his little sister but outdoor activities were greater diversions to him. He was a good brother but he didn't have time to sit down and listen to Opshora as she would have liked. There was camaraderie—she wanted more, she wanted him to hang out with her regularly, play games, take hikes on long trails that she enjoyed so much. Her father accompanied her when he could squeeze in some free time. Ruby didn't agree to Opshora's lone wanderings. She was cautious—afraid of unfounded faceless harms. Robin was older just by a year only, but Opshora expected too much from him and got disappointed in him, possibly.

However, there were many instances of family picnics, visiting friends and relatives, fun times at Leila's house—countless fights over Scrabble scores and harmless pranking. Robin was always there in the crowd but not solely for Opshora. She had to share him with her cousins and the entire clan. She craved his attention—wanted him to be her best friend. Robin's gregarious nature made him friends with everyone narrowing down the slot of brother-sister frontiers that she had emotionally reserved for them.

Robin simply didn't get it—failed to understand her needs.

Most of the time Opshora was by herself, studying, reading storybooks at home or listening to music. When she was in high school, some evenings on weekends when Leila was off duty, Opshora took the bus to be with her aunt. Leila's house was two blocks from the bus station. Even in winter evenings Opshora didn't mind the walk on the lighted streets bustling with stores, restaurants and people, carrying laughter with their strides. It was a safe neighborhood.

Leila's sons were busy with their own things but they were always a part of Opshora's life. Though a few years older, Opshora considered her cousins as her own brothers. They were no different than Robin. Leila looked forward to Opshora's visits. She loved Opshora like her very own—the daughter Leila always wanted. With her demanding schedule as a nurse, Leila had little time to cook. They ate instant cup noodles or Chinese delivery mostly and two scoops of ice cream as desert with half a banana each or a fist full of blue berries sprinkled over the succulent treat, or whichever fruit was available at home. Leila was aware of Opshora's love for ice cream so there were plenty of flavors to choose from, each time. Vanilla, chocolate, pistachio, strawberry flavors were stacked in the freezer. She had little concern about the boys' diets. They were happy with gorging down hot dogs, pizza and take-away Chinese or Indian food.

Dr. Mirza lived on and loved Indian cuisine that he ordered almost every evening. For lunch, both he and Leila ate salads at the hospital cafeteria. Ruby frequently sent home-cooked meals to her sister's family. He loved her food and waited for it to arrive at regular intervals.

He was extremely fond of Opshora. He had a hunger for a daughter as well. Sometimes after dinner he and Opshora talked for long hours. They discussed books, stories, movies and politics. On those nights he either drove her home or Opshora got permission from her parents to crash in for the night. He taught her how to play chess and poker. After she turned sixteen, he also introduced her to wine and let her taste a bit now and then without Ruby's knowledge.

"You shouldn't do this. Her mother wouldn't approve if she found out," Leila didn't support him.

"Opshora knows how to balance everything. Ruby has to understand the culture in which our kids are born into," was his casual response with a smile as he continued to puff at his pipe. "Even Quran says drinking isn't bad unless it becomes an addiction." He never deterred from his interpretation of his religion. He was against all kinds of bigotry—in lifestyle, ideology or practice.

Opshora grew up in the American culture with all the difficulties and pluses faced by minorities. They lived in a mixed neighborhood with mostly whites, some browns and a few blacks—a good blending of people belonging to upper middle-class and affluent economic brackets with equally diverse occupations. They were business owners, CEOs, executives, medical professionals and academics. Though she attended the neighborhood school, her father practiced as a doctor in the same area, Opshora was aware that she was different in every sense from the kids with whom she grew up. She looked different and was born in a family that followed the Muslim faith. She accompanied her family to the mosque for Eid prayers and sometimes on Fridays. Ruby was particular with her children about such attendance but MD Mirza seldom showed up for prayers. Except for Ruby no one in the family practiced the one-month-long fasting period that Muslims observe all over the world.

People knew Opshora and her family but her struggle to blend into the American culture continued. In school she was singled out as a kid of color like other non-white children, a handful of blacks and Asian Americans—belonging to Chinese and South-Asian races. Her chocolate-brown skin stood out unlike most of the students splashed in the paleness of Caucasian lineage. They were all different in appearance and heritage but unified beneath one flag. That's what she used to think in those times of innocence.

Opshora never forgot her first day in school. Ruby wanted the best for her children. She relentlessly went from one store to the other hunting for proper outfits for them. Back in her hometown children wore uniforms—usually blue frocks for girls and black pants and white shirts for boys. So Opshora landed in her class in a beautiful dress made of lace and silk in light shades of pink and mauve that Ruby had picked for her with much care. Opshora's shoes also matched the violet of her outfit. All the other kids wore T-shirts and shorts or pants—casual clothes. She stood out. Opshora didn't understand the reason but she didn't like it . . .

"You look like a fairy," her classmate Dana said.

"Are you going to a birthday party? Where are you going?" another girl asked. Opshora felt so alone. She wasn't like the rest of the girls in her class, and this trend kept following her. Robin did better that day. His integration was easier though his brown skin, dark eyes and jet-black hair stood out, too.

Opshora was saddened when most of her teachers stumbled over her name and decided an easy way out by calling her "Opps Mairza." Her last name was supposed to be pronounced "Meerza." They didn't want to make the effort—didn't care enough to respect the sanctity of her name. Her shortened new name got popularized, but Opshora hated it.

As a little girl she felt ashamed of her name. It was so different! All the other girls were either "Caroline" or "Lara" or "Melissa." She was upset with her parents.

"Aba, Can I get a new name?" the tiny Opshora asked her father after her first week in school. "You can call me Olivia," she had said with finality. It amused her parents at the time. They didn't peer deeper into the little girl's psyche.

As the years passed she began to feel mortified—her right to her name was violated. Her identity was deliberately made insignificant.

Her Spanish teacher Ana Lopez, however, cared and learned how to say her name correctly. Opshora liked this young woman who was instrumental in building her self-confidence, assisting her in standing up and claiming what was rightfully hers. She wanted to be like Miss Ana Lopez when she grew up.

Opshora would have liked to be friends with Clara, the beautiful popular girl in her class with the paleness of snowy-white skin, curly golden hair and deep blue eyes. Clara looked like the princess in the fairy tales she had read. Opshora's elementary school years were filled with a yearning to be Clara's friend. She didn't have the confidence to go and sit beside her because she could feel she wouldn't be accepted. Clara had a following of four to five girls—blonds and red heads with blue and hazel eyes, rosy cheeks like hers. She was always surrounded by them. They sat at the same table at lunch break. They did everything together. Opshora wasn't invited to be their friend. Those years, she wished she had pale skin, golden hair and blue eyes. She hated herself for being so different. Kids of color had their own groups—they were only a few in her school. So most of the time Opshora was mainly alone. This situation didn't change even in high school except the fact that there were more kids of color in her class and in the school.

Opshora was an "A" student, which possibly helped with some recognition among her classmates. Like her mother she was a math genius. She got noticed for her talents especially in her high school years but still didn't belong to the white girls' groups. She hung around with Tomo, a bi-racial kid of a Japanese American dad and Caucasian mom, Dexter, an African American boy, and Tina, who like her was the offspring of

South-Asian American parents. There were a few more other groups of kids of color. That was all. The bond that her group shared was their colored identity. Her real close friendship with Tomo began somewhat later in high school.

Robin, an equally good student made his mark in sports—basketball, football, swimming . . . he was unbeatable. He was also trendy, outgoing and good-looking. He had many followers. And his first name didn't sound strange. Being his sister in school added some feathers in Opshora's cap. However, she was a good runner and a school champion in that feat. She took to running because it didn't require too much interaction; she could practice on an individual level. The other reason was Ruby. She wanted her daughter to belong to a team like all other girls of her age. Participating in sports was a good way to blend, become a part of the milieu.

No matter how she tried, Opshora didn't belong . . . Tina made new friends in high school but Tomo and Dexter stayed in her group. There was some kind of subdued hostility towards her group from the white boys. The white girls totally ignored her—as if she didn't exist. The slim, rich white girls had no difficulty becoming popular and created their individual groups while Opshora battled with her identity crisis as well as the challenges of puberty—confusion and high-strung emotions. Her inner feelings were bottled up—she had no one to share them with who she could trust would understand her dilemma. Actually, she didn't even know how to express what she was feeling or label the issues under specific names. All she craved for was to be accepted.

An incident at that time shook her up. After math class was over Opshora stayed back in the empty classroom to do some reading. She had an hour to spend before Robin would be free. They walked home together in the afternoons. Though Robin would have liked to go home by himself, Ruby wouldn't hear of that. It was only about half a mile but she insisted Robin chaperone Opshora home. In the mornings MD Mirza dropped them off.

Opshora turned around at the sound of footsteps. Three boys had entered the room. They were big. White boys. They were senior to her. They looked at her with menacing smirks. They began to come closer.

"Hey brownie-bitch!" said the biggest in the group. The others laughed. Opshora froze. Then they circled her.

"Hey John, this beautiful bird needs her feathers ruffled," said one, laughing. John, the big boy, came forward and pushed her against the wall while the others kept laughing. Opshora fought back but didn't scream. John's knee was against her waist holding her back while with his hands he began groping her. Opshora made a fist and aimed a punch at his jaw but he caught her hand in a tight grasp, bruising her. It hurt.

"Hey, let her go! Right now!" Someone shouted in a big voice. It was Tomo. He had come back for some reason and found them. He had an athletic body and was a karate black belt. John pushed her and she fell down. Her head banged on the wall. Her arm got twisted a bit and she winced in sudden pain. And just like that the boys were gone. Tomo helped her to her feet. Her upper arm was sore. A deep bluish-violet bruise surfaced. She would have to hide it somehow from her mother. That was the thought that ate her. Tomo didn't say anything.

"Let's go," he said quietly. He gently pulled her up to her feet.

"Don't tell anyone. Nothing happened. Okay?" Opshora didn't want to become a subject of gossip or a joke. She didn't want to upset Robin, either. She was only fourteen but had the sense to realize that fanning this incident publicly would make matters worse. And she didn't want to admit it happened—she felt a strong sense of shame.

Tomo sometimes wore a scarf around his neck. He gave it

to her from his locker. Opshora wrapped it over the bruise. Hid it from everyone.

"Thanks. We are good," Opshora said to Tomo, again. He nodded silently. They became real friends henceforth.

Next year, Diana Burger joined her class. That changed the dynamics a lot. She was the daughter of a diplomat, a single mother who had Diana in her forties. Diana travelled around the world with her mother who finally retired and came to live in Arlington, close to where Opshora's family lived.

Diana was big for a fifteen-year-old, had a jovial laugh, high voice and had a mild acidic body odor. She sweated a lot. And she laughed a lot. Her bright blue eyes sparkled on her heavily freckled face. She and Opshora became friends instantly. Two misfits. Diana Burger was her first real white friend with a surname, which led to many jokes and laughter. Diana bore the teasing with indifference, tried to indicate she wasn't affected at all. Possibly that was her defense.

"These are harmless boogies. Don't care what they say ... what they laugh about ... Godknows and theirdark-souls!" Diana whispered casually, joining the words. Even her whisper was loud enough to be heard by others. "My name is as good as anyone else's. Plenty for them to somersault over." She taught Opshora how to shrug off meaningless yapping.

Mrs. Burger and Diana became regular weekend visitors at their place. They loved Ruby's cooking and her hospitality. Mrs. Burger usually brought wine and enjoyed it with MD Mirza. Though Ruby wasn't in favor of the drinking, she let it go. She really liked the no-nonsense former diplomat with the loud, deep throated laugh. On some instances Ruby also invited Linda and her husband Mark. With these people in her house, eating her home cooked food with admiration, and their friendship extended to her family, Ruby's faith in America was somewhat restored, and lessened her earlier staunch reservations.

It took Opshora years to understand why though born in

this country she was treated differently. And at one point she bravely accepted that like any other country, America was broken—abolishment of slavery didn't protect African Americans from brutality and extreme discrimination. Even the way they wore their hair was a cause to deny them entry into the mainstream society. The unnecessary wars overseas on the pretense of maintaining democracy in foreign lands ignoring gross injustices at home, the absence of adequate legislatures to ensure equality and equity for its own population projected a deep-set prejudiced system—persistent and heartless. It was an unfair world outside, and within its borders—a sobering fact that paled the wall of greatness boastfully safeguarded by the charlatans. When so many suffered in this country and others globally because of America's policies, how could it be really great?! It was hard for Opshora to come to terms with such hypocrisies.

She was definitely different. She ate rice for lunch and dinner without tiring; she wore Bengalee outfits at her cultural festivities. The two Eids were the main celebrations for her family unlike most Americans. Her family like the rest of the country of course celebrated Thanksgiving, Halloween, Easter and Christmas—accepted them as cultural and family reunion festivities. Eid wasn't a public holiday in the U.S. so they observed it on the first Saturday after the actual occasion—they wore new "deshi" or Bengalee attire, went to the mosque for prayers, cooked different varieties of food and ate dinner at Leila's place, without fail every year—Ruby packed all the food that she had cooked as Leila didn't cook much. That was the ritual they followed. Those used to be fun times! Gifts were exchanged and Dr. Mirza generously gave money to all the kids. They repeated this for both Eids and all through Opshora's growing up years. This routine changed somewhat as they all grew up and moved out.

They didn't know anyone from the Jewish community. So

Hanukkah didn't make it into their list of celebrations. They attended Diwali parties with their Hindu neighbors—helping to illuminate their houses with clay ghee lamps. They planned outings on Memorial Day weekends and loved the Fourth of July galas and fireworks. They enjoyed those occasions like any other American—whites, blacks and browns.

As she began to mature emotionally, Opshora embraced her surroundings, the unchangeable stumbling blocks of growing up in this amazing diverse culture, and learned to live and rejoice in her own heritage, enjoyed being who she was, different absolutely but a part of the modern, free America that had a place for everyone with some hiccoughs now and then, here and there. This was the only home she knew. She understood the flawed "America," and recognized the contradictions within her own self as well. Despite the challenges—her "love-hate" stand, she felt she belonged; it was her birthright to be an American. She was a proud citizen of this country.

Robin entered medical school while Opshora got into the University of Virginia to study socio-cultural anthropology. Undergraduate study was enjoyable, interesting but somewhat disengaging. Diana was accepted at Brown University.

"See, I like you so much that I got into Brown," She had said jokingly before heading to Rhode Island. However, she came home for every holiday and so their friendship wasn't affected. Tomo went to Chapel Hill. He was often back home on spring or summer breaks.

Though good in her studies, Opshora, unlike Robin, was undecided on a focused career path. Robin followed in the footsteps of their uncle, dad and older cousins and wanted to be a dedicated doctor. Opshora kept flirting with social science and anthropology. MD Mirza was lenient with his daughter and gave her time to grow up, make up her mind. Ruby was busy with her own work and relied on her husband's judgment. Though somewhat skeptical, Ruby trusted her daughter's good sense that she hoped would catch up with her in time.

Opshora plodded on and struggled. Robin fulfilled their parents' dreams, she was aware. She took some time off to work after graduation to discover life. She did internships paid and unpaid which helped her to gain experience, enhance her understanding of the world around her. By that time she moved into her unit in her parental house. Ruby was relieved. The thought of Opshora living by herself was too much for her. Sometimes during those years of indecisiveness Opshora felt she was lost—like a rudderless ship, adrift on turbulent waters.

Leila's three sons got married one after the other, in what were quickly formed commitments—the first one to a doctor, the second to a schoolteacher and the third to a banker. Only the banker was Caucasian while the other two belonged to South Asian heritage, born and brought up in the U.S. Leila had no qualms about interracial marriages and she welcomed all three of them with equal affection. The three women became a part of the Mirza family.

Robin was at Yale medical school—steadfast towards a life aspired. That's when Opshora finally made her mark. She got accepted at Columbia for her masters. She found her path, eventually. MD Mirza was overwhelmed and very proud. So was Ruby.

"I am thankful now! She is stubborn but in a good way. I wish she would think of marriage." Ruby was pleased but with some concerns. She had been trying very hard to get Opshora interested in a romantic life, made attempts to introduce her to sons and deserving male relatives of friends from their own culture. But Opshora mostly ignored such gestures.

"You need to step away from her, Ruby. She's a smart young woman now," MD Mirza said good-humoredly, not being judgmental or critical. He understood her well.

"A Bengalee mother doesn't know how to back off," Ruby had replied. She refused to step down from her stand. According to Ruby, a woman could accomplish many things, conquer the world but unless she found the right person to settle down with and create a family, her life would remain incomplete. She knew her philosophy about life wasn't very welcoming to her daughter and husband. Even Robin sometimes smiled at his mother's antics to rope Opshora.

Opshora was packed off to her new world stuffed with uncashed dreams, countless expectations—and recognition in her own family. She landed at Columbia University, New York.

The world around her was spinning at a whirlwind speed. Opshora began dating casually, sparsely, and of course not from her own culture. But she never brought anyone home to be introduced to the family as a potential and serious romantic partner. Studies claimed a big chunk of her time, her ever-evolving life. She discovered many like-minded young, scholarly thinkers around her and was intensely influenced by the wisdom of the academics. One day, she suddenly announced she was going off to Fiji to do an internship—course practicum requisite, to be completed in three months.

"It's a bold decision . . . but good," MD Mirza said.

"Are you sure you want to go there? Is it safe? Fiji people are cannibals I heard," Ruby wasn't sold to the idea.

"Ama, all is good there. Cannibalism is a story of the past. I intend to take a month's vacation in the islands after the practicum . . . experience the island culture. I will be back even before you miss me, Ama!" Opshora laughed. She was bubbling with excitement. Fiji was calling . . .

Robin met a fellow doctor from Indian heritage and got engaged. His fiancée Maya was of the Tamil ethnic group but followed the Muslim faith.

"I will try to teach her Bangla," Ruby was determined to like Maya—who would be her only son's wife, a part of the family. "I learnt English. Maya is a smart woman. She can pick up Bangla in no time."

Opshora missed the engagement party because she had already travelled out of the country.

# Part II.
## Fiji, 1987–1990

# CHAPTER FIVE

# Carry My Dreams
# As Your Own

Opshora arrived in Suva in 1987, a few weeks after Colonel Rabuka seized power in a bloodless coup. The country was still politically unstable, rumors and lies were widespread. However, Opshora didn't find the situation personally oppressive in anyway. The landscape was still breathtaking and the ocean still foamed into magical waves. At twenty-three, she didn't need much more than that.

It was supposed to be a four-month stint but Opshora stayed back three years. Because she fell in love. It was love at first sight—just a month after she landed in Suva, the heart of Fiji . . .

Four months later, after landing in Fiji, she informed her parents about her plans to get married. MD Mirza and Ruby got all the details in a letter from Opshora. That was the first time she had explained herself to her parents in such elaboration. In the lines they could almost hear her happy heartbeats.

She introduced Zayn, her fiancé in her letter to her parents. She gave her reasons for the decision to get married:

*"Zayn is a special person. He works with an airline as a ground staff, lives with his large extended family in a multi-*

*generational home in Suva. They are of limited means, modest in education but exceptional in island appeal and warmth.*

*What attracted me to him is his ability to understand me, accept me for who I am. His folks have made me feel at home the moment I met them—a beautiful family. I never felt so welcome anywhere in my entire life. Deep inside me a voice kept saying—'this is for you' and I trusted it. I have found my identity here . . . I hope you will understand . . .*

*And by the way, I have almost completed my practicum work—got an extension to submit it. So don't worry. I will do it when I am ready."*

Opshora didn't enclose any photographs. MD Mirza was thoughtful. He realized Opshora needed to be handled with extreme caution, gentle guidance, undying care and firm support. However, Ruby was devastated by the news.

"I can't believe this! What made her choose a Fijian man? Where did we go wrong?" She questioned a million times. She wept as she continued at the store and at home. To her it was an indication that in every possible way Opshora had rejected her own parents, especially Ruby.

"She hasn't yet finished her practicum! I have doubts if she will ever complete her masters," Ruby kept lamenting.

"She will come around Ruby. Let's have patience," MD Mirza said, though at heart he felt less certain at that moment. He knew his daughter, had faith in her but he was also aware of Opshora's independent nature. She needed their unconditional love and trust and she was sure to bounce back.

Zayn was fun. And Opshora found him intensely appealing. He was so different than the men she came across back at home. He was unlike any of the transitional boyfriends of her past life. He loved her passionately. He celebrated her awkwardness as diversity that commanded recognition and respect, not judgment for being unusual. Surprisingly, his Catholic family had no problem accepting her Muslim faith, which she hardly practiced. She was never religious. To her, religion was personal, a matter of choice. She had no hesitation attending church on Sundays with Zayn's entire family though her stand had always been sort of "hands off" regarding any faith. However, she had respect for those who followed their religion. Zayn's family instantly embraced her with all her unique-odd-foreign ways. They made her one of them, never treated her as lesser or an outsider.

Zayn was a cross breed as the Fijians called him. There were interracial marriages in his lineage. He was a product of Melanesian, Micronesian, Polynesian, Chinese and white European-Australian heritage. His complexion was faded golden brown, with curly sandy-hued hair and steely grey foggy eyes on an attractive face. He built his athletic body with regular vigorous workouts. He was proud of his looks. He turned heads whenever he made an entry, wherever. He knew his appeal and expounded it with his personal charms, cultivated mannerisms. He stood out in his casual island bula shirt with either colorful motifs of hibiscus or frangipani flowers, black *sulu* or kilt-like skirt worn by Fijian men, a cowry necklace peeking over his neckline and a sea-shell bracelet on his right wrist. He usually wore a fresh frangipani flower stuck behind his left ear like many island men. Very stylish, very Fijian, absolutely charming . . . and took her breath away the moment they met. Opshora could never forget how their paths crisscrossed . . .

Zayn breezed in, casually, silently into her life one morning at the Suva airport as Opshora was trying to rebook a flight to Nadi, that she had missed. It was a chance meeting. She was headed to Sigatoka from Nadi. All international flights landed at the Nadi airport and it served as a hub of all domestic flights as well.

They spoke. He looked over her documents. The airline

was refusing to reimburse or rebook her on the next available flight for some reason or another. Zayn offered her a seat in his small cubicle while he talked on the phone. It went on for sometime in the local language while she waited. Then he took all her documents and stepped out. She looked around his office. There were photographs of unknown faces—friends and family, possibly. She wondered whether he was married. There wasn't any particular photo suggesting that. All snapshots seemed casual, friendly, nothing intimate. Most islanders didn't wear wedding bands those days.

At that point while she was lost in her thoughts, he came back with his killer smile.

"All set. You are ready to board the evening flight," he said as he handed over the newly issued ticket and boarding pass.

"Wow! Thank you so much. How did you do it?" She was full of admiration.

"Trade secret," he laughed. She joined in.

"Do you have to go back to Suva?" The airport situated in Nausori was about eleven miles away from Suva.

"Hmm . . . not sure . . . What do you think?" Opshora wanted to know.

"Going back and returning for the 6 p.m. flight may not be conducive on this bad road with lunch time and late afternoon traffic," he said casually. "You would be on the road for about two hours and unnecessarily pay the cab fare."

"In that case I think I will walk around. Sit in a park, do some reading," she agreed. She could use the free hours to explore the area around the airport. It made more sense.

"Wise decision." He nodded. "New here?"

"Yes . . . Arrived two weeks ago—fresh off the boat," Opshora smiled. "I live in a house with three female friends, downtown Suva," she said as an afterthought. She didn't know why she had to mention her housemates to a stranger.

"It's nice to have friends in a new country. Where are you from?" Zayn's conversational tone was refreshing.

"I live in the U.S.," Opshora replied. It was almost getting to lunchtime.

"America is a beautiful country I am aware. Never been there, though." He smiled, again creating a wave inside her.

"Fiji is fascinating! It has character—a soul."

"Wow . . . wow . . . wow! You have fallen for the island country's charms like many other visitors," Zayn laughed out loud. "I hear such gushing words all the time."

"But it's true. Right?" Opshora challenged. He didn't answer.

"I am stepping out for a bite. You are welcome to join me," he offered instead with another heart-breaking grin. "I could introduce you to some authentic Fijian cuisines."

That was the beginning of their story. He killed her all over again with his smile.

They ate hot, spicy fish curry and steamed rice at a wall-less roadside eatery that day—beneath a flimsy roof made of leaves, under tall palm trees. The sun was merciless. The breeze was no match against the oozing humidity. Opshora's whole body was bathed in sweat. Her clothes clung to her.

"Here, drink this cold coconut water . . . it helps with hot food," he came to her rescue. He had watched her face reddening as she struggled with the spicy food.

"It's very tasty . . . but too hot for me," Opshora had to admit as she gratefully gulped the drink. His eyes rested gently on her face. She couldn't stop the soft blush as his gaze lingered.

Later in the evening Opshora landed at Nadi against the silhouetted shadows of the coconut trees. The distant shorelines were brightened by the moonlight and blazing stars. It was a new world at her life's threshold waiting to be discovered. She checked in at the nearby hotel, Raffles Gateway, across the road from the airport. She fell asleep amidst the overriding moldy smell in the tiny room in a narrow bed, on freshly laid linens, shown in by a very pleasant porter. After an hour she woke up and decided to take a bath. Her body felt cramped, a bit sore. The hot water took ages to come through the shower and the telephone didn't work.

Who would she have called that night? Not home to the U.S. as international calls were too expensive. Possibly she would have called Zayn. Before saying goodbye he had passed his home number on a chit of paper.

"In case there is any further problem . . . or not . . . you are welcome to call me, any time," he had said haltingly, expectancy escaping his voice.

"I am keeping it safely . . . in case there's any reason, or not, to call," she had smiled speaking in an even tone. At that both had laughed, their pretensions out in the open as they left the restaurant that smelt of spicy fish curry and rice and many other delightful culinary concoctions.

Opshora realized in her heart right then and there that she wanted to know more about this man who was already churning her insides with his smiles, his intense presence. He made it very obvious that he was interested in her. This discovery filled her with a sense of elation she had not known before in the company of any man. That was the beginning— intoxication by Zayn's persona.

After the night at Raffles, the morning appeared to be promising. She had a quick coffee and a piece of crispy bread with a handsome spreading of melted butter. She had overslept—tossed and turned for some time in the narrow bed. The silence of the night—broken by the intermittent songs of frogs and crickets outside—kept stirring her up from imminent drowse. As she struggled to stay asleep, her mind replayed every moment of her brief interlude with Zayn. It was a shocking realization—a total stranger had the power to occupy so much of her thoughts. She was finally in deep sleep when the first glow of the dawn came crashing in.

As Opshora stepped out in the open, she got a whiff of

the hot, humid air that held the faded incense of wildflowers and seaweed bathed in untamed sunrays relentlessly pounding on the plush deep horizon, tinted with vibrant hues of happiness. On that amazing morning looking out through the arched entrance of the hotel lobby, Opshora felt that this new universe that awaited her carried a message of bliss. She took a cab to Sigatoka.

Named after the river Sigatoka, the town was located on the island of Viti Levu, about forty miles from Nadi downtown. Sigatoka was incorporated as a town in 1959. Through the decades, the Sigatoka Valley remained famous for its high production of various kinds of vegetables, and was termed the "Salad Bowl" of Fiji, a title it proudly carried over the generations. Vast banana plantations adorned the township and continued in abundance all over the outlying villages. Opshora immediately fell in love with the surrounding rich green enclosures. She was told that from 1912 to 1923 the banana plantations were attacked by a severe fungal infection known as the yellow Sigatoka disease that ravaged the farmsteads. However, the disaster was overcome eventually. The lands also produced high volumes of sugar cane. She talked to villagers about their lifestyle, faith and culture, the information she needed for her practicum. The elders were very much respected and held key decision-making powers; family values included good morals, helping relatives and neighbors. Leading a virtuous life in the community was emphasized as its strength. The communal way of co-existence was favored and upheld. Opshora found this very much similar to her Asian upbringing, her own culture.

In addition to her course work requirements, she started gathering extra information for a separate publication to aptly share the richness of Fijian culture with the outside world from her own perspectives. It was too unique to ignore. The idea of this new book kicked in her brain, there and then.

It would be a great opportunity to write about the heritage of these amazing people enhanced by the mesmerizing anecdotes she was capturing.

The Fiji islands were known for practicing cannibalism in the past. Opshora was curious to know more on this matter and engaged with some elderly villagers to get their views and listen to their stories handed over the generations. It was a lively discussion in which they confirmed, in broken English, that many of their forefathers killed their enemies and ate them. They drank the blood of the corpse to be powerful. It was customary for the chief of the tribe to eat the heart and brain to absorb his enemy's knowledge and courage, followed by the ritual of prayers offered by a tribal priest, and celebration with dancing under the moonlight as the meat was cooked for the feast while the hungry villagers waited—and consumed later with slow diligence throughout the night. Opshora was both awed and revolted at the same time with the stories narrated with much pride and fun.

The literature reviews Opshora had done so far indicated several research sources that confirmed the case of Methodist missionary Reverend Thomas Baker who was killed and eaten in 1867 by the villagers of Nabutautau situated in Viti Levu—the largest of the Fijian islands. It's rumored that after devouring the missionary the village faced continuous bad crops as lands turned infertile. This misfortune made them listen to other Christian missionaries who preached against cannibalism. There were many fascinating tales that further colored the incredible Fiji islands, brewed in mysticism and countless wonders.

Opshora took photographs around the village—of the people and the plantations, the narrow streets and the houses standing against the distant low hills. Lavish green was splashed all over the landscape outlined by the turquoise of the Pacific Ocean. It was a different world altogether!

Later, in the evening, she strolled around Nadi town to

amuse herself and bought some local crafts. She roamed around the almost deserted streets and for no reason picked one bracelet made of shiny sapphire Paula shells and cowry, usually worn by Fijian men. For her, she chose a pair of dangling indigo blue oyster shell earrings.

Back in the hotel room, she buried herself in work but her mind sneaked off to the time she spent over lunch with Zayn, the laughter they shared, the brief exchanges that promised nameless hopes. Finally, though she knew he had left the office, she dialed his number with a nervous heart, shaky fingers. She left her name and hotel room number with his co-worker on duty. She couldn't muster the courage to call him at his home number.

Opshora woke up next morning with the sound of the phone ringing. Zayn was at the other end of the line. Her new life in the Pacific embraced her head on in the real sense as she said "hello" on the phone in a very sleepy voice.

When she returned four days later from her trip from Nadi, he was at her doorstep, waiting patiently.

Opshora shared a house with three other women, Lara, Jane and Laisani. They were her roommates and friends. They became her soul mates in a very short period. These three women had already rented a place together and were looking for another roommate. Opshora found out about them from the local YMCA and joined them happily. They all came from different places but youth was the common factor that bound them into one universe of existence at that point in time. Their friendship sparked from day one.

The spacious bungalow on top of a low hill belonged to Laisani's father, a reputable businessman. It was a bit rickety—the windows didn't fasten properly, the stone floor was uneven but the balcony faced the ocean. It captured an amazing view!

The four of them hung out together and didn't keep anything from each other. In that distant island Opshora found true friends. Unlike her, they were struggling in entry-level jobs but the cost of living was low in Suva, life was less complicated and full of fun. Lara was from New Zealand and worked with a shipping company as a clerk. Jane was Irish, from the U.K., and was with a sub-contracted project under the Ministry of Finance. Laisani was trying her luck with the judicial courts as a freshly graduated lawyer. She got her degree in Australia.

Laisani, as a native Fijian, was their guide. They discovered Suva following her lead—its nightlife spilled with local booze, quaint eateries, casual hints of romance now and then. They enjoyed countless good times on the open beaches under the night sky wrapped in utopian glee—that's what Opshora liked most. Lara had an old Canon camera she had brought with her—an inheritance from her grandfather. She often captured their moments of carefree merriment. She was a serious photographer. Her desire was to take up journalism in the future. The girls loved to pose for her and teased her relentlessly. In youth everything seemed a light-hearted matter:

"Hey Lara, don't forget to capture my smile at ninety degrees!"

"You need to focus more on my shapely legs! Two hoots to modesty, yahoooo!" Jane was the wildest one and came up with hilarious ideas.

"I look good in my right profile angle while in a sitting pose. Be careful of Jane. She tries to cover my face with her big boobs!"

The teasing went on and on. Often they would request a passer-by to take a group photo of them all. Lara couldn't master the auto-snap mode in the old camera.

Sometimes deep in the night the roommates would wake up at the sound of laughter from Jane's room. She was into extreme, casual flings and occasionally smuggled a spontaneous lover to her room. It was okay with everyone. They didn't chastise her. She didn't want anything serious and so her amorousness was kept buried in the dark of night. She didn't introduce any of her picks to her friends.

Laisani was seeing someone who she thought wouldn't get her clan's approval. So she vanished some weekends with her guy to some nearby island, away from prying eyes. Lara was undecided about forming any relationships. And Opshora found Zayn!

Opshora was too happy to go out with Zayn after she returned to Suva. She had plenty of vacant time and his charms were undeniable, of course.

She wanted to discover the mystery buried in his smiles . . . she wasn't able to shake him out of her thoughts because every time he looked at her she melted, her heart raced recklessly. They started dating seriously—it became an exciting new adventure for both.

After office hours, Zayn picked her up on the back of his motorbike and they sped through the Victoria Parade area to find a secluded corner of the endless beach, shielded by bushes. He knew so many cozy spots away from the public eyes, close to the waves. She was a good swimmer. The touch of the soft, lukewarm salty water on a hot day shined her skin, cleansed her soul. He taught her to ride the wild waves.

They walked to the water's edge hand in hand or sat down on the dampness of the sand to watch the last rays of the dying sun's brilliance dancing on the restless waters, constantly sprayed by the waves. And they talked. And laughed. They tried to discover each other as much as was allowed through the stories they shared—times lived in individual existences till their lives collided. They kissed and screamed out endearments drowning the sounds of the sudden huge waves. Life was transformed, became meaningful—ecstatic with fresh longings. She was totally infatuated with Fiji, deeply intrigued by her feelings for Zayn. He captivated her soul in such a short time!

Zayn charmed Opshora's friends the instant they met. He won their hearts by his love for Opshora, the genuine care he felt for her, his disarming smile. They understood Opshora's madness for Zayn.

Zayn found Opshora exciting, different from the women he had dated in the past. She was very Asian like the Indo-Fijians in appearance but so unlike them in upbringing, ideology and demeanor. She was a free spirit, genuine, a fun person—an uninhibited antidote to any intimidation. She openly voiced her views and could speak incessantly about the dreams she believed in, the hopes she cherished dearly. She could gurgle down a beer and engage men in debates on politics, sports, sexuality—after all, she was a researcher and in no time she became one of them. Her frankness made her charms irresistible, impossible to ignore. He had never before met anyone like her. Fijian men found her liberated attitudes fiercely appealing; women were fascinated by her fearless stands. In many ways she was more true to Western ways than her Asian heritage.

Zayn introduced her to his close inner group of buddies—three young men and two women he went to school with. They spent lazy weekends on the beach or had picnics in resort locations. They camped in the wilderness of Mount Korobaba and leapt into the ocean for a swim . . . and drank and danced under the starlit skies when night deepened. It almost became a routine.

Once he took Opshora on a night fishing expedition with his friends. It was a new experience for her. The waves danced with the moonlight on the silent, vast waters. The darkness of the night matched the intensity of the somber depth of the Pacific. The fish swarmed to the torchlights and were easy prey. Opshora felt sorry for the unsuspecting aquatic life lured so easily to their fates. She watched while the others were busy looting the waters, intoxicated with glee with their catch. Her heart was overcome by a sudden sadness. She didn't like the way Zayn and his friends were fishing. It was hard to brush away the tears. She didn't understand whether it was Zayn's nearness, homesickness or the fogginess of emotions growing towards him that made her sentimental over a practice so natural to the locals. She didn't know. She felt lost. Somehow she didn't enjoy being there.

Zayn noticed her silent withdrawal in the background and came around, held her close to him. He smelt of the sweetness of the salty waters, of fresh fish and adventure, wrapped in a caring meant only for her. At that moment she fell in love with him, fiercely—irrevocably. The awakening hit her. She clung to him as the boat rocked in the soft wind, cradling the gentle waves.

"I am sorry," he said searching the traces of pain in her eyes, meant every word he uttered. "I should have never brought you . . . this isn't the right adventure for you."

"I care for the fish more than the fun in killing them. I am crazy, I guess," she tried to smile—undo the guilt she sensed in his voice.

"No, you are not, my sea-shell princess. You are amazingly decent and kind. Rare and refreshing." He used to call her by adoring names.

"This is too Fijian . . . for you. I didn't even give it a thought before tonight. Cannibalism is still alive in our blood." He kissed her and held her close inhaling the dying fragrance of the blossomy shampoo in her hair.

"We are all cannibals in a sense . . . I mean we are carnivores . . . meat-eaters," Opshora whispered, comforted by Zayn's nearness. Both laughed and agreed.

Opshora felt safe in his arms. No one had ever held her like this before— protective, caring. It melted her heart—a candle against a flame.

❧

Her fieldwork for the practicum was almost complete as planned—only a few interviews remained. She had an extra month to complete the finishing touches and see more of Fiji before flying back to the U.S. Three months in Fiji had passed in the wink of an eye.

Now she had all the time in the world to know more of Zayn . . . he reigned in her heart.

# CHAPTER SIX

# Grains of Sand . . . and the Land of Hibiscus

Opshora was content. Life in the island country suited her, completed her. Zayn and she had been dating for almost two months—she had told him about her one-month vacation to visit the outlying islands. Zayn agreed to take time off to be with her. She knew that would be the opportunity to discuss their relationship further, make future plans—to check what he was thinking. She didn't want to deal with it in a hurry. She realized what she had with Zayn was rare, precious. She didn't want to jeopardize it in any way by abruptly departing from the island.

That's when tragedy struck. Her life took a 360-degree turn. And she made a life changing decision. It wasn't on impulse . . .

As agreed, Zayn rang the doorbell on that Saturday afternoon to pick Opshora up and drive her to the Pacific Harbor Hotel, which gloated in its legendary tradition and exquisiteness, fronting the ocean. He had the evening planned out—stroll on the seaside promenade, taste the beach vendors' cuisines for dinner and later lie on the damp sand closer to the water as the night deepened. At the wee hours of the morning when the entire Suva city was wrapped in the comfort of sleep, crawl back to it again. He also intended to tell Opshora how intense his feelings had grown for her . . . if she would consider rescheduling her trip back home, delay by a few more months, and consider some planning for the future. He wanted to know her better, test out the depth of what they were experiencing. He wasn't ready yet to let her go. In his heart he realized Opshora was a one-time gift. He might not find anyone like her, ever. He was willing to visit her in the U.S.—together think through a mechanism for a long-distance relationship if she felt the same way about him. He knew she was into him but wasn't sure enough about what her thoughts were for the future.

Zayn waited for some time but Opshora didn't answer the door. Maybe she was taking her time to get ready, or could have drowsed off he assumed. She was normally good with timing. The house was on a mound connected with the street below by a brick stairway—wide and shallow in depth. The grass and wild flowers crept over the old bricks, nestled between age-cracks. He walked back down the stairs for a quick cigarette puff in the meanwhile, prepared to wait. The sky gleamed against the floating clouds. It was serene, and had a calming effect. And at that moment Opshora appeared at the top of the stairs, against the unbolted door, distraught and confused—her hair caught the glow of the crimson sky behind her. Something was wrong. He threw away his cigarette and leaped up the stairs, crossing two at a time. In an instant he was besides her, holding her in his arms.

"Opshora, what's happened? What . . . "

By that time she was crying hysterically. She kept pounding her head against his chest while lamenting in a muffled voice. It took him several minutes to understand her.

"He had no chance . . . he just fell on the cold ground . . . oh! He died just like that," she kept repeating incoherently amidst a torrent of tears.

"Opshora! Opshora! Tell me . . .what happened?" He tried to figure out but she was dazed in her grief.

Finally, Zayn understood her uncle had died of a massive heart attack, while at work. She was very close to him, loved him as a second father, he knew from the stories she shared about her family. Her aunt Leila was dumb founded and the entire family was pulled into immense anguish at the unexpected tragedy. He died alone, among strangers and co-workers.

Zayn drove Opshora to the airport. She waited in his office cubicle for hours, drowned in her sorrow while he tried several airlines for a ticket. Zayn called his airline's offices to check if a flight was possible that night. All flights were booked; the tourist season was at its peak. He came back to her with the possibility of a wait list ticket with Qantas Airlines via Sydney late evening the next day with a transit of eighteen hours en route. Nothing was confirmed, she would be taking her chances of getting on that flight. It was also a very expensive option. By the time her plane touched down in her hometown, Dr. Mirza would be safely put to rest in his grave. She was too tired, too much in pain and wasted in her misery to try to go through the ordeal further. She called home instead of trying to fly back. No one picked up.

"I didn't get the ticket. I can't come home. I am so . . . so sorry," she whispered in a dull, mechanical tone to the impersonal answering machine option.

She was numb in her pain away from loved ones on the other side of the globe, across oceans. Like a zombie she followed Zayn to the car park. It began to drizzle and the pebble-strewn path to the open parking lot stung her bare feet. She forgot to wear her sandals when she came out with Zayn. She didn't recognize the car. He may have borrowed it from a friend at the airport because she remembered they rode here in his motorbike that made more noise than speed.

"Come, let's go in," she opened her eyes at Zayn's voice. They were parked at an unknown destination. She had no recollection of the drive. Possibly had dozed off in exhaustion while they drove. She couldn't recognize the place.

"This is my family home. I am taking you to my mom. She knows what to do," there was a calm assurance.

The door opened and the kindest of faces came out with outstretched arms. Without any hesitation Opshora submitted to Salote, the heavy bosomed body made of the softness of wool—the magnanimous woman who mothered Zayn and two of his siblings. Salote smelled of comfort mixed with the fragrance of flowers. Opshora cried as the warmth of the strong velvety arms encircled her and held her close, the gentle voice trying to ease her pain.

Though she tried she could never recall more about what followed that night. She only remembered the comfort, the healing outlines of the shadows, the hushed safety of the voices in the background.

She slept for sixteen hours without any interruption.

The news of Opshora's decision to get married came as a shock to her parents, her brother, Leila and her sons. Her parents read and re-read her letter in disbelief. They weren't able to attend as MD Mirza's practice was packed and Ruby's store was undergoing an expansion. Those were not the only reasons. It was also because Opshora informed them at the last minute—just three days before the wedding. Long distance travel required adequate planning. Ruby's passport needed to be renewed. MD Mirza's back up colleague was on leave.

Opshora would have liked her aunt to be beside her but it wasn't the best time for Leila to travel. She was still in mourning. She had buried Dr. Mirza just four weeks ago. The family was still trying to reemerge after the tragedy.

But Robin flew across the ocean to meet Zayn in person and landed in Fiji the night before the wedding. He conveyed their parents' blessings to Opshora. Though he chose his words carefully he couldn't fully hide their deep unhappiness and disappointment. That was the family mandate, which created more resistance in her. She knew how critical Ruby was, as she had always been with Opshora's choices, possibly also responsible for MD Mirza's silence towards her.

Robin tried his best, quite unsuccessfully, to smooth the rough feelings, though. Opshora smelled her parents' disapproval in his words. She knew she had failed them again.

"Are you pregnant? Is that the reason for the sudden marriage?" Robin wanted to know when they were finally alone and could catch up, amidst the last-minute preparations for the wedding.

"No! No!" She vehemently protested. "I love Zayn. My family has to understand this. Accept my decision . . . why can't anyone be happy for me?"

"But you know this man barely . . . only for three or four months? And you are marrying him!" Frustration was apparent in Robin's tone, doubt shone in his eyes.

"You don't need a lifetime to discover true love. It just happens, Robin. It's so genuine what we both feel. I am old enough to understand what's good for me."

"What about your studies?" He was interested in her future plans.

"What about it?" she countered.

"Our parents want you to complete your masters."

"I will. When I am ready. Please tell them to get out of my hair," was all she said.

Robin and Zayn were from two different universes. There was more awkwardness than camaraderie between them. Neither tried to break the barriers that separated them or search for commonalities that could bind them. But of course they had very little time to know each other, hang out or do activities together that men usually engaged in. Opshora was pained. She had expected more understanding from her brother. She blamed Robin mainly for his strange attitude towards Zayn. She knew her family was judgmental—Zayn didn't match their expectations.

They got married quietly on a beautiful day, as the bees were drunk on the summer blossoms; the waves broke gently on the shores. Opshora was giddy with happiness and excitement as the simple, endearing marriage ceremony was performed on the open beach with the sound of the ocean against the sands stirred by low breeze, under the soft glow of the dying sun. A family friend agreed to officiate the civil marriage outside of his stuffy registrar's office. A handful of relatives, close friends, and Opshora's three roommates attended. In spite of any misgivings, Robin's heart ached with affection as he witnessed his sister's happiness. Somehow this fantasy marriage turned into a reality.

Zayn's mother, Salote, wanted a Catholic wedding in her church. He convinced her not to put pressure on Opshora. Opshora preferred a civil marriage, as she wasn't into any religion. But she agreed to observe all rituals that were part of the island culture.

Zayn was married once earlier at barely twenty, got divorced after a year, followed by two more romantic associations that survived another couple of years, altogether. There were several very transitional relationships that fizzled out faster than they lasted. His emotional life wasn't in great shape. The women he was involved with were from his own community, same race, and followed a similar faith. Salote was anxious for him to be happy; she was additionally protective about him because he was the last born after two girls. She had hoped so much for him—a loving partner for life, healthy children, a happy, carefree existence. Opshora was totally the opposite to all the women in his life. As a mother

Salote was apprehensive, somewhat confused and doubtful about the future this young couple was weaving together, intoxicated in the passion of the moment, forgetful of the reality lying ahead. They were too different, belonged to diverse worlds. Opshora was so foreign, so unlike the island women in every possible way. Interracial marriages between Fijian men and women of Asian descent were quite rare, a very bold move. It didn't make sense to her but then none of Zayn's past romantic liaisons bore positive outcomes. She discussed this perceived threat with her married daughters, their husbands, her close friends, her sisters and the pastor she trusted most. Salote was a mother but above all she was wise and smart.

"Salote, you are a very intelligent woman. Times are changing and we have to open our hearts," the pastor's wisdom was too straightforward to be ignored. She listened to his advice and restrained her inner voices, decided to give Opshora a chance.

Opshora had flowers in her hair and wore a teal-colored cotton dress and strapless sandals adorned with vibrant beads. Zayn came in his usual attire with love in his eyes, passion tucked under his smiles. She trembled in anticipation as they stepped together to tie the knot. The butterflies in her stomach weren't born of doubt—but spelled feverish desire to be with Zayn. It was a simple event. Later, at his family home the real celebration began amidst music, food, drinking and dancing in a great fury of festivity. It was like an island fairy tale and she was the princess of the story. It was very new to her—the island vivacity, the intoxicating landscape and the amazing people.

"Mom and dad would like to visit. They miss you . . . they think their little girl is lost in this island country," Robin tried another angle to soften Opshora after the wedding was over.

"I am not lost. Nor am I a little girl. They chose not to attend my wedding . . . I will invite them over only when the time is right," she kept a defiant stance. At twenty-something she was still headstrong and a rebel.

"To be fair to them—you gave us a very short notice, sis. You can't blame parents." Robin's accusation was true. Opshora actually was relieved when their parents couldn't make it. She didn't want them here right now. Ruby might have sniffed more than there was in reality. She wasn't prepared for her mother's disapproval. She didn't want anything to spoil her happiness.

Robin was booked at a hotel in downtown Suva. During his brief stay in Fiji he came over to see Opshora every day at her new joint family residence. There were always people in the house—everyone welcomed Robin. There was a lot of food, drinking and merry making following the wedding. The newly married couple postponed their honeymoon till Robin's departure a week later. In a house full of people Robin didn't get any chance to speak alone to Opshora apart from a very few brief moments before she walked to the wedding altar.

On the day he was about to fly out, Opshora came to see him at his hotel. She wanted him to remember her as a happy, confident, married woman. Not as his defiant, immature little sister. Robin wasn't expecting her. He had bid farewell to her the night before. He was thinking of a lazy day strolling around Suva, as his flight was later in the evening. He was both surprised and happy to see Opshora outside his door.

They went for a long walk on the beach. The sun was merciful, lying low behind a curtain of clouds. The breeze was high, not oppressive. Early signs of a monsoon storm—a depression was forming somewhere. With the vastness of the ocean in the background, it was easy to talk. Both siblings felt at ease after years of built-up tension. Robin held Opshora with an arm around her shoulder, very much like he often used to do during their teenage growing up years. They hadn't been like this for ages, Opshora remembered with a shock.

"I am so glad you came, Robin," she was genuine. "I don't think I could get married without you. You have always been present on the best days of my life."

"And the worst," Robin said quietly. Opshora stiffened. Robin had to spoil everything, brush aside every laurel branch she offered. But she chose to ignore his jab.

"Opshora, I know I wasn't always available to hang out with you, but I loved it whenever we spent time together," Robin confessed, a bit pensive.

"Really? You were such an outdoor junkie those days!" Robin laughed at the way Opshora responded.

"Because of you I learned to be more attentive in chess as I played and lost to you!" They both laughed at Robin's frank admission.

"I enjoyed the times you joined me in hikes. Remember that trail we used to take from Georgetown? The wildflowers and ferns followed us with the trees . . . for miles and miles," Opshora was nostalgic.

"Yep. But I seldom went with you. Feel bad . . . But thanks for remembering the good memories," Robin sounded somewhat guilty.

"Don't be silly! Those were good times," Opshora was generous today. She wasn't sure when she would see her brother again. "Listen, there's a tiny eating place close to the water. Zayn and I discovered it when we first started dating. You will love their seafood dishes. Let's go there," Opshora proposed. It was still early for lunch but Robin decided he could do with that.

"I will race you," Opshora broke free from him and as it used to be in those long-lost years, they became kids again. Robin chased her, leaving deep footprints in the damp sand. When they reached the eatery, they were light-hearted, laughing their lungs out.

"To you, my incredible darling sister! And to our everlasting sibling rivalry and love!" Robin raised his glass at lunch.

It stung somewhere though it was said without malice. But again, Opshora ignored it.

They spent the whole day together. In the afternoon they returned to his hotel room. Opshora showered and wore Robin's extra clean pajamas and T-shirt like she sometimes used to in the good old days. The clothes hung loose—too big for her. She was tired and fell asleep on his bed while he did last minute packing. He watched his sister sleeping against the backdrop of the foaming waves outside his window. It was a peaceful picture—silently he wished all the best to Opshora, in her new life on this paradise island.

Opshora came to the airport with Robin. The flight was at eleven. The night was bright—it was full moon. A cool, pleasant breeze blew from the Pacific like a balm.

"Do you really need to stay out so long? Zayn wouldn't mind? It's getting late." He wanted to be sure.

"He wouldn't. It's Fiji. It's normal to be with my family. And it's very safe not like America. I will take a cab back home," she assured him. She stood against the glow of the streetlights caught up in her hair, eyes betraying hints of tears. That was the image Robin carried in his heart as he walked through airport security. He carried a strange ache in his heart for his sister as he kept walking . . . and as the Boeing jet pierced through the stars towards the Northern hemisphere.

Robin landed in the U.S., disheartened, somewhat sad. He didn't want to leave behind his sister on a forlorn island, so angry with the family, so alone, thousands of miles away. He wasn't sure of Zayn's motives, was perplexed by his large extended family. Their interactions were brief. There was politeness, no warmth. He didn't understand the island culture. Though he had vowed to keep in touch with Opshora, his hectic schedule in medical school was too overwhelming to give space to anyone—anything else. Sometimes he fell asleep while in the restroom or standing in line for coffee. Even a sixty-second nap was precious.

Opshora waited for his letter, his call. When nothing came she was hurt. She would have liked to reconnect with him. She tried to bury her hurt, shrug him off from her mind. "He has no time for me. Like always," her mind whispered with finality.

However, Ruby and MD Mirza were smart. They listened to Robin's narratives and analysis attentively and drew their own conclusions. They didn't want a total divorce from their only daughter's life. They began contacting her by phone. The line wasn't always good and it was expensive. But they didn't give up. They got to know Zayn as much as the phone connectivity allowed. They waited for an invitation to visit the couple, in time. Opshora wasn't ready for them. She never invited them. Then too many things happened and eventually the opportunity got lost.

Salote didn't understand Opshora that well. But ultimately she came to love this very alien young woman she mistrusted at the beginning. Salote and Opshora became allies with a promise to protect and nurture Zayn with their love for him.

Life with Zayn was very different, intense, rocky, turbulent. It was packed with manic passions and romantic adventures—any woman's dream. The first year flew in the speed of light, and after it was over, reality kicked in. The differences began to surface. Very slowly, almost imperceptibly at first, realization began to crawl in crowding their relationship. What she adored at the beginning as untamed excitement, infinite elation, became a liability as the months progressed. This unbridled gaiety involved unbound drinking, recurrent late-night parties and long, never ending hours in the company of strangers with whom she had very little in common. He just left her with them while he continued his alcohol-induced merry making in countless crammed bars beating with party music.

"Zayn, I don't like your drinking. You have to stop," she complained repeatedly, her heart starting to be clouded in furtive doubts that were hard to banish. "I don't recognize you when you are drunk!"

"I promise. I will stop. I will become better . . . as you want." He agreed without any protests. "I love you. You are most important to me." But Zayn was too complacent in his lifestyle. He walked back on his words. Unabashed. Opshora was always there, in his life, waiting for him. She took him back every time he misbehaved. That must have emboldened him to take her for granted.

"You got to restrain your drinking, Zayn. I feel helpless sitting among strangers all night. You forget I exist!" She had angrily retorted in some instances, disturbed at his heartlessness when he boozed. She was afraid of that dark side in him, didn't anymore find the caring man she married.

"Come on . . . I am always around you!" Zayn was quick to protest.

"You don't care about what matters to me. Not anymore . . . Don't spoil what we have, Zayn. It's good stuff." She was hurt and drained. The constant heartache of unpredictable ups and downs—she was losing him. It taxed their relationship, wrecking her peace of mind.

"My seashell . . . my rocky princess! Shh! Stop being melodramatic," he was beside her, and readily held her next to his heart. His murmurs melted all resistance. It carried a magic that bewitched her. He threw his charms without realizing how she was impacted. That was their ordinary routine caught in a torrent of emotions, folded in a façade of normalcy that didn't make sense to Opshora anymore.

# CHAPTER SEVEN

# *Storm*

Zayn made a promise only to break it. When he broke it, he became rowdier than in the past. When he drank, he lost control, he disregarded sensibility. One night on their way home in his drunkenness he went off track and hit a tree on the roadside. The car stopped with a loud throttle. Opshora was shaken. Zayn could barely keep his eyes open but he was scared as well. Luckily, they weren't spotted by any patrolling police as it was almost three in the morning. They sat in the car without speaking for hours till a passing vehicle noticed them and came to their assistance. Zayn was more restrained for about two weeks after this incident. But then he was back to his old habits soon enough.

Opshora slowly began to retreat away from him, helpless, humiliated. She was also a bit fearful sometimes. In his drunken recklessness he could get hurt. She couldn't turn to anyone. It was a shameful thing to admit about their gradually failing relationship, even to herself. In the Fijian culture, Zayn's behavior was looked upon as a silly male thing. Traditions were more liberal to accept delinquencies from the male of the species, always. Zayn was taking care of Opshora, responsible at work, not womanizing, and very much in love with her. People saw that and didn't understand why she was turning this into a bigger issue than it was.

"We value our men when they take care of the household, kids, relatives and parents. It's more than a husband-wife relationship." Salote didn't mince words. She was straightforward and tried to enlighten Opshora about the Fijian norm—the tradition that had been passed on from one generation to the other. That was the island way.

"Opshora, he loves you. You are so lucky that you are anchored tightly within his heart," Zayn's older sister Filo offered as advice. She was separated from her husband John for a year and was back at her parental home with her two children. John ran a shipping company and was too much into wine and women. Being a Catholic she didn't want a divorce but couldn't live with him and his relentless lies and cheating on her. Salote and the pastor were helping her with her dilemma and pain.

"Zayn's eyes hold only one face. Yours," Filo emphasized.

Opshora understood what Filo was saying, what others around her were hinting at. But an inner voice havocked her tranquility. She wasn't used to Zayn's ways, his love that was hurtful. She was brought up differently.

Men's misbehavior was not new to her. There were several kids from her school who lived with the pain of their parents' divorce due to spousal betrayals. She had seen this trend in her adult life, around her. But she had never witnessed her own father or uncle or older cousins breaking the ground rules that destroy family life. The men in her universe were firmly grounded in family values. There were differences but not enough to make cracks.

Opshora was intensely miserable—torn between anger and embarrassment, love and dejection, stupefied in frustration in herself, mostly. The problem was that still her heart foolishly fluttered for Zayn.

"Zayn, I can't do this anymore." She walked away from his arms sometimes, sad and disheartened. He was thoughtful, momentarily guilty. When sober he was so loving, attentive to her every wish. But by the next evening he was a slave to his recklessness. Opshora refused to go out with him. One night he came home drunk in the dead of night, slopped down at the foot of the bed and slept there, totally wasted. Finding him like that in the morning, she was full of tenderness and revulsion at the same time. She washed up, changed silently without waking him and tip toed out of the house. The entire day she sat in a tiny café at the edge of the beach near Victoria Parade reflecting on her life. She was sad, felt lonelier than ever before. She missed her family, the streets of home, the warmth of the life left behind so casually. The intoxicating aroma of her mother's kitchen, her father's ever present gentle laughter lingering in the background, Robin's arrested-adolescence kind of pranks sneaked into her heart, one by one. She drank loads of coffee as the memories pierced through her.

The incidents with Zayn kept recurring. After a recent meltdown with Zayn she called Lara, Jane and Laisani. She needed her friends. Laisani had moved out months ago but the other two girls were still sharing the same house.

"I feel lost," Opshora told them honestly, without any hesitation as they all met up for lunch. The bond with her friends remained unwavering though after her marriage she got busy with Zayn and her new life under Salote's roof she shared with so many others.

"I don't know where I am going with my life…Zayn… nothing is making sense." It was hard and painful to admit.

"Do you still love him?" Lara asked.

Opshora took a while before she replied while her friends waited patiently. It was a soul-searching question. She didn't know how to tell them . . .

"Yes. Yes, I do," she whispered. She was surprised at her shame to admit that she was still in love with Zayn.

They understood—her love and her pain. "We have been married over a year...but our differences seem insurmountable."

"From the bits and pieces you have been sharing from time to time, I've been thinking about you and Zayn," Jane confessed. "I didn't want to pry. But I worry for you, Opshora." The others were concerned too, and sad.

She stayed the night in her old bed in the house she had lived in with her friends. She didn't call home though she knew she should have. The next morning when she returned home Zayn had left for work. Others were out in their daily pursuits. Filo had taken her children to school. Only Salote was sitting on the balcony, stony-faced, waiting for her. Opshora was received with cold indifference by Salote as she entered the house. Salote didn't ask anything, didn't greet her. That was her rebuke for Opshora's irresponsible behavior.

With Zayn's extended family, Opshora managed to bridge the gaps, in spite of all cultural differences. However, there were some situations that had to be navigated with care—both by Opshora and Salote. Salote was fond of Opshora but wasn't willing to step in to chastise her grown up son. It didn't happen in Fiji. She felt Opshora needed to understand the fabric of this culture, the norms that bound the men and women in this society, and separated them in their individual roles. The "foreign airs" wouldn't resolve conflicts but pierce the much-valued harmony. It was essential to act mature and accept the reality. Island life was different. Salote made this very clear to Opshora.

"Coming back to me doesn't absolve him...he has a responsibility towards us, to create a life with me," Opshora had argued with Salote.

"You don't even realize what you have, Opshora," Salote shut her down. Opshora felt she was let down by Salote.

"This is how it is here, Opshora. Men get away with so much wrongdoing. Our society has double standards. It doesn't forgive a woman easily but turns a blind eye to men's missteps," Filo was more understanding. "I have endured a lot in my marriage with an unfaithful husband. He is not going to change. Eventually I know I will have to go back to him. But you have the power to choose to be happy or sad . . . make your marriage work," Filo said with firm gentleness. It seemed everyone's expectation was on her to take charge.

On weekdays both Zayn and Opshora were busy and came home late from work. She had taken a job at a school to teach history and English language to senior grade students. She liked her work and also began to labor over the book she was writing on Fiji. She decided to wrap up the last bit of work for her practicum. She was determined to complete her degree. She wrote to her professors. She also had plans to get her book published. This meant a few extra hours in the library in the evenings on most days. At the end of the day, Opshora felt like collapsing after the grueling hours with adolescents, trying to teach, manage their emotions, resolve conflicts sensibly, and stay focused. It wasn't an easy job to engage young minds and inspire them to learn, motivate them to behave responsibly in order to maintain the sanctity of collective harmony.

She was cut off from her own family and emotionally getting drained, beaten. Scanty phone calls bordered on civilities only—didn't delve into emotional domains. In any case, she couldn't come out honestly regarding her marital problems with her parents, separated by thousands of miles. She wasn't honest with Leila, either. They corresponded now and then. She vividly described the beauty and many mysteries of Fiji to her aunt but carefully shielded her life with Zayn. Leila never intruded so Opshora didn't reveal much.

Robin was caught up in his studies and didn't call or write as promised. Opshora didn't want to understand the demands of medical studies—she labeled him as heartless. On all those days and nights of sadness over Zayn she waited for her brother to check on her. For a long time she couldn't forgive him for letting her down, again.

Opshora felt sad. They argued often when they returned home from the pub. The entire household heard them at the dead of the night in that silent house. It was humiliating. There was no remedy. Conversation didn't progress much. The joy was all gone . . . Zayn transformed her in every possible way—with his love for her and his selfishness.

That's when family and friends advised her to have a baby. Experienced well-wishers swore that fatherhood could change men like Zayn—basically who were decent, warm and caring but struggling to be harnessed in domesticity. She shouldn't have to give up so easily, without a fight to save her marriage.

# CHAPTER EIGHT

# *Wheels of Change*

Zayn was a romantic. He trusted passion over linking of the souls. He thought Opshora would recognize his devotion towards their relationship and embrace him exactly as he was. She fell in love with him knowingly—his island charms and limitations. He believed his life away from home was very much his own and she shouldn't have any say in that. That was the men's domain, reserved for Fijian males where women seldom trod. He was conscious of his drunken behavior but stopped being ashamed of it gradually. Everyone drank and made a fool of themselves in public, now and then. It was to de-stress from everyday pressures at work, life in general—a malady to unwind. Such conduct was considered harmless. Society forgave and forgot these acts as a commonplace matter. It tolerated such behavior.

"I am just having a good time. Don't be so obsessed, princess. Stop, please. I will be sober tomorrow morning, promise," those were his usual drunken lines uttered with an occasional twinge of discomfort.

Opshora's life was crowded; there was too much happening in her orbit. Some matters never stayed private, in the boundary of their bedroom. And everyone had an opinion, some advice for her, not so much for Zayn. It choked her.

On that beautiful morning when the doctor confirmed she was pregnant, she was dancing with the clouds. With tons of happiness packed in her heart, Opshora bounced out of the clinic. The universe seemed different, bursting with joy, in tenderness, recognizing the new existence growing deep inside her. The news overrode all doubts, took away every ache. Her eyes could almost discern each speck of vivacious light landing softly on the awakened leaves of the lush palm trees. The blooms everywhere were rioting in color bursts that paled the sounds of the passing motors, the smell of dust on the streets, the monotony of the commuters stepping towards yet another loaded day—the canvas of predictability unfolding into Opshora's careless alacrity. The world around her was stirring with a new meaning. Impulsively she hopped into a taxi towards Naussori airport with a determination to surprise Zayn.

"I am so happy, so, so happy!" Zayn had folded her in his arms in tenderness, somber. His eyes gleamed with a hint of subdued tears. He was delighted. The old Zayn she knew and had fallen in love with was back again. In a flash all the stacked hurt vanished. His office cubicle seemed too small to hold the enormous joys they held in their hearts!

He took the day off. On his motorbike they rode towards the farthest corner of their favorite beach. They were like con-spiratorial teenagers dodging work. They hadn't been here since those dating times. On the way they had stopped to pick up take away lunch and fruit juice. Wine and beer were off the list. He cared for her, for their baby. Suddenly after so many wasted months their life together promised so much meaning. It was back on track. They lay on the beach. The damp sand was soothing.

"If it's a boy I will teach him to surf and go deep sea fishing," he announced.

"Why not to a girl? You are gender biased," she had teased.

"No, no . . . she would be exactly like you . . . beautiful . . . head full of dark hair, enchanting smile . . . Delicate from the outside, but strong of will . . . and mind. She will work to change the world. Change Fiji," he added thoughtfully, honestly. "But she can surf . . . and fish if she wants to." To that both had laughed.

"No night fishing," she added. He hugged her close and nodded.

Zayn had made her confident about the looks she had struggled with in her schoolgirl days. She assumed brown skin was dirty. In those teenage years the concept of beauty to her was palest of pale skin, blue eyes and auburn or golden hair—very much like Clara and her followers. She was embarrassed as her body developed curves; her full size breasts . . . healthy figure . . . she wanted to be pencil thin, flat like those popular girls in her class. She had to come all the way to this magical island to finally find out she was beautiful! The islanders called her "gorgeous." She didn't need the pale snow-white skin and blue eyes and golden hair anymore . . .

Later they threw back seashells and trapped fishes into the ocean. Covered the dead fishes under the damp sand. This was their favorite activity on the beach, always. They also collected clamshells and cowry. The beach was like a minefield of such treasures, a bounty hurled by the deep waters, relentlessly.

They were happy again. Very, very much together again—that evening. They came back home as the sky broke into a million stars.

The happiness of pregnancy spilled over into his life. He was content, willing to experience the exuberance that was changing their lives. Opshora became more accommodating, cheerful and relaxed as the pregnancy progressed—something that relieved him. He met her needs with care, respected her wishes. He was ready to change in his ways; he treasured their newfound happiness, and the harmony in their marriage. Their lives were steered away from the earlier rockiness to the lull of gratification found in a future both sought. The frequency of drinking was less, the pub-drunkenness stopped totally. He began inviting his close buddies to their home now and then to share a few glasses of whisky, sometimes sherry or port. Opshora had no objections to that.

"I told you Zayn is a good man," Filo reminded her often. "He can be a softy when he really gives his heart to someone. He has given his to you."

When she woke him up in the middle of the night he was startled into an unexpected confusion. The white bed sheet cringed under the depth of crimson. She was bleeding. He was confused, trembled in nervousness, hands shaking— body misaligned in the urgency of the moment. He was more afraid for her. The intensity of pain came later. Salote and the others were away at a wedding in Nadi town. The house was almost empty except for an elderly houseguest couple.

As he paced the hospital corridor outside the operation theatre, Zayn mourned for the lost baby, for Opshora whose happiness was crumbling by the minute. The elation of fatherhood had consumed him. Opshora believed their fate could be cemented together with children as the anchor. That prospect seemed hollow now. He felt defeated, wasted. And a formidable fear gripped his heart. He called his mother from the hospital and cried like a child when he heard Salote's voice on the other side of the line. He couldn't bear the load of loss anymore.

"Opshora is in a great shock. She has regained consciousness from anesthesia. But is forcing her mind to go back to her unconscious state. It's her defense mechanism. Doesn't want to face her pain," the elderly gynecologist was full of sympathy. "She needs care and understanding."

Opshora didn't want to get up from the hospital bed—wake up. Zayn brought her home a week later. Her eyes were vacant, hollow. She didn't speak a single word. Salote and Filo had abruptly left the wedding and returned home. They were eagerly waiting for her. Opshora didn't respond to their greetings. She walked past them and took refuge in her bed and slept and slept for many hours. She simply wanted to die.

Opshora's grief isolated her. She collected all the aches and tried to bury them in the deepest blues of her heart. She kept drowning and drowning in a fathomless pit of sorrow. She turned into a dead person, breathing only to live an existence pointless to her. Opshora felt the death of her baby was cruel, unnecessary, absolutely immoral—obscene. She didn't deserve this. She couldn't forget how her baby was cold, lay lifeless for hours in the safety of the womb until taken forcibly away from her. Zayn watched her, helpless.

In her pain Opshora became untouchable, an unyielding goddess of infinite sorrow.

"I am here . . . look at me. We can start all over again. We are still young," Zayn pleaded over and over. He wanted to cling to new hopes. She didn't respond to his pleas. Didn't stir to his caring efforts.

"I am tired," sometimes she whispered back as her empty eyes looked far away. He couldn't cross over into her life of loss, bridge the anguish that separated them. She was a changed person when she came back from the hospital burying her dreams.

Opshora took four months leave from work to recover and also to think. She was on strong sleeping pills at night and slept through half of the day mostly. Some days she would be gone for hours strolling on the beach or lost in the wilderness of streets all around the city. She lost weight, making her look much younger than she was. Hidden in her eyes was the sparkle of rage—ready to start a fire. There was a covert fury inside her that took over. She didn't cry—the tears froze into lumpy icebergs and nestled in her brain. Zayn reached out to her friends. Invited them to the house to be with Opshora, speak with her. Lara, Laisani and Jane came by. They understood her pain. But they couldn't help much

"Zayn, maybe you should think of sending her home to her mother? For some time . . . to recover?" Salote said, really worried for Opshora's mental wellbeing. The household agreed as they witnessed Opshora's unbearable agony. No one had the remedy for her anguish. They tiptoed around her. They were relieved when she slept or went out of the house. She walled herself in—didn't allow anyone to come near her.

"No. I will stay here. I'm not going anywhere," Opshora was calm when Zayn proposed a visit to the U.S. She couldn't think of going away. He was confused; he didn't know the art of persuasion, how to console a bereaved mother.

Salote invited a group of her elder female kin with a reputation for consoling bereft souls. They tried to talk to Opshora in their broken English. They sang hymns popular in times of grieving. Opshora sat among them like a statue curved out of stone. Her heart had become like a piece of rock. The women couldn't do much. Salote brought in her pastor. Opshora refused to get up from her bed. She took another sleeping pill and slept through the day. After that Zayn forbade his mother to try to cure Opshora.

"My son, I tried. I can't somehow break the circle of pain she has shut herself in," Salote was exasperated and sad and frustrated. Opshora had become a stranger in her sorrow.

"Give her time, Mama. Let her mourn. Let all the pain and aches get out of her and she will come around," Zayn told Salote. But Opshora's pain never died. It never lessened. It kept burning and burning and consumed her eventually . . .

Opshora didn't go back to the U.S., not even for a short visit to see her family. She didn't even attend Robin's wedding. Both Robin and his fiancee Maya were doing residency at the time and decided to tie the knot. Robin wrote to her to share the good news but she never responded. He wrote again. He was too late. His letters remained in a pile on top of Opshora's dresser, unopened.

"I have lost my baby, *Ama*," was all she could say to her mother in a broken choked voice over a partially dysfunctional telephone connection when Ruby could finally get hold of Opshora. "I am sorry I can't come to the wedding," she whispered fighting to keep the tears out of her voice.

Ruby was stunned. Opshora hadn't told her she was pregnant. Didn't know what to say. Being a mother Ruby was lost for words to comfort another grieving mother. There was a long silence as she absorbed the news. Her pain robbed her of her voice. In a flash Opshora's sadness travelled thousands of miles and landed in Ruby's heart, consumed her with agony. She was paralyzed in woe.

Opshora interpreted Ruby's silence as her displeasure for regretting to attend Robin's wedding. Countless thoughts floated through her mind as she waited patiently for her mother to say something. And she drew her conclusion that Ruby never understood her—not her joys or pains. Ruby, however, regained her composure and in a deliberate, steady voice offered to fly over to be with her but Opshora said "no." Then the line went dead. Ruby's calls were not answered anymore; her parents decided to give her some time to recover. They called Zayn but he didn't pick up their calls either.

Opshora refused to talk to her father, and never took calls from Robin or Leila. She shut herself into her world of isolation, crafted in immense gloom.

Opshora had carried her baby in the womb for almost six months, felt its heartbeat with her own each moment of its existence and then suddenly one morning all ended. Her inside gnawed with a strange hollowness—pierced with numbing aches unknown to her before. The pain lived with her in every breath, every heartbeat. There was no escape from it . . . sometimes she felt the baby was still inside her—she imagined she heard its heartbeats . . .

Then there were additional complications that began to choke the country. The political upheaval in Fiji escalated, undressed the gradual brewing of racial tension and tore open the myth of the "cohabitation" façade. Frictions became obvious, inevitable amidst age-old latent undercurrents. The seed of nationalism planted years ago began to sprout with intensity, devoid of rational thinking—seeped in mistrust and anger. Political agitation toxic with nationalistic populism dominated the lives of the population.

Fiji islands have a fascinating history—a multi-racial heritage. Fiji's first settlers arrived from the islands of Melanesia at least/about 3,500 years ago. On October 10, 1874 Fiji became a British Crown colony.

Sir Arthur Gordon was Fiji's first governor general and commander in chief. His policies restricted the involvement of Fiji natives in commercial and political developments that crafted the history of this island nation. Sale of land was not permitted—native Fijians were taxed in agricultural produce. In addition, they were governed through a system of indirect rule.

Indian laborers were brought in to work in the colonial sugar refineries and plantations. At the end of their tenure the migrants were encouraged to stay back and settle in Fiji. They didn't have lands and had restricted political rights. In 1920 Indians began strikes to voice their discontent and grievances.

Fiji was occupied by the allied forces during World War II. After the war was over, there was more agitation from the native Fijians and the Indian settlers as they were discriminated by the Europeans.

The constitution of 1966 ensured conciliation between the principles of parliamentary democracy and the ethnic divisions that prevailed in Fiji. On 10th October 1970 Fiji became an independent sovereign nation. However, in 1977, "Fiji for Fijians" movement became stronger.

In 1987, the Indian dominated National Federation Party formed a coalition with the new Labor party and this alliance won in the election. The newly formed government with Indian majority was resisted by the native-Fijians. It was shortly overthrown in a coup masterminded by Lt Col Rabuka who demanded stronger native-Fijian control in the government. A state of emergency was declared by the governor-general. He established full control of the government and initiated negotiations to diffuse the political differences and unite towards a civilian government. Lt Col Rebuka wasn't satisfied and took over the government in a second coup and executed a military rule. He revoked the 1970 constitution and declared Fiji a republic. Fiji was ousted from the Commonwealth. However, Rabuka formed a new civilian government. A new constitution to concentrate power in the hands of native-Fijians was declared on July 25, 1990.

The years following the coups on May 14 and September 28, 1987, were especially a dark period in Fiji dominated by ethnic unrest and political instability. Racial disharmony continued to soar.

Fiji's political situation was gradually intensifying with the passing of each day. It hurt people, it hurt the economy and the communal safety net. In 1989 the political instability had escalated so much that many ethnic Indians began fleeing from Fiji. The new constitution of 1990 proclaimed the dominance of indigenous Fijians, creating bigger divisions. While all this was happening around her, Opshora was wrapped up with her own life—not paying much attention to the world outside her doorstep. As her life was falling apart, so was Fiji, in some ways.

"Don't go out walking by yourself. Not a good time to be out on the street," Zayn cautioned. "Indians are targeted."

"I am an American, not an Indian," Opshora replied, somewhat defiant. She was totally unmindful of the tense environment in the country.

"Yes, I know. But to a common Fijian you are no different than an Indian woman. You look like one," he was worried for her, as she would wander out anytime—stay outside long after dark. In 1990 Fiji was about to erupt—it wasn't safe anymore. Though discussions were ongoing, and voices were raised in favor of political sobriety, there were disturbing elements in the society. Disharmony was not totally incidental. It was rooted in many unsettled grievances.

One night when she was walking back towards home she found three young native Fijian men following her. As she started to walk faster they increased their speed. The street was deserted, windswept, subdued in shadows under the paleness of the low voltage lights, sinister in stripped isolation. The sounds of the waves deafened the faint noise of motors in the distant background. She was all by herself and the three young men at her heels, following, gaining on her slowly. There were a few sparse houses but they were far away from the road. She doubted if she screamed whether the residents would be able to hear her. If the men had run they could have caught up with her but they decided to bait her, intimidate her in silent determination by stalking her, keeping a certain distance matching her pace. She didn't know what could have happened that night if two cars, one tailing the other hadn't ventured on the street at that point. The blaring music filled the emptiness of the night from rolled down car windows. They were partygoers, merry-making on their way. They were moving at a pretty low speed, possibly waiting for more cars belonging to the group to catch up. Their presence broke the spell of fear, the ambience of menace. Her pursuers quickly scurried to a side ally and vanished. She was saved from any kind of mishap.

Opshora was shaking inwardly as she entered her home. For the first time in Fiji she was really afraid that night. Zayn's caution sank in. The men could have beaten her up or raped her. There were some cases—reported and unreported incidents of assaults on women of Indo-Fijian race. It was a difficult time to be an Indian in the enchanting island country. Hatred embedded in mistrust was destroying its beauty and history of generosity and hospitality.

# CHAPTER NINE

# Many Shades of Grief

Home was becoming claustrophobic to Zayn. He felt Opshora didn't see him anymore, refused to acknowledge his pain, his presence. He was mourning for their baby, for Opshora's sorrow, their relationship, the lost million moments of togetherness. He couldn't cry out, couldn't unburden his overwhelming sadness to anyone—not to his mother or the pastor. He was unable to share his agony with Filo or even his closest friends. The only person with whom he wanted to cry was Opshora—the only person who mattered at this moment of intense pain. But she had turned away from him. She didn't want him to be near her.

The pub was a better place for solace, easy comfort. He began to go back more frequently after work and hung in there till his body could no longer stay awake. It became the routine on weeknights and weekends. Stealthily, he would return to his bed mostly in the dead of the night. By that time Opshora was lost to the world under the influence of sleeping pills. The loss of her baby and the changes hitting Fiji were insurmountable uphill battles. At the time, she was incapable of coping with any of them.

Zayn and Opshora almost stopped talking. It was only mere polite exchanges of a word or two, sometimes in passing. Nothing of any consequence. There wasn't much to hold on to.

Christine was at the bar waiting for Zayn that evening as on so many previous ones, in recent times. She had been a pillar of support. With her he was himself again— free of guilt, liberated from the legacy of pain that Opshora dumped on him. The load of grief was unbearable, too heavy to endure. With Christine he wasn't ashamed to order a few extra drinks, not sorry to get drunk. He could step back into a normal, regular universe that wasn't fogged by ever consuming sorrow. To her he could air his anger and anguish. She listened, all attentive—didn't intimidate him like Opshora did with the hollow-haunted look in her eyes that failed to register his existence.

While walking along Albert Park around Victoria Parade on that evening, Opshora saw a young couple entering a nearby restaurant. They held the hands of a toddler in between them. The little girl was stepping with caution as her tiny ponytail swayed in the breeze, excitedly repeating something after the parents. The meaningfulness and joy of the moments they were sharing together as a family startled Opshora with an intense unexpectedness, bizarre hopes. She kept staring at them till they vanished inside the building. In that instant she recognized life was too vast to be bewildered so much, to waste away. It was still possible to have a different outcome in life even though so much had happened—if only she made an effort it could change, eventually. All wasn't lost yet. In a weird way she still loved Zayn and she knew he did love her, too. Something could be salvaged if she tried with genuine energy, if both she and Zayn were committed to try to rebuild their lives from the ashes of the current catastrophe that had shattered them. She was stunned at the way these thoughts kept stirring her emotions. In a flash the happenings of the recent months sped through her mind. In that instant she knew what she had to do.

She half ran towards home all the way in a daze. She didn't dare to delay one more minute. She didn't want to risk her change of heart. The house was quiet and dark. Zayn wasn't back—possibly still at the nearby pub down the road. Dusk was creeping in. Salote could be at the church. Filo was out with her children. In haste Opshora left the house looking for Zayn. She needed to find him. The urgency was killing her.

After a whole day of stress Zayn was loosening up over a glass of vodka. Christine sat close to him with her glass. Her demeanor screamed out comfort. He wanted to talk tonight. She had to lean close to his mouth to hear him over the loud music and voices. Their knees touched as she balanced herself on the high bar stool. He had his one hand on her thigh to steady him—his head felt light, weightless. The other hand that held the glass was shaking, slightly. He was mildly drunk already.

Opshora spotted them as she stepped inside the bar. She stood glued at the entrance. She noted his hand resting on Christine's thigh, the conspiratorial intimacy they shared, the spontaneity of proximity. It seemed he had moved on— drifted away already from her, their lives. In a shock, she realized it was too late. She had allowed too much time to glide by. A cold spasm slowly began to rise in her heart paralyzing her brain. She stood staring at them, motionless not knowing what to do. At that moment Zayn looked up and saw her standing frozen at the doorway. Christine turned her face as well and noticed her. He tried to rise from his seat, call out her name but had to steady himself with a hand on Christine's shoulder.

Zayn had dated Christine in the past, when they were both in college. Opshora knew about it. He wanted to present a clean slate when he proposed and had told her about Christine. Now she was back again, in his life. Zayn didn't hesitate to jump into her arms when things got tough between him and Opshora. That's how Opshora interpreted the scene at the bar.

The music, the voices, sounds of laughter seemed to rebuke her. Opshora couldn't bear it any longer. She ran out of the pub. She had to get out of there, fast. It was a mistake—the life that had spilled out couldn't be gathered back into her bare fists anymore. He didn't come after her, or try to stop her.

When Zayn returned at midnight she was up unlike most days. She was waiting for him. The sound of the distant waves filled the stony silence of the room. The salty ocean air floated in. He hesitated at the doorway. She sat in the semi-darkness of the bedroom, commanding its stark gloom.

"Come here. Sit down," she was calm as she pointed to the edge of the bed near her. He dragged his heavy body swaggering unsteadily and sat down facing her.

"Zayn . . . I want a divorce," her voice was soft, her eyes were shining as the sliver of the light tiptoeing in through the open windows reflected in her trapped teardrops. She didn't complain about his drinking, his intimacy with Christine at the bar. His heart melted with tenderness. He realized in that instant once again the intensity of his love for her. He couldn't say anything—he was too drunk to trust himself to speak. He didn't want the words to come out wrong. She was waiting.

"I will see a divorce lawyer tomorrow," she sounded so cold, so callously unfeeling. "It's for the best. For both of us," she sighed.

"Okay. If you think so . . . have no objection. I want you to be happy," was all he could muster. He was fed up. He was at the breaking point. She made him feel like a worthless loafer at that moment. His head was dizzy. He climbed in bed and fell asleep immediately. When he woke up next morning she was gone. He felt bad, empty and ashamed of his behavior last night. He remembered the scene at the bar, the discussion in the bedroom later. He knew he had hurt her, needed to clarify that there was nothing more between him and Christine than mere camaraderie.

That evening he didn't go to the pub. She returned before sunset. She appeared to be tired but more composed. She had hidden her sadness much better in the failing daylight.

"I wanted to say sorry about last night. Nothing happened with Christine," he wanted to clear the air. "We are just friends."

"You don't have to explain anything to me." She sounded exhausted.

"I do. Because it matters to me . . . because I love you even if you don't believe me anymore, Opshora."

"Zayn, I can't deal with this now, please . . . please don't put more pressure on me," her voice broke but she quickly composed herself. "Tomorrow I am going away to Sigatoka. For a week. I am thinking of completing my practicum. Finish my book." Zayn didn't comment. He kept staring at the vacant wall.

"I wrote to my professors. Explained everything. They accepted my plea . . . will allow me to re-enroll." Opshora tried to break the loaded awkwardness. Her school understood about her situation. It took her many hours and many tears to write that moving letter exposing her inner agony to near strangers. It was extraordinarily difficult to craft those impossible words—*I lost my baby . . .*

"Do you have to go back to finish your masters? When?" Somehow Zayn managed to utter. He felt he needed to say something as Opshora had shared so much. This was the first time she had spoken to him directly in so long—provided information about herself.

"I . . . I really don't know . . . I have to do the groundwork first . . . finish the practicum. Not sure how to speed it up . . . my school has given me a lenient deadline. It's a special circumstance, they said."

Zayn noticed how Opshora spoke casually and wandered

into other things, tactfully avoiding any personal emotions. He felt like biting off his tongue for exposing his vulnerability to her a little while ago—he was almost begging her to accept his love that he offered so honestly. She didn't care anymore, it seemed. But his heart churned at the sight of her face, sound of her voice. He couldn't discern what she was saying. He had to control his impulse to jump towards her and take her in his arms. He was afraid of her coldness, her rejection, and her nearness. She was like an ice maiden built out of tons and tons of sharp icicles, frozen in dense frost—the queen reigning in the land of melancholy.

Opshora left a note for him next morning listing down the documents and information the divorce lawyer had asked for. The lawyer's name and contacts were at the bottom of the page. Zayn had already met her—Laisani Fong. Opshora sought out her friend as her divorce lawyer. Laisani was a casual acquaintance—Zayn had met her with Opshora's other friends a few times at their house after the wedding. He never got a chance to warm up to Opshora's friends as their interactions were extremely brief. One part of him was angry, the other part felt empty and sad. He decided to drop by Laisani's office on his way to work.

In the evening, he went back to the pub where Christine waited for him. He was frightened of the emptiness of his bedroom without Opshora's habitual presence. The void was overwhelming, harsh.

Opshora returned after fifteen days, twice as long as planned. She had already called Salote and informed her about the delay. She had needed more time than anticipated for her work. So, Zayn couldn't reproach her.

He smelled her faint perfume in the empty bedroom air and knew she was back. He had missed her by minutes as she had gone out immediately after returning home. He was surprised to find a strong elation beginning to grow in his heart even after the conversation they had on divorce. But nothing had changed. That evening when he returned home, Opshora was already in a drug-induced sleep.

She worked at the library most of the time for the next two weeks and came home late. Zayn was careful not to come back too drunk and was home prior to her return. They exchanged brief civilities before crashing into bed. After their recent cold showdown they had begun to speak again—not much though but better than totally silent. Zayn's hopes flickered.

Opshora went to her school and resigned from her teaching job. The principal was reluctant to accept her resignation and proposed a six month-sabbatical at the end of which she could rejoin. She offered Opshora a lifeline to return to work.

"Think this over, Opshora. You have done wonders with the senior students. You inspire them. The parents are happy. It's all because of you. We don't want to lose you." But Opshora had made other plans.

" I can't . . . I feel empty inside," was the closest she could share. In time she and the principal had become friends and professional allies.

"I am almost your mother's age. I know time gives one the strength to move forward though the aches remain buried inside. Healing doesn't always happen. Only coping mechanisms kick in." She stopped to look at Opshora fighting back tears, her face averted towards the open window that caught the sunlight on the waves of the Pacific.

"The ocean brings high waves to the shores but also is tranquil when the wind dies . . . Don't run away from turmoil, Opshora. In some form or the other they will always shadow our lives." The principal couldn't be more direct. Her words were grounded in realism, and philosophical.

It was sad to say goodbye but there was no other option for Opshora at that particular time in her life. She enjoyed working at the school. It had become her second existence in

Suva. The care and respect from her students kept her going through the difficult months of loneliness in her marriage, in her overwhelming isolation from her family back in the U.S.

"You will think over my proposal, right?" The principal asked again.

"Yes, I will. I am so thankful for your understanding and kindness." Opshora walked back home with a heavy heart. She realized her love for Fiji was massive, heart wrenching. It made her sad.

Opshora went back to Sigatoka again. Her absence in some ways brought back the normal rhythm in the house. The old sense of carefree life began to resume. The cloud of sorrow burdening their lives was lifted. The family went about relieved, and stopped consciously looking over their shoulders to make sure Opshora wasn't disturbed, interrupted in her mourning. Voices were not hushed, laughter not subdued anymore. It was like being liberated from the burden of woe, of the guilt of embracing their normal lives.

After their initial discussion, Opshora hadn't brought up the issue of divorce though Zayn provided all the information to her lawyer as she had asked. Laisani was someone who understood her. Opshora knew she could trust her. They were good friends in addition to Laisani being a good lawyer. Lara and Jane were aware about her estranged relationship with Zayn, her heartbreaks and about the loss of her baby. Apart from them she didn't have real friends in Fiji. They were her sisters for life!

Days passed, uneventful. Opshora spent most of her time working on her practicum and her book. She was in and out of Suva. She contained all her pain inside her and tried to project calm. Zayn was careful. He returned home mostly sober and avoided Christine and the pub. He went out with his childhood friends and male cousins sometimes to break the stress. They played poker and drank at someone's home.

# CHAPTER TEN

# *Pale Incense, Faded Colors*

Zayn was surprised to see Opshora waiting in his office cubicle. His heart leapt in joy when he noted the familiar posture on the chair, the delicate curve of the neck, the hairline . . . she was staring outside at the adjacent garden, through the large glass window.

"Hey, what's up? When did you return from Sigatoka?" Zayn failed to suppress his joy at seeing her. He greeted her with a broad smile.

"Hi." Opshora smiled back. Her eyes carried deepened dark circles, and exhaustion. Her face looked dry, limp. The paleness of the smile broke his heart.

"I came back two hours ago. Dropped my bags at home and headed to your office," she said with a hint of a smile. She pushed her unruly hair back from her forehead with one hand as she always did—the familiar sight Zayn loved so much. With a shock he remembered he hadn't actually looked at her in recent months.

"Here," she bent down and pulled an envelope from her handbag that lay slumped at her feet. She showed it to Zayn. It was a ticket to Washington, D.C., through L.A.

"I am leaving on Sunday night. Exactly five days from now." Her voice was distant but gentle.

"I see. It's one way," he confirmed. "When are you returning?"

"I wanted you to be the first to know." She came to his office to catch him when he was sober, during work hours—it was obvious.

"You are not coming back." He figured out.

"Yep. I have completed all data collection . . . whatever I needed." Was there a very slight hesitation? Zayn wasn't sure. "I will finish the writing from D.C. Want to submit my practicum by end of the year," she added, still somewhat preoccupied in her thoughts.

"You just want to leave? Just like that?" He confronted her in passive aggressiveness, didn't raise his voice, though. It pierced through her. She didn't respond. "Don't want to consider our marriage? No?" he asked again.

Time stood still. She looked out of the window, again. The frangipani tree in the garden was defiant in bloom—bent under the burden of countless flowers. The dragonflies were drifting aimlessly in the breeze. Opshora kept gazing outside, into the emerald hue of the shrubs and plants and grass. His eyes followed her.

"It's worth a try, Opshora," he pleaded shamelessly. He hesitated to say out loud "consider our love." He was so obsessed with the fear of being rejected that he held back.

"I have thought and thought . . . this is for the best, Zayn." She faced him now. He hated her professorial wisdom, her definitive tone. When she used it, he lost the argument. It made him angry, feeling impotent and useless.

"Okay. I will let you decide then—for both of us," his voice sounded hollow, strange to his own ears.

"I have to go now. Lots to do. Pack . . . say goodbyes. I have met with Laisani. As my lawyer she will take actions as required. In my absence."

"When will you tell mama?"

Opshora inhaled sharply. Then sighed, "Soon. Maybe tomorrow . . . "

"Leave your ticket with me? I will try to upgrade it to a business class," he said.

"That's not necessary, really."

"Let me at least do this for you. I want you to travel in comfort," Zayn said in earnestness.

She handed him the ticket and stepped out.

"See you at home? I may be late," she said from the doorway as if talking to a co-worker. She sounded flippant, perhaps jovial because she had been able to inform Zayn about her decision. And the most difficult ordeal was over. All was done, finally! She had been dreading a face-to-face with him.

She hit the road. A load had lifted but it didn't make her truly happy. Her heart felt soggy—damp and soiled like a muddy puddle. She kept walking as her eyes blurred with tears. The wind was getting high and pushed her forward with a force. Suddenly the sky darkened and raindrops were pouring. Opshora walked in the rain for an hour. Her tears mingled with the rain and kept falling unabashed.

Zayn stood in his office stupefied, clutching the ticket. The faint perfume Opshora wore filled his cubicle—she left it behind.

"She's going away," Salote said as they ate dinner together. Zayn didn't comment. Opshora wasn't home yet. She was out on her round of goodbyes, possibly.

"You will let her go? Like that? You won't do anything?" Salote was angry. Opshora had informed her about her departure that morning. She didn't know whether to cry or laugh or get angry with Opshora.

"What do you want me to do? Lock her up?" he countered calmly. Sometimes Salote failed to understand her son.

Zayn finished his food. It was tasteless, dry in his mouth. "I can't force a dead relationship . . . she has stopped loving me, Mama." Zayn sounded helpless, like a little boy afraid to go outside alone in the dark.

"If I were you, I wouldn't take it lying down like this," Salote's eyes flashed.

"I am not you, Mama. I can't fight the impossible," Zayn said in a near whisper and left the dining table. He couldn't tell his mother about the upcoming divorce. He couldn't tell her how his heart was punched.

He stayed home, in his bedroom. Opshora was still out. He started to get worried but didn't know where she was or what to do. The crickets and frogs outside kept conversing or crying or calling to each other . . . Zayn couldn't figure out which and fell asleep at some point.

When he woke up much later towards the wee hours of the morning he found Opshora's sleeping body against him. Her back had slid into the curve of his body, her familiar faded scent filled his lungs as he inhaled. Her breathing was even, peaceful. Her warmth could be felt through his clothes. He remained motionless, afraid that he might wake her up if he moved. One side of his body became numb in that cramped position but he was determined to keep her close to him while she slept. He would have to let her go out of his life, and soon. He pretended to be asleep when she finally woke up in the morning and tip toed to the bathroom. He left the bedroom before she came out.

Opshora met with her friends—Jane, Laisani and Lara. She called the meeting with the intention to say goodbye. She hadn't broken the full news to them when she invited them to lunch at their favorite restaurant. Over the phone she couldn't yet tell them about her decision to leave Fiji for good. Only Laisani was aware of her divorce proceedings. By then both Lara and Jane had moved into more deserving employments after initial months of internships. Laisani was already established in her profession. All her friends seemed more at ease with their lives.

Since she got married, Opshora had maintained connections with them sort of on and off, as her life got busy with many complications. But her friends were aware of her struggles in her interracial marriage. They were in essence her only friends outside of Zayn's family and circle. Whenever there was something to share, they came together—met over lunch or late afternoon coffee. Opshora liked to meet her friends outside her home in a more carefree environment. Even if these get-togethers weren't that frequent in the recent months, Opshora's friends knew what was happening. They deeply cared for her. They mourned with Opshora for the loss of her baby. They understood her loss.

"I think it's a wise decision to visit your family, Opshora," Lara said. "I am leaving end of next month." She held Opshora's hand in hers. "My mom isn't too well. She needs me." They talked a bit more. Ordered food.

"I have to break some news . . . I got engaged, girls! Last month!" Jane said at one point, her voice bursting with excitement and happiness. She kept this to herself all this while—was hesitant to share her good news as Opshora was still struggling with her pain.

"What?!" Laisani, Lara and Opshora pounced on Jane. After months of her life stagnating, Opshora's heart pumped with pure joy. In shock, she realized she still had the capacity to be happy for others. Jane showed her engagement ring, beaming.

"Tell us the details, still-waters!" Her friends almost cried in unison.

"Met Noah at work. He is Australian . . . a consultant with the Ministry of Finance. His contract is good for another two years. We will decide what to do after that," Jane blushed, smiled in happiness.

"When is the wedding?" Opshora wanted to know.

"We are planning in spring of next year."

"I will have to fly back for the wedding," Lara's commitment was instant.

"I am sorry . . . I will miss it," Opshora's tone was flat. She looked away.

"What's that supposed to mean?" Jane asked.

"I am leaving—not coming back."

"Holy cow!" Lara whistled softly.

"I thought you were going back for a little while to recuperate!" Jane was equally shocked.

"You are leaving Zayn?" Lara's question was straightforward. Opshora nodded. Laisani kept quiet. She hadn't shared the news with anyone. Opshora was entitled to client-attorney privilege.

In brief words Opshora gave her friends enough insights. She was honest about her love for Zayn, the cultural struggles and her immense sorrow. They didn't pry, but supported her in her decision.

One chapter of her life ended.

Opshora said goodbye to the family at home. Salote's hug felt aloof but Opshora wasn't offended. She understood she had hurt the good people who loved her and accepted her as family.

"Do you think this is the right thing for you?" Salote had asked Opshora when she first told her about leaving Zayn. "Opshora, you're blind not to see his love for you," she added. There was no anger, only deep sadness.

"I don't know what's right . . . what's wrong at this point, Mama. I know I am drowning," Opshora had responded honestly.

"Both of you are so young . . . there will still be many more chances to become parents," Salote's voice held care. "I had two miscarriages. Many women I know had such misfortunes . . . it is quite common, Opshora."

Opshora didn't know what to say. She remained silent,

curled inside her cocoon, untouchable, very alone. "It would be good to spend some time with your family . . . but come back, Opshora. This is your home now."

Salote had witnessed her pain—over Zayn, and later at the loss of her baby. She still struggled to understand Opshora's uncompromising stand regarding Zayn.

It took Opshora ages to reach the airport, as the traffic was bad. Cars were bumper to bumper on the narrow, broken roads. People were impatient and honking or trying to pass from the wrong side which intensified the traffic jam. There were no police, no system, as always. Opshora's impatience was mild compared to the others around her but she began to feel trapped. In any case, she had ample time to catch her flight. Finally, as suddenly as it had started the traffic jam loosened. The taxi sped on the road along with the other commuters.

As promised, Zayn stood at the airport main entrance, waiting patiently for her. He looked exactly the same the first time she met him three years ago—in a flowery blue and white bula shirt with hibiscus motifs and black sulu or kilt, wearing a cowry necklace and a bracelet on his right wrist made of Paula shells—handsome and elegant.

His hair was ablaze from the lights reflected from the airport behind him. Tiny beads of perspiration were forming on his forehead at the hairline like a garland of diamonds—very much like stars at dying twilight in a cloudless sky. It was warm but breezy. He stood there, for her. Only for her, one more time.

Her heart felt heavy, like a rock. The pain was ruthless. A part of her wanted to cancel her trip. It didn't feel right. But she kept quiet, immobilized in the fear that if she spoke she would say something that she would regret later. He helped her with the luggage and through express check-in. He knew almost everyone at the airport. By the time all was done, the boarding announcement was heard in the background.

"You are upgraded all the way to D.C. Short transit in L.A." He handed over her ticket and boarding pass. His smile held sadness. She wanted to scream out, *Thank you for loving me, letting me love you, for giving me a taste of the "Fijian magical-madness" that I will always treasure . . .*

"Thank you. For everything . . . Good-bye, Zayn!" She said instead, equally sad.

"I will always love you, Opshora!" his voice carried many tears, mountains of heartache. She hugged him. He held her tightly against his chest suppressing a sob, kissed her on the lips after many months, without any hesitation or fear of rebuke. She came into his arms easily, as of habit.

"I love you, Zayn. I will never forget my life in Fiji . . . I messed up real bad." She moved away, walked towards the gate. Her thin body mingled amidst the crowd of other travelers. She had lost heaps of pounds since the miscarriage. Zayn's heart broke as he watched her so wasted, so anguished . . .

When she looked back one last time before entering through the boarding gate, she found him standing where she had left him, transfixed. The warmth of his mouth stayed with her all the way back home.

Opshora landed in Washington D.C., on November 25, 1990.

PART III.
WASHINGTON, D.C.,
SPRING 2015 (CONTINUED)

# CHAPTER ELEVEN

# Coffee and Cupcakes, Dusts of Cinnamon...

Antonio whistles cheerfully, beating egg whites for a new dish he is trying to perfect. He hears his mother Isabella's voice in the pantry chastising one of the kitchen staff. She can be pretty sharp when she perceives rules are broken. She is a true Italian matriarch in many ways. She is proud of her heritage and at every conceivable opportunity doesn't hesitate to tout it.

"Mamma Mia!" Antonio says softly under his breath.

Like many Italians, Antonio's forefathers arrived in San Francisco as immigrants in search of new opportunities in the late 1800s. They were escaping the hardships and oppressive taxation system imposed on southern Italy following the Italian unification in 1861. After their first few years of struggle, most of his family moved to Baltimore and then towards the middle of the 20th century, they settled in Montgomery county and around that area, just a few miles away from D.C. At present, Antonio's parents and his married sister live in Silver Spring, one of the suburban cities.

At the time of en masse migration from Italy, only a handful of his ancestors were literate. It was easy for them to pick up the language and understand the lay of the land. But the rest of the clan was uneducated and found employment as lowly paid laborers in factories, eateries and local businesses. In social status they were closer to the blacks. The cost of living was high. The scanty money they earned wasn't enough. Antonio's great grandparents had little education but excellent culinary skills and business brains. They borrowed a small amount of money from fellow countrymen and opened up a make-shift eatery in one corner of Baltimore harbor mainly to cater to the needs of the Italian laborers. Not a fancy restaurant—just some wooden benches for outdoor seating during the warm seasons. For winter they had placed a few tables and chairs that tightly fit in the small room half of which was taken over by the kitchen. In any case, during lunch time rush hour customers didn't have time to linger around for too long.

The rent of the place was cheap. It was soup and Italian bread and pasta at the beginning. They added pizza to the menu and sandwiches. Meatballs were inexpensive and easy to make which was added and became an instant hit with the low earning customers, though in Italy no one ate meatballs with spaghetti those days. It was an American addition that gained immediate popularity and became a permanent extension to Italian cuisine.

Word of mouth spread. Locals also began frequenting the place in search of delicious food at low cost. Only after two years the reputation of their food grew so much that they were forced to move to a bigger, better place in the same neighborhood with proper seating arrangements. Decor, crockery and furniture were bought to make the place more appealing. A couple of waitresses were hired to assist and appease the ambience. They were daughters from the family, and Italian friends. The price of food went up with the new facelift. However, the Italian laborers always got a discount on their orders. Only the Americans were charged the higher rates. That's how the journey began for the Russo family and through generations they stuck to the restaurant business. Later when Antonio's father, Marco, took over the family restaurant, he expanded the business further as wholesalers of packaged Italian food—confectionary, jams, jelly, bread, frozen pizza, varieties of hot sauces and pickles. There were always enough working hands within the extended family to keep the wheels of the business in motion, mouths that needed to be fed, alongside catering to ardent patrons to be satiated with the flavor and taste of authentic Italian cuisine! The best thing was that the money flow remained within their own community. Eventually, more Italian eateries sprung up across the country started by members of the large clan and followers.

Marco relocated the restaurant to D.C. and renamed it as Pasta Paradiso. Along with his extended family members, Antonio grew up listening to the fascinating history of his forefathers' migration to the states. The stories changed somewhat each time someone brought them up at family gatherings. Even then everyone acknowledged that there were some strong elements of truth that remained inherent no matter how much transformation of facts happened over time.

Today where DuPont Circle stands was once home to a brickyard and slaughterhouse. In 1871, the US Army Corps of Engineers started constructing the traffic circle, which was then called the "Pacific Circle." Congress renamed it as "DuPont Circle" on February 25, 1882. At the same time it also authorized a memorial statue of Samuel Francis Du Pont to acknowledge his services as a Rear Admiral during the Civil War. Launt Thompson, an American sculptor created the statue which was unveiled on December 20, 1884. Flowers and trees were planted in the encircling park for added charm.

Several members of the Du Pont family sought permission to remove the statue to Rock Ford Park, Wilmington in 1917.

They believed that it wasn't the best way to show respect to a war hero. They commissioned Henry Bacon and Daniel Chester French to design the fountain to decorate the DuPont Circle of present day. The work was completed in 1920. The fountain depicts carvings of three classical figures symbolizing the sea, the stars and the wind.

Opshora steps out of the metro station and walks over to the Dupont Circle park. She doesn't see Antonio anywhere. She keeps waiting. The wall clock on the opposite street corner shows fifteen minutes after five. Maybe he has forgotten all about their rendezvous, who knows? Possibly she has been stood up. It definitely dampens her ego. Not great to be dumped. She tells herself she is too mature to be offended by a casual acquaintance, that she doesn't mind that much. She wanders in the park enjoying the summer evening along with many others. One could never feel alone in this place. Voices and laughter from the crowds mingle with the delightful aroma from the nearby cafes creating a carnival mood—lively, mobile, fun-filled.

She barely knows Antonio, so no use holding anything against him. She keeps strolling, observes the evening crowd pouring in. From their body language she assumes many could be tourists, possibly—domestic and international. Millions of visitors flock to D.C. all year round. She decides to hang at Kramers bookstore, have coffee, linger around to check the new arrivals and then grab a bite at their café-restaurant as the night deepens. The food is really good there. She is a regular patron. They have maintained their standard over the years. The Japanese platter is her favorite. That's when she notices Antonio—entering through the other end of the park. He offers her an embarrassed smile as he comes closer.

"You must have been thinking Italians are no good. Always late . . . Or maybe I wasn't serious," he eyes her intently to check her reaction.

He is better dressed today. White crisp plain shirt, dark blue formal pants and intense mahogany-colored polished shoes. Clean shaven, stubbles banished. He has an attractive, honest kind of face—she notes.

"I was a bit disenchanted. Was weighing in . . . some not so favorable thoughts, I must admit. Mentally was planning the evening by myself," she returns his look with a smile.

"We Italians, always spoilers of fun!" He mocks and both laugh. "Thank you, Signorina for not quitting on me." He gently touches her elbow and guides her towards the park entrance on 19th Street. They cross the road and walk past the large bookstore that sells used books. It has a commendable collection. Opshora frequents it, often.

As promised, he takes her to a petite, snug café exploding with the aroma of good, strong coffee. There are confectioneries—Danish, pastries, croissants, banana bread, fruit tarts, apple pie and dark chocolate cake displayed craftily near the counter in a glass enclosure. He points towards them but she shakes her head in refusal. He orders cappuccino for her, macchiato for him, and a piece of soft chocolate mousse cake. The service is fast.

"Yesterday I was distraught . . . was like the village idiot of Trump-country circus!" Opshora laughs at his statement all over again—his comical reference to the current political absurdity heating up each day during the election process. "My universe was chaotic, very erratic . . . nothing was making sense. Believe me, laughing with you in the park made me forget my miseries. And I knew I had to see you again," he says looking at the dying steam of the scalding drinks. She waits for him to continue.

"My sixteen-year-old daughter ran away with a car mechanic day before yesterday. I didn't know about her whereabouts when we met in the park . . . She lives with her mother mostly. My ex-wife called to give the bad news," he pauses, stirring the macchiato unnecessarily. "I was angry. Heartbroken. Maria is a fool, a baby. Not ready for love yet," he speaks, frustrated. Opshora sits quietly. Not knowing how to react. A gust of lukewarm air steps inside the café with a group of new customers. The chime on the door alerted their arrival. Antonio follows her gaze and then looks back to her.

"We were thinking the worst . . . then Maria suddenly turned up late last night. No word of what had happened. Shut herself in her room since. Possibly sleeping."

"I am sorry . . . really," Opshora doesn't know what else to say.

"I told Ashley, my ex-wife, that's her name, I will see Maria later tonight. Don't understand women," he shakes his head. Exasperation deepens in his tone. "Anyway, I don't want to bore you with my life story."

"It's okay. I don't mind listening. If it helps," she says, genuinely.

"I just met you . . . and I am already crying on your shoulder." He laughs somewhat embarrassed. "Don't want to scare you away with my problems."

They sip their drinks. He gently pushes the cake towards her. After a slight hesitation she takes a small bite with the spoon, a delightful muddy mass drowned in remnants of dark chocolate. Her mouth fills with the taste of sweet joy, which kicks her blood stream up with a slow surge of euphoria. He keeps watching her.

"Like it, right?" his tone is definitive. She nods in agreement.

"Right choice," Opshora manages to utter somehow with her mouth full.

"I will bake a real cake for you. It will melt in your mouth before it touches the tongue."

She licks her lips to clean away the tinge of chocolate. He keeps watching.

"What kind of cake do you fancy? Chocolate? Lemon cake . . . cheesecake . . ." he says again. "I learned to bake from my grandma. What a lady she was!" Antonio blows a kiss upwards, possibly towards heaven where he believes the old lady is currently residing. Opshora finds it amusing. How people without any question have full trust in something that hasn't been proven to exist. Blind faith!

"Why do you have your hair in a knot today?" His eyes sweep over her. "I liked the way it was yesterday, falling over your neck and side of the face . . . ahh, I see! You want to show me your earrings?" He moves towards her right slightly, and with his left hand softly touches the sparkling ruby in one of the dangling earrings. She pushes his hand away. He is a lefty.

"Come on. Let me look at it. I like it. The silver setting is *beautifoool,*" he says. She blushes faintly, not sure of the reason. She is amazed to note that she still has some bashfulness left in her. His gesture was quite intimate, sudden, and she wasn't prepared for it.

"You are well dressed today," she teases mainly to divert the attention towards him. She feels awkward under his penetrating gaze.

"I wanted you to notice me today. Took proper care, right?" He laughs at his own joke. "Yesterday was a chance meeting. I had no preparation to impress you." He is cheeky. He makes her smile. "You haven't said much about yourself, though. I am talking and talking all this time." He becomes serious now.

"What is there about me?" she asks. He waits. She remembers his curiosity about her marital status.

"I was married to a Fijian man . . . once upon a time. I went to Fiji for three months for an internship, initially. Requirement for my masters course but stayed back to be with this guy. I fell in love. Fiercely." Antonio doesn't take his eyes off her. And she looks away.

"What happened?" his voice is caring.

"Took me three years to understand . . . got burnt. My

marriage fell apart . . . I fell apart . . . came back to my angry parents. Concentrated on my studies. It was an uphill struggle. But it was in the 1990s—it was a different me," Opshora says in a low tone, sounding like a whisper to her own ears.

"And?"

"Resumed my life. Got a divorce. My mom is stubbornly dead-against interracial marriages. She thinks I should have never done it. That was years ago—another lifetime. Maybe you were not even born when all this was happening to me," she gets back to teasing, trying to lighten the mood.

"Come on! You look like a spring-chicken to me."

"I turned fifty-one this year. How old are you?" Opshora wants to put matters straight.

"I am forty-four," he says calmly.

"I thought so. You look young," her voice is equally calm.

"Huh? Young? At forty-four? You are the first one in years who has called me young!" He laughs, genuinely amused. "Does it matter?"

Opshora doesn't respond to his question.

"Once you cross forty, you don't age anymore . . . further. Everyone becomes middle aged—you, me, him," Antonio points towards one of the older cafe staff. His tone is comical and they both laugh.

"OK. There is more . . . in addition to freelancing— writing jobs, some teaching assignments . . . I co-own a small crafts store on 17th street. It's called 'Beads and Bracelets.' My business partner runs it, mainly."

"A man?" Antonio blurts out. She nods.

"He's just a business partner?" Antonio is too curious.

"Yea. A gentleman . . ." she doesn't avert her eyes this time. "He's gay," she says again. But also is surprised at herself for revealing the sexual orientation of her business partner.

Opshora takes a sip from the cup and turns to face Antonio directly now. She upsets the spoon which falls on the floor with a small thud splattering around some of the dark mousse that lingered on its curvy form. He bends down to pick it up, puts it back on the table silently. She doesn't apologize for her clumsiness.

"The point I was trying to make earlier is . . . I am much older."

"You don't look your age, signorina. No matter how hard you try! Not a single line around your eyes, mouth. I thought you are barely 40. Why are we talking about age? Age is in the mind . . . not in your heart . . . how you feel, that's what matters. Here," he adds placing both his hands on his chest passionately.

She smiles at his fervent retort. They sit in silence. For some moments.

"Marriage is not for everyone. Not a bad thing that you came out of it," he says thoughtfully after a minute's awkwardness. She nods.

"We were young. Ashley Walker, my ex, and I when we got married. She was a head turner. I really fell for her . . . hook, line and sinker. My family was against our marriage. She's not Italian," he smiled again. "We can be very racist, like everyone else. Italians think they are the best."

"So what happened?" It's her turn now. She asks more out of politeness to continue the conversation, than curiosity.

"Arguments, fights, walking out of the house, moving back in . . . there was no peace. There was no sense, all foolishness. She was unfaithful sometimes." His eyes span over the café, and glance the outlines of buildings on the street silhouetted against the large windows as the evening gathers outside. Opshora doesn't understand what woman in her right mind could cheat on a Greek god like handsome Antonio . . . maybe there is more behind the handsome face, funny, pleasant personality. In any case she hardly knows him. He must be putting up his best to impress her, who knows? But in any case, what happens in a marriage is very personal for the people who are in it.

"We were trying for a baby. Italians like large families. She doesn't. Anyway, after several miscarriages Maria was born," he says. Opshora's heart almost misses a beat at the mention of miscarriages—even after all the years of pain she thought she had left the aches behind.

"We were happy for years after that," he sounds thoughtful. "Then she started to get bored. Again. We broke up this time for good. Maria was only nine." His smile is forced.

"I am sorry," she says.

"Our divorce messed up Maria. So . . . so much." There is hurt in his voice mixed with a hint of desperation. "Her grades started to go down. She challenges her mom in every ruling and breaks boundaries."

"Maria lives with her mother?"

"Yes. We settled on that. We thought it was in her best interest. But . . . Ashley isn't always truthful about what happens between the two of them. Keeps it a secret from me, my extended family." Antonio shrugs. "We all want to help."

They linger in the café for another hour. Twilight begins to gently wrap the treetops and the buildings down the street. The noises of the motor vehicles and pedestrians sound faint from inside the café. They talk about inconsequential stuff, move on to life in general—growing up as minorities in the U.S. —the struggles Antonio's ancestors faced after migration and especially his father's generation during World War II when Italians were looked upon with mistrust though his family had already lived in the U.S. for decades and were American citizens. 120,000 Japanese-Americans were forced out of their homes and held in internment camps by an executive order (9066) signed by President Roosevelt following the bombing of Pearl Harbor. They were allowed four days to two weeks to prepare for their forced relocation. Their incarceration was a dark time in this country's history. It also called for compulsory relocation of over 10,000 Italians, placed them under watchful eyes of the government. Italians had to be careful fearing they could be targeted with treason charges anytime. Though Americans, the movements of more than 600,000 Italians nationwide were restricted.

"Italians were not considered white enough or true Americans. It was a tough time to be of Italian race at that time in this country," Antonio adds.

"Well, Muslims went through almost the same experience after 9/11. Similar treatment, suspicion, fear, hatred . . . It was a bad time to be brown-skinned in the U.S., and of Muslim faith," Opshora reflects. "It still somewhat continues in some form after over a decade has passed. Even if I don't practice any religion, I don't like the people of my community to be maligned for their faith—or of any faiths . . . thus generalized."

"Well Jesus was an Arab. Not the blue-eyed, white dude that Christians like to believe. And Moses was Egyptian." Antonio winks. "Immigrants will always be treated with fear and mistrust." The streetlights glow brighter against the approaching night.

They talk some more. Antonio casually expresses that he and his family would like to publish a book about the restaurant. The book could capture the story of the Italian heritage of the Russo family, highlight the signature dishes popular on the menu, and include some tips on the admired recipes.

"Opshora, you have great writing skills. I looked up your book on Fiji and some other titles with anthropological focus."

"Huh?" Opshora is surprised now.

"Oh, I googled you. It's the age of Internet . . . your past, present unfolded smoothly on my computer screen." Antonio smiles and makes a gesture of salute. "Hail, Bill Gates. Steve

Jobs! . . . for making our lives easy." Antonio's theatrics force a hearty laugh from Opshora. "But nothing about your Fiji life, a pity," he utters the words in an inoffensive way. "Jokes aside. I think you would be the best person . . . would you be at least interested to consider this as a writing assignment?"

"No, I don't think I have the necessary skills to write a cookbook," she rejects the idea instantly. "I am an anthropologist, a researcher. Not a foody talent."

"It's not about food only. You can talk about Italian culture, lifestyle, particular details about our signature cuisines . . . how we introduced them . . . overall history of Italian food, recipes . . . this smells of anthropology! You can turn it into an experiment—about our people," he tries to entice her by making a strong point. "My entire family will assist . . . and all the restaurant staff would be able to contribute something."

They keep debating. "This will be the story of succeeding as Italian Americans. A story of immigrants." He wouldn't take no for an answer. So, finally she agrees to think through the proposition, still quite hesitant. Though she has never written anything related to cooking or eateries, in her mind she reasons she could do an anthropological piece focusing on historical facts—the struggles of Italian immigrants when they first arrived, their perseverance through the time of World War II, what makes them tick in modern America. She could highlight peoples' food habits, behavior around specific cuisine selection, include some anecdotes about Antonio's restaurant, its establishment and customers' preference for his eatery. She hesitantly agrees.

Antonio promises to discuss the concept further with his family and arrange a meeting with them and her in the upcoming weeks.

"Don't think I am doing this to see more of you. I am serious about the book," he says, flashing his captivating smile.

"You better be," she warns him mockingly.

"But I would like to see you. Really. Cross my heart," he says softly. She thinks he is rather funny. He notes down the name of her store, promises to drop in to check it out.

Antonio takes leave as the night settles down on the D.C. skyline, complacent and inevitable. The drive to his ex-wife's house would take roughly about forty-five minutes because of heavy traffic. She lives in Bethesda.

Antonio seems decent and genuine—attributes that Opshora always finds attractive in a man. Something had definitely clicked between them when she met him at the park, she realizes.

Opshora takes P Street, doesn't go to Kramer's for dinner as initially planned and walks back home all the way, light-hearted.

# CHAPTER TWELVE

# Beginning of a Romance

Antonio doesn't call after their tete-a-tete at Dupont Circle. Deep down in her heart a little hope wanted to rise up but she crushes it, deliberately. She had enjoyed the two meetings with him but those have led to nothing. Maybe he isn't so serious about the book after all or has second thoughts regarding seeing her again. She decides it's best to carry on with her own life, pretend Antonio never happened.

Surprisingly, she does get caught up with Antonio. He has been in her thoughts at leisure hours and especially late at night when she struggles with insomnia. She decides to shake off all thoughts of Antonio and concentrate on her laptop. Her writing hasn't progressed much recently. Work has piled up with her mind meandering in empty daydreams.

A couple of days in the week Opshora is at the Beads and Bracelets store. She spends about half a day each time. She likes to do her writing assignments from there while helping her business partner with the sales. Chris, the co-owner of the store, is a very passionate gay man in his mid-forties who is constantly falling in and out of love. She met him through a common friend years ago and instantly they took to each other. Their chemistry worked, they bonded. Somehow the people who introduced them faded into the background while they continued to be friends and started the business together.

Opshora hasn't been to the store as regularly as expected. She has constantly failed to keep up with her share of the bargain—her agreement with Chris. He actually owns seventy percent of the store. He makes major decisions and sometimes forgets to inform her about his strategies. When Opshora discovers the changes by accident she doesn't bother to question him. She has full trust in his business judgment. She has none. Their friendship and business involvement hence has stayed smooth over the years. She invested in the store because she likes the ambience and Chris. The regular revenue gives her a bit of extra financial freedom that she needs from time to time.

Somehow work hasn't been on her mind lately. She is aware it's unfair to Chris. He is a happy, nice person, extremely empathetic and readily gives much grace to Opshora. He is a good listener and an amazing hugger. She doesn't want to stereotype him, either as some believe LGBTQ (lesbian, gay, bi-sexual, transgender, queer) people are usually upright and nice because they are the most marginalized and incapable of vice, while others condemn them as sinners, bad elements—not to be trusted. To her the issue is LGBTQs are like any other group of people with their fair share of burdens—virtues and vices and dilemmas and joys and sorrows.

Chris has been Opshora's sounding board for decades. He has held her in his arms and calmed her down, cried with her in her pain and silently stood beside her like a rock, all along. She has been there for him always, as well. During his past heartbreaks, she helped him back on his feet and gently walked him out of his miseries. They are like the opposite sides of a coin—each mirroring the life's journey of the other, in the closest contexts, though poles apart in their philosophy about life.

He doesn't complain much in general unless his threshold of emotional resilience is tripped. He is a happy go lucky kind of a person. His living quarters are above the store—a spacious studio apartment, set with large windows, a full bath, a comfortable kitchenette and a luxurious walk-in closet. It's not easy to find a place these days in D.C. with so much space to store clothes and suitcases, and personal belongings that need to be hidden away for aesthetic purposes.

Chris has two cats and an abundance of indoor plants. On weekends he sometimes has assignments to perform as a drag queen in a gay club. He loves these nocturnal adventures that pump him with extra adrenaline. Gloating on the thrills of those events makes up for many vacant moments of aloneness, making them bearable. It is also an additional source of income though he doesn't care for the money as much. His talent is recognized and he is on the list of several prestigious gay clubs. He derives gratification in this creative outlet, as a hobby.

The name of their store Beads and Bracelets truly compliments the merchandise it offers to customers. They sell different kinds of beads made of glass, clay, wood; semi-precious gems, as well as ethnic jewelry, arts and crafts, quilts, rugs, used and new books and magazines. Paintings of aspiring artists are also sold there. It's like a creative-hub- boutique that offers a mini universe of artistic paraphernalia. Sometimes painters are present in the store to talk to prospective buyers, market their products and give out tips on painting to budding artists, interested listeners and learners. The store is decorated craftily with ethnic stuff, seasonal flowers in pots, old delicate carpets and indoor greeneries, stylishly positioned. Chris' sense of interior decoration is par excellence.

On the extreme end of the store are a handful of hefty floor cushions, wooden stools and rattan chairs for patrons to relax and go through the collection of books. The store provides free wifi to attract customers. The two-story building that houses the store belonged to Chris' family. He inherited the place from his grandmother who gave it to him, her gay grandson before she passed away over a decade ago as a protest to her own son who refused to embrace Chris' homosexuality. To a southern Christian conservative, Chris as a son is like a punishment, an unceasing reminder of evil. So his father turned away like many in his society. Before that he did try to instill the thought of conversion therapy, which Chris rejected. Chris' mom is a constant support in his life but he seldom visits his parents due to the fall out with his dad. She is in frail health for years and the only contact he has with her is through phone calls. His two sisters are lukewarm to his gay status so he maintains a distance from them as well. The both brothers in law consider him as a possible bad influence on their adolescent children. Chris is extremely fond of his two nephews and a niece, born to the sisters but he is wise to limit his contacts with them. He craves to be with his family but they aren't fully ready for him. It's a hard, isolated life for many, misunderstood because of their sexual preferences. Opshora has been his best friend for years.

As Beads and Bracelets is more popular than the nearby cafes a coffee corner is now under consideration to further add to the allure of the craft store. People are allowed to breeze in with their coffee and laptops, any time, and many do that. Chris also provides customers with local news, gossips, tips on sightseeing and names of restaurants if they care to ask his advice.

Opshora finds Chris in a real cross mood as she steps inside the store one late morning after hiding away for almost a week. She has walked from home—three and a half miles, exactly. It's a beautiful morning outside, sunny but breezy, bliss on a hot day. She heads towards the chairs to catch her breath, and cool off. The air-con is stronger in that part of the large store.

"Beautiful, here is a lemonade I made for you," Chris says gruffly as he practically thrusts the cold drink towards her. The sweat on the outside of the glass glitters in the light, and runs with a slow trickle downwards.

"Oh, lovely! Very thoughtful!" she doesn't comment on his mood or offer any apologies for being late today, or her sparse presence at the store for days. That would open the floodgate of stifled reproaches packaged in honeyed words, a miserable effort to hide his displeasure caused by momentary calamities. Opshora knows it all—it happens all the time with Chris. She needed the time away to complete her writing assignments undisturbed. She knows him too well not to meddle when he is in a foul mood—that's inviting disaster. He will open up when he cools down enough to be an amicable companion. She is sure of that. She walks away from him and sits down on the large floor cushion in the farthest corner. As she sips the lemonade she hears his footsteps crossing over towards her spot.

"This country is so messed up!" he remarks. He pulls a stool and sits close by with his drink.

She waits patiently as he first picks up a tiny scrap from the floor, positions his glass on the edge of the nearby glass-top side table, freeing his other hand and smooths a wrinkle on the rug. He is a nitpicker in the literary sense when it involves keeping the store or his life in proper shape. He likes to see order in everything but life doesn't unfold in a straight line, unblemished. Disarray annoys him—the reason he is often frustrated with disappointments that pop up in his life like poppies in summer, now and then, which he can't control.

"You know, this man I met? Older . . . he had such amazing deep, amber eyes." There he goes again, she thinks, trying not to avert her eyes from his earnest stare. She doesn't want to hurt him more. He gets wounded easily.

"Anyway, we had drinks, vintage Merlot . . . some soft

intimacies at the bar. Then he said he had to go back to his wife!" Chris almost shrieks out followed with a shrug to emphasize his scandalous reaction. "Why did he lead me on? I was thinking of a cozy night back here, more drinks . . . "

"It's good that he backed off before you got too deep," she offers gently.

"I have been lonely, honey-bun," he sounds desolate, subdued. "It's so cold, alone at night." A slow sadness stirs up in his deep hazel eyes

Opshora puts down her glass and holds both his hands in hers. Her right hand touches the iciness over his palm grasping his lemonade. He leans closer towards her, possibly trying to seek assurance from the nearness. She understands fully. He has been in disastrous relationships every few years that created tumultuous aftermaths. The recoveries have taxed him heavily. His broken heartbeats echoed his agony each time as he lingered long over the aches, the testing times.

"I am so sorry, my friend. What more can I say?" Opshora is genuine with her affection for Chris.

"He should have decided what he wanted . . . I told him that. Gave him a piece of my mind . . . He can't have it both ways . . . just like that."

"Bi-sexuality is common, Chris."

"I understand that. But this guy was not forth coming." He is still upset, agonized over last night.

The chime at the entrance sounds at that moment announcing a customer's presence. Opshora is relieved. Chris leaps up to his feet and heads towards the counter. A group of tourists reign over the store for the next hour. They chat in their native tongue, they sound like Scandinavians. They go around the store gently touching the delicate rugs and admiring the maze of paintings and merchandise heaped on the floor, stacked on the racks with style. They examine the numerous other exhibits. They are generous with their picks and purchases, and linger on while shopping. They talk to Opshora, laugh with Chris. He can be amazingly warm and funny with complete strangers—a rare asset that boosts business. After the rocky beginning with Chris' low beat mood it has turned out to be a good day for trade. So, his mood is uplifted.

"Crisis over . . . !" Opshora mutters to herself.

"Oh, sugar bun-bun . . . " Chris uses this endearment when he is happy and when he opens his heart to her, and when he is upset. Opshora has to decide on her pick, judging his mood of the moment.

"A guy called . . . wanted to talk to you."

"What guy? Shit! Shit! Shit! I have lost my phone. I am expecting a call from Michigan University. They want me to take some classes," Opshora remembers.

Opshora has been searching for her phone all over her place without much success for days. This is the fifth time she has misplaced her phone in the last six months. She is considering giving up on cell phones totally but she knows her parents' reaction. They would possibly buy her a new set. South Asian parents like to be present even in the lives of their adult offspring, always. Also, a cell is a must in order to live on temporary assignments.

"Allow me to finish, sweet face. Don't distract me with your cringes and cries . . . the nice-voice-guy on the phone said you agreed to write a book for him. He was trying to contact you—without success." Chris pauses to check Opshora's reaction and continues. "He didn't know what I know now about your cell mishap . . . harmless moron you entrapped recently with your guiles?!" He is cheeky and finishes with a smirk.

"Hey, don't make this sound sexy! I am heart-broken at my loss. I mean my phone."

"Call him. He sounded a cross breed between desperation and *mesmerization,*" he throws over his shoulder, teasingly.

"That's not a word as far as I can recall. Mesmerization!" Opshora makes a face at him as she pushes around the chairs, upturns the rugs in irritation, looking for her missing phone.

After a thorough search of the store the culprit is finally detected behind a pile of photo frames lying in silent compliance. Perhaps when she sat on the floor, the cell must have dropped out of her lap or from the kiondo. She is in the habit of pulling out things haphazardly from the bag. The mess inside is always alive as a rule of thumb. The phone is dead. So the next fifteen minutes they search for her charger.

"Why do you keep a Samsung? Migrate to iPhone like all smarties," he says exasperated as he pulls out her charger from under a bundle of goodies, finally.

"We could have shared my iPhone charger you know? Instead of this treasure hunt."

"You are a techie, my friend. I am not. I like to keep things simple." She hurries towards an outlet with the charger.

"Yes, messy kind of simplicity. You beat me every time with your talent!" More teasing comes from Chris.

Six missed calls flash on the screen as she plugs in. Two are from her aunt Leila, four from Antonio. Quite encouraging. He has been trying to seek her out. Her ego soars like that of an adolescent girl.

"Thank God you are alive!" Antonio's voice booms from the other side of the line. Opshora chuckles inwardly visualizing his expression, gestures of throwing his hands up in the air to make a point or in frustration, or both. She likes what she hears.

"I was about to give up on you . . . well, before that I would have passed by your store, for sure," he adds.

"Why didn't you? I have been working mostly from the store," Opshora lies. "I lost my phone," she adds in a small voice, ready to hear some more teasing words.

"Really? And you are a *professore*? Claim to be a PhD?"

"What's the connection between all that and a missing phone?" She has a hard time controlling her laughter. It takes him a few seconds to grasp the sound of her mirth.

"Come on! Don't make it a trifle . . . can't understand how one loses a phone in this century! You are no better than my Maria," he manages to say somehow, though almost lost for words and takes a pause. Opshora waits. "She needs it all the time but misplaces it every few minutes . . . anyway, I missed you. Believe me. It has never happened to me before, Signorina." Opshora hears his serious proclamation.

"C'mon . . . you hardly know me." She tries to stay on a teasing level.

"Signorina, you have to allow me to know more of you . . . " He has additional news for her to chew on. "Meeting with my family at Pasta Paradiso on next Tuesday? That's our restaurant. You have to see it physically, interact with all of us to gather ideas for the book."

"I haven't given it a thought yet," Opshora mumbles weakly.

"No worries. We will all think together. OK? Meet with the main actors. That's the first step. Alright?" Antonio's enthusiasm is boundless. At the end, she gives in and agrees to his plan. He invites her to a date afterwards.

"Next time I will cook dinner for you . . ."

"What next time? I don't think . . ." Opshora tries to intervene.

"Hear me out, please . . ." Antonio pleads. "I will take you to a special place after the meeting is over," Antonio sounds eager. "We will need a break from my family . . . They are prying, unruly, they like only their own ideas, I promise you. Don't listen, much," he cautions. Opshora tries to understand his flurry of words. He doesn't spare his folks in preparing her for her upcoming ordeal. She somehow likes his frankness.

"I am taking a cigarette break now . . . we can talk. Tell me what were you doing all this time?" He switches into a conversational mood.

"Working. What else? Now at the store . . . Trying for an assignment in Michigan. I think I will get it." *Not mooning over you*—in her mind she utters.

"Oh, wow!" He is impressed. "How long will you be gone?"

"Several weeks, I guess," she says casually, not giving him the entire information. "Any success with Maria? . . . Pardon me, I shouldn't be prying," she bites her tongue right after the words are out.

"You should ask . . . you have every right to know . . . as we are seeing each other."

"No, we are not dating. One swallow doesn't make a summer," she clarifies. She doesn't want to step into the trap of dating so fast.

"I don't know what kind of stupid birds swallows are . . . never seen any . . . to an Italian having a good heart to heart opening up with coffee constitutes dating. I respect your different view, though."

"Don't pull your Italian stuff on me."

"You mean my charm? Come on, admit it! *Incantata*! You are enchanted! Ha . . . ha. . . I have bewitched you—sweet, sweet, *tesoro*!" He laughs heartily.

"I will check the Italian words you have just used on me. Have to go now. Can't anymore deny the customers . . . my maddening charms," she laughs.

"Yea, kill them with kindness . . . not too much, not too little. The right proportion . . . Don't use what you did on me . . . I am already murdered . . . Ciao."

"Ciao." She repeats, laughing softly and hangs up.

"That was interesting!" Chris had crept behind silently and was listening. He does it often, just like a teenage sibling.

"Not what you think," she tosses at him and moves away.

"Throw me some beef . . . BFF . . . this is a famished beast . . ." he waits, expectant. She doesn't respond. "You need music and dancing and wine and fragrance in your life, sugar-face!" Chris says after a while.

"I am happy the way things are. And who says I don't have music and dancing . . . etcetera, etcetera . . ." she makes a face.

Antonio calls again—three more times in the next five days before the grand meeting with his family. She is a bit surprised but likes it.

"Hello, taking a cigarette break. Thought I would check on you . . . ," he says on the first call with a hint of hesitancy. "I am serving a new cuisine tonight," he volunteers after the initial exchanges of greetings.

"Something I would fancy?"

"Oh yes . . . it's asparagus and cheese tart, a small portion of linguini with avocado and mussels to go with it . . . as a combination dish, on the side." He is passionate about culinary topics.

"You smoke a lot . . . ," Opshora remarks on his second call.

"No, not really. Maximum three cigarettes a day . . . , " he is apologetic. "It's an excuse to call you," he finally confesses making her smile on the other end of the line.

"Awestruck by your honesty!"

"You are not laughing at me, no?" He is a good guesser. Luckily, it isn't a video call. He detects the minute traces of hidden amusement in her tone. She is impressed. But then chefs have extra sensitivity—to pick up the reactions of costumers to their culinary creations. If the food doesn't appease the appetite, the rejection becomes personal.

"No. Not laughing. A tiny bit amused, only." Opshora is honest with him. They talk for fifteen minutes, bantering, playful and laughing over small things.

From then on she makes sure not to take Antonio's calls from inside the store. She steps out in the pretext of a stroll around the time she expects his calls. That way, she manages to avoid Chris' hawk ears. It is too early to delve into any serious thinking, and stomach more teasing from him, of course!

"I like talking to you. Look forward to my cigarette breaks," he admits on the third call. To be honest, she was actually waiting for the call and looking at the phone screen, checking the time. He has called exactly at his usual time—11:30 a.m. sharp.

"I enjoy our brief chats," she has to give him some rope, some assurances of her growing interest in him. Men are vulnerable when they make the first moves.

"Ahh . . . Signorina . . . you made it worth it to kill my lungs with poison!" he sounds pleased.

"No, it's no excuse to smoke, my friend," she protests. She is crestfallen when the call ends. Antonio can't be away from his kitchen for too long.

She wished Antonio could call at night when she is home, at leisure. But evenings are packed for a busy chef like him. Even on his off days he is on stand-by for any kind of emergencies—for unexpected crowds or to be the extra pair of hands to his supporting second chef. He has given her the full picture from the beginning.

"The life of a chef isn't easy. It's always full of people, work, food and demands!" He had sighed.

# CHAPTER THIRTEEN

# *Caramel Canapés with Cognac—A Recipe for Catastrophe*

Opshora picks her outfit carefully—a fitted soft pink silk shirt with a black pencil skirt that does justice to her curviness. She picks a stone-studded slim necklace and matching silver earrings set with ruby and deepest blue lapis stones as accessories. With black, sleek high-heeled shoes matching the outfit she feels chic, confident. She never had an Italian friend or even a colleague. From her limited knowledge about Italians she knows the women are usually elegant and beautiful. First impressions matter and so she carefully prepares for the meeting.

She remembers Antonio's comments about her hair and smiles. She decides to take a chance. She lets her hair loose, unruly—a dark mess caressing her neck, falling down her shoulders and back. In fact, the careless way of wearing her hair gives her quite a trendy look. Every summer she is determined to chop off her mane into a manageable bob but somehow hasn't been able to act on it, so far. D.C. is too hot, too uncomfortable for a big mass of hair—it gets sweaty, damp and itchy within twenty-four hours of shampooing and grooming. Her hair-cutting dilemma has been a constant factor, though. In her teenage years, Ruby vetoed against shortening it and that was the rule.

With care she darkens her eyes with mascara, and applies a soft shade of violet lipstick complimenting the colors of her clothes. A dash of Chanel Mademoiselle perfume and a quick last look in the tall wall mirror and she is all ready to meet Antonio's family. She takes the red line metro to Dupont Circle and heads towards the Pasta Paradiso restaurant. The fifteen minute walk to the eatery sobers up her nervous heartbeats and galloping pulse.

"*Benvenuto*! Welcome, welcome! *Mia Ragazza*," says Russo senior, as he is the first to spot her. She likes him calling her 'my girl'—it sounds pleasant, friendly.

"Hello," Opshora takes his outstretched hand. He grips hers in a strong, warm handshake and holds it longer than necessary.

"Marco Russo," he says in an earnest, rich voice. He is a big man and hobbles under his massive weight.

"You are here! Welcome to Pasta Paradiso!" Antonio surfaces from nowhere and imprisons her in a tight embrace. He kisses both her cheeks. "You look absolutely stunning!" He whispers before releasing her.

Opshora is overwhelmed at this welcoming gesture and smiles uncertainly, looking around. Hearing voices, more faces appear. Isabella Russo, Antonio's mother, meekly kisses her cheeks; Rosa, his sister's hug is warm. Then there are embraces from her ten-year-old daughter Lola and nine-year-old son Jacob, her husband Carlo and Antonio's younger brother, Alberto—with a killing resemblance to the mythological Greek god, Apollo. He is the youngest born. The whole family assembles to talk to her.

"We'll have a drink first . . ." Isabella leads them to a narrow, cozy place—glasses and wine bottles are stacked on a bar top, snugly packed inside the corridor between the kitchen and the restaurant area. Luckily, the entire wall is made of glass—a French window that offers a peek into the grounds outside laden with seasonal blooms and thickets of greenery complementing the ambience of homeliness inside. The aroma of cheese and sauces from the kitchen fills the air with pleasantness, not overbearing, not in spicy stings. Opshora is ushered here gently. Wine is poured generously into spotless crystal glasses at commendable speed by Carlo and Alberto who head the group.

"To our new book on *cucine*," Marco Russo raises his glass.

"To the new book on *cucine*," the chorus echoes as each person joins in.

"We are happy that you agreed to write this book for us," Carlo is earnest. "This will be a great marketing strategy for the restaurant." His jovial face and friendly tone are reassuring. Opshora likes him instantly.

"We will need good photographs of our popular dishes, restaurant, customers, kitchen . . ." Antonio informs the group.

"Do we have to dress up?" Rosa tries to squirm in.

"Come, on! Give me a break, Rosa *amore*," Carlo speaks over her with fond teasing.

"Hey, hey, hey . . ." Rosa shoves Alberto away as he tries to open his mouth in support of his brother-in-law. "Hold on . . . let me finish! We pose . . . as models?"

"Don't try wearing your scanty, tight red dress, Rosa! Carlo will murder you . . . " Alberto now chips in.

"He likes it, he . . . ask him. Now!" Rosa pushes back.

"Bedroom only, *amore* . . . but . . ." Carlo laughs harmlessly.

They keep interrupting each other. The teasing goes on for several minutes. Antonio winks at Opshora, and throws up his hands in the air displaying his helplessness and also to prove his earlier point about his family.

"Manners, manners . . ." Isabella attempts to restrain the playfulness. "Let's be serious for one moment. Family!"

"Okay, okay, put on your scanty rags, Rosa. You will look sexy," Alberto laughs. Rosa throws him a dirty look.

"Don't gloat on your looks, little brother! You were born with it—not your accomplishment," Rosa corners Alberto. Marco smiles. Alberto takes after him much more than his other two siblings.

"What did I tell you? See? They don't listen. Always yap, yap, yap," Antonio leans towards Opshora and whispers. The bantering continues.

Antonio raises his hand up indicating everyone to stop and listen to Opshora. He fails so he picks up his glass and beats a spoon against it signaling everyone to attention. It works this time. "Let Opshora speak, gals and guys, *grazie!*"

"Hi again. No, no modeling style for photographs . . . I don't think it's necessary. Being natural is a more attractive selling point. More appealing, actually," Opshora finally enters into the conversation. "Rosa, you are gorgeous as you are." Rosa beams and gives thumbs up as Alberto rolls his eyes. Carlo puts his arms around his wife in affection. "I will also need anecdotes, old photographs, insights about family history," Opshora adds.

"Mamma mia . . . !" Alberto chimes in. "I have lots of stuff. Skeletons . . . you may call them. I can share with you," he winks, laughing. "Want to see Antonio in his bare bum at two? A beauty . . . *bellezza!*" he says again. Another round of teasing and laughter follows. Mock protests erupt. Opshora begins to relax and laughs with the rest. It's a loving family gathering that steals her heart. Then and there her commitment to the project is cemented.

She finally gets the initial assurances from everyone of their cooperation. The prospect of the book sounds realistic. She talks a bit on her thoughts on the content—a mixed script that would describe cuisine and the native Italian and migrant Italian cultures as the foundation of the book, including some exotic recipes heightened by good snapshots of the cooked favorites, followed with interviews of the family and staff. She requests them to discuss further as a family and decide what they would like to say, and then she will speak with each of them individually to work on the initial draft. There are murmurs and then agreement to her proposition. An easy victory, so far!

All this while Isabella remains quiet, withdrawn and keeps observing Opshora. She becomes aware of Antonio's mother sizing her up—calculating the risks ahead in a probable romantic liaison between the "foreign" woman and her son, perhaps. As his mother, Isabella has little difficulty in detecting her son's attraction for Opshora. Opshora reads the stress, traces of resistance in Isabella's measured smiles, muted glances, stiff body language. *Oh shit . . . I have stirred the hornet's nest,* Opshora says inwardly, feeling slightly uncomfortable.

"We must talk more . . . come over sometime and I will make you a real Italian lasagna," Isabella extends an invitation to Opshora taking advantage of a gap in the conversation. She has a heavy Italian accent though her English is perfect.

"She makes the best, mind you. Better accept her invitation. She's very miserly with it," Rosa adds, laughing. Possibly she guesses the underlying reasons behind the invite.

" . . . And calculative, always has a hidden motive, my dear mamma," Alberto says in a low voice, careful not to upset his mother too much with his loose tongue. "So be prepared, my friend," he concludes. Opshora understands she needs Isabella as an ally should she consider continuing any kind of relationship with Antonio.

"Papa . . . pappo!" Every head turns to the source of the

sunny voice that breaks the intense conversation. A very stylish teenager in a scantily tight skirt, low-necked see through sleeveless top with leopard motifs, and fashionably messy hair walks into their space mounted on a pair of black, shiny stilettos.

"*Benvenuto!* Welcome, *mia ragazza!*" Marco comes forward with outstretched arms.

"Maria! *Benvenuto mio caro!* So glad you could make it," Antonio exclaims. His voice holds unabashed joy.

"*Nonna! Nonno!*" Maria disentangles herself from the ongoing embraces and manages to hug Isabella. Then she turns around and greets everyone. "Hi!"

"Hello," she shakes hands with Opshora and casts a cold glance towards her in the awkwardness of adolescence as expected, already prejudiced possibly. Another rough meeting . . .Opshora's brain murmurs in amusement.

In an attempt to cover her nervousness Maria smiles and the lights glitter on her braces paling the soft freckles spread over the tip of her nose and cheeks. She is a beauty, no doubt, despite these little obstacles, Opshora notes. Maria doesn't engage in any direct conversation with Opshora but hangs on to her father's arm distinctly proclaiming her possessiveness. Opshora can feel Maria's passive hostility. It must be stemming out of emotional anxieties regarding her parents' estranged relationship.

Opshora understands and decides not to be too bothered. She finds the family dynamics quite interesting. Her own family is very different— her relationship with Robin, the cousins and their families seems restrained compared to Antonio's. She has never seen such kind of emotional warmth. She lacks closeness with everyone except Leila and her own father. In any case, nothing has really happened between her and Antonio to trigger off any alarms. She is highly amused, rather.

Finally, they are on their own—Opshora and Antonio.

They head out to dinner. Starlight begins to arrive over the pierced curtain of clouds, flirting callously with the moon and dances on the canvas of the vast horizon. They approach the bend in 18th Street. Antonio takes her hand in his. She doesn't mind. He cautiously walks her through the pedestrian crossings and they arrive at the restaurant of their choice for the evening. Of course, Antonio has selected the place and didn't tell her anything to keep it a surprise. Opshora is okay with it. After all he is a highly skilled chef, a master of the culinary cosmos. He had made the reservation two days ago to avoid any last-minute hitches since this eatery is popular for its authentic food. They are seated at a corner table, adjacent to the window, quiet and secluded from the usual mayhem. He orders a bottle of Shiraz, to begin the evening, and a small platter of Parmesan spinach balls as appetizer.

"Not Italian. Hmm . . . Australian red wine." Opshora muses.

"I thought something foreign would be good . . ." Antonio smiles. "Actually I like this one. Want to try it?" Opshora nods. "I can order some cognac, for later." He has thought out everything.

The soft music in the background slowly oozes over to their space. The easy presence of the waiters combined with the distant aroma of food and her racing pulse create a symphony of comfort mixed in opposites. The luxury of moments with Antonio at this place, at this time seems overwhelmingly genuine. They leisurely sip the wine. The mood sets in.

"What do you suggest?" Opshora asks as she skims through the menu, biting into a Parmesan spinach ball.

"What do you want to eat? Fish? Lamb? Chicken? Seafood?"

"Seafood would do."

"I suggest seafood paella. It has tiger shrimps, squids, scallops and mussels cooked to perfection, simmered in a spicy sauce. Ooomph . . . *mamma mia!* Very tasty, mmmm!" he whispers and at the same time licks his lips allowing a delicious sound to escape out. Opshora has to smile.

"If you're not that hungry, try Maryland crab cakes or seafood chowder with a salad or baked potato . . . hmmm . . . let's see . . . blackened salmon in garlic, lemon herb butter sauce or white sauce is good, too. But go for paella. It's the best here. I can assist with the excess," he encourages her.

They end up ordering the seafood paella and a plate of crab cakes on a bed of crispy lettuce, scallions and sliced tomatoes from the vine. They create their own salad—a mix of herbs, romaine, cherry tomatoes, goat cheese, pine nuts and sliced almonds sprinkled with Russian dressing.

"Why are you trying to over feed me?" Opshora is in a teasing mood.

"I like women who eat well. Relish food. I am a cook. Remember? My first love is with food." Opshora watches Antonio. He looks relaxed, caring. The anxiety she had seen in him earlier has evaporated.

"We are not driving. Let's have more wine. What do you say . . . enjoy the night?" Antonio's smile is tender as he looks intensely at her over the rim of his wine glass. She boldly locks eyes with him. His charm seems to be working on her, more at this instant. Or perhaps the wine has gone into her brain. She is unsure now.

He orders another bottle of red wine. She feels lighthearted. The humdrum flavor of the day is left behind, forgotten in the folds of the past before the evening started with Antonio. She is glad she agreed to this date with him. She hasn't dated in the real sense for a long time, actually. So far, she is liking this new experience.

He picks up piece of shrimp or fish now and then with a running commentary about its specialty and feeds her with his spoon, lurching his long arms from the other side of the table. It's intimate, different. It somewhat brings back slices of her life with Zayn when things were uncomplicated.

"Ahh . . . *Tesoro*, try this bite." He calls her "sweetheart" in Italian if she isn't mistaken. He may not mean anything. It may be a casual habit. But she enjoys the pampering, loves the savory food. The endearment sounds so natural in his native tongue. They hang around late drinking the last drops of their wine and continue to talk and laugh as the night ages.

"I think we need to leave," she observes, taking into account the almost deserted restaurant.

"Okay, let's go." He gets up, helps her out of her chair and keeps holding her hand. She doesn't mind, even this time.

"Where will you go?" he asks.

"Back home, where else? It's late."

"Let's walk towards 18th Street first. We need some air to clear our heads. There is a small park . . . I love that place." He leads her by the hand.

"I will need to call an Uber," Opshora tries to remind herself.

"Yes, we will. Or I can drive you back. But first let's find the park."

Opshora doesn't know where his car is parked. They walked to the restaurant from Pasta Paradiso.

They keep walking under the stars, on streets surrounded by beautiful archaic houses, his arms around her, holding her close. The city is still alive; people walk by, soft music from nearby houses spills onto the road. A faint breeze starts to break and rustle the treetops resting against the night. They continue to stroll, enjoying each other's company in silence, bodies brushing against each other.

"Want to come over to my place?" he wants to know. She nods in agreement. Tonight, she doesn't mind anything. It's too beautiful a night to end now, somewhat immoral to kill the possibilities of footsteps that may wander into right directions . . . Besides, she realizes she is attracted to Antonio. Maddeningly. It heightened while they ate dinner. He reached her heart through her stomach—the thought sounded funny in her head. In any case, she doesn't want to be alone on a night like this. She has been alone for a very long time.

And they walk through some back alleys taking a short cut to his residence. He lives on the top floor of the Pasta Paradiso, miles away from his parents' home, to keep his autonomy and peace. He isn't fond of family meddling in his daily existence. They find the lights of the eatery dimmed as it's closed to customers but the sounds of cleaning continue inside. They hear voices coming from the kitchen. A small team of assistants are organizing stuff in preparation for the next day. The restaurant will reopen at 11:30 tomorrow morning as usual. Antonio is careful not to draw any attention and gestures that they need to tip toe up the stairs to his rooms.

"Family is gone for the night. Good." Antonio whispers as they climb the stairs. Opshora controls her giggles with difficulty.

Antonio's living room is spacious with large windows, sparse furniture. A big television is mounted against the inner wall. Beautifully hand-crafted floor rugs cover some of the empty spaces. On one side is a small low table with two timber stools on opposite sides that serve as a dining space; two place mats are laid on the table ready for the next occasion of eating. The tiny kitchen is just across, separated by a transparent sliding partition.

He leads her into the bedroom. It's cozy, fitted with a king-sized bed facing a large window, which forms the entire front wall. The curtains are pulled away allowing streetlights to feed into the room. There are no high-rise buildings across the street that can invade the privacy of the room. Other than the bed it's bare, hermit-modest. Two semi-closed doors on the sidewall indicate a bathroom and a walk-in closet. Opshora likes the simplicity of the room, the snug ambience. The air con hums in the background. He doesn't switch on the light but gently gathers her in his arms and begins to kiss her. The somewhat faint taste of the red wine they drank still alive on his lips fills her mouth with sweet warmth. She kisses him back, fervently. He holds her closely and then they are on the bed. He fumbles with her shirt buttons.

"Out of practice," he whispers. She laughs at the hilarity of the situation. He stifles her laughter with another long, passionate kiss.

"You are beautiful! I love your silky, chocolate skin." His breath is warm on her face, on her neck. She wraps her arms around him tightly, craves his nearness.

"I don't have a condom," he explains after several minutes of passionate exploring. She sits up on the bed.

"We can't," she refuses to go further.

"No? Sure?" She nods. He gets out of bed, searches the drawers.

"Even if you are as old as you claim? Ahh . . . *tesoro* you amaze me . . . " he teases, gently.

"Yes! Always a risk," she throws a pillow at him that he dodges. It falls on the floor with a muted thud.

"There's a twenty four-hour CVS close by. Next street. Let's go there. I will buy enough supplies," he proposes. They get up, quickly put their clothes back on and carefully climb down the stairs. The kitchen lights are still on, the voices monotonously engaged.

"We are drunk," Opshora remarks resigned as they walk long minutes in circles around the streets unable to find the store. She has a hard time stopping from bursting out in giggles all over again. She feels silly. Light-headed. The wine has really kicked in.

"I guess I agree." His lazy yawn confirms her observation. They both are tired. It has been quite a night so far.

"These high heels are killing me! Shall we rest a bit?" she suggests pointing to a bench beside some thickets, beds of flowers, alluring in the shadows of tall trees. Antonio carries her shoes as she treads barefoot.

The grass is soothing under her feet. It seems like a tiny

park. D.C. is famous for parks and flowers and trees. Countless colors—all throughout different seasons. He holds her close and they lounge on the bench. Her head resting against his shoulder, her body nestled against his, they fall asleep.

When the sun lights up the early dawn sky with a crimson glow they quietly return to Antonio's apartment and sleep for hours till the sounds of cars stir the morning. The smell of a new day invades their space. Opshora wakes up after nine, washes up, uses the extra toothbrush Antonio has kept for her near the sink faucet. When she steps out of the bathroom he is already waiting with steaming coffee. He is in his dark blue dressing gown, barefoot, hair tousled, eyes still holding the last tiny traces of lost sleep. They sit on the low stools facing each other and smile. It's a funny situation.

"What a night!" he exclaims. "Next time you are here I will be fully prepared for you. Cross my heart," he makes a mock solemn face. "No mistakes!" They laugh together.

"How do you plan to smuggle me out now?" She is curious.

"Italians gossip, gossip, gossip. It doesn't do them any good. I was just trying to be careful last night. Maybe because the wine knocked out my brain. It doesn't matter, actually."

"At daytime it doesn't? At late night it does. Got it," Opshora quips, smiling.

"You missed that I referred to the wine and the craziness it created in my head," he lounges forward and kisses her, long, slow.

"You can come and go any time. You can stay here as long as you like. I am not afraid of the gossip, not anymore," he is serious.

"What changed in the last five to six hours?" She is curious.

"I am saner now . . . We are adults. We do what we choose. It's our lives," he says matter of fact. She gets up.

"Got to go. Have a meeting . . . a life and a store to run. And writing to address." Opshora gathers her stuff.

"When can I see you again?" he asks.

"Why?"

"I will tell you at our next date. Fair game?" He is playful.

Opshora doesn't respond. She stops him from following her downstairs. They kiss at the door and bid goodbye. She doesn't meet anyone on her way out and in a minute is on the street, leaving the reminiscence of the night at Antonio's.

After Opshora walks out of the building, Antonio is seized with a strange kind of euphoria that he tries to bury within. He is happy. He quickly showers, changes and runs down the stairs whistling in a cheerful mood. Glances are exchanged and smiles break on faces in the kitchen.

"Boss got it last night," someone says and the men clap.

"Nailed it finally, eh, Antonio boss?"

"C'mon, mind your business," Antonio tries to be brisk, miserably failing to brush off the voices and the laughter, and the meaningful glances that follow. He tries not to smile, though inwardly he is amused.

"He will go easy on us now, boys! The power of *sesso!*" The voices keep teasing. They assume he got laid last night.

"No! No sesso, *idioti,*" He didn't have sex with Opshora.. . . the idiots are thinking ahead, unnecessarily connecting dots because of their hormonal male brains.

"Boss was writing poetry the whole night as the lady waited patiently, *mamma mia!*" Laughter and whistles fill the kitchen.

Antonio doesn't pay any more attention to his staff. Let them laugh at him. He concentrates on the menu showing a flash of his teeth in surrender. The entire kitchen has been buzzing since morning. Someone must have spotted them last night or Opshora getting out of his residence in the morning hours. They have drawn the conclusion based on evidence, of course. He can't blame them. Best to brace the tide with smiles.

"Poop-face turned into apple-cherry blossom . . . Cinderella spell," someone whispers loud enough to be heard by everyone. A fresh spell of laughter breaks out.

Was that his nickname in the kitchen? Poop-face? He thought he was better liked by staff—Antonio wonders, and pretends he hasn't heard the comment. If he ignores the initial whispers and gossip, it might die down altogether. After all, Opshora would be working with many of the staff for the book. But his mind flies on wings and he keeps whistling. He orders a flower bouquet to be delivered to the Beads and Bracelets store. Hours roll on; he gets busy in the web of creating lasagna, zuppa e salsa, ravioli and spaghetti and more . . . every minute expecting to hear from Opshora. But she doesn't call.

Opshora gets a good look at herself in the glass door reflection as she enters the Starbucks on K Street for her meeting in downtown D.C. Her silk shirt is wrinkled beyond repair as it was underneath Antonio the entire time they were asleep. The skirt bears no signs of last night, no secrets to give out. She finds one earring is missing. Must be lying on Antonio's bedroom floor somewhere. She heaves a sigh of resignation, and accepts that her disheveled appearance can't be altered now. Too late to care. People are polite and hide their surprise or whatever, and dive into the discussion right away. It's on the research report she has been working on for a non-profit organization. The meeting goes well, as planned. She manages to get an extension on the deadline to rework and finalize the draft.

She lingers over another cappuccino after the meeting is over before venturing out towards Beads and Bracelets. She decides to walk to the store in order to process the night spent with Antonio.

# CHAPTER FOURTEEN

# Realization . . . Taking Stock

"Someone got lucky last night!" Are the welcoming words Opshora hears as she steps inside the store. She quickly takes off her shoes and heads towards her usual corner.

Chris follows her. His gaze is inspectional. He takes into account her wrinkled silk shirt, flushed countenance, and failed attempt to avoid a face-to-face encounter with him, her body language.

"Mind your own business. Nosy . . . get out of my hair!"

"Ok my Pinocchio! Tumble-ass! I rest my case," he is a connoisseur of words as always and teases in a solemn tone. "I have some extra T-shirts upstairs in the closet that may become you, I think. You can change if you want to. I'm just offering you a graceful option."

Opshora is too happy to grab the lifeline presented and escapes from his intense scrutiny. She is not ready to talk, yet. Chris loves a gossip, juicy details. She knows her appearance is a bit "too untamed" even for the crafty store. Chris' residence has always been a sanctuary.

"Ahh bestie, forgot to give you . . . this arrived some time ago." Chris brings out a bouquet of white lilies and roses, wrapped in an exotic faint fragrance.

'*Tesoro, for you,* Antonio'—simple, honest expression in economic use of words, projecting voluminous underlined possibilities. She likes the flowers, the words on the card—sprawled over its entire space with genuine feelings. It touches her heart somewhere.

"Food … flowers … wrinkled shirt … lethal combo, dear," Chris says in passing with a hint of laughter. Opshora doesn't humor him with details.

"Curiosity killed the cat," Opshora matches his playful taunting.

After the store closes, she rings the bell at Leila's house. She hasn't been to see her aunt recently. And tonight she thought the emptiness of her apartment might be too weighty, crassly appalling. Leila opens the door at the first ring as if she was waiting all this while on the other side of the door for her. Opshora drops her bag on the floor and at the expiration of the first hug runs upstairs for a shower while Leila heats up food.

"You will find a freshly washed yellow skirt, blue tie-dye printed top on hangers, in the closet outside the bathroom. You have to do with them. Too much color? Mind it those are mine," she says over her shoulder. For a woman of eighty, Leila is still classy in her choice of clothes. She buys mostly from Banana Republic and designer clothes from fancy, expensive stores in Georgetown.

She didn't comment on Opshora's appearance, and she never has. She didn't even ask why Opshora has showed up suddenly without prior notice. She has remained a comfort zone for her niece whenever Opshora needed her, knocked at her door, with a smile or totally disheveled. She always patiently waits for Opshora to explain a situation or offer details only if she chooses to unlike Ruby whose impatience to help though well meant, sometimes becomes overwhelming. This has defined the relationship between the mother and the daughter, distancing and painful to both. Ruby wants to wipe away every hurt from Opshora's life even if she doesn't want her mother to intervene.

Leila's uncritical stand has intensified a close bond with Opshora over the years as she continues to navigate through life's glacial aches and turbulences, simplicities and surprises.

The sound of running water lasts long, giving Leila enough time to be ready with dinner. A simple menu of steamed rice, shrimp and broccoli in garlic sauce, mixed potato and peas curry—take-away from the restaurant around the bend. She makes a salad as an addition. Dessert is pistachio ice cream and coffee. A very unusual combination but it has worked for both for years and she keeps the tradition going at every visit of her niece. Sometimes they also try pecan or vanilla adding a dash of sliced banana for ecstasy.

"Ah! My colors become you!" Leila glances at her niece, amused.

"I love your clothes, missy. You know that . . ." Leila has been "missy" to Opshora since she could speak. She picked it up from her aunt as Leila used that endearment jestingly when she was a little girl.

"Humbled." They both laugh at the way Leila utters the word.

"What a delightful menu," Opshora remarks sitting opposite Leila. The next several minutes they concentrate on the dinner, passing the dishes, heaping food on their plates. She is really hungry now. She had several cups of coffee and nibbled on half a blueberry muffin from Chris' kitchen after the seafood paella she ate with Antonio the night before. They chitchat on trifles, matters of no real significance, laugh over everyday news and gossip.

"Missy, I have met someone . . ." Opshora finally has the courage to verbally acknowledge her association with Antonio to someone beyond her inner self. She has tried to brush off the whole idea of Antonio as inconsequential, but doubts keep surfacing about her assessment of the situation. In a nutshell, without specific details, she introduces him to Leila.

"I am attracted to him, missy. No use faking as if it doesn't matter."

"What do you want to do about it?" Leila is curious.

"I am afraid, confused . . . not sure it's right. I don't want to get entangled in a casual relationship . . . I need to be careful about romantic disasters." Flashes of memories come back to her . . . she dated Tomo for a while on the rebound from Fiji. "Is he the right choice? The whole thing seems so absurd, so sudden."

Opshora sips her coffee after spooning some of the pistachio ice cream into her mouth. Her teeth react at the sudden touch of warmth before the tinge of iciness has died down totally. She has to take another sip to neutralize the effect.

"What's the problem with a casual relationship? What are you afraid of? Even if it's temporary, it can take away the brunt of loneliness," Leila says gently. Opshora doesn't respond.

"Zayn? Still?" Leila hits the nail on the head. Opshora nods. "Unless you give it a chance, how can you be certain, darling?"

"I have been burnt badly, missy." Opshora's voice sounds worn out.

"I know . . . Life is yin and yang. Darkness breaks at sunlight, always," Leila puts in quietly. "If my memory isn't totally bonkers, I don't think I am aware of any decent relationships you have had for years."

Opshora smiles at the use of the word "decent" by her aunt. It's true—the universe around her has moved on, transformed in many ways but she has been hung up on Zayn. He has clouded any prospect of any kind of romantic associations.

"Look at me, missy. I am a total failure. At fifty one, like a rudderless boat in vast, rough waters." Opshora tries to smile again, but traces of buried pain abruptly spark and own her eyes. "Zayn, my life in Fiji, will always remain an inseparable part of me. So hard to forget."

"Who says you are a failure? You are not broken! You have never played the victim . . . You've done what's right for you and that's the way to go." Leila's steady voice stabilizes Opshora. "But you have to remember, Zayn is in the past. Don't let him mess with your life anymore."

"Antonio is forty-four . . . much younger."

"Does age matter when people are safely adults?" They both laugh at the way Leila emphasizes on "safely."

"I need to go away. Think this through," Opshora sobers up.

"Really?"

"Really." Opshora is certain now.

"What about a visit to your nephew and niece in that case? To take your mind off of it—let the steam out. " Leila suggests. "But how long can you run away?" She knows the answer but still asks.

Opshora calls Robin later that night. It's lovely to catch up with her brother after many months.

"It's late . . . I know," she is apologetic.

"I am glad you called. I was reading in bed. You can call me anytime, you know that," the warmth in Robin's voice touches her.

"I know Robin. You have been a good brother to me, always . . ."

"Misunderstood, sometimes?" Robin jests.

"Yes. Many factors played a role," Opshora admits. "Deep down I have been envious at the way you have handled your life." Opshora is surprised at this self-revelation. She feels a bit guilty for having pushed Robin away, always suspecting an underlying meaning to whatever he says. She decides then and there to be more open-minded about her brother, stop dissecting his every gesture.

"There are bumps in my life as well, Opshora. I try to manage and survive," Robin is serious. His honesty almost drives her to tears. "It happens in everyone's life, now and then. In many ways you are stronger than I am . . . you approach difficulties without inhibitions," he pauses giving Opshora enough time to ponder his words. His honesty is astonishing.

"Maya is here. She would like to say hello," he adds, possibly to divert the flow of the discussion. He is a man of few words unlike Opshora, and always surgically precise.

Opshora says a quick "hello" to Maya and hangs up. Maya has been quite neutral and pleasant, always refraining from being overtly critical about her sister-in-law. Opshora feels she should have invested much more in strengthening their relationship. When their lives crossed, Opshora was carrying too much baggage and trying to move away from Zayn, the Fiji days. Robin's stand regarding her fierce love for Zayn also created distance which over the years had been bridged to a great extent though the remnant of heartaches sometimes overshadowed the new-found tranquility in her relationship with her brother. He mostly ignores such wrinkles for which Opshora is grateful. Otherwise, the distance would have widened. However, she is glad to have had an open conversation with Robin tonight.

Opshora switches off her cell phone. She will have to discuss the absentee time with Chris but she is sure they will be able to work something out. He is a solid friend and compassionate and genuinely understanding.

Chris is more than a friend, more of a younger brother. He has filled up her old school-girl friend Diana's place—though she regularly keeps in touch, she lives in another state—not available to accompany Opshora to kill an idle morning in a history museum, or watch a sentimental movie or silly soap-operas on TV or to go shopping or satisfy any impulsive desire. Chris is happy to be with her on such occasions. He doesn't mind at all. In fact she finds his taste in clothes modern and immaculately classy. He has guided her in making the right selections at countless expeditions to the mall.

Opshora knows she will have to call Diana sometime soon to give an update of the recent developments with Antonio otherwise she will put up a phone-fight. In her extremely busy schedule as a professional, mothering two teenagers and taking care of a husband, Diana doesn't like to miss out on anything. She has a habit of calling Opshora at the most odd hours . . . to catch up. She forgets the three-hour time difference she has with the east coast.

Sounds of very faint music infiltrate Opshora's room from Leila's. Her aunt doesn't sleep well since Dr. Mirza passed away. Resorting to music soothes her emptiness at night and she is able to succumb to a few hours of unconscious existence, eventually. Opshora is used to this routine and slowly drifts off after hours of emotional turmoil and fatigue.

# CHAPTER FIFTEEN

# One Slice of Onion, Two Drops of Lemon, a Whisper of Tears

Maya meets Opshora outside the Port Jefferson railway station with Bella and Liam. She has taken the afternoon off. Opshora wanted to take an Uber from the station but Maya wouldn't hear of it.

"No way!" She had protested. "It will give me an excuse to take a break from work. We will be waiting to see you soon."

Port Jefferson is a beautiful town embraced by the blue shoreline—it got its name in 1836. In the well-preserved saltbox and brick homes, the magic of bygone days is traceable, unmistakably proclaiming the glories of the past. History corroborates that shipbuilders constructed their homes here while battles were fought with the British to keep the independence of the newly formed republic. Opshora has travelled on this route before—from New York's Penn station catching the trains operated by the Long Island Rail Road. Both Robin and Maya work at the Stony Brooke hospital. They moved to Long Island right after Bella was born. Though her visits haven't been as steady as she desired, the children are somehow drawn to Opshora. She never forgets their birthdays and festive occasions to shower them with presents that they treasure. She researches and invests her time well to pick up gifts that would take their breath away.

The breeze from the ocean greets Opshora as she steps out of the train. The kids come running to her arms as they spot her on the railway platform

"I am so glad you have come," whispers Bella hiding her face against Opshora in a tight embrace, inhaling the fading exotic perfume that encircles her. That's the best part Bella loves about her free-spirited aunt. Bella is also fond of Opshora's carefree, hearty chuckles at the funny stories that she shares about her friends, school and teachers. Her tiny life becomes a magnanimous canvas of fun when she is with Opshora.

Liam likes to sniff at his aunt's hair and vibrant scarves she wears casually around her neck. Sometimes his nose ventures too close to her dangling earrings. He loves the scent of his aunt, the sound of her laughter. It has the ring of many waterfalls, carries the echo of unbridled promises of absolute fun.

"Liam! Get back!" Bella pushes her brother away as he is up to his usual gimmicks. "Stop sniffing like a dog." He looks like a studious geek. The sunlight reflects on his glasses, touches his thoughtful deep brown eyes.

"It's okay. He has missed me. Let him familiarize himself with me. I love his professorial inquisitiveness," Opshora smiles and lovingly draws her nephew into the fold of her arms. Liam's face brightens up at this appreciation. He sticks out his tongue at his sister gleefully, content at his small victory.

Maya and Robin have a lovely house on a slope. It's an old architectural marvel built a century ago, has more bedrooms than they need—large bay windows, stonewalls and ocean-facing wide balconies. They have renovated it keeping the archaic spirit of the house untouched and alive. The house is about twenty-minutes drive from the railway station. Maya maneuvers through numerous side alleys to take a short cut.

Robin is pleased to see her. He changes from his hospital gear and joins everyone after a quick shower. He is late today, after last moment emergencies. In the next hour the food and the flippant talks lighten up Opshora's mood. She momentarily forgets her life in D.C., Antonio and her new found attraction and dilemma regarding him.

Four days pass. Still no calls. No news of Opshora. Antonio has been waiting to hear from her. The nights keep aging, the shadows on the streets deepen but she doesn't return his calls. The scent of newfound happiness begins to ebb away. Antonio gets restless, cranky. He shouts at the assistant chefs constantly, bangs the cooking pots against the kitchen sink, throws tomatoes in a fit of rage at a helper at a peak hour one evening. Isabella and Marco are away on a break for two weeks to visit a close friend. Rosa and Carlo witness Antonio's mood swings, as does the entire kitchen staff. The gossip about Opshora's sudden departure from Antonio's horizon has reached their ears as well. They are weary, worried and suffer his temper tantrums in troubled silence. Only Alberto is nonchalant.

"Boss bro, shall I go and check where Signorina is?" he inquires.

"No, mind your own business." Antonio is irritated with himself, with Opshora and his irrational reaction to her withdrawal from his life. He barely knows her but she has the power to disturb his normal life. He is surprised at this discovery and angry about it.

Opshora hasn't even acknowledged the flowers he sent her. It was a message—confirmation of the appeal this relationship holds for him. And he assumed it was the same from her side as well. She is totally nuts not to understand his romantic advances, not to reciprocate with his honest intent. He isn't sure what has turned her off.

Meanwhile, he calls her cell phone only to be silenced by the automated voice mail system. He doesn't leave any message. She has suddenly disappeared, without notice.

"Boss, signorina has gone off on a break to New York," assistant chef Marcello informs him on the sixth day.

"Says who?" Antonio doesn't understand why people can't leave him alone.

"I passed by her store this morning before coming to work. Signora Rosa sent me to get news, boss."

By that time Antonio had called Opshora three times and finally in a tortuous voice left a message, only one time.

"Antonio here . . . um . . . hope you're okay? Um . . . No news . . . call me? Missing you. Addio." The automated voice prompting him to leave a message intimidated him no doubt.

During his cigarette break he calls the Beads and Bracelets store to check on Marcello's news. Chris gives him the eagerly awaited information.

"Opshora is visiting family. She is expected back to work around mid next week. Possibly five more days to go . . . I will tell her you called. Any message? Who is this?"

"No . . . no one. No message. Just checking. Ciao." Antonio hangs up hastily. It was an awkward conversation. He makes an instant mental calculation. Anyway, some news is better than none.

He is annoyed with himself for having exposed his vulnerability to the world. Carlo has tried to drag him to drink a shot or two without much success. Luckily, his parents aren't here to witness the debacle. He is relieved about that. Maria hasn't ventured near him so far, either; she's been too busy with studying for tests. Ashley called to give an update about her behavior and it seems the teenager is manageable for now. Even this news doesn't lift his spirits. He fails to understand why Opshora's silence is such a big deal. He is uneasy at her sudden disappearance. He wonders whether she was too disappointed in him on the date night. He couldn't prove his prowess, for sure. He got drunk and missed the opportunity with her. Women are crazy creatures, wrapped up in strange ways that are considered normal only by them. The kitchen is weary of him, but perhaps they also pity him in his extremely wasted mid-life crisis. Who knows?

Opshora is fond of the walk on the dock around the harbor. This has always been an attraction of Port Jefferson in addition to the allure of Bella and Liam. She has visited Robin in the past especially to be with the children. She loves seeing them grow up. Both Robin and Maya have very busy lives. They balance it to the best so that the kids can have a meaningful space in their hectic schedules. In the morning Robin drops them at school. They take the school bus back home. During the daytime, only the nanny is in the house. She comes around lunchtime and stays with the children till Maya is back from the hospital in the early evening.

There is so much to see and do around Port Jefferson village. Cultural events occur throughout the year. The place stays alive even in the heart of winter, entombed under snow. The parks and beaches have their own appeal. For hours she hangs around the dock watching the boats coming inshore, sailing away, the sea gulls drifting in the winds. She is never tired of listening to the songs of the waters, the waves breaking on the sands—a most rewarding lazy escape to recharge and heal. It's a very different landscape than Fiji but deep down the salty smell of the waves takes her back to Suva's beaches. Grief is a strange emotion—it brings people together, it also drives them apart. The ache is dulled now and she is more objective about her feelings buried in the past. She has transitioned back to her life in America—her birthplace, nestled inside its folds.

Opshora kills time exploring the town—the East Main Street, the tiny interesting stores, the Mather museum. The ferry to Bridgeport, riding over the exhilarating mass of waves, is a unique feeling every time she travels over the bay. She tries to push away any thoughts of Antonio—and sober up from any kind of fantasies.

The quaint eateries offer all sorts of culinary delights. Very special, very authentic to Long Island's tradition. Opshora's favorite is the Pasta Pasta restaurant, famous for its ambience, innovative food creations sensational to the palate, exciting dessert menu and an amazing wine list. The kids like the place as well. Bella is adventurous with her orders but Liam sticks mainly to pizza. For dessert, they all love tiramisu and classic crème brulee, baked vanilla custard with a brittle sugar glaze. The restaurant has been operating in Port Jefferson for over twenty years, creating a revolution in gastronomy. They also sometimes try the Toast Coffee house, which is a delightful eatery for the standard options or the Tiger Lily Café on East Main Street noteworthy especially for their interior décor, vegetarian cuisine, and other soulful ethnic dishes.

Opshora works at night after the entire household goes to sleep. It's easier to manage her insomnia and also get work done. Chris has been generous about her time away from the store. She speaks to him on Skype on some nights. He is a night bird and they giggle for hours on over silly things. . . They hardly discuss business or Antonio:

"I owe you, my friend. I will work my ass off when I am back." Opshora promises. Chris smiles to that and affectionately gives her a virtual hug.

"Come back recharged, sweet-face! I love you more when you keep smiling. Good night. Now sleep tight."

"How's your writing coming along?" Robin asks as they eat dinner. He feels guilty for not having kept more in touch with his sister in recent times, even though she has visited from time to time.

"It continues," Opshora doesn't give any specifics, but skirts around the issue.

"What plans now?"

"No plans," she is straightforward. Truthful. That's how her life has been all these past years. It doesn't belong to any definite frame.

"Good, good. That's okay . . . flexibility isn't a bad thing. Our jobs get boring. We can't command our time," he tries to sound jovial. Opshora is certain that he has taken her response as a snub, which it wasn't at all.

"Try some okra. I cooked it specially the way you like it—with shrimp and green chilies, a dash of cilantro," Maya chimes in breaking the frigid situation. She is a great cook and cooks with a loving fury. Opshora takes a helping, not just to please her but because it's really tasty.

"Tilapia sear-fried is great . . . like it? Want some more?" Robin searches for a good piece of fish in the serving platter, picks the right one and heaps it on her plate. The attention diverts back to food. The environment normalizes. They tease Maya. She constantly experiments with cooking.

"This is what I call soulful food . . . well done Maya," Robin compliments her, emphasizing the word "soulful." She detects a hint of teasing but still passionately explains how food heals.

"Food is love, comfort. Food heals, neutralizes and rejuvenates. Brings happiness. A shared family meal brings people together. At the hospital, we are borrowing ideas from non-profit projects that have had success with the curative power of food—as medicine," Maya has a point. "Cooking is an art. Food becomes a spiritual experience when cooked with creative rage." Unknowingly, Maya brings back Antonio all over again. Opshora remembers the passion he invests in his culinary universe. She has been trying to run away from him, escape into a horizon where she doesn't have to deal with emotions he is stirring in her, the fears she is unwilling to confront.

So far, Opshora has been doing quite well in her long wanderings around the town. Time spent with the children has been meaningful, bonding. She is enjoying the family outings, meals, and interactions. But soon she will have to face what awaits her. She can't run away for too long.

"I intend to go back day after tomorrow. It has been very refreshing so far. Thank you for having me here . . . at such a short notice."

"Stay a few more days." Robin's invitation is genuine.

"It has been over a week," Opshora reminds them, herself.

"Really? I can't believe it. The kids are going be heartbroken!" Maya's emphatic.

"I will miss them. Really. But got to get back to my life," Opshora says.

"What's the hurry? What do you have to do?" Robin asks.

"I do work for a living. It may not be glorified but pays my bills." The tension returns. "I will come back. I love to be here," Opshora adds hurriedly, a little ashamed of her hasty reaction, all over again. Robin's remark was possibly innocent. She has become overly sensitive—a good realization. Maya is a healing presence. She desperately tries to break the awkwardness whenever the situation arises. The phone rings at that moment giving everyone a respite from the charged atmosphere. It's from the hospital for Robin.

The day of departure arrives. Opshora bids goodbye to Robin in the morning. It is cordial. Robin makes coffee for her and they sit together for some moments, sipping from their mugs. By not saying much they say a lot. Opshora was truly embarrassed for snapping at Robin two nights ago. Though she wanted to, she couldn't bring herself to apologize to her brother.

"Come back again. I really enjoyed our time together." Robin kisses the top of her head as he leaves for the hospital. Opshora is touched. She has a hard time blinking back her tears.

"Opshora, you will always have a home with us, you know that, right?" Maya has guessed something is amiss this time.

"I appreciate this, Maya . . . very much. I wish we could spend some more time together." This is Opshora's way of admitting her prior mistake in not investing in her relationship with Maya. In the past, she refused to treat Maya as a person—independent of Robin. She never gave Maya much chance to be close to her. Maya has stomached Opshora's attitude with patience and maturity without any complaint. She has encouraged her children to bond with Opshora.

"Sometimes I feel I could do better. I don't know how or what I actually want." To her own ears the words sound despondent.

"I am only a dial away . . ." Maya says softly. She doesn't ask any questions or offer any suggestions.

Opshora waits till the kids are back from school to say a final goodbye to them before leaving. Liam is okay with such separations and bears them with stoic wisdom. For a nine-year-old he is too cool. He knows Opshora will be back again, she will remember to send sensational gifts wrapped in beautiful packages safely stored inside brown cardboard boxes delivered duly by UPS. He waits for those moments. Bella is unable to stop her tears every time Opshora departs. It breaks Opshora's heart to see her niece crying at goodbyes.

She calls Uber and heads towards the station. There are only a handful of travelers at this time of the day. The train pulls ahead. The beautiful town falls back slowly, and vanishes behind its tail line as the powerful engine surges forward on serpentine tracks.

In about an hour Opshora lands at Penn Station. She walks a block and waits for her bus at a nearby café. She switches on her cell phone and calls Chris.

"Welcome back to the world of the commoners . . . oozing

puss in boils, farts contained in the backfire of jalopies . . . the stench of rowdy, disgusting sewage drowned in the Potomac . . ." Chris is overjoyed. His outrageous words convey his unbridled expression of delight.

"Stop being obnoxious or I will hang up," Opshora threatens with a laugh.

"Can I expect you tomorrow at the store?" he is eager.

"Of course! Let me first successfully launch myself into my home, partner." She should be home before midnight barring any mishaps on the road.

"I have news . . . I met someone!" By the sound of his voice she had guessed the sudden surge of euphoria had a stronger base than the news of her re-emergence in his world. There is more to his cheerfulness than her return. She promises to lend her full attention at their upcoming meeting.

She hangs up and scrolls through missed calls and text messages. Five texts are from her mother. Ruby has tried to be casual, asking her how she was doing, how was work, her expected day of return back home. All this while she has been in contact with her son regularly, Opshora is certain she had access to all the updates. She forgives Ruby for her pretenses. After all her mother does care. Ruby genuinely worries for Opshora even though Opshora is slightly over half a century old. Too old and too much of a rebel, still!

She finds the missed calls from Antonio and his sole stumbling message in the voice mail. She listens to it four times. The stark simplicity blended with undisguised honesty in those words touches her. She understands the uneasiness with which he had spoken to the machine, cautiously—in expressing his emotion but at the same time trying not to sound too needy, reveal too much.

# CHAPTER SIXTEEN

# You Are the Butter on My Bread

"She's here. I seated her at the end of the room, close to the windows," the head waiter reports to Rosa the next evening.

Opshora didn't call Antonio, but on a sudden whim just showed up at the restaurant. He is not aware of her return. She wanted to surprise him. Now she is not so sure whether it was a good idea to barge in without any notice. While she waits the dilemma grows stronger.

"Ciao! How are you?" Rosa bends down to kiss Opshora's cheeks as she places the breadbasket and a glass of red wine carefully in front of her. After exchanging greetings Opshora feels somewhat silly.

"I shouldn't have come. Maybe I should leave," she says. Something in Rosa's mannerisms tells her that people know about her vanishing act on Antonio; it came at a cost.

"No, you mustn't do any such thing, dear! Drink the wine. It's really good. On the house . . . Antonio is on his way." Rosa brushes off her dilemma. No one has told Antonio about Opshora's presence yet. Rosa heads toward the kitchen to give him the news in person.

Back in the kitchen, Antonio is sweating over the rising heat as he stirs his signature dishes risotto ai gamberoni, and capon margo. The saffron and the shrimps have to be cooked to perfection—perfezione as Antonio likes to call it. It's a busy evening. He has been breezing through the kitchen frequently overseeing the work of the assistant chefs in between his own creations. The orders are piling up mostly for his signature dishes. The assistants prepare under his hawk eyes. There is no scope to mess up anything. Mistakes are not accepted here. And these days Antonio has much less patience.

"Antonio's Ingredients for Risotto ai gamberoni" is printed on a scrap of colorful hand-dyed recycled paper placed on each table:

*Risotto:* 3–4 tablespoons extra virgin olive oil; 2 shallots, small diced; 2 cloves garlic, minced; 2 cups Arborio rice; ¼ teaspoon saffron threads; ¼ cup of dry white wine; 6 cups of fish or vegetable stock, simmering; 2½ tablespoons of butter; ⅓ cup heavy cream; ⅓ cup freshly grated Parmesan cheese; Salt (start with ¾ tsp-add to taste) and freshly ground white pepper.

*Shrimp:* 4½ tablespoons of butter; 18 pieces of large shrimp (size 16/20) raw, peeled and deveined; ¼ cup of dry white wine; 1½ tablespoons lobster base, purchased; ¼ cup water (room temperature).

*Garnish:* ¼ bunch parsley, finely chopped; 1 onion, thinly sliced, lightly floured and fried.

*The process:* In a large saucepan over medium heat, warm oil and sauté shallots and garlic for 4 minutes. Add rice and stir, about 3 minutes. Add saffron and wine and stir until liquid is completely absorbed. Add stock to rice a ladleful at a time, stirring frequently after each addition. Make sure rice never gets dry. Season with salt and pepper. When the rice is tender to the bite, after about 20 minutes, add butter, heavy cream and Parmesan cheese and mix well; set aside and keep warm.

For shrimp, in a sauté pan over medium heat, melt butter

and sauté shrimp for two minutes on each side. Deglaze with white wine, stir in lobster base and water and simmer for 5 minutes. Remove shrimp from sauce and pass through a sieve. Whisk butter into sauce a little at a time. Arrange risotto in warmed appetizer plates and top with three shrimp. Drizzle with sauce and garnish and chopped parsley and fried onions.

"Antonio, she is here," Rosa informs him.

"What? Move . . . get out of the way," Antonio keeps monitoring his cooking on the stove over the rising cloud of steam. He is too busy to listen to meaningless utterances. All tables are seated and waiting. Hungry people to feed.

"I said Opshora's here," Rosa shouts over the noise of steaming pots and murmurs coming from every corner of the busy kitchen. A whistle pierces the background clatter of hissing and banging with the pans. Antonio forgets to stir the food for several seconds. Uncertainty clouds his eyes momentarily. Then he comes to his senses.

"Marcello, take over here," he gets out of his apron and throws it on the pile of vegetables waiting at one side to be chopped. He wipes his face on the back of his shirtsleeve.

"You look a sight. Go and wash up. She is waiting for you. I will keep an eye." Rosa's heart goes out to her brother. She gives him a kind smile and shove and heads back towards the seating area. Impatient customers are waiting for tables.

It takes Antonio ten minutes to make himself presentable enough to Opshora. He crosses through the labyrinth of crowded tables searching for her and spots her instantly, staring out at the night through the large window, eyes fixated on the streetlights outlined by the darkness beyond, her back towards him. She looks fragile under the gentle, pale light of the eatery—wearing her vulnerability in the soft neckline entangled in her messy hair above the pale peach colored low-cut top. Antonio stands a few feet away from her, staring, nonplussed. At that point she suddenly turns her head and their eyes meet. In a second he is beside her. He pulls up an empty chair and sits next to her. Before she can say anything her hands are in his warm, tight clasp and he kisses them ardently.

"Let's get out of here," she whispers, a troubled look in her eyes.

"Okay," he whispers back.

Much later as she lies in his arms, Opshora listens to Antonio's steady heartbeats. He has dozed off. The air con got a bit chilly and the warmth from his bare body against hers offers comfort. She tries to think what happened in this room . . . she doesn't regret it. Antonio's touch has burnt her body with the kind of feelings she thought weren't possible after Zayn.

"*Ti amo . . . Ti amo . . . la mia belezza . . .* I missed you so much . . . became insane without you . . ." he had murmured as he made love to her. She didn't understand the endearments, whatever he was uttering, but understood the language of his passion. She couldn't hold out and reciprocated with equal urgency.

"Shall we eat something?" He opens his eyes as dawn breaks in through the cracks in the blinds. She nods. She hasn't eaten in hours. She couldn't as the anxiety of meeting with Antonio took away her peace of mind, her appetite. They skipped dinner last night. Food was the last thing on their minds.

"I am going to make you a king's breakfast," he jumps out of bed and wraps a sarong around himself.

"No, I want a queen's breakfast," she teases, laughing.

"My mistake. I will make a Queen Elizabeth breakfast for you, your highness! Your wish is my command," he responds in mock seriousness.

The upper part of his torso bare, he walks towards the kitchen. She keeps looking at him, with tenderness in her eyes.

"I know what you're thinking," he throws to her, over his shoulders.

"Don't get so cock-sure," she challenges.

"Come over and see what I am going to cook for you. A big brunch, I have decided."

"When?" she pretends surprise.

"Just now. A quick change of plan because I want to pamper you." He has all the ingredients inside the fridge—ready to be cooked.

"Fickle minded. I was bracing myself for an innovative breakfast."

Opshora lazes in the bed for some more minutes listening to the sounds of pots and pans in the kitchen. She likes the candor of his bedroom that witnessed their first night together. She hadn't planned the night to turn out the way it did. But she is glad it did. She missed him. She is falling for him . . .

She can hear Antonio whistling cheerfully as he stirs the cooking. She picks up his shirt from the floor where it was dumped earlier in haste, puts it on and follows the sounds of Antonio, the aroma of the food. He stops in midair as she approaches with bare feet, in his shirt too loose on her, coming short at her thighs, the outline of her taut breasts visible through the soft fabric, her dark hair falling down her back, some strands astray inside the shirt collar hugging her neck.

"*Bellissima* signorina! . . . you're beautiful," his eyes follow her. He momentarily forgets to stir whatever is on the stove.

"Hey Signor! Concentrate on your cooking. I am famished."

"Sure, my beauty." He smiles at her and hands her a mug of steaming coffee while the food is cooked on the stovetop on high flame.

"In my school days I hated my looks. The other girls were so white, golden or redheads . . . slim and tall. I felt ugly in my dirty-brown skin," Opshora says, sipping her coffee.

"No way!" Antonio is shocked. "I love the brown about you. Reminds me of caramel . . . chocolate mousse."

"All you think of is food!" Opshora laughs.

"Opshora, food is life, food is love for me. Feeding the hungry is my oath. The only truth I believe in."

Antonio serves the spicy spaghetti alle vongole. Opshora isn't fond of mussels so he has used pink shrimp imported from Thailand instead and tossed in extra jalapeno for additional hot flavor, garnishing it with freshly chopped cilantro as the finishing touch. He has opened a bottle of red wine to complete the meal.

"How are you going to defend your spotless moral character to the kitchen staff after all this?" she asks as they start eating.

"Well, they would want some facts, definitely," his smile is wicked. He pours the wine in their glasses.

"No! You can't," she almost screams in protest.

"It's a man's world, *tesoro*. We are guided by a brotherhood code. We all follow rules. Can't back out."

"Oh my God! How am I going to deal with them now? I have to work with your team, remember?" Her face is aflame in embarrassment.

"Those are dirty, hungry men. But I will spare the gory details," he smiles again with a wink. She throws the wine from her glass at him. He gets up and imprisons her in his arms so tightly that she is unable to move.

"Look at me, *mio caro* . . . my darling . . . I won't dishonor you. But will have to give the starving wolves something otherwise they are going to write their own stories about us. Full of bullshit! And keep laughing behind our backs. Trust me?"

She nods in agreement. With a kiss on her forehead he releases her.

The drafting of the cookbook progresses quite well. She sits down for in-depth interviews with each of the family members.

"Mr. Russo, I would like you to tell me stories—about your

family, the business, your children . . . customers will need to understand who you are . . . it's a marketing strategy to tell personal stories—to make it more authentic and appealing." Opshora puts down the terms at their first meeting. Isabella's turn is a week later as she has been extremely busy and couldn't make time before that.

"Call me Marco, *mia ragazza*," he reminds her again. "I have set up a small table in the backyard garden for us. We eat lunch as we talk?" He walks slowly, showing the way. His knees work harder to carry his enormous weight.

A simple lunch is laid out—soup, Italian bread and salad. Opshora likes the herb-mixed olive oil for dipping the bread.

"Good, right? Isabella is gifted with all kinds of recipes for sauces and unique cooking," he informs. "She likes to work alone. Very independent . . . I met her at a church charity years ago and she stabbed my heart." Marco smiles. "I was on vacation . . . staying with my mom's distant relatives in Rome." Marco pauses as Opshora waits, interested to hear the story.

"I stayed the entire summer in Rome for her . . . I was never a religious man before. Became super pious so that I could meet her every Sunday at church!" Marco has a warm, infectious laugh. Opshora is taken in by his charms. "And I was one fourth my current size those days." They laugh again.

"Does Isabella go back to Italy often?" Opshora asks.

"Yes, every summer . . . this restaurant is my life. We expanded it together with care, little by little." He discusses Pasta Paradiso, about his heritage and beyond. Marco is warm towards her and speaks with passion about his work, his life, the Italian clan he was born into. There is pride in his voice for being of Italian race, a descendant of immigrants.

"I have never met someone like you before," he remarks at one point.

"In what ways? Good or not so good? . . ." Opshora frames her question in half jest.

"Italians are very territorial. They are rigid in their ways . . . protective about their families, culture . . . relationships . . . it's complicated." There is slight hesitancy in his tone. In a gentle way he is alerting her, possibly. Opshora doesn't know what to say. She waits for his next words.

"You are a brilliant woman, mia raggaza. A doctorate! No one in my family has a PhD. Antonio dropped out of college . . . all he ever wants is to cook," he says again.

"I am the only PhD in my family," Opshora smiles. Then something comes over her and she adds, "I like Antonio. I like him a lot. I am not thinking anything—beyond that." Opshora shakes her head, wants to assure him. Her face is aflame. And an ache slowly begins to consume her heart. After that the discussion becomes forced. They talk about a few more things—polite, inconsequential matters. The earlier camaraderie is somewhat broken.

She gathers her stuff and leaps to her feet. "I have to go now. I enjoyed our conversation. It was very helpful for the book. Loved the food. Please tell Isabella her herb mixed olive oil is amazing."

Marco gets up. He smiles and gently kisses her hands as they bid goodbye. She sees the tenderness in his pale blue eyes.

"Here, I picked this wine for you to take back home," he says gently and hands her the bottle with another kind smile. She returns his smile and walks out on the street clutching the wine bottle.

Late at night Antonio calls her. She mutes the television and stands facing the window, her favorite spot as she takes the call—looking at the silent night outside.

"Why did you leave without seeing me?" he asks. "I was hoping you would pass by the kitchen. I wanted you to taste something I was experimenting with." Antonio's thoughts border on his love for cooking, usually.

"I thought you were busy," Opshora lies. She couldn't tell

him about the heaviness she felt in her heart after speaking with Marco.

"I was busy but Marcello was ready to cover for me. I could have snuck out for a couple of hours before the evening rush kicked in . . . for a quick kiss . . . a little time with you at my apartment." Opshora doesn't say anything. "Where are you now? At home? I am coming," he says matter of fact.

"No. It's late," Opshora protests.

"Are you sleepy?"

"No," she is truthful now.

"Then I am coming. We are going for a long drive." Antonio hangs up.

The time on her phone shows close to eleven. At this time of night with low traffic he may be outside her door in thirty minutes. Opshora puts on her sandals and grabs her bag. She sits on the front porch and waits for Antonio. About twenty-five minutes later he shows up. He must have driven at seventy miles an hour. Ruby, at that moment for no reason looks out of the window before going to bed. She finds Opshora getting into a white car.

"At this time of the night she is going out," she declares to her husband in a low voice.

"Hmm . . . she is a mature woman, Ruby," MD Mirza doesn't look up from the medical journal he is reading in bed.

They speed through the silent night. The complacent sky strewn with gazillion stars and the almost full moon keeps up with them. Antonio has come directly from the restaurant. She gets comfort from the cheese aroma he is wrapped in, the result of hours of laboring in the kitchen but she likes it. They don't say anything. He begins to whistle.

"In your shorts, sleeveless top and those sandals you look like a school girl," he says with a brief glance at her.

"Antonio, why are you here?"

"I wanted to see you. I missed you." He pulls the car in a

deserted side ally and turns to face her. "I want to kiss you. Hold you. Now. I smell of cheese!" At this she starts laughing. They undo their seat belts.

"You turn everything into fun with your theatrics," she closes her eyes in the comfort of his arms. Her heart wants the clock to stop—immortalize this moment with Antonio on this night beneath the streetlights.

"Don't come too close . . . even the moonlight can't hide away my wrinkles," Opshora attempts to joke, eyes closed, head leaning against his shoulder. Antonio doesn't rise to her bait.

"Don't mind what my father says . . . or anyone for that matter," he whispers and comes closer. He has guessed all right. He kisses her tears away and holds her tightly. She can hear his racing heartbeats.

Alberto flirts with Opshora non-stop with mischievous boldness in spite of Antonio's open displeasure. Alberto brings Italian desserts to share with her when they meet to discuss the book, or sometimes he smuggles a bottle of fine vintage red wine. Opshora tries not to get diverted by his overt attentions but he is the best among the clan with ideas and stories. Most of the time he is semi-serious and she accepts his funny ways with a pinch of salt. She is no teenager and is perfectly able to keep him at bay.

"Principessa, come to me if boss bro breaks your heart. I will always be here for you," he declares at opportune moments with a little bit of teasing, some seriousness.

"Alas, you are too young for me. I am in no mood for babysitting," Opshora pushes him away with equal candor.

Alberto is three years junior to Antonio, childless and divorced. His wife had a long-standing health condition and wanted to get out of the marriage. No one in the family talks about her. He has been cautious with romantic affiliations but has had a few discreet relationships, which never materialized into marriage. Her sons' divorces were hard for Isabella, a staunch believer of the Catholic faith. Marco accepted the changes with stoic grace as part of the baggage—of separation from their native country, the undiluted culture of Italian traditions.

"Not joking. He is a master of breaking hearts. My brother," Alberto has broached playfully, in more than one occasion, using different tactics. "He can do it simultaneously as he stirs pasta . . . he is a connoisseur . . . in cooking, heart breaking . . . "

Opshora doesn't want to take his warnings seriously but can't totally brush it away. Somewhere it sticks and the ache begins. Perhaps this is his way of warning her? Pointing out Antonio's outlook regarding commitments? But she is not even sure she wants any commitment from him at this point. She is uncertain about her own feelings. But even then the pain remains.

"Don't continue to be a nuisance, brother," Antonio cautions whenever he hears such utterances.

"My two brothers have a history . . . it's complex. But we've learned to live with it," Rosa is frank with Opshora.

From Rosa, Opshora discovers that initially Ashley had dated Alberto. Alberto introduced the two on their third date and from then the story changed. Ashley chose the older brother and eventually tied the knot. The family was against the match. They warned Antonio. Ashley's heritage, her way of life was totally different and on top of that the Alberto angle hung over the scenario. However, Antonio went ahead. He listened to his heart. The bittersweet rivalry between the brothers began from there. Eventually, Alberto moved on and found someone else. He got married which lasted only a handful of years. Rosa didn't provide any thing more beyond this. Opshora doesn't like prying and she didn't probe any further. That was the end of the discussion about Alberto's life. But Rosa doesn't hesitate to talk about Ashley. . .

The first few years were good between Antonio and Ashley, and Maria was born. Ashley was happy, preoccupied at the beginning then motherhood started to feel like a burden. Antonio was busy as ever with the restaurant. To Ashley it seemed she and Maria were less important—second to his extravagant attachment to cooking. Isabella and Marco tried to help in raising Maria. A live-in Italian nanny was hired. Ashley began drinking, clubbing with friends. Her relationship with Antonio soured and after several incidents of infidelity initiated from her side, she ended their relationship in a bitter divorce and custody battle.

Alberto never tried to win her back to get even with his brother, though Ashley hints constantly about such a possibility. She is open to a casual involvement but Alberto stays away from her. He has no intention of igniting any romance between them. He moved on when she dumped him for his brother.

Alberto met Nora . . . by then some years had passed. He had learned to resist his feelings for Ashley.

Nora was from Italian-Jewish descent. Her family had migrated to the U.S. during World War II. It was a blow to Isabella and her undying Catholic faith. There was hesitancy to embrace Nora with open arms. Surprisingly, Antonio was the first one to welcome her in the family and made sure she was treated well by everyone. Rosa and Carlo joined him. Ashley was indifferent and maintained her distance.

Nora's folks were wealthy. She was one of the directors of their family-owned shipping sand oil business. Her parents were elderly and sickly. Her only brother had moved to the west coast with a young family. So the care of their parents fell on Nora.

Aberto met her at a book fair in New York. He was on a business trip and walked to the fair out of boredom. He loved art and literature and sometimes tried to write when he could. He got attracted to her the first time their eyes met. They spoke.

"Paulo Coelho is my favorite," Alberto commented as they stood in line to pay. Nora was buying *The Alchemist* by Coelho.

"I like his writing. I have actually read this title. Misplaced my copy . . . so couldn't resist buying a replacement," Nora smiled sweetly. Her face transformed with the smile. Her hazel-colored eyes, clear skin and jet-black, shoulder length curly hair looked exotic. She was pencil thin, wore a floral summer dress that halted just below her knees, and low-heeled leather pump shoes. She looked young, delicate. They got to talking and walked out of the fair together.

"I am getting hungry . . . any place you can suggest? Care for a bite?" Alberto was straightforward. Surprisingly, Nora wasn't put off.

They sat down at an open-air restaurant to eat roast beef sandwiches with salad and fries, a quarter of a mile from the book fair venue. It was a hot, summer day. Alberto had never been to this side of the city before. He has been to New York a few times but work kept him occupied. He didn't have much time for sightseeing.

"You don't live here? Where are you from?"

"I am of Italian descent, as you can see," Aberto began a bit comically and made Nora laugh. He liked the sound of her laughter. It was like spring water splashing against pebbles.

"I am an Italian, too. But born and bred in New York." Nora said. Then she looked straight at him. "I am a practicing Jew."

Their relationship grew fast. They spoke on the phone regularly and he began returning to the magical city every other weekend. It wasn't easy to get away from the restaurant and Isabella's ironclad demands to be committed to the business. However, the rest of the family strongly supported him and Rosa and Antonio took over his workload during his escapades to New York. Nora invited Alberto to meet her parents after they had been dating for five months.

The big iron gate of the huge mansion in Manhattan spoke for itself—Alberto realized how out of league Nora was for him. Her parents didn't hide their displeasure about Alberto's difference in background and his faith.

"Marry me," Alberto proposed to Nora the same night when he said goodbye to her after the torturous introduction-dinner with her parents.

"You don't even know me well enough . . . ," Nora was hesitant.

"I want to build my life with you, Nora. I am certain about that."

To the dismay of Isabella and Nora's parents, Nora and Alberto got married two months later. It was a civil wedding. Alberto shuttled regularly for the next three months between D.C. and New York, they found a nice, cozy apartment around D.C. and Nora and he began their lives together in their new surroundings.

Nora was liked by everyone in the Russo family. Even Isabella liked her though initially she had many reservations.

"She is paper-thin! So flat! Italian men like curves," she had commented to Rosa after her first meeting with Nora.

"Mamma, they are in love. Can't you see that? With all the beauty and curves and money, Ashley is giving hell to Antonio," Rosa had responded emphatically. By that time Ashley and Antonio had begun fighting again, openly, to the distress of the family. "And Nora is an Italian."

"Luckily, yes! She is Italian." Isabella was glad about that fact. To her, Ashley's problems with Antonio were escalating because she didn't understand the Italian ways. Ashley was brought up as a Protestant.

"I wish Nora were a Catholic like us, not a Jew. They don't celebrate Christmas . . . but she will have to learn."

"They don't do so many things like us, Mamma. But that doesn't make her lesser," Rosa added firmly. She had gone through her share of battles with her parents when she fell in love with Carlo.

The next two years went okay. Nora fit in well in her new life. She remained very close to her parents and from time to time travelled back to see them. She was always their daughter and ready to be with them whenever they needed her. Then she fell sick.

The shadows began to grow deeper and deeper . . .

The sibling contention between the brothers sometimes burps up from beneath layers of adequately spread balms thickened over the rough years. Many things have been forgiven and forgotten, as they were all young those days. Rosa and Carlo are in a happy conjugal union. She got lucky compared to her two brothers. Their children are growing up to be normal, healthy kids—both in school and at home.

# CHAPTER SEVENTEEN

# *Doubts*

Antonio gives his apartment key to Opshora. She isn't prepared for this.

"Why? I don't need this . . . I would like you to open the door when I knock," she remarks. It's too much, too soon. Things are moving very fast.

"*Tesoro,* nothing will make me happier if you spend Tuesdays at my place, if you can . . . as much as possible. That's my only day off from the restaurant. I want to keep it for us. I am not forcing you to move in . . . but I would love you to be with me," he literally pleads. "I'm tired of my empty, busy life."

She finally gives in. Keeps Antonio's apartment key in her kiondo. Sometimes she stays through Monday and Tuesday nights. She knows Ruby is dying to find out what is happening. Ruby notices Opshora's absences on some weeknights. Curiosity almost kills her but she refrains from prying.

"She will tell us when she is ready," MD Mirza advises.

After her initial discussion with Leila, Opshora hasn't said anything further to her aunt about Antonio. So, her family is in the dark though they guess something is happening in Opshora's life. They wait for her to break the news.

Antonio is happy with their present arrangement. Their time together is packed with much laughter and stories, and soul-searching moments—many things to share! He wasn't aware he could talk so much about himself, his past.

He has become more patient, more receptive to others. His inner joy is transforming him into a more composed person. A part of Opshora wants to be with him but deep down she is hounded by unknown fears. Though she knows it's baseless— she doesn't feel at peace.

"What am I doing, Chris?" Opshora sounds lost. She is unsure about her relationship with Antonio. They haven't discussed much in-depth—nothing about any kind of commitment or a future together.

"Partner, why do you need a logical explanation to everything? Life happens . . . just go with the flow . . . enjoy this moment in time," Chris is more philosophical about relationships.

"What if . . . he . . . Antonio suddenly decides to walk away?" She doesn't know why she is so bothered at this thought. She knew from the very start that this was a casual involvement. She never expected more. Neither does Antonio, she guesses.

"Well if that happens, you go your way. That's how it works, precious. Zayn walked away but you didn't fall apart," Chris comments, matter of fact. "You picked up your life from there and did what you wanted to." Then he turns around, takes a step towards Opshora and inspects her face closely. He gives out a low whistle. She pushes him away.

"Mamma Mia . . . you are in love with this guy! Serious!" he says soberly. Opshora doesn't respond. She keeps her eyes averted, examining her bracelet. The Paula shells in it catch the light and shine in intensity.

"Listen, my darling. It's always worth taking a risk. He may prove to be a mature, genuine person and value your feelings for him or be a total idiot, a jerk, and fail to see the real you. It can happen. This world is full of imbeciles." Chris' wisdom doesn't take the lurking doubts away. They intensify.

". . . But that shouldn't make you afraid of taking chances, honey-bomb," he says again, gently.

Next day, Opshora meets with Isabella to interview her on the book and to taste her lasagna. Their scheduled meeting was postponed a few times due to Isabella's hectic work pressure. She is diplomatic—gives Opshora many good tips and anecdotes. She is also open with her recipes and volunteers to teach Opshora. Isabella is deliberately friendly. Opshora remembers Alberto's warning—"If she is too pleasant be careful. She has an ulterior motive. I know my mother too well."

"Antonio's life has been topsy-turvy . . . *sottosopra* . . . it has been tough with Ashley . . . now Maria," Isabella comments in a casual tone at one point. Opshora understands more is going to come.

"Maria needs the love of both parents. Their separation is tearing her apart. Poor girl. Antonio has to behave more maturely . . . like a father. Nothing good will come out of what he is doing . . . he is too old for casual involvements," her voice trails off. She avoids facing Opshora—gazes outside.

"Isabella, why are you telling me this?"

Isabella doesn't answer her question. "Antonio has never been steady in romantic attachments. He is my son but I know he is not up to taking responsibilities. Too emotional." Isabella provides additional information with a smile in her eyes, steel in her voice. "Alberto—that one is different. Doggedly committed . . . but he is unlucky in matters of the heart as well."

"There isn't anything to worry about . . . I wouldn't if I were you," Opshora smiles and manages to say without betraying her inner emotions. She understands Isabella and is not upset. Only, greater sadness grips her heart.

She doesn't go to Antonio's place though it's a Tuesday. Her nerves are rattled. She switches off her cell phone and heads towards Georgetown to Leila's to eat ice cream with her—a bowl of vanilla with blueberries sprinkled on top or maybe the one with lots and lots of crushed pistachio. The comfort food that has helped her through tough times . . .

Very late that night she switches her phone back on. There are no texts from Antonio or missed calls or any voice mail.

Next morning she texts him: "Got busy. Sorry couldn't come by." She has deliberately decided to shrug off her blues and act mature. He texts back immediately: "Understand fully. Drop in whenever you can. Missing you." The cloud from her mind immediately lifts. She feels calmer. *Grow up, Opshora. You are just another person in Antonio's life at this juncture. Don't eat your heart out over him . . . ,* she keeps repeating.

Opshora gets an offer to join Howard University as an adjunct faculty—a temporary position. Her days start getting busier. Though fully engaged with the restaurant during six days of the week, Antonio keeps his off days totally dedicated to Opshora. With her dilemma mounting as the weeks progress, she shows up whenever she can at his place. The routine gets established fairly well without any complication. Antonio accepts her busy schedule and is happy with whatever of her time he gets. Except for Leila no one in Opshora's family knows about Antonio's existence. Opshora keeps her life totally private. She is aware that Isabella is watching her and disapproves her relationship with Antonio. Opshora tries to be as discreet as possible and takes care so that their paths don't cross.

"I am an adult and so are you. No one should push their noses into our business, *tesoro* . . . I would like to keep it like that. So stop worrying. Don't mind mamma," Antonio firmly brushes away any uncomfortable thoughts. Though she hadn't given him any details of her lunch meeting with

Isabella, Antonio assumes something has happened between the two women on that day. He doesn't pry.

The work on the book continues, though slowly at first, it picks up momentum eventually. The constant whistles and jokes made by kitchen staff at his expense hinting at his nocturnal triumphs, Antonio now ignores with a broad smile. He knows everything comes at a cost. Opshora maintains a strict professional stance when she speaks with some of the kitchen staff for the book. She quite likes Marcello—the second senior chef and Antonio's right hand.

That's when Maria tries to make an even stronger entry back into her father's life. Opshora understands where she is coming from, recognizes the insecurities that the teenager is battling with. Opshora empathizes with Maria, knows she is hurting. With a vengeance, Maria attempts to disrupt Antonio's regular routine, tries to claim her father's attention. She demands his presence in a more prominent way. Her possessiveness about Antonio becomes like an obsession but he tries to balance it. Time with Opshora is important to him but at the same time he wants to be a responsible, caring parent to Maria. Ashley keeps floating into Maria's life between her casual boyfriends, clubbing and late nights unable to be a constant anchor to her daughter. Opshora recoils at Maria's stark hostility. She is saddened at the unnecessary tension created by the father-daughter relationship, which ultimately begins to impact everyone in their orbit.

"Go, go to her. She is just a child, Antonio," Opshora has compassion for Maria and recognizes Antonio's predicament.

"*Tesoro* . . . I am grateful to you. You are a mature person, generous. But look at Ashley . . . what's she doing? She's the adult in Maria's life. Oh, Maria . . . Maria . . . oh *Dio!* . . . My life is in a mess!" Maria's imposed emotional demand is too much for Antonio. "I don't want to lose you," he declares suddenly turning to her. He takes her in his arms, holds her tightly.

"I am not going anywhere," Opshora rests her head against his chest. She tries to calm him down.

"I lead a very busy life. I can't give you much time. You are such an accomplished woman, Opshora. Our worlds are so different. And I keep thinking you are so out of my league . . . I don't even fully understand the smart stuff you say. I get scared sometimes."

Opshora doesn't know what to say. Everything Antonio says rings so true. Their lives are poles apart. An ache eats her.

"I get scared, too . . . sometimes," she whispers truthfully. She doesn't tell him about her fears—her tears at the thought of letting him go.

On Tuesday nights whenever Antonio returns to Opshora in the safety of his apartment away from prying eyes ready to enjoy his time with her, the phone starts to ring, usually. Maria has her own way of finding out about Opshora's presence at Antonio's place. The interruptions have become almost a regular affair. It's either Ashley having a problem in managing Maria's rage or rebellion or it's a call from the daughter asking her father to pick her up from a friend's house or a disco club. Sometimes she calls to report about a fight with Ashley expecting Antonio to rescue her from her mother's house. She chooses the most inappropriate times to catch Antonio's attention.

"It's not easy to be a father. You have more responsibilities to your daughter than to others." Opshora overhears Isabella talking to her son one afternoon. She mostly speaks in English with her heavy accent when discussing important matters. She uses her commanding tone to add gravity to the issues she addresses.

"You didn't answer the phone, Antonio. At three in the morning she walked for an hour to take a cab home!" Isabella's voice rises in indignation. Then she adds some words in Italian that Opshora doesn't understand.

"Mamma, I fell asleep. Was tired, my phone was out of

charge. Why is Maria out so late? You can't put all the blame on me," Antonio protests.

"It's a dangerous world out there for a young girl to be alone at night, Antonio!"

"That's her doing. She chooses to be difficult. I can't do this anymore," Antonio isn't repentant.

"Talk to her. Find out what's happening. Listen to Maria, *mio figlio*. You walk away now, you will lose her forever." Isabella doesn't give up. The conversation continues.

Silently Opshora moves away. She feels guilty for lingering on. She feels a storm is brewing, somewhere on the horizon—an unexpected turn of events beyond her grasp. She is claustrophobic; it's hard to breathe. The walls seem to close in.

She hits the street and walks faster and faster. She wants to be away from Pasta Paradiso, from Antonio, from Isabella . . .

Both Opshora and Antonio are roped into the ensuing stress. Opshora's inner voice tells her to walk away—return to her previous sane existence of predicted pluses and minuses that life offers before it's too late. The novelty of involvement with Antonio is fraught with misery and doubts and additional complications.

"Let's get away . . . I need a break. I can't do this anymore, *tesoro*." Antonio proposes. "My life isn't easy. I am dumping unnecessary burden on you."

"What about your kitchen?"

"Marcelo can take over . . . and mama and Rosa are there. One week isn't asking too much." Antonio has thought through his escapade.

Opshora agrees. Quality time exclusively with Antonio away from others may help her to understand what's happening to their relationship, if it has any prospect. At this point in her life Opshora is totally unprepared to be caught up in this web of uncertainty, stress and strange family dynamics. The more she is in Antonio's life, the more she is confused. Antonio's baggage is too weighty. He hasn't ever vocalized any thoughts of commitment, or hinted about the future—may be this is all a pastime for him.

Opshora feels she is in a mess, like a "watermelon-sugary-syrup dipped in tamarind" kind of muddle. But she is also aware of a fondness growing inside her steadily for Antonio, for months. There is a strange kind of ache blended in euphoria that is almost consuming her. She feels vulnerable, emotionally drained. The recent months with him have brought immense joy but with an equal share of burden as well. A week away from their current cluttered, busy lives sounds alluring and full of promise.

# CHAPTER EIGHTEEN

# A Pinch of Tajin, a Shot of Tequila, Lime Juice for a Good Margarita and for the Soul

As planned, Antonio picks up Opshora from Georgetown, early morning before the sunrays hit the half-asleep city. She has stayed the night at Leila's house. She doesn't invite him in or introduce him to her aunt. She can't do so before she breaks the news to Ruby. Her mother may decide that Antonio will have to be presented properly to the entire clan, which includes Robin and Maya when they are in town. Opshora hasn't even discussed this prospect with Antonio. She has no clue regarding how he feels about meeting her side of the family. She has met his because of the book writing. Anyway, Opshora decides to cross the bridge when the time is right. But she is certain that Ruby would never forgive her if she introduces Antonio casually to Leila before her own family. *I am fifty-one years old and I still have to deal with this shit? I am grandmother material.* Her brain keeps hammering with profound irritation dreading a possible encounter with her folks and Antonio.

They drive all the way towards the Indian Lake. He has been craving to be alone with her far away from his crowded existence—in some place undisturbed by the discomfitures of the mundane. But the luxury of taking a real break from the kitchen isn't always easy. He hasn't taken any time off in recent years. Public holidays mean more rush in the restaurant so he has to be in the kitchen while the entire country vacations.

Antonio has made all preparations for this trip well ahead of time. For weeks he intensified his training of Marcello, his assistant chef, and a team to support him. He has introduced Marcello gradually to all his tricks and weaponized him adequately with the wizardry of his culinary secrets to take over the kitchen in his temporary absence. In addition, Isabella herself is an excellent cook and oversees the quality control whenever Antonio needs an extra pair of eyes and a culinary brain to ensure all is on track. So, he has no qualms to fearlessly leave the kitchen to her, and Marcello as her knight ready for the gastronomic battles of the days ahead.

Anyhow, Isabella isn't too happy about his vacation. When she finds out that Antonio is going away with Opshora, she is rather surprised. However, she doesn't say anything to him. She expresses her displeasure only to Rosa.

"What is he doing? He is so blind." She uses unnecessary force in stirring the white sauce on the stove. Rosa keeps mum. She knows her mother too well to arouse her agitation further by commenting.

"Mama isn't very happy. So play it diplomatically, big bro!" She warns her brother.

Opshora and Antonio cross the city's borders in hours. In a rented car they drive toward upstate New York. The plan is to stay overnight at a motel to break the journey, get some rest and then at daybreak continue to the cottage he has reserved close to the lake. For the return journey they are booked on an American Airlines flight.

"So glad we came . . . for years I imagined a vacation in a cottage in the lap of Indian Lake. Lost to the world for a few days, mio tesoro. Now finally it's happening." Antonio looks pleased as he navigates on the highway guided by the GPS. His cheerful whistling is infectious. Opshora's mood lifts up.

"How come you never did it?" she is curious.

"Busy, busy . . . and then Ashley wasn't very enthusiastic about rustic cottages. She's more for sandy beaches, five-star hotels in exotic places where she can show off her bikini clad sexy self—in love with herself!" He laughs. "I am flattered you agreed to come with me."

"Hey, remember? I am an anthropologist by profession. I love to be outdoors. Meet people—dig cultures." Opshora laughs with him. "I enjoy traveling around this country. So vast—so much to see, so much history to learn from. Each state seems like a separate nation."

As they travel hundreds and hundreds of miles together, she discovers a very different Antonio. He is relaxed. Smiles more often than scowls. Gone is his edginess along with the tense vibes. He hasn't even smoked a single cigarette since they hit the road.

"Do you want to take the steering wheel?" he asks. Opshora usually avoids driving if she can. In D.C. taking the public transport—metro, bus or Uber makes more sense. For long distances she prefers air travel.

"I could . . . but I can't guarantee where we will end up."

"Even with the GPS?" he jests.

"Yep . . . my brain is too creative and will defeat the navigational guidance. It follows its own sense of geography . . . it's sure to take an unchartered exit or a destination resulting in a totally shocking outcome."

Antonio tries his best to woo her with the small solaces available on the spot as they speed through small towns. At lunchtime they stop at a Panera joint to eat French baguette with broccoli cheddar soup. They step into a local diner for dinner before pulling up at the motel for the night. Easy, everyday common food—tuna sandwiches, fries, cold beer or red wine. Luckily, some diners in New York serve alcohol.

Antonio loosens up and stretches his limbs. It has been a long drive. By tomorrow mid-day they will reach the cottage. Later, she falls asleep against his body in the somewhat swanky bedroom on the top floor of the homely motel that offers a faint musky smell along with its comforts.

Opshora immediately falls in love with the cottage built around the edge of Indian Lake in a breath-taking spot covered by trees and grassy mounds, lulled by the pleasant breeze that carries the scent of the cool, placid waters. The cottages are scattered in a big fenceless compound hidden by tall pines and wild thickets. Their cottage is towards the end of the grounds, closer to the waters. Opshora likes the way the wooden deck juts out. The sudden wind creates soft waves on the water—the ripples glimmer in the sun—visible through thick bushes that grow near their cottage.

The cottage is comfortable, it is rustic. Its roof and floors are made of strong planks of uneven wood. It is late summer but the slow wind rising from the lake is slightly chilly at night. The moonlight compensates as they stand on the deck inhaling the fragrance of wildflowers, the sound of deep silence.

"Tonight I ordered the moon for you," Antonio whispers and makes Opshora smile.

"I give you the fireflies," Opshora whispers back. They watch, fascinated, the tiny flecks of light from lost fireflies cradled against the vast depth of the night.

She feels drunk at his nearness, the magical landscape drenched in moonlight. They make love under the stars on the deck. The warmth of their bodies swats out the stains of chilliness in the air.

For over a decade Opshora hasn't had a real lover. A year after her return from Fiji she began seeing Tomo—he remained a friend since her high school days. By that time she had completed her masters with distinction. There was too much time on her hands. She didn't have a plan for the future.

She didn't apply for any jobs, either. Tomo was working in D.C. at the time. Initially it felt like spending time with an old friend. They met frequently—whenever she was sad or happy or bored, he was there for her. She had taken the metro countless times to meet with him after work. They hung around the parks and bars late on those amazing empty nights. Then they started dating in the real sense—romance crept into their unbridled friendship. She dated Tomo for about a year. She was broken after her separation with Zayn. Tomo was the only one she could relate to—who understood her pain. He held the key to her present.

Tomo and Opshora were in touch even after leaving high school. Like Opshora, Tomo knew how hard it was for immigrant kids, especially kids of color to fit in. Years later she learned about his grandparents who with their children ended up in an internment camp in Arizona in 1942. Tomo grew up listening to those stories told many times over.

While they were dating, Tomo got a better job in New York. Opshora moved in with him for six months ignoring Ruby's strong disapproval. Opshora didn't care about what her community thought. She was sure people were gossiping behind her back. She knew it tormented Ruby no end. But Tomo's studio apartment in the heart of Manhattan meant a massive amount of freedom at the time. And she was afraid of waking up alone in the dark, in the middle of the night. Tomo's presence next to her was comforting.

It was possibly too hasty after the Fiji saga. She was still somewhat in shock. She couldn't love Tomo the way he loved her. She did care for him. She didn't try to find a job in New York. Trotting through busy Manhattan was the only thing that interested her. Soon the idle hours began eating her comatose neurons. She felt the city was too big, too noisy, too fast. She couldn't keep up—she was getting lost. She wanted to believe Tomo was good for her, though not the best. Initially, she had thought if she could learn to love Tomo it would be an antidote to take away the pains of her life lived with Zayn . . . the vacant nights, the hollow waking hours. She was ashamed to admit to even herself that she picked Tomo on the rebound and wasn't ready to commit to him whole-heartedly. There was a vacuum she carried in her heart that he couldn't alter. She couldn't continue living in New York for much longer and returned home. Tomo was heartbroken. He was committed to their relationship but understood her enough to let her go.

She and Tomo remained friends. He still carries a torch for her in an insane, strange way. She had hurt him badly but he didn't complain. He never left New York. He got promotions over the years and now heads the company where he joined as a junior executive all those years ago. He calls her often—for a friendly chat. Whenever he is in town he makes sure to drop in and check on Opshora. They have dinner without any expectations. He never married.

After Tomo, Opshora has been alone mostly except for a couple of very casual flings. Those died in the infancy days of the game. She found dating tiresome. Ruby and her friends never gave up and still connive to find a suitable husband for her, but she has learned to avoid such traps without offending anyone especially the unsuspecting strangers thrown in her path.

Zayn's memories keeps rushing back into her mind as she lies next to Antonio. The moon and the whisper of the waters in the breeze stir old remembrances. The two men are worlds apart. She struggles to drown thoughts of Zayn. She couldn't stop loving him even when it hurt. With Antonio it's a very different experience. She is content one moment and restless the next. She didn't think it would be possible to love any-one after Zayn. Her passions went bankrupt she believed; for years she thought happiness wasn't meant for her. But Antonio seems to be a reality now. In this idyllic setting, as she can trace Antonio's heartbeats next to hers, life seems full of possibilities. She tries to push away all doubts. They seem absurd, somewhat.

"I love you," Antonio turns towards her and declares. He sounds dead serious. Opshora is taken aback at the urgency in his voice. She doesn't say anything. She isn't sure if he expects her to reciprocate. She is still hesitant to bare her heart. Too afraid to be hurt. "Bellisima . . . you will learn to love me." With his hands he cups her face towards him, looks into her eyes in the sparkle of the pale moonlight. "You love me . . . I know you do," he murmurs without waiting for a response from her.

At the touch of his lips caressing her neck Opshora feels safe. She wants to live again; she wants to be happy like others, fulfilled in Antonio's love. With this realization, her mind begins to unwind. She snuggles closer and falls into a deep, deep sleep on the deck, against Antonio. When she wakes up in the morning, she finds herself in bed. He had carried her inside, careful not to wake her up. She smells the aroma of coffee, hears the sounds of his whistling and movements in the tiny kitchen. The wooden floorboards creak in harmony under his feet.

"Good morning, bellisima!" he greets her with a mug of coffee. While cooking he must have kept an eye on her.

"I am making breakfast—fried eggs, mushrooms stirred in cheese . . . French baguette and butter."

"Queen Elizabeth breakfast?"

"Of course. Can't treat you to a lesser one. There is a nice grocery store in the corner, up the hill," he mentions.

"You went there by yourself!

"Yes my sleeping beauty, while you were lost in dreams . . . I wanted to create this gastronomic miracle for you."

Antonio expresses his love by cooking. Other men send flowers or fancy gifts to the women they desire but Antonio, since she really began to know him has been cooking and baking for her. Every now and then he showers her with pastries or brownies or chocolate mousses or cakes and fruit tarts that he crafts dipped in his deep care for her.

"Hmmm . . . thanks. I will shower instantly and appear in my best self, properly attired for the grand occasion," she leaps out of bed, naked as the quilt falls away. He had covered her under it, didn't fuss to clothe her while asleep.

"I like this better though," he winks. She quickly gets inside the bathroom and closes the door. The next few minutes she busies herself to face the amazing lazy dawn—allows the warm water from the shower to wash away the night.

They explore the grounds and around the shore of the lake during daylight, rest under the sunny sky spread out on the velvet-smooth grass. He takes her to the grocery store up the hill to pick up a few essentials. It is run by an elderly couple. Opshora gets polite stares from the other few middle-aged customers as she moves around the narrow aisles and low shelves that hold limited merchandise. This place is buried in the heart of rural America and she stands out like she did in school. The same is true for the many professional meetings she has attended over the years. She belongs to a tiny fraction of a presence most of the time . . . In this tiny township far away from cosmopolitan life, Opshora draws attention, again. She is still a rarity in her brown skin.

"Bellissima cioccolato you are so special. They are not used to seeing someone like you. You have taken their breath away . . . along with mine," Antonio teases.

"You mean I am spectacular because I'm not white?" She is amused about it—like always—after her awkward teen years.

"Look at the old man. His eyes will pop out . . . he must be thinking why me, not him. We both are white but I get the cioccolato," Antonio whispers comically.

"Your thoughts are corrupt, signor," Opshora struggles hard to stifle a laugh.

"Nope. You are like a movie star here," he keeps going.

"You have a beautiful smile, dear," the old lady at the

counter comments as Opshora pays with cash. Antonio winks again as she looks up. She bites her lower lip to stop laughing out loud. That would have been a disaster. The old lady was genuine in her compliment.

Back at the cottage they talk about their lives, trying to fill up the numerous blanks with stories before their lives crossed paths. Their culture, childhood memories, camping, college days, dating experiences, friendships and heartbreaks are all poured out in their heart-to-heart conversations.

"How come you never had a real boyfriend in school? Be honest. This is our discovery process. Full disclosures," he reminds her.

"What is a real boyfriend?"

"You know what I mean?" He winks. "Stealer of your virginity?"

"I was a virgin for a very long time . . . it never entered my head to throw it away—just like an old dress." She tells him about Ruby's paranoia to conform to their culture and faith, her reactions about Opshora's friends from the opposite gender in school. "I was somewhat conditioned by my mother's inhibitions. I also rebelled so much because of that."

"She sounds tough," Antonio comments.

"Wait till you have the encounter of the third kind with her," Opshora jokes.

"Opshora, I would like to meet her. I am serious." He surprises Opshora, again. He has declared his love and now this. She had thought Antonio wanted to keep their relationship casual.

"We can think of something to make that happen," Opshora responds cautiously. She knows Ruby would need to be handled with care. Endorsement from her would be hard to come by.

Ruby never approved of her choices in boys when Opshora first became aware of the opposite gender. Her mother always found some fault with them and justifications for her critical opinions. At fourteen, Opshora had an African American boyfriend, Brian. His family had moved to the neighborhood recently and they became friends from the first day he joined Opshora's school. The relationship was entirely platonic. They never even kissed. There were several instances of hand holding in the semi-darkness of the movie theatre, warm hugs in open daylight but that was all they ventured into. They shared a common interest in books, sports, music and people. Unlike her other class friends she wasn't yet into experimenting with sex. Virginity was precious, sacred to her as taught by Ruby as the most important pillar of Bengalee family values. Even then Ruby was extremely critical, suspicious of Opshora.

"*Ama*, I like him. I am not planning to marry him." She tried to defend Brian but Ruby didn't get off her back.

"You know how our people will talk if they see you with a black boy ... tongues will wag," was her stand. Ruby brought up the cultural differences constantly. The number of South Asian families was growing in their neighborhood. Ruby was an active member of the community.

"He is a decent person. His folks are genuine, honest people. Why do you stereotype him?" Opshora had retorted angrily, her face burnt in embarrassment. She thought Ruby's views were mean, prejudiced like so many people she came across in school, in the community—both people of color and "off color."

"What's your problem, *Ama*?"

"I am sure Brian is a nice boy and has a great family. But his background is very different from ours," Ruby retorted. "We follow the rules of our culture." That was her defense.

Racism existed in some form or the other in every culture—that was Opshora's take, learned early in life. Brian's ethnicity was the stumbling block, definitely. Her father had to intervene eventually but by that time some damage was done. Ruby's reservations exhausted Opshora. She decided to walk away from the friendship, hurt, ashamed to be thus persuaded because of Ruby's myopic views. Brian's family moved to Pittsburg the year after and he faded from her life completely.

In her tenth grade she actually got to know Tomo Yamaguchi. It just happened. They were in the same class since elementary school but weren't close, though belonged to the same group with a few more kids of color. A school outing brought them together. Brian had left the school by then. She was late for an educational expedition to the Smithsonian American Art Museum and managed to hop into the bus at the last minute. The only empty seat was beside Tomo. They talked during the entire bus ride. She found him to be interesting, shy but smart. From that day they became friends. This happened a few months before she was attacked by three white boys.

Tomo was extra sharp in Math and helped her with breaking the toughest equations. After she invited him home to study together, Ruby commented that Japanese boys are always their mom's puppets.

"You know, their faith is different from us. Not right either for a Bengalee girl," Ruby further added, matter of fact. That was the only time Tomo ever came home for a visit.

"He is not my boyfriend. Just a friend who happens to be a male, *Ama*," was Opshora's justification. And it was true at the time.

She kept him away from her mother's world. They stayed friends. Ruby couldn't take that away from her. Her affair with Tomo shocked Ruby. She was sad beyond cure.

Opshora eventually understood Ruby's stand. All her efforts were to protect her daughter from the harshness of societal bigotries. So at one point Opshora partially forgave her mother, sort of.

⚜

Antonio squints his eyes when Opshora talks about Tomo.

"Tomo Yamaguchi, huh? Friend from school? Do you still keep in touch with him? So he works in New York? Convenient distance."

"Yes. We catch up on emails, texts, phone calls or usually over a meal whenever he is in town," she explains.

"So what's the catch?" Antonio is jerked into attention.

"I dated him for some time—after I came back from Fiji. I thought I was in love with him—could make it work. It wasn't enough. We broke up eventually."

"Hmm . . . I see." Antonio remains quiet for some minutes. "He is Japanese," Antonio tries to brush him off.

"So? What's your point?"

"He is too short. If you wear high heels he will fall under your arm pits," he remarks.

"Stop your assumptions. You haven't even met him. He isn't short. You don't know about the depth of his mind," she defends Tomo.

"What depth? Japan is all ocean and sushi. Not good for health—too much seafood. They smell of fish." Antonio shrugs.

"You smell of cheese," she teases. "Tomo was born in the U.S. His mom is white. Oh! You are jealous." She finds it rather flattering. He does care enough for her and is envious of an invisible adversary.

The days run out faster than they anticipated. On the last night they eat dinner on the deck. The sky looks stormy under the burden of trillions of twinkling stars. The wind rises high. The treetops eclipse the moon, helplessly swaying in ceaseless intensity. In the distance, the shallow waves in the lake sparkle in the gloomy moonlight. Opshora's heart is full with a different kind of ache—borne out of her feelings for Antonio . . . the moments crafted in love. No matter what, she has fallen in love with this strangely funny man. But she decides to keep it closeted. Tears well up in her eyes.

"Why? *Bellissima . . .*" He kisses away her tears, not needing any answers. He knows.

Opshora has been drifting and drifting for years—the chapter of Zayn in her life never reached a full closure. She carefully kept that part locked away from everyone. Even though she told Antonio many aspects of her relationship with Zayn, there are things she isn't able to talk about yet. It's her life, her pains, her memories, to which no one has entry.

Her heart is full of love for Antonio, and countless hesitations.

# CHAPTER NINETEEN

# Encounters—
# Strange and Surprising

"Antonio said he loves me, Chris," Opshora tells Chris the day after she returns from her vacation.

"You didn't know?" Chris looks straight at her. "You can't read the signs, partner," his voice is calm, extremely serious.

"How long have you known?" Opshora is surprised.

"On your behalf I have been receiving all those pastries and cakes and tarts from him for months." There is laughter in his voice. His old self is back. "When a man starts feeding a woman like the way Antonio does, there is only one conclusion."

"Is it that obvious?" She has been so blind. Isabella and Marco and the others must have witnessed enough evidence of Antonio's growing fondness for her. *Shit, how could I miss this?*—Opshora is shocked at her cluelessness.

"Any plans? What are you going to do now?"

"No plans. Mind you own business, nosy." Opshora shakes him off and concentrates on her laptop. She needs to complete the final draft of the cookbook to share with Antonio and the family. She is way behind.

Antonio keeps expressing his desire to meet Opshora's

folks. In her mind she debates with the idea—chalks out the pros and cons. She can't shake off his declaration of love for her at the cottage. He hasn't mentioned it at all since they came back. But she knows the truth now and finally decides to give him more access into her personal life, agrees to introduce him to her parents properly. She is sure it was a missed opportunity to keep Zayn away from her family. If they knew him, things might have happened differently.

Surprisingly, Ruby shows interest in meeting Antonio after Opshora shares a bit about him, tells her who he is. Though the mother and daughter have treaded many hurdles in life and reached absolutely contradictory milestones, Ruby is now more accommodating, solemnly pacified in her mature age. After having navigated through tough times and good times, Opshora has made some sort of peace with her mother. Ruby has accepted that. However, she calls Robin late that night to air her doubts, voice her feelings. She is troubled.

"He is a cook. On top of that an Italian! She is a PhD and he is a college drop out! How's that? How is this going to work?" her deep sigh at the end of the sentence explains volumes. Robin listens, is thoughtful. He understands his mother's reservations but doesn't embrace them whole-heartedly. He is on speakerphone so that Maya is able to participate in the discussion.

"*Ama,* Antonio is a famous chef not a meager cook. He gets excellent reviews. He is in a solid restaurant business," he tries to clarify as he glances at Maya's phone. She has quickly Google-searched Antonio. "Cross cultural unions are happening all the time, *Ama,*" he adds. Ruby doesn't respond.

"Opshora's not getting any younger. She has been battling alone for too long. We could feel her loneliness so much this time. Let her go ahead with this one, *Ama,*" Maya almost pleads. "Even if it doesn't continue forever. Nothing lasts a lifetime. Only by taking risks one can find out . . . "

Maya is a reputable pediatric doctor and smart. Ruby pays

much more attention to her intellect than her own daughter's judgment though Opshora holds a doctorate from Columbia. To her, Opshora's brain is lightweight when it comes to romantic relationships. Opshora makes outrageous associations. Ruby admires Maya for her sensibility—making a successful life with Robin, excelling in her own profession while bringing up two wonderful children. She also brought inheritance money with her into their marriage. She is a model of prosperity and wisdom. Ruby listens though her inhibitions do not die down entirely.

"He is seven years younger than her. She just turned 51," Ruby's uncertainty continues.

"Opshora is not your little girl anymore, *Ama*. You can't tell her what to do," Robin speaks in his professional voice trying to be firm now. When everything fails, he has to take charge. "It's America. Here no one bothers so much about such stuff. Best to support her."

Next day, Ruby and MD Mirza officially invite Antonio to their home. They request Opshora to convey the invitation to Antonio. Opshora promises to ask him to confirm a date and time suitable to him.

⚜

Opshora bumps into Ashley, as she is about to enter the restaurant to show the final draft of the cookbook to Alberto. She also needs to discuss some changes with him. Antonio, the day before, agreed to any modifications that she feels are necessary. He has given her a blanket endorsement for improving the quality, style and tempo as the author. The book is coming along nicely with most expectations reflected in the stories. But she feels another pair of eyes and a creative brain might help her. Alberto is full of innovative ideas.

"Hello! So you are back from your vacation with Antonio." Ashley stretches out her hand. Opshora takes it and the handshake is a quick, sudden touch.

"Yes, almost two weeks ago."

Ashley is still a striking woman, tall, pear shaped hips, thick golden hair outlining the face, steely dark blue eyes. She is only a year younger than Antonio. "Glad we meet, finally," she smiles. Opshora smiles back.

"I kept missing you . . . heard so much about you. Was dying to see what Antonio came up with this time," Ashley speaks again.

"A professore?" Opshora jokes mimicking Antonio, and laughs. Ashley doesn't. "A mature brown woman of no consequence, I am afraid," Opshora adds further with an extra frank smile. Her voice is matter of fact, holds no malice. Ashley doesn't return the smile.

"Care for a cup of coffee?" Ashley's arched eyebrows are raised in inquiry. Opshora understands there is more to it. But she still accepts. She doesn't have any womanly curiosity or any envy regarding Ashley. Antonio had shared enough about his life with her.

They walk over to the nearby Starbucks across the road. Ashley chooses a corner table, away from the crowd. The aroma of strong coffee blended with stifled murmurs floats inside the café. They order an Americano tall for Opshora, espresso for Ashley.

"Antonio's priorities are all mixed up. He refuses to take his share of the responsibility," Ashley says as they sit down with their coffee, on opposite sides of the table. Her voice is low, icy. Opshora doesn't know what is expected of her. She listens in silence. Ashely looks at her and smiles. It doesn't reach her eyes—is mechanical and cold.

"It's a difficult time for Maria. She needs steady parental support, especially from her father who she looks up to so much," Ashley chooses her words carefully. "Antonio is good at diluting his part. He loves to play the victim . . . blame someone else for his problems." Her words hold veiled warnings.

"Why are you telling me all this, Ashley?" Opshora maintains her composure. "Why don't you speak with Antonio? What are you asking of me?"

"Oh, nothing, nothing. No one can deter him. He chooses what benefits him most, our Antonio. Doesn't mind who gets trampled." Ashley looks away. "He is ruthless . . . selfish," she continues with finality. Opshora is at a loss. An awkward silence creeps in.

"Ashley, not sure what to say . . . I don't want to be rude but I have seen a very caring side of Antonio. I believe Maria is always the first in his mind."

"Really? I am surprised. He is a good actor." Ashley throws her frosty smile again. Then she moves closer. Her face is only inches away from Opshora's. "How long do you think he will be like this? He changes his women the way he throws away old recipes . . . he dumped me as if I don't matter."

"I don't think there is anything further for us to discuss. Thanks for the lovely chat, though." Opshora has stomached enough. She puts down the half-finished cup. Her mind is filled with distaste. She walks out of the café without giving Ashley any chance to spread poison further. Ashley follows her.

"I am sorry . . . I didn't want to . . . I thought . . . you know . . . Antonio is so heartless . . . " Ashley fumbles with words. "I didn't want to offend you. I mean it, really." Her tone doesn't reflect what she is saying.

"I am sorry too, Ashley . . . Do me a favor? Please don't drag me into your family theatrics. Goodbye." Opshora starts walking away. Right now she wants a gulf of distance from this woman's hostility.

At that point Carlo spots them from the restaurant window across the street. He gives a low whistle and gestures to Rosa.

"What the hell is going on? What are they up to?" He never liked Ashley who always tries to see through him, has difficulty in respecting him as a member of the family.

Ashley considers Carlo as an outsider and is intensely hostile towards him. She believes Antonio's mind got corrupted against her because of Carlo's influence. Once he caught her red-handed in one of her infamous episodes of infidelity and promptly reported back to Antonio. Ashley was furious when she found out and since then she stopped speaking with Carlo—gives him venom looks whenever they come across each other, mainly at the restaurant where most family meetings are held.

"Opshora doesn't look very happy . . . what did the ex-wife tell her?" Rosa tries to comprehend. "Let's not breathe a word to Antonio." By that time Opshora is halfway down the road, out of eyesight and vanishes amidst the street crowd. She doesn't go back to the restaurant as planned.

"Are you okay?" Chris inquires politely, concerned at Opshora's disheveled appearance. After her encounter with Ashley she has walked all the way to Beads and Bracelets. She is distressed at the way the odds are solidifying around her life. She hated her encounter with Ashley.

"Do I look okay?" Opshora starts crying. She hasn't cried like this in years.

Chris is at her side in seconds and holds her close. He lets her cry against his shoulder. In a few minutes Opshora shakes up her head, smiles at him through her tears.

"Better now? A good cry is always the best elixir to wash away built-up problems," he says. She nods in agreement.

"Good. That was rather quick, though. I am getting coffee. Let's chat a bit more," He says and is back in minutes with two mugs full. They sit down side-by-side and sip the coffee.

"By the way Ooopps . . . your hair smells super good . . . what shampoo do you use?" Chris tries to break the silence. Opshora pushes him away as they both laugh.

Chris doesn't pry. He doesn't want to know what happened. Opshora is grateful to him for that. She has a meeting at Howard University but needed an emotional break after her incident with Ashley who forced her to look into the uncertainties with Antonio, all over again. At the cottage he did tell her he loves her. He sounded genuine . . . And Opshora was sure about it till she spoke with Ashley.

Opshora feels lost—is somewhat afraid to trust her instincts about Antonio. There is some truth in what Ashley accused him of. Alberto sometimes shares about Antonio's lifestyle—crafting cuisine and casual involvements with women. Opshora has shown no interest in Antonio's past, trying to indicate very clearly that whatever Alberto hints at doesn't work on her.

"My big bro can't say no to anything in a skirt . . . a concoction of wine, women and good food is THE recipe for his life," Alberto has uttered several times since she got to know him.

"Antonio, what's this talk about all these women and you . . . as Alberto harps on every time I meet him?" Opshora had asked point blank.

"After Ashley and I broke up I had some casual flings . . . nothing serious. That's the past. You are the present, tesoro. Let's not speak of what is long gone."

That settled all the turbulence, all doubts at the time. . .but the misery of suspicions is back now. Fear needs no reason.

Antonio cooks a lovely dinner. They carry the food onto the rooftop to eat in candlelight reflecting against the brilliance of the night sky and the murmurs of the streets below. After dinner is over, they sit there for a long time without speaking, feeling the night. He holds her close, she feels safe. Her eyelids get heavy with sleep, in the comfort of his nearness against her body. The effect of the wine they drank starts to sink in. He gently leads her back into the bedroom and they lie holding each other as he begins to kiss her slow, purposefully. That's when the phone rings—disrupting, annoying.

The magic breaks. Antonio glances at the number on the screen.

"It's Maria. Got to take it," he whispers getting out of the bed and walking to the living room. Maria has called again so late at night. Through the open door Opshora hears Antonio's voice. He is forceful, annoyed. A phone fight starts, obviously.

"You don't get to tell me what I should or shouldn't do. You don't dictate my life. I choose what I want, what is good for me!" He hangs up, finally.

He comes to bed and kisses her, holds her close. His hands are on her.

"I am tired. I need to sleep . . . I have work early in the morning," she kisses him on both cheeks, turns away and closes her eyes. She has had enough drama in the last few days from his family.

"Okay, rest, tesoro." He accepts her lame excuse. It is like a rejection. With a heavy heart he lies down beside her. Thoughtful, uneasy, angry at everything beyond his control. He wishes things were different for him this time, that there was more support from the family.

Opshora lies awake beside Antonio, pretending to be asleep. She can hardly breathe under the heavy load of pain. Recent events have been gradually infecting the sweetness of feelings she has been carrying, seeped in promises. What if she is a casual fling in his life? The silent tears begin to fall but she doesn't move. She doesn't want to draw Antonio's attention. The salty drops sting her cheeks, stain her heart. Something begins to die within her. A hollow eats her heart like an empty song. Playing the same tune over and over.

While such emotional turmoil is going on, Ruby finalizes the date for Antonio's dinner with the family. Days have passed by since Opshora told her parents about Antonio. Ruby is now unwilling to delay it any further.

Maya and Robin have come for a visit with the children for the weekend. Opshora guesses it is planned well ahead in order for them to participate at the family dinner. It is too good a coincidence to have happened without any manipulation. Antonio accepts the invitation, decides on leaving the kitchen to Marcello for one more evening.

Antonio arrives at her parents' house, very punctual. He wants to make an impression. He looks handsome in his white full sleeved, open collared shirt, blue denims, and dark burgundy shoes. He has been growing his hair and the curls lie casually on his neckline, over his forehead. His intense eyes look animated in the excitement of the moment. Whenever he glances at Opshora, his eyes soften with a tender spark, giving away his love for her. He is a total hit—everyone likes him immediately though they find his mannerism, heritage and ethnicity are matters that would require some more understanding to get used to. But they are okay with it. Opshora is surprised at her mother being so taken by Antonio. He pays special attention to Ruby and is genuine in his admiration for her cooking. He had brought a big bouquet of one hundred white roses for Ruby and a large box full of pastries and tarts for the others. Ruby is floored by his flowers. And his attention.

"Signora Ruby . . . may I call you that? You are a gem of a cook . . . in the selection of spices and herbs and special condiments you used in the lamb korma, absolute perfezione! I would be honored to be your student." His humility conquers Ruby's heart in an instant. He heartily eats the Bengalee food prepared in his honor.

Her father animatedly discusses Italian history with him. Antonio is well read on his native culture, and his people who arrived at the American shores in boats more than a century ago.

"We are immigrants, like you and many others, Dr. Mirza.

Italians were not even considered white in the U.S. before the twentieth century. We suffered during World War II—mistrusted, prosecuted, persecuted," Antonio says.

"Well, so did the Japanese. It was shameful . . . we went through that phase after 9/11. People of Muslim faith were treated as traitors overnight," MD Mirza agrees. "You can't generalize . . . can't put everyone in the same basket. Immigrants of all faiths and colors have contributed to the making of this country."

Opshora still remembers the horror of that day—the massacre at the World Trade Center. A handful of Saudi Arabian nationals masterminded and carried out the mass murders . . . the fear and uncertainties . . . and what followed afterwards. The peace that Muslim Americans found living in this country was wiped out in an instant. They were terrified. And America was enraged, afraid. They wanted to blame someone. Some ignorant, angry Americans spewed hate against fellow Americans who followed a different faith, who looked different but were as innocent of any crime as anyone. Brown people were harassed, attacked all over the US. In fear of repercussions many Muslim men shaved off their beards, women in hijaab or headscarves stayed indoors, afraid of the vulgarity and threats thrown at them. Many Americans were confused. Sikh-Americans, mistaken as "Muslims," got murdered in rage in several states as the Sikh men are bearded and wear turbans in their heads as a part of their tradition. The profanity continued. Some unity surfaced at one point. Some believed America is beautiful because of its diversity; some others sought scapegoats. It was an uncertain time.

"We Italians faced our share . . . starting with the Columbus Day. It was supposed to be a one time national celebration after eleven Italians were lynched. And to calm diplomatic tensions with Italy . . . Then came World War II . . . the suspicion and discrimination my dad's generation faced during that time is inexcusable."

"Sometimes I think America's democracy hangs by a thin thread," Opshora adds to the conversation.

"Agree . . . look at how African Americans are treated . . .This guy Trump is a joke. Is this First Amendment right to say outrageous things? Republicans better watch out. But he is going to create trouble for immigrants," Antonio warns.

"Do you think he will win? In any case democracy here is better than in other countries!" Maya voices.

"Better than Cuba, Russia . . .Venezuela," Everyone nods in agreement with MD Mirza's comment.

"I wish he was kicked out during the primary," Maya says. "There are more likeable republicans than Trump. They could give a chance to John Kesich . . ."

"Maybe Hillary will wipe him out. We will know in four months," Leila puts in.

"Not so sure. Is this country ready for a woman leader yet?" Robin is doubtful.

"Mama Mia! Let destiny take over . . . and we venture into something less depressing." Everyone laughs at the comical way Antonio diverts the discussion. "Is football a safe topic?"

Robin and Antonio tease each other on cricket and football—Italians are passionate about both sports.

"We have won the FIFA world cup several times," he proudly reminds the group. "Italians are also ranked 28th by the ICC."

"You guys are good," Robin accepts Antonio's claims. "We love football and cricket. Though I was born here, I learned about these games from our community of South Asian Americans."

"Americans don't understand football or cricket. Our blood boils as players pick up bats, hit the balls . . . baseball? Not a real game for men . . . I played basket ball in school, though. Football is soccer here, what the heck . . . disastro! Simply disastro!" he punches Italian words to make a point. A goodhearted laughter follows his comment.

No one mentions that both Ruby and MD Mirza are base-ball fans. He is an ardent supporter of New York Yankees while she is for Boston Red Sox.

"Where did you learn these games? Opshora told us you were born here," Robin asks.

"Like you, my Italian American uncles and grand pops taught us."

Ruby and Maya are curious about some specific recipes and they sit down with Antonio, picking his brain while MD Mirza and Robin are in deep conversation over current economic policies.

"Glad I am having a much better time with you, great ladies—grandi signore . . . discussing recipes instead of dry politics," Antonio winks and charms them with his smile.

Opshora keeps busy with the children. Best to give the family time to get to know Antonio, especially her mother. She wants this episode to succeed.

The two women learn how to make Italian white sauce, and ravioli. In return Ruby shares the lamb korma recipe with him as well as a South Asian way of cooking pilau. He notes down everything in a small notebook he carries in his shirt pocket.

"Signora Ruby, Signora Maya always remember heavy cream, parmigiano are basics. Always pick up fresh from the market," he reminds. "But the main ingredient of true Italian cooking is love . . . lots and lots of it . . . add a pinch of madness . . . a drop of tear or two . . . and no problema!" The women begin to laugh at his advice. "Believe me . . . every dish I cook is mixed with love and slices of my heart. That's the magic."

After dessert, with his coffee mug in hand, Antonio walks to the corner where Leila is sitting. With a smile she pats the empty place beside her for him to sit.

"She holds you in her heart," Antonio says quietly.

"I know. She is very special," Leila utters almost in a whisper.

"I know," Antonio whispers back.

When it is time to take leave he shakes hands with the men, kisses the cheeks of the women, hugs the children and lands a kiss on Opshora's lips as the family looks on. She doesn't care. She hadn't alerted him about the Bengalee culture of no public display of passionate emotions. Her mother is visibly uneasy but the others simply don't mind.

Opshora walks him to her apartment through the outside entrance, up the spiral stairs made of rot iron. Before she can switch on the lights he kisses her—half carries her to the sofa and they make love in the semi-darkness broken by the headlights of occasional passing cars that stamp their marks on the large windows.

"What if they come looking for us?" she says in a half whisper.

"I don't care. Let them get a shock," he responds in between kisses as she tries to suppress a giggle.

"Stop laughing. I can't concentrate if you giggle so much when I am obsessing over you," he says in mock seriousness. They lie there for a long time nestled against each other, passion spent, comfortable in the knowledge of the other's nearness.

"Can I spend the night with you?" he asks.

"No."

"I will wake them up when I drive away. Our secret will be out. That's no good." He is playful.

"We will go down stealthily. In silence. You can pull out of the drive without starting the engine. It's on the slope . . ." Opshora cautions.

"How do you know all this?" he is impressed.

"Both Robin and I grew up in this house, remember?" Opshora says with a straight face. Antonio gives a low whistle

"Bellissima?" He calls out softly after some time.

"Yeah?"

"You know that I love you, right?" Antonio whispers.

"Yes, I know. And I love you, too," Opshora says tenderly. They lie in the quiet darkness some more minutes.

"Would your mom be very disappointed if she finds out I stayed over?" he breaks the silence. Tries his case again.

"Yes. She is a fanatic regarding preservation of Bengalee culture. She suffers from ostrich syndrome. Even though I am half a century old she can't let go. My virtue is important to her."

"Don't say that. Don't bring up your age for no reason. That's unladylike. You are gorgeous. And apologies from me to Signora Ruby—I already slept with her daughter."

Antonio puts on his clothes and climbs down the spiral stairs silently.

# CHAPTER TWENTY

# The Book— and Untold Stories

The book is almost ready. Opshora's agent has been negotiating with a reputable publisher, which has finally confirmed the publication of limited copies with some conditions on promotional activities and royalties. On behalf of Antonio and his family she signs off on the deal. All they want is for the first edition of the published book to generate publicity for the restaurant and retain the good ratings. They are not so concerned with profits from the sale of the book—the restaurant would be benefitting enough if the book gets good reviews, for sure. She assists in launching of the book.

The book opens with an introduction on Antonio and his culinary skills, followed by the story of the Russo family and Pasta Paradiso, emphasizing the historical background of its establishment decades ago casting some light on the migration of Italians to the U.S. Each chapter presents a city in Italy famous for its specialty cuisines, portrays interesting aspects of the daily life of its people, their traditions, their stories, followed by selected authentic recipes popular in that region which are now served in Pasta Paradiso cooked by Antonio and his team's magical touch. Photographs of the eatery, signature dishes, and anecdotes are captured in the text shared by the family, staff and customers. Opshora picks the most appealing anecdotes as opening lines for each chapter.

*"This is my life. I started this ristorante with a floor space of six tables and a kitchen in the back. Now I can sit twenty tables . . . even then the customers have to wait in line to eat here on weekends and holidays." —Marco.*

*"I hate it when my sauce gets too thick some days. The customers don't understand the difference and relish it. But I cry in the restroom and put extra makeup to hide my tears . . . I am an incorrigible perfectionist!!" —Isabella*

*"I am a food activist. I fight to bring authenticity blended in exotic taste to the table. I want to woo my customers with what I cook with love and some madness—pazza, some heartaches. My food is special—offered to special people. By the way, every customer is special at Pasta Paradiso." —Antonio*

*"Carlo hates it when I wear my tight red dress as we receive customers, and I assist in seating them. But I get lots of admiring looks from both women and men . . . I know some men return . . . (Carlo, don't kill me!). I am not going to give up my red dress. It adds to the charms of Pasta Paradiso." —Rosa*

*"Pasta Paradiso is my rendezvous with destiny! I have to live up to its standard. I better behave." —Alberto*

*"I am available for every odd assignment around the restaurant. I taste the food, the wine and my heart is full of love for the restaurant and my family." —Carlo*

*"I am Maria. I never get tired of eating lots and lots of pasta in this restaurant because my nonna cooks it with her care and skill." —Maria*

Opshora liked the way Maria expressed her feelings and used her exact words. It sounded genuine and she coined them in the book.

Glossy paper, vibrant colors and fonts are picked to give the book a creative look. Artistic styles and motifs are used with a traditional Italian flavor to heighten its appeal. The first round of congratulations is spontaneous as everyone crowds over the near final mock-up. Isabella beams at her snapshots of the kitchen and the accurateness of her recipes she has carefully dictated.

"I like it," she declares. "Thank you. You have captured the true spirit of Pasta Paradiso."

"Hear! Hear! You have tamed the lioness," Alberto whispers to Opshora while the rest of the family pores over the pages, talking over each other as always.

"So the main hurdle is crossed!" Opshora mutters. She feels relieved. Deep down she had some worries regarding Isabella's approval.

"Opshora, signora . . . you have done a good job!" Isabella adds now and smiles at Opshora with sincerity, for the first time. Her voice holds genuine admiration. Marco comes around to her and gives her a hug.

"I look so good in my red dress! Oh, Opshora you make me happy! You are a genius." Rosa's hug is tight and genuine.

"Let Carlo have a good look first, sister. We may have a murder on our hands I bet," Alberto teases Rosa amidst sincere laughter.

"I don't like what you said about me," Maria's displeasure shows.

"I used what you said, Maria. Those are your exact words. But we can still edit this if you change your mind," Opshora offers.

"But this is good, bellissima," Marco puts in.

"I like it. It's . . . so you, Maria. I agree with pappo," Rosa supports Marco.

"It's so childish. I am not a baby. I hate it!" Maria storms out of the room.

"Maria! You can't leave like that! Come back and tell us what you want," Antonio tries in vain to intervene.

The room falls silent. Awkwardness creeps in. Alberto gets up and in his usual manner kisses Opshora's cheeks.

"You did good my friend." He holds her longer than necessary and winks. Antonio's slow scowl begins to appear. Opshora smiles inwardly. Somehow the brotherly non-verbal scuffles amuse her.

Opshora feels good. Her work is almost over. She has won the family's approval. Now they know her main intention was to do this book professionally and not use it as a pretext to continue dating Antonio. Of course, she loves that part as well. She is in love with him.

The next day, Maria has another showdown. This time with Antonio at the restaurant before the evening crowd begins to gather. From the beginning she has eyed the book-writing as a gimmick used by her father to seduce the family in Opshora's favor. Somewhere, she has been feeling redundant in the process of creating the book. She openly expressed her dislike about her quote. Though Opshora has tried to get an edit of her anecdote, Maria hasn't shown much interest, and wasn't forthcoming with any further contribution. Her melt down is triggered by discovering the family's robust approval of Opshora's efforts with the cookbook, their acknowledgment about its potential to their business. Everyone has been talking about Opshora's good work. Even her grandmother's indifference towards Opshora is dissolving, creating a bridge towards her acceptance in the inner circle of the family. Unfounded suspicion about Opshora's motives breeds jealousy in Maria. And Maria loses it . . .

"Papo, you don't care for me anymore. You are busy with the cookbook, blinded by the girlfriend. You have no time—so don't give me sermons about my behavior," Maria is heard yelling a response to something Antonio has said.

In a fit of seething rage, she kicks at a bucket of water, throws a basket of vegetables and fruits all over the kitchen, behaves like a spoiled brat while the kitchen staff watch, waiting for the next step of the drama to unfold.

"It's not true! You are unmanageable, untruthful, lying to me all this while like your mamma!" Antonio shouts back. Carlo and Alberto step in at the commotion to check but stay on the sidelines, not interfering.

"Keep her out of it," Maria's voice is high. "Don't blame her for anything and everything."

"Why? I speak the truth."

"She is like this because of you, papo. You broke her."

"Maria, it's a damn lie. You know it," Antonio spits out in anger.

"I am never, ever going to come back to you! You are blind, selfish. Mamma is right," screaming, she runs out of the restaurant.

"Okay, don't! I don't want to deal with your rebellion every day! You are full of drama . . . I am tired!" Antonio shouts back at her from the entrance of the eatery as Maria stops a cab and gets in. The family gathers at the entrance.

"Antonio, this isn't going to work. You have to calm her down first. You can't abandon her. She is your first responsibility," Isabella shakes her head in disapproval. Her disappointment in Antonio is undisguised. Both watch helplessly as the cab speeds away in the busy street.

"Her mother has some role to play. Stop blaming me," he responds heatedly.

"Boss bro, we all know what her mamma is like!" Alberto injects.

"Pazza! Pazza—a crazy woman, her mamma! I always said that," Marco now joins them and says in exasperation.

"Never liked her," Carlo chips in but stops saying more as Rosa throws a warning glance towards him. She doesn't want him to be pulled into the family melodrama.

"Where is Maria going? You need to find out. Not again to the mechanic?" Rosa raises the alarm.

"She has been seeing this guy. He is not fit for her. Uneducated, so much older! She is sneaky, lying to us! I told her I will stop her allowance if she doesn't cut off with him," Antonio wipes the sweat from his forehead with the back of his palm.

"So the fireworks!" Alberto gives out a low whistle.

"She feels rejected by your new life, my son," Isabella remarks. "Maybe that is the reason for her rebellion."

"Can't be helped mamma! I have a right to be happy. She is not a child anymore."

The heated argument and counter squabbles continue for some time. Each one has a different solution, dissimilar view. Agreement isn't reached on any proposition. Antonio goes back to the kitchen, fuming and frustrated. With a fury he concentrates on his cooking.

"We need to do something about the mechanic. What do you think?" Carlo looks at Alberto as the family disperses. "Put the fear of God in him?"

"No. Stay out of it . . . " Alberto doesn't agree.

A week later Maria runs away. Ashley isn't home when it happens. She has travelled out of state to attend a friend's wedding. Her life has always been full with her job, clubbing and socializing. The school calls Antonio in the afternoon after being unable to reach Ashley to inform her that Maria has skipped her classes from mid-morning without notifying the school authorities. This wasn't the first time Maria absconded from her classes like this and Ashley had been duly informed each time. This is news to Antonio! The principal warns of a possible suspension.

Antonio has joint custody of his daughter but agreed to Maria's decision to live with Ashley, closer to her school. He thought it would be easier for the girl to have some stability, instead of dragging her back and forth every two weeks between two households. At the time it seemed a good decision that Maria chose to stay with her mother. Antonio's life has always been busy though Isabella and Marco expressed their willingness to give support in every way at the time. Maria wanted to be with her mother.

# CHAPTER TWENTY-ONE

# Shadows Grow Darker
# in the Scent of Pines

Ashley rushes back to meet with the Russo family in the evening of the same day after Maria's disappearance. She had been compelled to drive four hours in heavy traffic as soon as she got Maria's news. Antonio's angry voicemail forced her to return to D.C.

"Maria has never done this before. What happened? Can anyone tell me?" Ashley says as she steps inside the restaurant where the family has gathered. Her accusatory tone is directed towards Antonio.

The fatigue and lines under her eyes due to late nights are visible. She looks annoyed, disheveled by the suddenness of the incident but more so because of Antonio's anger and the family's concern over Maria's disappearance.

"Stop lying Ashley. This isn't the first time," Antonio throws out. Ashley is taken by surprise.

"You should have been on guard. Checked on her whereabouts better," Isabella hisses in subdued rage. Her nostrils flare as she speaks, betraying her inner turmoil.

"I ran away at fifteen with my tennis coach. It's not a big deal. Really. I realized the folly and came back home after a day. My parents weren't bothered," Ashley says trying to keep a casual tone.

"Come on, Ashley! It's different these days . . . men have become perverts. We are Italians—unlike your filthy rich folks." Antonio is choked both in anger and a gut punching worry. He spits on the floor.

"Don't make a big deal of it. That's what I am saying. And don't you dare insult my family!" Ashley fights back in defiance.

"What if she is in trouble? Don't underestimate the risks. You left a fifteen-year-old alone in the house?" Antonio rejects her excuses. "You should have told us about going out of state."

"My neighbor watched over her. She usually does that. And stop accusing me right away! Where were you? You are always missing in action." Ashley's eyes flash at him.

"Ashley, it was your decision, Maria's decision that she would be best placed with you. So I gave up on the custody battle. I trusted you," Antonio says in frustration. "You haven't been a good role model to a teenager."

"Neither have you . . . what good example have you been setting? Not giving her the attention she needs . . . busy . . . too besotted with your foreign lover," Ashley hurls back emphasizing on the word "foreign."

"Keep Opshora . . . my life out of this, please! And for the record she is as good an American as you are. She was born here. So don't utter unfounded nonsense!" Antonio doesn't plead with her. He commands her to stop. She shrugs, nonchalant. The family watches.

"You could have informed us about your travel. Ashley, you are a mother, the guardian! You were irresponsible," Isabella doesn't mince words. Ashley winces momentarily then shrugs again in defiance because this wasn't the first time she had left Maria by herself without alerting the family. Nothing of any significance happened in the past.

"Maria will be back when ready, okay? Let's not make it a big issue." With that wisdom Ashley walks out of the restaurant, drives away leaving the family bewildered.

"She looked as if woke up from a long night of partying," Alberto comments. No one disagrees with him. "We need to take some concrete steps . . . Maria isn't safe with her anymore."

"Let's hope she hasn't gone back to the mechanic. That would be a real troublesome matter," Rosa chips in. She is very worried for her niece.

"What shall we do? Report to the police?" Antonio asks the family. After considerable debate and dialogue the collective consensus is to wait till the next morning. Maria may show up, as Ashley believes.

"It's so wrong . . . so wrong! She is so wrong for Maria," Alberto says aloud.

Years ago when Alberto met Ashley at a party, he found her recklessness absolutely attractive. She came from an affluent, cultured background unlike Alberto whose folks were hard working, struggling middle class. Ashley's father owned several financially profitable corporate businesses and her mother was a CEO in a reputable bank. Ashley was the only child of her highly successful parents and had everything going for her at the time Alberto met her. She was an undergrad at a private university and was a good student. Alberto attended a community college and worked at the family restaurant in between his classes. There was a hell of a gap in background between them. And that's what she found so appealing.

He was drawn to her bizarre lifestyle of non-stop partying, drinking and drugs. He got pulled into her unruly crowd and was grateful when she agreed to go out with him. Despite everything, he fell in love with her because he understood her, discovered a beautiful mind inside her outward rebellion. Her stunning appearance drew crowds. Alberto was too happy to join her cult of admirers.

Her choosing Antonio over him sobered Alberto. He thought it cured him of Ashley—it restrained him from making a fool of himself in public but he struggled with his love for her secretly for a long time and couldn't forgive his brother for his treachery. When he introduced them, Antonio was fully aware of Alberto's feelings towards Ashley. She might not have seen it or chose not to see it. It was too early in their relationship and Alberto hadn't had the chance to declare his love for her openly. But for onlookers, he wore his heart on his sleeve. Watching his brother and Ashley together was tormenting. He coped with their laughter and time with the family in stoic silence and with an outward display of a nonchalant attitude. He suffered. He thought, in time, Antonio would tire of her. The bombshell fell when Ashley and Antonio declared their intention to marry.

Ashley became an unavoidable presence from then on. A constant source of torment to Alberto. The worst thing was, whenever Ashley and Antonio had fights, she would try to taunt Alberto with her attempts to flirt. He could have taken the opportunities to get even with his brother but by then he knew Ashley was self–destructive and it was best to keep away from her. He distanced himself from Antonio and the rest of the family.

The Russo family is anxious about Maria as they prepare for the day. Life has to go on—the restaurant will have to operate on its regular schedule. Still there is no news from Maria. Antonio keeps glancing at his phone as he works. He can't fully concentrate and feels an unease gripping his brain.

When Opshora steps into the restaurant in the evening she almost smells the asphyxiated staleness in the environment, a charged-up setting for something waiting to happen. It seems a storm is increasingly building up to strike down anytime. Between Alberto and Carlo, she gets a report of the happenings—Maria's running away and the family's reactions and fears.

"Maria is having problems accepting changes around her," Carlo comments. He has had enough of the mother and the daughter, both he believes are rowdy and headstrong. "One needs to grow up. This isn't the way to bring up a teenager! If you ask me, Ashley is hopeless as a mother."

"Maria is still a child actually . . . our boss bro and Ashley should have talked to her more. Listened to the issues bothering her. She is disturbed by boss bro's romantic adventures," Alberto's words hit Opshora like a blow. She doesn't know whether the family is blaming her for Antonio's digressions. "But she needs firm supervision, if you ask me. She is spoiled, totally," Alberto adds casually.

Opshora has been disappointed with Maria's attitude toward her. She is openly hostile towards Opshora. Her insecurities over her father may have made her more rebellious in addition to the normal emotional confusions of adolescence. Opshora somewhat accepts her own share of responsibility in not being able to deescalate the tension between her and Maria. She could have reached out, tried harder to reassure the teenager that she isn't a threat in anyway—they can coexist in Antonio's life. Initially, Maria hadn't been eager at all to speak with her though Opshora attempted to engage her several times in the pretext of collecting the girl's views on the cookbook. Maria resisted purposefully. She gave some lines for the book, but still wasn't happy.

Opshora would have liked to be friends with Maria.

She is greeted with cool aloofness by Isabella and after a few seconds she vanishes somewhere for the entire evening possibly to avoid Opshora. Rosa has been very positive about her brother's new love life from the beginning and gives a pat on Opshora's shoulder in camaraderie.

"Mama will come around. Don't worry," Rosa is genuine. "It's one of her airs . . . we are used to it." But Opshora isn't used to Isabella's ways. She hardly knows the older woman. Warmth never happened between them.

"That girl is a mess, I tell you . . . she is more of Ashley than us," Rosa speaks with honesty. "I wonder if any of us could have had any influence on her. Running away? Hmmm . . . now don't feel guilty, Opshora. She may be having fun with her mechanic while we sweat here for her."

Marco's smile is thin tonight. He looks tired, somewhat defeated, sweating under his heavy weight as he goes about dragging his aching knees. Carlo whisks between tables with some errands, thoughtful. So is Rosa. She wears her distress on her face. Only Alberto is unaffected. He continues to whistle as he organizes the wine bottles for the evening guests.

"Signorina, how are you faring? This will lift the mood. . . " Alberto starts humming, "la la la la . . ." Then he turns towards Opshora and offers her a drink. "This is to clear your head." Opshora fails to understand him. Only a few minutes ago he had hinted at her relationship with Antonio as Maria's source of distress.

"You sure? I feel lousy, already." Opshora gulps down whatever Alberto gives her. A slow warmth begins to flow through her brain and limbs and reaches her heart.

"It's working," she affirms. "So you think I am causing unhappiness in your family?" The wine starts to speak and she moves away before saying more things she would regret later.

"I wasn't blaming you . . . my target was boss bro. Apologies, dear signorina."

Opshora doesn't see Antonio anywhere. He must be busy in the kitchen. That's a place she doesn't venture into. She knows if she does there would be soft whistles, low chuckles . . . subtle looks. The staff are still amused by Antonio's romantic life. His crew wouldn't give her an easy pass for sure.

Maria lives in a world of fantasy, all fired up by raging

hormones like any other teenager around her, Opshora gets that. There are too many triggers in her life in addition to the stressors amplified by her estranged parents' situation. Ashley hasn't been the complete mother—unable to guide and supervise her as her own needs often clash with her daughter's. Maria usually gets second preference, which she finds hard to accept.

Antonio on the other hand has moved on, his life is on a plateau of contentment in his soaring professional achievements. He has discovered harmony and happiness in his relationship with Opshora. His life finally is on a fresh track, has new meaning. Maria interprets this as a rejection from her father's life. She tries to push back assuming she is second best to him as well. She is afraid of being redundant in the lives of both her parents. She resents her situation, feels they have abandoned her. Maria has Opshora's full sympathy. But Opshora is unable to untangle the vicious knots that tie their lives at this juncture.

Unlike other times, dinner is brief, quiet. Antonio heats up a dish of pasta he has brought from the kitchen downstairs. He is not in the mood to cook dinner tonight. Opshora understands his mental condition but doesn't know how to help him. He left the kitchen to Marcello, an hour early. He is disturbed. The stress is too much. Maria hasn't contacted anyone yet.

They don't talk much—only remark on trifles in monosyllables. He almost finishes an entire bottle of wine. Opshora has only one glass to soothe her jumpy pulse. A strange stream of muted angst keeps rising. Both try to grasp a sliver of composure that is non-existent. That night they go to bed in silence.

"Tesoro, my sweet, I am tired. Will sleep," he kisses her lightly on the forehead and slumps on the bed.

She cleans up the table, loads the dishwasher. The night looks strange outside. The streetlights spread brilliance on the trees looming over them. Opshora looks out through the window for a longtime, watching the slow-moving cars, the carefree pedestrians. People are going back home or to their hotels possibly. D.C. is full of visitors all year around. People flock here for conferences, while some are just curious tourists or residents—students, executives. The streets would become deserted soon.

When she enters the bedroom, Antonio is in deep sleep, snoring softly. Opshora feels helpless at the way life events are going against her—all over again. A shadow hangs over her newfound happiness. It's hard to ignore the omen she senses in the air.

Next day in the afternoon Antonio files an official missing person's report with the police despite Ashley's claim that it is totally unnecessary. Ashley is angry because the family ignored her opinion. She screams at Antonio on the phone. The police promise to alert patrol cars to look out for a missing minor but at the same time advise the family to have patience as they believe in such kinds of cases most of the runaway kids usually return on their own accord within a week. They don't think she is in any danger yet.

Two more days pass but no one hears from Maria. The family is desperate. It seems she has vanished. Isabella's nephew is in the police force in D.C. He has been in regular contact with the family. The police are still unsuccessful in tracing Maria.

The past four days have been a testing period for Opshora, and the entire Russo family. Every evening Opshora has returned to Antonio's place. At daytime she goes to work directly from there. She knows he needs her. He is appreciative of her presence—his eyes light up when she lingers for a second at the kitchen entrance to let him know she will be waiting for him upstairs. There are no faint whistles or laughter any more at her presence. The news has reached the kitchen. She doesn't hang around in the restaurant, to avoid the family. The atmosphere feels electric—ominous before a thunderstorm breaks.

Isabella and Marco talk in low tones; Rosa and Carlo barely say anything. Antonio buries himself in the kitchen. The kitchen crew is full of empathy for him and waits with the others for Maria's news. The police have advised the family to lie low, keep up their hopes. According to them it's not yet time to go public or advertise in any way about Maria's disappearance. They start making initial contacts with her school and close peers in the meanwhile as a first step.

From the information they gather they are convinced she has run away with someone, possibly a boyfriend and would contact the family soon. But this isn't enough consolation for the Russo family. The tension keeps growing.

Though Antonio doesn't talk about Maria, Opshora understands he is uneasy about the way they had parted. He is gratified to see Opshora at the apartment when he returns late at night, exhausted, crestfallen, brooding over his failed parental connectivity, his daughter's rejection.

On the fifth night after Maria's disastrous walk out, Opshora is startled awake from her deep sleep by Antonio's cell phone. He is quick to grab it and listens, jerked into instant attention. It's three in the morning. In the charred darkness of the room his face remains overcast. She can't read his expressions—catches only broken pieces of his monosyllables almost in whispers. After several minutes he sighs and hangs up and starts to get into his clothes.

"It was Ashley. Police called her . . . they found Maria. She bashed her car against a tree an hour ago. Possibly drunk. No one is hurt. Thank God for that! She has a minor concussion," Antonio's voice is flat, devoid of emotions—very unlike him. "I am going to the hospital."

"Shall I come with you?"

"No, you stay here. I will take Alberto. He may still be up," his voice quivers slightly now. She sees the trouble in his eyes. She tries to reach for him to assure him. He abruptly moves away to avoid her touch.

"I let five days go by without going after her! My little girl!" His self-reproach rings through the apartment as he rushes out. He forgets that even the police failed to find Maria though her disappearance was reported early enough.

Alberto lives three houses from the restaurant. He shares it with another housemate, an elderly single man. He has been renting this house for many years right after Pasta Paradiso moved to this current location. She hears Antonio's footsteps fading on the stairs; she hears the faint sound of the car's engine driving away in the darkness. She knows she has to wait for the next episode that will dictate what happens. The night hangs in there with her. She lies awake till the sun glows outside. They're the longest hours she has lived in recent years. Then she drowses off.

The kitchen stirs around seven in the morning. She hears Carlo's voice, the sound of Isabella's car. Her car backfires when she takes the narrow space to park, and as the engine is switched off it dies with a loud throttled noise.

Carlo has plenty of experience with automobiles but hasn't been able to diagnose the problem with Isabelle's car. He worked at his father's garage and apprenticed under him in a small town in the south of Italy. When Rosa fell in love with him years ago he was a college drop-out, a vagabond who came to the U.S. to attend a wedding of a cousin and to backpack around the country for sightseeing and also to search for economic opportunities. He was fed up with the stagnant, limp life back in Italy and was keen for a change. He met Rosa at the wedding ceremony, as she was a friend of his cousin's bride. Instantly they fell in love and decided to marry soon afterwards, both barely in their early twenties. Marco Russo and Isabella were dead against the match. But Rosa was determined. Carlo was the man of her dreams. She threatened to run away with him. She had a history of misfortune with romantic love. At least Carlo was from their own culture and had the potential to be polished into some usefulness in time. So, unhappily the family embraced Carlo, gave him a job in the restaurant.

Rosa was already helping in the evenings, as she was about to complete undergrad studies. Isabella had her hands full. Rosa and Carlo got married and right after nine months their first child was born. Rosa completed her studies simultaneously.

Rosa's parents gave the down payment for the house that she and Carlo moved into, across the street from Isabella and Marco. So she never left her parents in the real sense. They could cross over to her threshold whenever they wanted and she welcomed their constant presence in her life. Isabella desired it earnestly and became indispensable to her daughter. She helped with babysitting when the children were young and later whenever her services were needed.

Even at present, as the matriarch in the family, she has full control over her daughter's household. She goes back everyday a few minutes before the school bus arrives around four in the afternoon where she receives them, feeds them and makes sure they do their homework. Their part-time nanny takes over from seven when Isabella returns to the restaurant. Rosa and Carlo take turns to go back home around nine every evening to relieve the nanny and tuck the kids in bed. On weekends both children come to the restaurant with their parents armed with books and games. They either hang around in the back room beside the kitchen or at Antonio's apartment till the eatery is closed and it's time to return home. Sometimes they help with small errands in the restaurant and learn a few trade tricks. Everyone lends a hand in the family-owned restaurant. Their grandparents believe it's good to get business-savvy early on. Rosa is also a partner in the family business.

Opshora hears Alberto's voice floating in through the window and is jolted back from her thoughts. They have returned. Antonio didn't call her from the hospital. She was expecting him to update her about Maria's condition. Though it's still early she hops out of the bed, showers and makes coffee.

She finishes her drink and leaves some in the pot for Antonio. He will need it. She doesn't have any appetite for breakfast. A knot has formed in the pit of her stomach; she is flustered and nervous. Unless she finds out how Maria is doing she will be unable to concentrate on anything. She keeps waiting. He doesn't come to the apartment, to her. So she climbs down the stairs at some point. The sounds of several voices pierce through the walls of the side room and reach her on the stairs. They speak in Italian and English at the same time.

"I . . . ahmm . . . Maria . . . " Alberto's voice is inaudible, dipped in distress. Opshora freezes at the entrance. More talking. Isabella speaks in her native tongue for some time. Opshora is unable to understand her. Some arguing continues, amidst raised voices—and a backdrop of murmurs. The whole family has gathered. Opshora stands frozen on the stairs. She can't move. She doesn't know how long she has been standing there. From where she is, Opshora is able to get a partial view of the room.

"Mamma! Mamma! . . ." Antonio sounds broken at this point, he rushes to Isabella's outstretched arms. She gathers him close, his face is on her lap. He weeps uncontrollably, silently. He is her little boy again.

"Ah . . . Antonio, Antonio, *mio figlio* . . . ahh," She hugs him close and attempts to soothe him, trying to shield him from his woes, take away his hurts. She cries with Antonio. Opshora's eyes register the scene. She wants to flee but her feet are glued to the ground. She stands in silence watching the mother and the son—witnessing their suffering.

"Antonio, you have to correct this. You have to make Maria understand she is important to you over everything," Isabella tries to hush him as she speaks. She speaks in her professional voice in English. Others in the room start to talk at the same time; each has their own theory about Maria's situation. There is some clamor.

"Maria needs you more than anyone now . . . this cannot go on, mio figlio. It's not easy to be a parent. Maria's interest should come first. Nothing else matters," Isabella's tone is firm.

"She is so broken . . . my little Maria. So shaken . . . confused. She is a baby. I should have protected her better. I should have given more time to her," Antonio almost chokes with emotion.

"We must try harder to make her feel she is loved, she is important to us . . . she can turn to us and not run away from us. We are family. Start all over again, *mio figlio*. Forget what happened . . ." Marco puts in.

"Things got to change from now on," someone echoes.

Marco says something again in the background. Soundlessly, Opshora walks away.

# CHAPTER TWENTY-TWO

# In a Time of Countless Losses and Wins

"He has been calling, Opshora. Why don't you return his calls?" Chris says cautiously. The news doesn't make her cheerful.

Chris doesn't have the details. But from the way Opshora has been behaving lately spells trouble. He is visibly concerned.

"I have lost my cell phone," Opshora is truthful. She doesn't know if Antonio has tried to reach her on her cell. "I will have to get a new one."

"You can use the land line. He called twice at the store so far, to be accurate . . . yesterday and the day before. You were away," Chris adds gently.

"He allowed more than a week to pass by before dialing me," she keeps uttering in her mind, over and over again. "Sorry you have to face this, Chris. I promise I will deal with it, soon," she says in a flat tone.

"Nothing to be sorry about—just passing the info, bestie," he says with caution.

"I am getting a bit worried about you." Opshora ignores his comment and steps outside for a stroll, to get her thinking straight.

Opshora hasn't been back to Antonio's place since she

stepped out on the morning after Maria's accident. She has been doing some soul searching in the meanwhile—whether her relationship with Antonio is worth saving, whether this is what she really wants. Her life has been eventful in some good ways, with a few hitches, here and there, along with a dash of heartaches but somehow she has been able to tread on the path that aligned with her philosophy. Though all the decisions she's taken haven't matched her expectations, she has managed to live her life so far. She has coped with the consequences fully knowing they have been of her own choosing. After her life with Zayn ended, she has tried to leave all remnants behind . . . she didn't want to look back. Now she feels like a spectator, as if an outsider in the universe she occupied with Antonio. It seems all is over. She is numb. And it hurts. She is unable to feel good. "I am too old for all this . . . this is not for me . . . Antonio is not for me," Opshora repeats to herself and concludes, finally.

Inhibitions have pulled her back from reaching out to Antonio and Pasta Paradiso, so far. Actually, deep down she has been expecting Antonio to come looking for her. He knows where she can be found but Antonio hasn't knocked at her door. There is no way to find out whether he is still trying her on her cell phone. She has failed to retrieve the lost device. In a way, she is sort of relieved—she doesn't know what to say to Antonio at this moment of emotional turmoil. However, later in the afternoon when Chris goes out for lunch she pulls up enough courage and calls the Pasta Paradiso from the store. Alberto picks up.

"Oh, ciao. Boss bro isn't in. Possibly out somewhere for a smoke break," Alberto's greets her. Opshora called knowing fully well about the timing of Antonio's cigarette breaks. She politely inquires after everyone, doesn't particularly ask about Antonio.

Alberto updates her with all the news—Maria is better, was released from the hospital after a day. She has a sprained ankle and is currently convalescing under Isabella's care. Antonio paid for the damages to the car and is trying to spend more time with his daughter amidst his extremely busy schedule. Ashley is in and out and relieved to have Maria off her hands, for the time being. Life is promising to gradually return to normal for the family.

"Come by sometime. Printed copies of the cookbook were delivered yesterday! Looks amazing. Good work, Opshora! We need to talk about promotional issues," Alberto continues—maybe as a pretext to include her back into the fold of their lives. He welcomed her into the family the first day they met and has remained a friend all along.

"I will. I have to submit an assignment first so under pressure," she lies. "I wanted to pass by but couldn't . . ." another lame attempt to clarify the reason for her long absence. Alberto possibly understands the pretension but doesn't comment. They chitchat some more.

Opshora wants to give the family enough time to recover and reunite with Maria now at center stage. That's how she tries to justify her actions to herself—her reason for not contacting Antonio. But she is still confused.

"What's up signorina? Boss Bro isn't chasing you anymore?" he sounds curious. "I don't think I have seen you around in recent weeks . . . it's a good strategy to lie low till the bubbles settle down a bit. But don't wait out too long."

"I told you I am busy. But thanks for the advice."

"Any message for him? I could tell him you are pining for him . . ." Opshora hears him laugh.

"I miss teasing you," he admits honestly. And he continues talking and talking . . .

*Antonio must be having second thoughts about us* . . . in her mind Opshora keeps obsessing, and loses track of what Alberto has been saying.

"Call him," is Alberto's friendly advice. "He is under tremendous work pressure. We have several big bookings. Then there is Maria . . . Marcelo is down with the flu . . ." his voice trails off in the background. Opshora's mind wanders into a web of doubts.

"Got to go. Bye," she says mechanically at one point. Something has changed, definitely.

The country is in turmoil. Opshora finds it matches her inner turbulence. She can't escape. Like many others, she feels trapped in the acridness of uncertainty, anxiety and alarm. The nation is divided—"What kind of America is it going to be after Obama?

. . . why wasn't Bernie the choice?" Some wonder. No one knows . . . America has become more fragmented since Hilary Clinton officially was declared the presidential nominee of the Democratic Party on July 26, 2016, and the Republicans nominated Donald Trump. He turns politics nastier than ever. Politics dominates social gatherings, creeps inside offices and homes. Family members are divided; politics destroys friendships, alienates one from the other. Trump continues to incite his supporters with falsehoods—sucking out the oxygen round the clock giving no peace to anyone.

"Trump is hitting the airwaves with lies and misogynistic, racist dog-whistles," Chris is worried. "If he wins it is going to be a different world for you and me, bestie."

"Don't worry, partner. Hilary may still win. The election is only weeks away. We will find out soon," Opshora says with a false sense of calm that she doesn't feel. Like others around her, she is exhausted by the name-calling and misleading filth that the Trump campaign keeps propagating. Her inner restlessness solidifies in the current scenario that projects a bleak transition towards extreme negativity. It is so un-American but many disgruntled potential voters embrace it. It shows how fragmented the country is.

"I worry Opps. You are a brown woman and I am gay. It will be a tough place for the likes of us." It is hard to counter this fact. "We are endangered species in Trump's universe, Opshora," Chris adds in a low voice.

News of gay bashings, attacks on the transgender population and people of color, including followers of Muslim and Jewish faiths begin to escalate. The political pot keeps brewing. Living around D.C. she feels safe but her friends and family caution Opshora to be careful on her lone walks back home at nighttime. Suddenly, the memories of Fiji during the turbulent times rush back to her mind. It's no different . . . She can now understand Zayn's fears about her safety. But at the time she had mostly ignored the danger.

Days pass. Opshora continues with her life—working amidst sadness at separation from Antonio. Desperation builds up as she keeps missing him—his teasing, the warmth of his embrace, the flavor of cheese that clings to his hair after work. And some nights she is tempted to call him . . . to have a heart-to-heart talk, to ask him what went wrong. The realization that Antonio hasn't sought her out kills her. Only a handful of miles are keeping them apart. If he really wanted to be with her, he could have easily crossed this distance anytime. In any case, she doesn't try to contact him, either. Her irrational thoughts have deepened—maybe he considers her too much trouble? Got tired of her . . .

Opshora can't get Pasta Paradiso out of her head—Antonio, Alberto, Rosa and the others cram into her thoughts spontaneously. She is often tortured with the idea that she is to be blamed for some of Maria's emotional uncertainties and actions. She wonders if Antonio blames her as well. Though no one has said anything to her, deep down she has been aware of Isabella's disapproval, accusations reflected in the aloofness towards her, in Marco's body language—both wearied by Maria's constant negativity and irrational emotional demonstrations on so many instances.

Alberto has been nonchalant throughout Maria's disturbances and Rosa and Carlo have appeared to be neutral. Antonio, on the other hand, had refused to acknowledge the building up of tension. He believed that by ignoring it things would fall back to normalcy. He could have addressed the hostilities and calmed Maria by listening to her, by being more attentive to erase her unreasonable fears. He could have defended Opshora better to his family. But he has done nothing, stood on the sideline waiting for a catastrophe to happen. Opshora now holds Antonio fully responsible and is angry for being drawn into the family-battle of resentments. She is hurt and exhausted at the impact it has on her. She wishes Antonio had protected her from the spikes of antagonism thrown at her, and helped to heal Maria's wounds.

"Here, it just arrived," Chris hands over a box of pastries with the label of Pasta Paradiso. Must be Antonio's apologies masked in the sweet delights he baked for her, wrapped carefully under layers of butter, sugar, vanilla and cream asking for her forgiveness? An attempt to balm her aches after weeks and weeks of silence? Camouflaged repentance? But there is no card with it—only a box of sweet temptations.

She takes the packet and trashes it in abrupt fury. It breaks the spasms of brooding that have dominated her mind since Maria's incident. After all this time of waiting Antonio has the guts to send her pastries? He is too proud or stupid to show up in person? A sudden rage consumes her. An overwhelming ache breaks her. But she doesn't care anymore. She marches out of the store leaving a bewildered Chris staring after her. She didn't even look what was inside the box. She doesn't want apologies from Antonio. Like Zayn, he has hurt her, failed her most when she needed to be comforted, reassured of his love. He has wounded her trust, allowed others to invade the sanctity of their relationship. He has defined where they stand.

The fall wind embraces her as she hits the road—it is chilly and erratic. There aren't many pedestrians at this hour and she cries as much as she wants but the tears don't stop. She loses track of time and when totally exhausted sits in an abandoned part of a park to cry her heart out even more in an attempt to cure her heart of Antonio. She weeps for the hopes destroyed. The good cry calms her down, steels her mind. She sits there till the stars break on the D.C. sky. She walks towards home in the twilight, weeping. The long walk steadies her.

She is surprised to find the lights on and her father standing beside the window in her living room. He looks up at the sound of her footsteps; tender sparks hover in his weary eyes.

"I came to check if you are okay. We haven't seen much of you lately," he states simply, not inquisitive, not accusatory. He has an envelope in his hand. She knows instantly what is inside. She takes it from him, stands still without opening it.

"You don't want to see what it is?" he asks gently. His voice gives her the strength to tear the edge of the packet and rescue the trapped letter. Her face becomes ashen as she reads. He looks at her inquiringly.

"I got the faculty job at Stony Brook SUNY," she says in a low tone. Her interview had gone well but she is surprised at the offer. She needs this job, badly—she needs to get away from D.C., far away from Antonio. "They want me to join in the next fall semester."

"It's great news. You wanted it," he says in an equally soft tone. "I am proud of you, Opshora!"

"No, you are not. I have always been a disappointment to you, *Ama*, Robin . . ." MD Mirza listens without interrupting her.

"'Robin is your golden boy. He has a spotless career, doctor wife . . . as Ama wanted. He has a great family. I never lived up to your expectations. My life is a big mess," she is confrontational, unnecessary at that point. Tears sting her eyelids. MD Mirza watches her, pained, waits for several minutes giving her time to regain composure.

"You are wrong," he is gentle but firm. "Robin is predicable. You bring surprises. Good ones. I read your book on Fiji . . . Shows how much you loved Zayn, his family, the ocean and the islands—to create it. A patient gave me a copy," he pauses to catch his breath. "It was published years ago but I didn't know of its existence."

Opshora keeps staring at her hands in fear of the betraying tears that are too close to escaping, running wild. After many years of working, shelving and reworking, she conquered her inhibitions and finally published the book on Fiji and the extraordinary heritage of the people of that island country. She continues to listen to her father unable to utter a single word.

"You are the only PhD in our clan. You went to Columbia, achieved so much, my dear girl! We love you. We care for you. We should have expressed more, our appreciation for you."

At that point Opshora breaks down completely. MD Mirza holds her in his arms and afterwards for a long time they sit on the sofa listening to the songs of the crickets outside, the deepening of the night as the wind begins to rise.

"*Aba*, I broke up with Antonio," she finally says, voice muffled under the load of tears, the weight of her loss. She has been drowning in her heartbreak, hitting the bottom but Antonio is gone from her life. It is a shocking realization—it sobers her but the ache doesn't go away.

"I know," MD Mirza says calmly.

"I am leaving for Michigan soon. Will be there for the spring semester," she informs him in a whisper, her head resting against her father's chest.

"I am happy for you . . . if that's what you want to do," he whispers back.

After that day Antonio altogether stops contacting her or trying to reach her at the store landline. But she can't be so sure if he has given up totally because she doesn't have a cell phone anymore and isn't in a hurry to get a new one. He doesn't pass by the store looking for her or send pastries to appease her. Opshora breaks up with Antonio without speaking to him.

A week later, on November 3, 2016, Hilary Clinton loses the election to Donald Trump.

The cookbook gets good reviews. Alberto calls at the store to invite her to the official promotional launching but she explains she can't attend. The publishing agent would be there to assist. She will be away in Michigan at the time. She didn't connive it—it is a coincidence that the dates just clashed. She also suspects that it is a ploy to get Opshora and Antonio to face each other. Maybe Rosa and Carlo are involved in it as well.

The day before she is about to head out to Michigan, Opshora bumps into Carlo at the Safeway store in Georgetown while struggling to carry a packet of toilet rolls in a plastic shopping bag too small to contain it. She is embarrassed to be found out with intimate, undignified stuff like toilet paper. There is a Safeway branch somewhere on 18th Street closer to Pasta Paradiso but Carlo has chosen to be at the Georgetown branch on this particular day and time she is shopping there. Bad coincidence.

"Can I give you a ride?" he asks politely.

"No, no, thanks. I will take an Uber," Opshora tries to avoid talking to him further.

Anyway, he lingers on. Though she doesn't ask, he informs her that Maria is more stable, is attending school properly, she has broken off for good with the mechanic. And she is trying hard to get her parents back together. But Antonio is holding out though the entire family thinks it is a good idea to try again for the sake of harmony, for Maria. The restaurant is doing well; everyone is in good health.

"I know how difficult it was for you . . . Ashley is a mean woman! Her filthily rich parents live in the same house leading separate lives. All her needs and troubles were soothed with money while growing up. So what do you expect?" Carlo spills the beans. It's news to Opshora. No one had breathed about this to her in all the months she has known the family. "So she knows no other ways." Opshora has nothing to say. She listens unwillingly. Once Carlo starts talking it is hard to stop him.

"Maria is no better . . . a spoiled brat if you ask me though Isabella thinks the world about her. Don't worry. Antonio will see sense . . . soon," he adds. It is obvious that Antonio hasn't discussed anything about them. Carlo doesn't know that it is she who broke up with Antonio, not the other way round.

"Oh, I am good actually. Ciao!" She walks away quickly. Carlo, somewhat confused, heads towards the car park. He isn't sure if he has offended Opshora.

On her way back home Opshora wonders why Carlo was giving her all the details of their lives. Was he giving her some hints? A message? He never really liked Ashley and prefers her to be away from the family.

After this chance meeting with Carlo, Opshora writes to Antonio, a brief apology.

*Dear Antonio,*

*Saluti! I am sorry I didn't return your calls or try to meet you and allowed months to pass . . . I believe you have the right to know about the reasons for my silence. It's more than overdue. Over four months (almost) have gone by since I walked out of your apartment.*

*There is no mistake—I have fallen in love with you but it's also true your family wants you to stand by Maria, especially while she is so vulnerable. That's a huge responsibility and my presence wouldn't have helped with her emotional uncertainties, which under the circumstances may be normal for a teenager who wants her father's full attention, to heal out of a broken home. She needs you much more.*

*I think it's best for us to not complicate matters further—go our own ways for the time being. I know you will understand. I lived every moment I was with you. Not a single day goes by when I don't think of you . . . think of the amazing time we shared. Please accept my apology for my long silence.*

*I didn't want to cause you pain, though I did, I know. Believe me it wasn't intentional. I never doubted your love for me.*

*By the way, I would have liked to come over for the book launch but I will be away to Michigan on an assignment during that time. I am sure you will have a great launch and enjoy the book. I am glad I had the honor to work on it.*

*Ti amosempre—will always love you, (See, my Italian improved!)*

*Opshora*

*P.S. I truly lost my cell phone this time. Will get a new one soon, possibly. And I did return your call and spoke with Alberto instead as you were not in. I didn't leave any message for you, though. Also, thanks for the pastries.*

On second thought, Opshora acknowledges receipt of the pastries. She knows Antonio had taken special care to bake the ones she loves.

Antonio doesn't respond to her letter. He never calls the store again. Never bakes any more pastries exclusively for her.

She gets a new cell phone eventually and changes the number. The months glide away too quickly—like being caught in a whirlpool. It feels like a lifetime, though.

Opshora notices the good ratings and reviews of Pasta Paradiso often online and in newspapers. The cookbook has indeed given it an additional glamour—a new boost. She is happy for Antonio, glad that she could be of some help. Isabella may be satisfied now discovering that Opshora's involvement with her son did have a silver lining. The cookbook is a good promotional strategy for the restaurant.

"I am really sad," Chris had said several times after she broke the news of her job at Stony Brook.

"You are not heart broken, come on . . . think of visiting me on long weekends, vacations. Port Jefferson is breath taking round the year, even when buried under snow. I would love to have you stay with me, anytime, partner." Her genuine invitation cheers him up.

For the store they decide to hire a new staff member to take over some of Opshora's work. Beads and Bracelets was doing well for years now. And in a way, they both agree that more systematic assistance is required for running it. Lately, her commitment to the store has ebbed away because of her assignments. Chris has been sweet about it—never complained. He also is excited about new plans to expand the merchandise in additional categories, focusing on tourist attractions. She is relieved at the pleasantness Chris extends regarding her move. The guilty twinge she has been struggling with is lessened.

Opshora's family has come to terms with her breakup with Antonio. They respect her privacy and don't inquire about details. In a way Ruby thinks it's for the best. She was worried about the cultural differences. In addition to his Catholic faith, Antonio's lack of formal educational qualifications pricked like a thorn every time she thought about a looming marriage scenario. She was afraid of gossips that such a match would have unleashed in the Bengalee community. Ruby wants to be proud of her children and deeply cares for societal endorsements.

Right from the moment she came to know about Opshora's relationship with Antonio, Ruby doubted whether he would be able to hold her daughter's interest for long. Opshora is a smart, mature woman and highly sensitive intellectually and emotionally. To Ruby, interracial unions are recipes for disaster. Moreover, the age difference between the couple also bothered her. She deems it's a must for the man to be older than the woman in a romantic affiliation.

Ruby was aware of Opshora's intimate relationship with Antonio, and it made her uncomfortable. She feared there would be repercussions for sinful living—a union not sanctified by marriage. So all is good now. Though she somewhat liked Antonio, his departure from her daughter's life has eased her worries.

"Apa, it's for the best, I think. Antonio was no match for Opshora. She is too accomplished, too independent. I don't think a half-educated Italian could handle her," she had voiced her ideas to Leila right after Opshora's break up. "There is a reason it ended."

Once again her daughter surprises her by bagging the job at Stony Brook University. She is happy for Opshora and definitely relieved that she narrowly escaped the unwanted romantic liaison before more damage was done.

"Missy, you promise to visit me soon, right?" Opshora crashes in at Leila's the night before she travels to Stony Brook.

"Promise. Cross my heart. But tell me how are you now?" Leila has been worrying for Opshora.

"I am still struggling . . . to forget Antonio. I thought he was good for me. We were good," Opshora is honest with Leila.

"Is it a lost cause?"

"We are poles apart, Missy. Opposites can't always hold attraction—can create disruption. Don't look so pitiful!" Opshora gets up and hugs Leila. She somehow always smells of cinnamon and rosebuds. Opshora grew up with this scent of her aunt. "And don't worry for me. I will get through this. Just you wait and see."

"You are a survivor. That's so inspiring about you," Leila kisses Opshora's cheeks affectionately.

"Some mornings I wake up . . . my fighting spirits are fierce. And on other days I feel old, defeated and scared of being so alone. I ask myself why could I not find the recipe for happiness?"

"My dear, you are not old. You just turned fifty two . . . it is a mature age no doubt but it holds immense possibilities. Stony Brook may be the best for you," Leila's gentle, firm voice steadies Opshora.

So her brief tango with Antonio really ends, abruptly, at the cost of many aches, countless tears.

# Part IV.
# Stony Brook, 2017

# CHAPTER TWENTY-THREE

# *You Know How I Feel*

In August of 2017, Opshora moves to Stony Brook to begin teaching in the fall semester. Initially she stays with Maya and Robin. They offer her their old sedan to drive to work. It's kept in the garage as their third car. They also line up some apartments for her to check.

"I don't want to grow roots so fast. I'm not buying anything yet. My gypsy lifestyle is like a permanent stain—hard to get rid of," laughingly she proclaims to Maya and Robin. She eyes the neighborhood around the East Main Street, and finally makes a selection. Ruby is glad that Opshora will be living close to Robin. She is aware of the stressful relationship between the siblings and hopes it will be repaired finally.

A new chapter in her life unfolds at Port Jefferson. It's lovely to see Bella and Liam again, pick up the old threads of sibling ties with Robin, strengthen rapport with Maya. As she strolls the streets of the tiny town, she has ample time to dissect her past life, which in essence still holds some flavors of the happiness she experienced with Antonio. Over and over again she tries to think of various scenarios, chances she overlooked which could have yielded a very different result had she been more mindful. The ache for Antonio doesn't go away. The worst thing is, he brings back memories of Zayn as well.

Anyway, the semester classes start and she gets busy soon enough. Her apartment is on the top floor of a quaint two-story house on the E. Main Street. The ground floor is rented by three female masters students. On some nights she hears their voices, their laughter while the rain splashes against her windows keeping her awake. Once upon a time her life was equally carefree. The time she lived in Suva with her three housemates resurfaces and the aches return. Opshora also misses Diana and her two adorable children. She admires Diana for keeping a balance in her top executive job and a happy marriage. At least they call each other often and Opshora has visited her several times in San Francisco. Mrs. Burger lives in an apartment close to Diana so her visits to the East Coast have almost ceased unless she is on official business.

The rain keeps her awake. The raindrops carry the sound of laughter of the young women from the floor below. Opshora dials Diana.

"Opshora!! What a surprise! Why haven't you visited us this year?" Diana shrieks. Then they talk for almost an hour, giggle like the old times . . .

The view from her balcony is spectacular. This is what she wanted. She calls Chris and describes the scene to entice him to visit her.

"If you come here, you wouldn't want to leave my friend, trust me!" Opshora is enthusiastic. Chris is glad to detect the cheerful tone. "And here the restaurants cook the food with their heart," she almost bites her tongue the moment the words are out. She doesn't want to remember Antonio . . .

In Port Jefferson, she begins to breathe again, live again despite the pains. Despite the despairs, she begins to heal.

❦

Robin drives them all to D.C. in his large eight-seater for the Christmas break. MD Mirza and Ruby are overjoyed. Leila has already moved in with them for a week for the occasion. It's always fun to be together during such family reunions. Leila doesn't want to miss anything. Her sons with their families don't visit her every year. They had spent last Christmas with her. She intends to be with them in San Francisco in spring.

Opshora has missed her Arlington residence every single day. She came back here from Fiji and learned to pick up her life, gathered the courage to move forward. While away in Port Jefferson, her heart constantly longed for the place that has been home to her, always. In her absence Ruby kept her residence exactly the way Opshora had left it. Ruby had it cleaned from time to time and watered the indoor plants.

Leila, Bella and Liam opt to stay with Opshora upstairs. The weather has turned bitterly cold and windy. Winter has come early this year. It begins to snow at night after the kids are in bed. Opshora makes a round of coffee. Her parents, Maya and Robin join in and laze in her living room trying to catch up. After a long time the discords have been weeded away, it seems to her. It is heartwarming to be back and laugh with the family as "many times told" jokes are shared along with popular past anecdotes. The light from her window spreads over the white snow and sparkles with the shadows.

"2017 is almost gone. What a year!" Robin exclaims. "But I am glad despite everything we are okay. We are so happy to have Opshora living near us."

After many years Opshora and Robin are finally comfortable with each other. Opshora in fact looks forward to spending time with her brother and usually shows up to join the family dinners on Saturdays. Bella and Liam are a constant source of happiness to her. Once or twice a week she takes them out for long walks that usually end at the port with clam chowder soup and crab sandwich or seafood pizza with a finishing touch of chocolate ice cream. On the way back they take an Uber. Opshora drops the kids at home and returns to her place. If Robin and Maya are free she hangs around to catch up with them over coffee or some herbal tea that Maya favors. Between her job and her regular habits—writing, reading and long walks around the port—life is decent. Sometimes the whiff of freshly cooked pasta or paella from the nearby restaurants brings back Antonio. But she pushes thoughts of him away. Life with him was too complicated. She wants to breathe without the heartaches that are the bedfellows of his memory . . .

A white Christmas is in the forecast. It is not so common in the greater D.C. area, though. It's spoiled by brief spells of snow now and then unlike New York where winter is long, dreary and freezing. Opshora enjoys the snow when the house is full of people, aroma of food and steaming coffee.

The kids are excited and make plans to go snow balling. Chris and his new boyfriend Toby have been invited for Christmas lunch. They first met when Opshora was still in Michigan, winding up her teaching assignment. Toby has already moved in with Chris. Opshora wants to express her gratitude to Chris in person for the kindness he has showered her with during all the years of their friendship and her move to Stony Brook. She also wants to meet his new flame. Chris has been like family to her, protective, compassionate.

Chris briefed her about his new romantic adventure in detail. She attentively listened to all the emotional ups and downs of his courtship with Toby and sometimes advised him. She is accustomed to Chris' tales of the heart. The least she could do this time was to firmly stand beside him as his relationship progressed—a penance for abandoning him so abruptly. She owed this one to Chris.

Chris has a beautiful soul—honest, genuine and extremely

caring. In his simplicity he spontaneously opens the gate to his heart to people. He gets exploited easily and often but continues to dish out goodness to whoever comes across him. Opshora admires him for who he is. His connection with his family is complex—his homosexuality defined him to the people he loves most. Opshora knows he is famished for love.

Surprisingly Ruby is more generous with others than she has been with her own children regarding conforming to norms. She has no problems accepting Chris and his boyfriend. As long as any such "different-kind-of behavior" isn't embraced by her own family, she doesn't mind.

When her kids were teenagers Ruby had carefully observed them, searched through their things while they were in school looking for signs of discordant behaviors that would single them out as not "normal" in her community. She was petrified by the possibility of deviations that could ostracize her children, as the culture around her was brutal to anyone who was different. Acceptance in her own community was important to Ruby and she had tried her best to conform to the codes of conduct. She, however, had little control over the discrimination she and her children faced like many immigrants around her—which to her dismay continues even in the present time in some form or another.

Ruby didn't want to understand gayism, or lesbian preferences. People in her orbit labeled homosexuality as immoral, condemned by religion—there was hardly any informed discussion about this topic. It was an uncomfortable issue and so shunned or ignored. Ruby craved to be accepted—among her mosque, temple and church going friends. So her children could not afford to deviate in any way. She wanted them to have heterosexual unions, houses full of kids to carry on with the family name as dictated by the Bengalee tradition. She never had any Jewish friends but knew that the synagogue denounces homosexuality.

Opshora recognizes that Ruby isn't a narrow-minded person or a bad mother. Her family is important to Ruby above everything. She wants to protect them at any cost. Ruby left her parents and brothers and friends and relatives and the tiny town where she lived till eighteen to create a life in the U.S. Leila was the only family here. Being cut off from her known world, the intense isolation in an alien culture while trying to blend into her new homeland, influenced her stand on many issues. Separation from her mother and loved ones created an incurable, everlasting emotional starvation in Ruby. It followed her throughout her life—made her vulnerable. So when she became a mother all she could think of was to be in the lives of her children, be there for them and keep them safe from any kind of harm. The community she belongs to in the U.S. though multi-cultural is mostly comprised of immigrants like herself who have suffered from similar dilemmas and have fiercely tried to remain true to the traditions they brought from their birth places—the benchmark of societal morality. They constantly struggle to engrain into their children their heritage, at the same time allowing them to embrace the society they are born into in the U.S. Ruby's psychological journey has made her complex. Opshora understands it but still has difficulty in dealing with Ruby's worldviews. Every time she has an emotional clash with her mother, she promises to retrace her steps to find common ground. But the tussles continue . . . the crevasse between them widens.

Opshora wakes up to a beautiful sunny day after a night of snowfall. The sunlight pierces through every pore of the white cottony fluffiness that has gathered around the backyards, evergreen pines, brown-bare branches, the sidewalks, the rooftops as far as the eyes can capture. The early morning's miserly warmth fails to defeat the iciness that lingers strong and alert, filling up the crooks and corners. The whiff of coffee and the sounds of giggles grow stronger prompting her to venture out of bed. Leila extends her a mug of freshly brewed coffee. The children jump over her bed almost at the risk of spilling the hot drink. Leila pulls the curtains aside and the brilliance of the sun crashes in, unabashed.

Since morning Ruby has been laboring in the kitchen. Everyone's favorite is on the menu. Chicken roast, lamb korma, baked salmon in tom yam sauce, Pilau rice, stir fried vegetables, Russian salad, freshly baked French bread, three kinds of cheese—all lined up for the Christmas brunch. Caramel pudding and strawberries with ice cream are for dessert, her grandchildren's "love-food." She likes to serve a robust meal.

In the Bengalee tradition, food is central to all celebrations. With great care she stirs the lamb over the leaping flames. A sudden ache tears through her as she remembers Antonio's advice—to cook with love and the taste is bound to be *perfezionare*—perfect! She had seen sparks in Opshora's eyes every time he looked at her, and she couldn't help notice the way he wore his heart on his sleeve for her daughter. But even then things went all wrong. Though relieved, she can't banish some sadness at the failed relationship. She was doubtful at the time but somehow wanted to believe it would work.

Ruby turns around at the sound of Leila's footsteps. "I wish he was here today beside Opshora. Sometimes I think I am too narrow-minded. I care more for societal acceptance . . . than happiness," Ruby utters in despair. "I am so confused . . . what do I want and what I don't? Why isn't she destined to be happy?"

"That's how it is meant to be, Ruby, I guess . . . I wish I knew the answer. I wish I could say there is a reason for things to happen," Leila responds. "Opshora is happy in her own way, though."

Ruby's eyes are fixed on the cauldron of lamb korma now simmering on the stovetop as her mind races with sad thoughts.

"I can't break the riddle," Leila says gently.

"He is a Catholic," Ruby speaks after several seconds of silence, both sisters lost in their own worlds. "Maybe it's good they broke up. Too much difference . . . " she halts, reaffirming her justification.

"What's religion when two people in love do not see it as an obstacle?" Leila has always curbed her own culture's influence in defining who she is.

Ruby almost agrees with Leila. She lives in a universe of contradictions, not always sure what should be the right choice. "I wish Maa was still alive. I could get some guidance from her on how to be a good mother. I think I have failed Opshora."

"You are a great mother, Ruby. You have brought up two extraordinary human beings. You have fought to make yourself belong in an alien culture . . . after all these years, you keep MD Mirza's smile ever present." Leila is genuine. "I wish we didn't have to steal you away from the family like we did."

"No *apa!* I don't blame you at all. And neither should you. I met MD Mirza because I came here. You created my life for me . . . my happiness. I wouldn't have wanted anyone but him," Ruby smiles kindly at her sister. The sounds of laughter and voices from the dining room invade the kitchen.

Ruby stirs the vegetables with undivided attention, her mind caught up in the past, searching for her frailties that might have influenced Opshora's behaviors, modeling her daughter's life or fate.

Opshora in many ways inherited more of Leila's stands than Ruby's. Till today it remains a faint bone of contention between the sisters. Opshora runs to Leila for guidance or to discuss her problems. She never seeks her own mother's assistance. Ruby wanted to see Opshora mirror her. The more she tried, the further she drove Opshora away—to embrace her aunt's ways more and more. It pains Ruby, always.

"She went for a Fijian man. Then there was a Japanese . . . now an Italian. I wish she had tried to find a good Muslim man from our Bengalee culture," Ruby sighs. Opshora is on her mind. Opshora's lonely life especially during these happy times of festivities and family occasions saddens Ruby.

"Religion is a very personal thing. It's immoral to drag it into the public arena," Leila adds. Her position is clear.

"You think inter-faith marriages can succeed? When do you decide what faith your kids should follow?" Ruby voices her doubts once again.

"Ruby, Christianity, Islam, Buddhism, Judaism, Hinduism . . . all these faiths are meant to be followed as a way of life, not to be a measurement stick—one faith is not greater or lesser than another. Bastardization of faith, religion, is happening to reap personal benefits. Politics of self-interest is the motto these days," Leila says patiently, in a more understanding tone. Words form in her mind that she can't verbalize—*which planet are you from, Ruby?* She loves her sister but sometimes feels burdened by Ruby's biases.

Ruby has been torn on faith-related debates, on the pros and cons of conforming to one's religion. She tried to make her children understand the religion they were born into, embrace it as true believers. She has taken them to the mosque on Fridays and Eid prayers; she didn't forget to attend religious ceremonies herself, especially funerals and sacred events. But she has never vilified other faiths though she strongly considers conforming to a common faith is a binding force in a marriage and creates harmony. She has never quite agreed with Leila's relaxed definition of religion.

"You know apa, when Opshora came back from Fiji I wanted to hold her, wanted to talk to her . . . her eyes were burning with anger . . . broken in grief," Ruby says again softly as if speaking to herself. "I couldn't simply bring up the loss of the baby with her. I was afraid of her sorrow—so immense, so heart wrecking."

Leila understands what Ruby is saying. Opshora refused to open up to her as well. She kept waiting with the hope that one day Opshora would be able to master her pains and reach out. She never did. Never talked about her miscarriage . . .

Chris and Toby arrive exactly on time. Chris is extremely punctual, always. The pair get out of their car with a bouquet of white lilies and a large cheesecake with strawberry topping, Christmas gifts in colorful wraps, and wearing huge, brilliant smiles. Opshora immediately falls in love with Toby, a six foot three, large-framed, pleasant guy. She submits defenselessly to Toby's bear hug. After the preliminary introductions are over, they crowd into the family living room around the Christmas tree. With help from Maya and Leila, the kids have decorated the plastic tree. Opshora is against buying a real Christmas tree. She believes loving trees is much more in the spirit of Christmas and the environment than chopping down live treetops for the occasion. So, Ruby keeps this plastic replica bought from Wal-Mart decades ago, stored in the basement. It's brought out every Christmas and redecorated. Coffee and snacks are passed around as everyone comfortably settles down.

"What do you make of him?" Chris asks Opshora after the meal while Toby is engrossed in discussions with Leila, Ruby and the men. Toby has an easy, comfortable way of engaging with others that she finds refreshing. He is much older than Chris unlike his former boyfriends.

"Chris, I believe he is the one. Hold on to him."

"I think so too. I am tired of loneliness, betrayals . . . and heartbreaks. I don't think I can do that anymore. Like me, Toby has gone through his share of rough times." His eyes shine with a hint of either muted tears or intense bliss. Opshora can't define it. She hugs Chris. With all her heart she wishes Toby is permanent, the happiness they share keeps on radiating in their lives.

Toby works at a bank as his day job. In the evenings, he

plays music at a gay bar and café in downtown D.C. Like many, he had tremendous difficulties in finding himself, accepting his true identity and coming out. For years he believed something was wrong with him and was afraid to listen to his inner voice. He dated girls as a suppressant to his pent-up emotions, and didn't have the courage to fight back the normalcy thrown at him by the society he grew up in. To make things worse, his dad, as a pastor, had always been a strong advocate of the conversion theory or therapy for the "derailed" souls about whom he regularly preached from the pulpit among his church parishioners. So, Toby got married in his thirties to banish the demons of his desires and tried to blend in. The marriage was a disaster from the beginning and it fell through after a few months but he had to hang in there as his wife of six months, Caroline, was pregnant. He couldn't tell her who he was, couldn't abandon her and waited till she gave birth.

He named his daughter Lulu. He looked up the meaning of the name—*an amazing girl, beautiful in every way, independent, caring; her eyes can light up any dark day, she will never forget you.* Lulu is the spark in his life, the incessant joy, indisputably sacred, very precious.

When Lulu was five, he and Caroline broke up. Toby had to confess to Caroline about his homosexual thoughts—the desire to live a free life. The divorce was amicable and he agreed to Caroline's conditions. But she is stingy regarding his blocks of time with Lulu, allowing him to be a father for only limited blocks of time. She couldn't forgive him for deceiving her, for the humiliation he caused. She didn't understand his desire to come out and disrupt the world around him. For Lulu's sake she decided to be civil. Toby agreed to every rule she had set up—the least he could do for hurting her. He pays alimony and avoided going to court for custody or to figure out his financial responsibilities.

Toby understood Lulu needed a stable home, and an

enabling environment to grow. Caroline was the best option for her. With him, there was little hope, and fiercer battles to fight against being ostracized or labeled as a freak. Living with a gay father could be a bloodier uphill path for a girl to fit into her own domain. He didn't want that for his daughter. He had taken enough bullets throughout his life for being himself.

Toby explored different relationships after he separated with Caroline, went through a phase of doubts and low self-esteem. He tried to be discreet and live as a gay person at the same time. It was difficult. Finally, he accepted who he was and came out to a wider circle of people he knew and was instantly disowned by his family. His father forbade his siblings to be in contact with him. So Toby drifted away further and further from home, from his loved ones and cruised through years of emotional turmoil, self-reflections, self-reproaches and sometimes some blissful experiences. Whatever difficulties he had, he maintained a stable connection with Lulu. He is grateful to Caroline for allowing him to be a father to his daughter. At fifty plus years, he finally has found Chris . . . in ten minutes Chris shares Toby's entire life's journey with Opshora.

"How are you?" Chris waits earnestly for an answer. Opshora looks away.

"I am getting there. I like my job, living in Port Jefferson, I guess. Too early to form a solid reaction," there is slight hesitation in her voice. "But I have to make this work, Chris. This is my life now. I can't keep floating." They sit in silence, comfortable to have each other as close buddies.

"I know I shouldn't tell you this . . . Maria and her mother came to the store for Christmas shopping. I recognized them from the photo I saw online from your cookbook launch. But they didn't know me of course," he speaks after some time, looks apologetic for passing on the information. "The girl looked happy."

"I have outgrown that phase of my life . . . mostly, Chris." Opshora responds with forced calmness but he can hear the sound of hurt in her mirthless voice. The ache is still there no matter how guarded she is, how well she tries to camouflage it.

"Can't believe I haven't seen you for so long! 2017 will be over by next week!" Chris changes the subject.

Opshora feels guilty for not having invited Chris even once to her new home. He has no complaints against her, too busy to notice. Because he is happy—he has got Toby now!

"Her braces are gone . . . she has beautiful teeth, really!" he adds after a brief pause, still thinking of Maria. He can't back off . . . has to tell Opshora. Both laugh at that and break away from the discomfiture.

"How do you know she wore braces?"

"I guessed . . . and I wanted to make you laugh, bestie," Chris puts his arms around Opshora. She has grown thinner. He can almost feel her shoulder blades under her sweater.

"I have missed you bad," is all she is able to say in a choked voice.

After coffee and dessert are served they gather around the Christmas tree to open gifts. Children are spoiled with electronic toys, digital games and books. Opshora's gifts for her mother and aunt are identical woolen shawls she picked from a quaint store in Port Jefferson. For her father she brought a signed copy of her book, *Fiji: A Lost Paradise in the Sapphire Horizon*. In addition to the charms of Fiji and its rich cultural heritage, Opshora has highlighted the political and racial disharmony in her book.

"This was long in the waiting," Opshora's smile is laced with apology.

"It was worth the wait. And it's signed by the author!" Her father smiles back as he flips through the pages, his eyes proudly lingering on her signature.

Maya and Robin get premium tickets for the Broadway

show "School of Rock" that they were planning to watch for months. In their busy work schedules and parenting routine it's not easy for them to get away to such exclusive escapades.

"I checked your schedules with your assistants before buying the tickets . . . and I am volunteering to babysit on the show night. An extended part of the package deal. If you want to spend the night in Manhattan and return the next day, my services are further offered," Opshora declares amidst roars of laughter and hugs.

"For you," they hand over her gift. It's a check for three thousand dollars. Their card says: "Take a break."

"We rummaged our brains . . . to give you something meaningful and so we decided, you must get away for a while. Go mountain climbing, or diving or on a spiritual quest in a remote island," Maya says.

"Opps, you can go scuba diving in the Maldives. The beaches have white sand and the water is sparkling. Can I come with you? It's good to have a man around in a foreign country," Liam throws in with hope in his tone.

"Silly! It's for her alone. It's her break." He gets a shove from his sister and hearty laughter from the adults in response.

"I would want no one as my bodyguard and guardian angel other than you . . . if I ever decide on the proposed scuba diving," Opshora draws her nephew close in her arms. He is embarrassed at the attention he gets, trying to understand the adults' reaction to his sincere proposition. In his geography class he has been studying about different cultures and countries. He knows about Opshora's stint in Fiji and thought the Maldives would make her happy.

Opshora's parents give her a bedside hand-woven Tibetan rug to take back to Port Jefferson. From Leila she gets a pair of lapis and pearl studded silver earrings. Chris and Toby get a hand-crafted ceramic kettle with four matching mugs from the entire family. More gifts are passed around amidst fun and laughter and murmurs.

"I have something for each of you because you are so unique. And for your generosity in having us over today," Toby says solemnly.

Chris unzips a bag he had carried in, and out comes a beautifully hand painted wooden flute. Toby blows life into the flute with passion, fills the house with magical melodies. He mesmerizes the audience, playing one tune after the other. The music is profound, enthralling, deeply touching. At the end, he plays "Jai Ho" created by India's Oscar-winning composer, A.R Rahman. The applauding continues for over a minute after he bows.

"Amazing! Amazing!" MD Mirza utters, voicing everyone's reaction. Toby encircles Chris in his arms affectionately. Chris continues to beam, proud and in love. Opshora knows this is it. He has finally found Toby. The partner of his dreams!

# CHAPTER TWENTY-FOUR

# On Home Grounds—
# Mist of Coffee on a
# Sparkling Dawn!

The next day while the house is still asleep, Opshora takes a walk to Georgetown. The snow on the sidewalks has melted. Some soft snow still hang on the chasms of bare branches. Her favorite P Street hasn't changed a bit; neither have the houses, narrow cobbled lanes and tiny kiosks along the roadside. She strolls through the streets adorned with barren, dark brown trees robbed of their lusciousness of warmth— her famished glances suck in the known ambience. Though the plants have lost their green to the winter, their naked loveliness has a unique appeal. The leafless branches create their own beauty of loss. How she missed all of this!

The exercise helps her to bear the cold better. Luckily, there is no wind. She stops to rest at Lamont Park, around 16th Street. She has wandered for hours, almost over four miles from home. The cool breeze against her flushed cheeks is welcoming as she leans on the back of the wooden bench on the curbside, to rest her tired feet. At home people must be wondering about her whereabouts so she texts Leila. Her absence shouldn't raise unnecessary worries. She decides to give a surprise visit to Chris. The store is open today.

She hesitates before stepping inside Beads and Bracelets. The store looks exactly as she left it months ago. Chris isn't at the store yet. Maybe he overslept or is taking a half day off. He didn't tell her, though. Opshora introduces herself to the girl working in the store.

"I have heard so much about you from Chris! I am Cara," the new manager welcomes her and extends her hand with a bubbly smile. She grasps Opshora's hand in a firm, friendly grip.

"What a beautiful name!"

"My mom visited Rome in her youth. It's Italian and Cornish in origin—means beloved," Cara smiles again. The smile reaches her eyes giving them brilliance.

She inspects the new additions to the merchandise, Cara following at her heels. The semiprecious stone beads, hand crafted exclusive jewelry made of Paula shells, clay, stone and wood artifacts dazzle on the shelves. There is a collection of exquisite raw silk bedspreads and quilts piled up in one corner, some on display. The entire lot has been imported mainly from Asia. The store's sales have doubled since last year. Good that they found Cara.

"We also have a new supply of Native American charms and ornaments. You know, I found out they began jewelry making about 12,000 years ago—they have a way with turquoise. Come this way, I will show you," Cara uses her saleswoman's voice. Opshora skims through the display, gently touches a semiprecious stone-studded pendant.

"Native American artists and jewelers are inspired by their surroundings and culture. The butterfly is a common theme— it's an image of transformation, a messenger from the spirit world. A snake is a positive symbol representing healing, re-birth and good luck," Opshora says smiling at a bemused Cara.

"You will see plentiful use of both butterfly and snake motifs in Native American ornaments . . . they have a mastery with beads and seashells and stones," Opshora adds as she looks closely at the designs.

"Wow!" is all Cara can say.

Opshora decides to wait for Chris. He will possibly be in the store by lunchtime. They could have a bite somewhere close by if he is up to it, laugh over popular gossip, talk a bit more about his love life. She doesn't have much to offer about hers. She hasn't dated anyone after she walked away from Antonio.

Chris has been giving her tips on romantic wizardry but she had brushed it off, so far. She looks around the store holding much affection in her heart for the place they built together, years ago, step-by-step.

On New Year's Eve Robin takes everyone out to dinner at a Thai restaurant. The family has carefully avoided any Italian eatery though they all love Italian food. They order basil, shrimp fried rice with added tofu, whole fish in lemon garlic sauce, chicken cooked in green curry paste and coconut cream—a robust, satisfying meal for everyone. They return home right after dinner to watch the count down on CNN. Both Ruby and Leila are addicted to Anderson Cooper's hosting of the event and have watched it without fail for years. Opshora remembers the times when she used to celebrate New Year's Eve with the older Mirza and the cousins . . . Those were good days, unbridled happy times.

Bella and Liam are allowed to stay up late tonight. Time like this with the entire family is precious. Whenever Robin visits the parents with his family during the winter holidays, Opshora loves to be home, hanging around them. Otherwise on some occasions she spends the New Year's evening with Leila if she isn't on the west coast with her sons for the holiday season. Other times instead of being alone she goes with Chris and his crowd to a gay club or with Tomo and a group of local friends if he happens to be in town. Most from their generation have moved away but usually during the holiday season many come back to be with their families.

She enjoys the drinks, music, dancing and the mayhem that helps her to drown the memories, the temptation to fall into despair trying to dissect the good and the bad that happened to her in the past year and decades before that. Such times bring back memories of Zayn, the dull pain of the baby she lost. She wants to escape from all of that and partying is the best remedy in creating forgetfulness. However, she seldom is absent from the family reunions—the times with Robin, Maya and the kids. These are extraordinary, caring times that she doesn't want to miss at all.

Opshora doesn't have many close female friends any more except for Diana and the friends she made in Fiji. They try to keep in touch. Internet eases the connectivity but they have busy lives with kids and spouses. The time difference especially with Fiji is an additional obstacle. She is now concentrating on building stronger ties with Maya. It's a comfortable relationship with her as Opshora is close to Bella and Liam. They are the bridge between the two adult women.

"Happy 2018!" The family shouts out together. They all hug and kiss and laugh as midnight strikes.

2017 peels off from the calendar. A new year looms ahead—each one on his or her own timeline, to embrace their destiny or dare it . . . forcing changes, or not . . .

Robin with Maya and the kids are scheduled to drive back to Port Jefferson around midday after the new year's excitement has rubbed off over a good night's sleep and rest followed by a hearty lunch spread out by Ruby. She got up early to prepare the meal. Opshora will be staying two more weeks. She plans to take the Amtrak from Union station to New York's Penn Station. Then to Port Jefferson on LIRR trains. She has promised to spend some time at the store to work with Chris and Cara to address some outstanding issues.

But she also intends to spend some of her own time to enjoy her favorite joints in downtown D.C. and Georgetown, and explore the wintry trails before she heads back to work. The long walks through P Street allure her. Winter has its own beauty and D.C. excels in it. A couple of nights at Leila's are also in her plans.

After the goodbyes, Opshora braces herself for a long evening touring around Dupont Circle. She feels like a tourist in her hometown though she was away for only a few months. The Red Line is on schedule, so the metro is the best option to D.C. Her father has gone out to meet friends. He practices part time these days—only twice a week. At eighty-six he is still very fit and looks ten years younger than his actual age. Ruby is back to her convenience store. Opshora plans to kill the evening with class and style, finishing it with the taste of a lovely dinner at the Kramers bookstore "Afterwords Café" like the old times followed by several solid hours of skimming through new arrivals on the bookshelves—a post dinner respite. If the weather permits she could even wander around Connecticut Avenue. It's fascinating under the intense night sky. She could either take the metro back home or hop into an UberPool ride. The comforts of a cosmopolitan life in a big city!

Opshora invites Leila to join her at dinner but Leila prefers to be in the safe warmth of the house. Arthritis in her knees behaves badly in the cold so Opshora is all by herself to face the upcoming evening.

Both the cafe and the Kramers bookstore are crowded tonight. She is lucky to get a corner table within ten minutes of waiting. She orders a glass of Merlot and her favorite blackened salmon fillet—Cajun-spiced with braised beans, sweet corn succotash, hot pepper jam and chimichurri. It's a house specialty culinary creation. The space around her is jam-packed with voices, unabashed laughter, a vibrancy of colors and unknown faces. Best place to be your own self, unpretentious and of course gluttonous, forced to simply enjoy the life contained in such special moments of existence. She begins to unwind. "Ahh . . . it's so good to be back! In 2018!" she whispers to herself. She didn't need to. The murmurs and laughter around her have consumed the silence weaving a symphony of cheerfulness.

It's almost ten when she finally drags herself towards the bookshelves. The new arrivals are interesting, some are intriguing, enticing—others offer mundane flavors. She really gets turned on by the smell of newly published books, it captivates the brain cells and awakens the spirit; of course the holes it makes in the purse is a serious matter. Every day new authors surface. There is so much in this universe to write about. She is completely lost, exploring the pages—and doesn't remember how long she has been standing in this corner of the store, engrossed in a book she discovered quite by accident. As she maneuvers through the lines, she travels to an unknown land, cruises in different time zones with people from another era . . . At that point she is forced to acknowledge the gentle signals of fatigue from her overexerted back—a soft kind of ache flows from the knees upwards to the torso. A reality sign of mature years. She resigns to it and begins to return to the present. That's when she also becomes conscious of him . . .

She looks up. Antonio is right there four or five feet away leaning against a bookshelf, staring directly at her, measuring her up. What is he doing here at this time of the night—the first thought that invades her brain. He should be dazzling in his kitchen on a night like this. He looks thinner, not much changed otherwise; hair slightly tousled as always, eyes somewhat troubled . . . in a blue shirt faintly wrinkled—wearing his heartwarming smile. It creates a sudden ache inside her. They meet face to face, finally. In a shock she realizes she broke up with him a year ago.

"Ciao," she speaks first. In an instant he is beside her in two giant steps and grasps her hands.

"Ciao . . . *Tesoro!*" his voice is charged with emotion. Opshora doesn't try to disentangle her hands.

"How are you, Antonio?" she says, rather.

"Why do you want to know? What do you care?" he replies in a low, deliberate manner. She doesn't respond, just returns his look, troubled now.

"You are a coward, *signorina*," he throws at her. He can't control himself anymore, no matter how hard he tries. There is suppressed rage in his voice, passive aggression.

She doesn't know why she expected to find him exactly where she left him in their relationship.

Opshora feels stressed. His tone changes abruptly—he adds softly, "You just took off when life got harder."

"What do you mean?" Opshora is taken aback.

"You couldn't face me, hid from truth. You couldn't tell me to my face . . . you broke up with me in a letter, Opshora!"

"That was the best option. For both of us, at the time," Opshora tries to defend her action.

"No, no, no . . . Maybe for you. You had no right to decide for me! Is this a common practice with you, *professore*? To run away?" His eyes bear down into her, piercing her with a strange force. There is so much intense emotion in them. She is unable to decode it. "You were so callous, heartless! You didn't care."

She flinches involuntarily as the vehemence in his accusations hit her. His naked hurt he lays out for her to see. She has broken him no doubt but she has been suffering, too. She stands still in front of him, perplexed not knowing what to do next. What could take away the pain? At her horror, she finds tears welling up in her eyes, uncontrollably. She turns around and abruptly hurries out of the store. She doesn't want him to see her misery, not anymore.

On her way out she pushes through the crowd that has gathered around the counter somewhat blocking the entrance. She continues shoving away whoever is in her way. People have lined up to buy some new bestsellers, or something. She doesn't care. She has to get out, run far, far away, fast. Once out of the door, she exhales vigorously; the overpowering tears now begin to stream down her cheeks, falling down on her bosom with a waterfall velocity. The brutal cold hits her. She has left her overcoat behind in the store, slumped against the corner of the shelf where she was reading. The frostiness bites through her but she is too consumed in her pain to notice.

She keeps walking faster and faster, away from the store, reckless in her wandering. She stops at the signal, and waits to cross the street. Traffic is rare but she still stops out of habit and also to catch her breath. Someone taps on her shoulder and she turns around. Antonio has followed her. He has her coat. He gently helps her in it. He sees her tears now. She is caught red handed, ashamed of her weakness, humiliation born out of teardrops.

"*Tesoro* . . ." He puts his arms around her and together they cross the street as the signal changes.

"Don't cry. Please. Please . . . I am so sorry to have hurt you," he says with deepest solemnity. Through the thickness of the coat she almost feels the warmth of his body, slightly brushing against her. Opshora halts for a moment and then breaks into fresh tears, her body heaves with the intensity of her anguish, shaking uncontrollably. Her heart seems to break in pent-up pains.

Antonio takes her in his arms and lets her cry, her face buried in his chest. He can almost hear her heartbeats racing rapidly. They stand motionless as the few passersby fade away in the distance. People are going home as the cold swallows the night. The air infused with the blinking rays of streetlights form a halo of fierce iciness, and nestles down on the barren lanes crisscrossed around them. He gives her his handkerchief. He is from an older age. Very few carry cotton handkerchiefs these days, is all Opshora can think of at that instant. She tries to wipe away her hurt, the damage of the tears.

"Let's go," he says now.

"Where to?" There is a slight tremor in her voice dwarfed by the deep sigh that escapes her.

"Come with me," his hands firmly on her shoulder, he leads.

She doesn't have any will power left to protest or inquire further. Together they walk through the freezing cold, under the stark sky breaking with stars, among leafless trees and near empty streets waltzing with the silent night.

"Come, let's go up," he says after endless steps they have walked on the semi-dark streets.

"It's a gay bar," Opshora's voice holds mammoth calmness, not a single trace of surprise.

"I live upstairs."

"Over a gay bar?" Strains of music and murmurs of voices mingled with the aroma of cigars and wine and life spill out through the doors, intoxicating and pleasant . . . and engulfs them.

"I moved out. Had issues with the landlord. Didn't want to live there anymore . . . Wanted some distance from the restaurant in my spare time, as well."

"I loved your old apartment, though," Opshora manages to say, almost in a raspy whisper.

They climb the narrow stairs together. He still has his arms around her so they have to take each step slowly, with careful precision, as he tries to adjust his body by turning slightly towards her to fit into the space on the scanty staircase.

The apartment is more spacious than his previous one. He releases her to switch on the tall table lamp in the corner. The sudden light takes away the frozen darkness of the room. The heating is welcoming, embracing them in a sunny comfort. All his furniture and rugs are here. The plants in the pots are in robust health; some rebel, creeping branches hugged by the windowsills are busy scrambling towards the sunlight. Specks of colors from careless blossoms have broken out through barricades of green. The low dining table aligned with two facing wooden stools have also made their way into his new residence. A faint residue of mixed scents from downstairs invades the place. He takes her coat and then they sit on the sofa, face to face. He brushes away a stray eyelash from her cheek imprisoned in the soft dampness of a near-dry teardrop. She grasps his hands in hers and keeps holding. Their gazes lock. They look straight into the others' eyes, hands entwined.

"I didn't know any other way . . . " she starts to speak.

"So you ran away? Again?" he interrupts her. His voice doesn't hold the taste of bitterness anymore.

"It was too much . . . Maria, Ashley . . . I couldn't fit in. I tried and tried and kept failing and failing..." He listens intently. "Isabella..." He smiles now at the mention of his mother.

"I took care of her . . . rented my place above a gay bar, see?" He winks. They both laugh out loud, and keep on laughing. The sound of their laughter melts the iciness; a whiff of fresh, clear air washes away some of the awkwardness, the twinges of pain.

"She is a devout Catholic. She has totally made herself scarce. Doesn't come here to snoop into my life, control me." They laugh again.

"It's heartless, Antonio. She cares for you," Opshora's protest is genuine.

"She cares too much. I know she will never forgive me but I had to get away. From my family . . . their smothering, interfering cares." He is straightforward.

He tells her that Maria is doing okay, has accepted responsibility for her share of trouble making and now is trying to make amends by focusing on her studies. Ashley though unrepentant, has agreed to the family's decree to establish more parental control with care for Maria's well being. She made a commitment to inform Isabella whenever she needed support and to drop off Maria at her grandparents' if she has to go out of town or plans to stay the night with her date. The mechanic in Maria's life is a thing of the past. Alberto and Carlo took care of that.

"They threatened the mechanic?" Opshora asks though she already knows the answer.

"Some of my dad's relatives through marriage lines still have connections with Sicily. Our Mr. Mechanic was informed regarding their notoriety. That's all. He chose to be smart. Just vanished." Antonio flashes his smile, amusement riding into his eyes.

He makes coffee. The aroma of freshly brewing coffee spirals through the apartment, subduing some of the tangs from the gay bar. She is thankful for the moment, to get another chance to be with Antonio, to right all the mistakes. They sip their drinks, each deep in thoughts.

"You know, a week before you abruptly left me, I was thinking of proposing to you. I know you are still afraid of tying the knot . . ." Antonio sighs.

"Oh, Antonio! I can't agree to marriage . . . couldn't have. You know that. I harbor too much sorrow. I am afraid it's bound to stain whatever happiness may come my way. I am jinxed." Opshora sighs as well. They sit in silence. Then she speaks again. "I thought I was losing you. I wasn't sure if you wanted me anymore."

"Tesoro, I never wanted anyone more, ever. The time I was with you was the happiest in my life. When I declared my love for you at the cottage, I meant every word. But you were hesitant. I understood and was waiting for you to come around. I almost proposed to you there but stopped," he explains. "I planned the vacation with that purpose in my mind—to test you, actually. You were not ready."

"I am so, so broken, Antonio!" The tears fall again. His

heart breaks in tenderness as he looks at her face, painted with sadness, distant.

"Oh, I have made you cry again!" He gently wipes her tears away. "Opshora, look at me. I am here . . . I never stopped loving you. I was waiting for you. I will always be with you if you let me," he whispers, holds her tight. "I was too busy, too flustered at the time we were together. I wish I had taken more care to preserve what I had."

"You know . . . at one point I felt old. Ashley is so beautiful . . . so much younger." Opshora almost speaks to herself, finally admits her emotional insecurity. She is relieved after having voiced it to Antonio. It has bothered her no end all this while.

"Tesoro, when I look at you, I see only an amazing, beautiful person . . . very extraordinarily weird, if I think hard," he laughs. "You are the bowl of pot to my druggie heart." Opshora launches a teasing punch to his chest. "I fell out of love with Ashley a long time ago."

They continue to talk. He tells her that after she left, his life had become empty, flavorless—very mechanical without her. "I cooked and cooked . . . cooked away my life. Nothing tasted good. And I complained . . . and behaved badly with the kitchen crew. I still trouble them," Antonio confesses. His voice calms her inner turmoil. Resting her head against him feels good. She is glad she found him at the bookstore.

"I am so sorry I wasn't there for you—though I was aware of the constant aggression from mamma, Maria and Ashley," he declares with sincerity. "I thought ignoring the negativities and problems would make them go away. . . I expected them to wear out, eventually. Actually, I didn't know how to handle them. I was weak. I was scared."

"Rosa accepted me as a friend, though. So did her kids, and the other three men," Opshora adds with some sadness. She wishes she were not resisted so much. "If only I were given a chance for your sake. Isabella, Maria and Ashley broke my confidence with their hostility."

The three Russo women's aggression was often buried in small gestures, a glance or words but sometimes also quite blatant, exposed in a cruel way. "They made me feel  lesser, clumsy . . . unsophisticated," Opshora is honest.

"I allowed them to hurt you. I am so sorry," Antonio reasserts. His failure to diffuse the angst embedded in his family dynamics ultimately created savage cracks in his own relationship with Opshora. He paid quite a heavy price.

"I sent you a note . . . with the pastries delivered at your store. You didn't see that? It was inside. I thought you would understand the cues about my feelings for you."

"Nope. I was so angry. I trashed it." Opshora is truthful. "What did you write?"

"Oh, *tesoro,* you threw out my labor of love! You are impossible, always!" Antonio teases. "It was sort of a cross between an apology and a love letter, very economical."

"Miser! Calculative!" Opshora laughs. Antonio joins her. They talk a bit more. The night ages as the icy wind blows outside on the silent streets.

"Do you want me to take you home? You are welcome to stay over. I still have my old shirt you prefer to wear at night. Stay?" He doesn't want to pressure her into anything but he doesn't want to let her go out of his life again, either. He has missed her, he has longed for her on lonely endless nights, happy days when he created miracles in the kitchen . . . but was often sad when he couldn't share the triumphs with her.

Opshora agrees to stay. She wants his nearness more than anything in the world right now. Nothing else matters. It's too late to disturb Leila, so she texts her father but doesn't disclose anything about Antonio. He may think she is crashing at Chris' place. She doesn't want anyone to worry. Ruby may conjure up fantasies but she decides to live with that.

Later, they cuddle in the bed, lying side-by-side drawing comfort from the warmth of their familiarity.

"You don't have to agree to marry me. Just don't leave me, again," he whispers. "We can think of other possibilities for a shared life, more permanent, with a total commitment to be happy. We don't need documentation."

"I have to go back to Stony Brook, you know that," Opshora states, clear-cut. He nods cradling her head on his shoulder.

"But you can join me there," Opshora adds emphatically. She is all fired up now. She is ready to put up a fight to keep him in her life.

"You mean leave Pasta Paradiso?" Antonio is surprised.

"You can open a branch in Port Jefferson. It's a heartwarming place. You always talked about starting your own eatery."

"Port Jefferson . . . it's a great idea. Yes, I want to get out of here. Start afresh. I want you in my life, above all," he whispers again, kissing her neck, inhaling the scent of her tousled hair. Determination is very obvious in his tone. They talk about the possibilities in Port Jefferson.

"I don't want to lose you, either, not anymore, Antonio," Opshora whispers, eyes heavy with sleep.

"You know we must actually thank Maria for our reunion. I went to Kramers to get a book she wanted," Antonio confides. "At the end, she became the catalyst . . ."

Listening to each other's quiet breathing and the steady beatings of their hearts they fall asleep. It has been an extremely exhausting encounter.

It snows more while they sleep. The brilliance of the sun rays covering a translucent blanket of whiteness is almost blinding as they peek outside through the window holding their coffee mugs in the morning. Opshora is glad that she is there, right beside him and it's not a dream. She smiles to catch his eyes to make sure last night was real; the promises made etched in heartaches are still true. She feels loved, content, finally after years and years of emotional aimless floating through time. Zayn seems another existence, though the love for him remains buried in today's happiness . . .

On that icy, exotic morning, Opshora steps out on the street. The gay bar and Antonio's residence fall behind as do the Starbucks, the Pho Asian restaurant and the cheerful crowds that stomp ahead across the narrow vibrant alley. She keeps walking, with a smile, sparks in her eyes drowning the vibrant sunlight dancing on the snow.

# PART V.
## PORT JEFFERSON,
## SUMMER 2018

# CHAPTER TWENTY-FIVE

# One Spoon of Lemon Zest, Two Counts of Laughter

Pasta Paradiso in Port Jefferson is a riot of many voices, intoxicated with the aroma of exquisite food specialties. The staff in the kitchen are busy creating an orchestra of culinary magic. Antonio stands on the terrace of the restaurant and looks at the ships sailing on the distant horizon splashed by the incredible turquoise blue waves as he takes a quick cigarette break. He has promised Opshora that he would cut down on cigarettes to only two per day. The stress of over-work, running the operation and frequent management of business-hiccoughs forces him to seek a cigarette now and then. He had opened the restaurant in spring, and now in late summer it's already making headlines.

Marcelo has joined him amidst cold disapproval from Isabella but Antonio made sure the kitchen crew at the D.C. eatery was well equipped before he made the final move. Other than Marcelo, he had left the entire trained team behind. Rosa and Carlo have renewed additional commitments to be vigilant. Alberto and Marco have also stepped in more robustly. In fact, they encouraged Antonio to start afresh at Port Jefferson. It was the right move at the right time. So, "Pasta Paradiso—Port Jefferson" was born five months after he bumped into Opshora on that cold January night of 2018.

Antonio moved here with a clear intention—he wanted a life with Opshora, he wanted to make her happy, he wanted love in his life. He doesn't regret his decision, neither is he apologetic for taking this giant step. This is where he belongs, waking up every morning beside her against the mess of her tangled hair, gorgeous smile, eclectic oddities—she is his life-line in a bizarre, magical way.

Opshora is amazed at the happy closure of her emotionally turbulent times with Antonio. The aches inside have subsided. The memories of the past are kinder on her pains. She doesn't have to banish the past in entirety anymore like she used to. She can now pick the remembrances she wants, especially the fond ones undiluted by sad thoughts. This newfound emotional stability is liberating.

Antonio has moved in with her. They have bought a house together. She is more than sure that her father and Leila have reined in Ruby from offering advice regarding decorum, etc., etc., and her judgmental observations. Opshora can do without it. She knows Robin and Maya have also played a strong hand in reasoning with Ruby to let Opshora lead her own life, and be happy with the choices she has decided to make.

Ruby's concerns and prejudices come from a place of love she has for her daughter, Opshora is aware but she believes that for greater harmony, adjustments are necessary. Ruby finally agrees to abide by this rule and resists trespassing into Opshora's life as prompted by the family. However, she would have liked to see Opshora and Antonio married before moving in together. She genuinely likes Antonio now. And her reservations about inter-racial, inter-faith unions aren't so fanatic anymore. He has managed to change her views with his humor and gentleness and softened her rigid measurement stick of acceptability. Ruby ultimately resigns to the concept of living together as a necessity of modernization, a nonremovable clause of migrating to the U.S., a penalty or a sacrifice at the altar of the American dream, possibly. This is Opshora's country of birth. She doesn't know any other country as her own. Except for the three years in Fiji she hasn't been away anywhere longer than a month. Binding her to archaic cultural norms while she is a mature person is beyond the scope of parental jurisdiction, Ruby now accepts this with great stoicism. Antonio and she often speak on the phone mainly to discuss recipes. He is experimenting with a fusion of Bengalee-Italian dishes and appreciates Ruby's guidance.

Opshora is relieved to find her mother eventually taking a sober step back from her life, and is less critical of her current lifestyle. But she also knows Isabella harbors the same kind of reservations, expectations and desires and has to learn to embrace her son's choice as well. Two mothers from two different cultures are not very dissimilar where their offspring are concerned, even though both Opshora and Antonio are very adult, very mature people.

Opshora has been working hard—practicing to improve her cooking skills, including the lamb korma recipe from her mother.

"*Ama,* I am cooking your lamb korma for dinner tonight. Can you walk me through the steps as I cook?" Opshora admits honestly.

"Nothing to worry about if you follow my recipe. Of course I am here for you." Ruby is taken aback and immensely happy when Opshora shows such an interest. Finally her PhD degree holder daughter needs her help—an extremely gratifying feeling!

"Call me when you begin to cook. We can do it together," she further adds.

"I am nervous, *Ama.* Antonio is a terrific chef," Opshora doesn't feel confident.

"Don't be nervous. It's a Bengalee curry—you have it in your blood. He's Italian, a foreigner. He can't match it," Ruby assures her daughter. Ruby still considers white folks as foreigners in their own country! She makes Opshora smile.

In fact, Opshora calls Ruby several times to perfect the nuances of cooking this special dish. She wants to surprise Antonio, bowl him over on his own home ground of expertise. She doesn't have much claim on his time these days, as he is almost never free. He labors to the extreme, seven days a week to make sure Pasta Paradiso-Port Jefferson soars beyond expectations—the pride he has masterminded to create. But tonight he has promised to eat with her.

Opshora and Antonio are happy though busy. On rare evenings when he makes it home before midnight, with a glass of red wine she loves to stand on the terrace with him. It's bathed by the soft breeze that dances around the landscape in silent suddenness, and bounces back on the waters tracing outlines of the ships cruising on the waves. His nearness is precious, the intimacy very special. She lives for these moments—they fire up her life.

Robin and Maya are engaged in their hectic schedules and parenting. Liam and Bella are regulars at Pasta Paradiso. Antonio is good with kids and both of them are allowed in the kitchen while their orders are prepared. They love to hang around while he cooks. They have learned a few tricks from his kitchen. Whenever they are free they come over to spend time with Opshora. Watching them growing up is a rare stroke of luck—she knows that and is grateful for getting this opportunity.

MD Mirza continues with his part-time practice. He has visited Opshora twice. He and Antonio get into passionate discussions on cricket and football over beer whenever they get a chance. Antonio wishes he had more free time to hang around. Maya jokingly has adopted him as a new family member in MD Mirza's brood. Ruby hasn't been here yet as she is too occupied with her business. She has bought another

7-Eleven in the next neighborhood. Between managing two stores she hardly has a spare moment to do anything else, even her time to rest is restricted.

Chris and Toby are still very much in love. They got married quietly—a destination wedding in the Maldives. They remembered to mail a postcard to Liam from Male (Maaley), the capital, giving him a few details about this amazing island nation. Liam was absolutely charmed to learn that the airport is situated in a separate island from the main capital where their hotel was. Motorboats are the means of transportation from one island to another.

"Cool!" was the only comment he made as he stared at the postcard. Very proudly he showed it around. He earned his friends' respect as he took it to school for all to see.

Chris and Toby are in the process of adopting a baby girl. Opshora is excited for them. They want her to be the godmother. Opshora knows she can't have any children of her own—the ache haunts her still.

"We have Liam and Bella. And of course Maria. How many more do we need, *tesoro?* You will see Maria is going to come around more . . . and you two will end up being great friends." Antonio understands her pain. He held her gently when she broke the news of Chris and Toby's adoption of a baby. "Kids are pain in the ass . . ." he had tried to joke and made her smile despite the aches.

The Beads and Bracelets store is doing extremely well. Toby has taken an early retirement from the bank and joined the store as a full-time manager to take care of new businesses to support Chris; Cara is still with the store but plans to go back to school in the fall. Toby wants to concentrate his full attention to their daughter when the adoption goes through. He spends his time in reorganizing the store's management with his professional wisdom. Caroline has relaxed her grip a bit and allows Lulu to visit Toby more often. It's also because

Lulu at seventeen clearly informed her mom how much she values her father in her life and wants to be with him. So Caroline has been forced to accept the changes.

Leila's arthritis bothers her these days. She is seeing a physiotherapist. Her sons want her to join them in San Francisco and give up the house. She isn't considering a move, yet. This is where she started her life as a young woman with Dr. Mirza, brought up her three sons. D.C. is home to her.

Rosa and Carlo came over with the kids for a visit and to give moral support to Antonio when Pasta Paradiso-Port Jefferson was inaugurated officially. They helped with the opening night, serving food and wine alongside the staff. The children ran errands as well. There was mayhem that night—murmurs and laughter, a crowded floor and servers running around with everlasting, vivacious smiles on their tired faces amidst the steam of delicious aroma oozing out from every corner. The restaurant got excellent reviews and ratings. Alberto called to wish them luck. He calls often and also talks to Opshora. They discuss life in general, philosophy in particular. The relationship between the brothers is gradually improving. It shows possibilities for growth.

The cookbook climbs to a national bestseller's list to Opshora's surprise and horror that she keeps well hidden. She would have liked less association with culinary science though she is immensely proud of the work Antonio does. She considers him the greatest among all chefs.

Isabella hasn't yet reached out but Maria has called and briefly talked to her.

"I . . . I am doing a writing project for my school . . . I am thinking of a visit to Port Jefferson . . . maybe . . . " Maria has expressed with shyness, with some timidity in between her stammers.

"It's a great idea! There is so much history, art and cultural stuff here . . . food for creative thoughts . . . ," Opshora enthusiastically invites her to spend two weeks in late summer. Maria accepts.

"I could help you if you want," Opshora proposes genuinely, glad that the ice between them is melting.

"I would like that," the teenager responds without hesitancy.

Opshora hopes that finally they may have a civil kind of a relationship, and Maria would accept her as her father's partner.

Opshora is aware that Antonio calls his father for advice, now and then. The bond between them never waned. He is hopeful that Isabella is going to come around, one day. Having a better relationship with Maria may influence Isabella to value Opshora's position in her son's life.

For Opshora, the demons of the past are harnessed and the pain is mostly appeased now. She knows Zayn deserves a long-pending explanation that she never provided. In their limited communication in the days before she left Fiji, she didn't totally account for her decisions, neither did she give him an adequate hearing to defend his side. So much between them remained unsaid, shrouded in unspoken hurt. She writes to him after decades. It is challenging; it is emotional as the memories crash in, scrambled with many flavors of pain and laughter. After numerous drafts she finally manages a few decent paragraphs.

*Dear Zayn,*

*I didn't realize it would be so difficult to write to you. And finally I would have the strength after such a long time . . .*

*I remember—everything between us used to be spontaneous before all rusted away . . . when my heart started to break. At the time the pain was too raw, my loss was inconsolable. I was looking to blame someone and I chose you to be the receiver of my punches. My sorrow was so engross-*

*ing that I thought yours was lesser. In my audacity I believed I had the sole right to mourn, and grieve alone. I left you behind.*

*I am writing today—daring to apologize, to seek forgiveness for hurting you. I am so, so sorry!*

*I was numb with anguish and didn't know any other way to recognize your presence than to strike you with fury for 'my' loss, which was our loss, rightfully in essence. I was blinded by grief, overlooked yours. You are not to be accused for the way life took over, designed our fates. This is all I have to say. It has taken me many years to gather the courage finally to reach out to you, as you can see.*

*I am working my way towards peace. I wrestle, even today with the demons of my past. But I know I am now on the right track. I hope with all my heart's desire that you have also found yours. We were meant to meet, destined to fall in love and create our incredible joys and extraordinary sorrows. I am coming to terms with all of that.*

*I wish you all the best that heaven and earth can ever boast of. (Forgive the blasphemy! Never felt at ease with religiosity.)*

*Above all, my love for you lives. I keep it stored safely deep in my heart. All the hurt in the world couldn't 'hurt' it . . . I don't know if our baby was a girl or a boy . . . if the baby had lived, s/he would have been about twenty eight years old now . . .*

*Take care. Would love to get an update of your life if you are up to it. Otherwise, I won't hold it against you.*

*Yours, ever, with love,*

*Opshora*

She sends her letter via registered mail. She wants it to reach Zayn. Without his forgiveness she can't be totally free of the burdens she has been carrying over the years. She waits nervously for a response. Her expectation rises every time she checks the mailbox, skims through the mail. She waits and waits. Zayn doesn't write back. She doesn't have the nerve to track her letter. So far the post office hasn't sent her the receipt from the receiver. Maybe they couldn't find Zayn? He could have moved out of Fiji. She remembers how he spoke about a transfer to the Sydney office, in the past. What if he is based there now? Overseas letters need time, she is aware. As the days drag on, her expectations begin to wear off, get subdued.

"I am glad you are doing this," Antonio had remarked softly kissing her on the forehead when she informed him about the letter. "I am so proud of you—not easy but I believe it needs to be done." Opshora had finally shared most of her Fiji stories with him.

"As long as you don't poke the sushi man, I am okay. Remember, he smells of fish?" he had added as an afterthought to lighten the situation. Opshora had pushed him away, laughing.

Before heading out to the restaurant Antonio brings the mail in while Opshora is at work. Some Tuesdays he lazes a bit longer in the mornings at home, takes a half day off, drinks a few more extra cups of espresso to boost him for the hard work ahead. He spends a bit of his time caring for the plants, watering, pruning. Opshora likes them to grow totally wild, clamber all over the place, undisciplined. At the risk of her disapproval, he usually tidies up the plants. She gets disturbed by symmetry, order, but in the culinary world measurements and regimentation have meanings, essential for creation. Born out of rules, the equilibrium is reached and magic happens.

Opshora has to run inside the house in the light drizzle as she gets out of the Uber. She couldn't walk back home today because the sky has been weepy since midday. Antonio takes the car to the restaurant. They still use the borrowed car from Robin and Maya. They gave it to Opshora.

"As your dowry from us," Maya has told Antonio jokingly. "In our culture the bride is given something valuable in cash or kind to take to her new home. It's called dowry . . . So don't worry about the car."

In the horizon there is a glow, which means a promise of a break from the rain. The sun is possibly getting ready to appear in the next hour or so. With her hands still covered in gentle raindrops she casually fingers through the mail laid aside on the dining table by Antonio. He has also bought a box of scented candles she loves and left it beside the mail.

Then she sees it. There! She recognizes Zayn's sprawling neat handwriting on the envelope addressed to her. She stands there, motionless. Her mind travels in a flash to the day, years ago when she received an envelope from him, the last time. It was her divorce letter—thunderstruck she had stood in the middle of the room cradling the letter to her breaking heart. She knew it was bound to happen eventually but when she received the legal document, surprisingly she wasn't ready. Severance from Zayn was excruciating. It shattered her world. Somehow she had believed he wouldn't be so prompt. He would hold on to the thin thread that still existed between them. It hurt her. The life she knew with him crumbled in an instant, leaving her with only dejection and a stabbing pain. She went into a deep, dark depression for years and years.

With trembling, discordant fingers she opens the letter. On white, flawless paper Zayn's lines dance in front of her eyes. She takes to the sofa to read.

*Bula Opshora,* (No endearments, only normal courtesy she notices, crestfallen. He used to call her by so many delightful names!)

*What a surprise! Almost after more than two decades! I had given up all hopes of any contacts with you, ever ... and then suddenly you pop up. It's bizarre, but pleasant. You were always unpredictable, strange in a very sweet kind of way, if my memories of you are still accurate! I must admit truthfully my heart leapt in joy when I opened your letter. I read and re read it many times—you can't even guess. I didn't know how to react. I was happy one moment and the next I wept, and then due to sheer exhaustion borne out of my emotions, I distanced myself from you. But I know you mean every word. I am so, so glad you wrote, finally. You have freed me from my pains.*

*I googled you (never thought of doing so in all the years since you left me). You are all over the Internet. Still very beautiful! Exactly the way I remember you—want to remember you. So much happened but the spark in your eyes remains— fiery, impossible.*

*I could give the entire world even today to understand the mystery in your smile . . . it bewitched me in my younger days. Your magic still works—across oceans, through the Internet, and the words laid down in the letter. Believe me!*

*I was angry when you suffered alone, when you left me in one blind corner of your life when all the changes were happening. I was miserable because I couldn't communicate with you— make you understand my love for you, and the pain I carried at our loss . . . of the baby and the life we wanted together. I wish I had tried harder to understand you, to force you to see me, somehow. I was there beside you all the time for you to notice me. I was young—we were young and we made mistakes. I will leave it at that.*

*Let me give you a quick update (you deserve to know this). I am now heading my travel agency and fly often to Sydney and Europe to oversee the branch offices. I married Christine. It was destined though I stopped seeing her totally after you left. When we were married, I never cheated on you with her. At the time my heart had no space to love anyone but you. You have to take my word for it.*

*I drifted away from Christine for three years after we said goodbye but she didn't give up. We reunited and dated for another three years before I decided to make a commitment. We tied the knot, eventually. We fell into the rhythms of marriage, learnt the ups and downs but by then we were mature enough to settle our differences through dialogues. We made up our minds very early that we wanted to stay together, no matter how challenging it was going to be. Do I love her? This is something I don't want to dig into—neither does she. We are happy together and that's what matters now. Love is not always the prerequisite to happiness.*

*We have two amazing daughters. We became parents after a decade in our marriage. I was afraid . . . pregnancy ruined my chances with you. But the second time I was lucky. The older daughter is named Lily. She is a wonderful, sober girl and makes sensible choices like her mother. Our younger one is called Malaika. It means angel in the Swahili language. Malaika reminds me of you—free spirited, beautiful, impulsive and extraordinarily impossible. I have taught her to ride the wild waves.*

*My mother passed away eight years ago. I should have informed you. She loved you, in her own way. I know you cared for her deeply, as well. She was angry and hurt because you were stubborn in your decision to leave Fiji. But I believe that's how it was meant to be. She led a full life, was happy with all of us at the end.*

*By the way, Antonio seems to be nice. I like the way his arm is over your shoulder in the photograph taken at the entrance of your restaurant—it came up as I searched. I feel he loves you. I can hear the sounds of laughter in your eyes. You look happy with him—always so gorgeous!*

*I wish you all the joy and peace. I am proud of you. I am*

*reading your book on Fiji. I can relate so much with your every word.*

*I never stopped loving you. By the way—the baby was a girl. You were so distraught that your doctor advised us to tell you later and we didn't for some reason . . . will you ever be able to forgive me for that?*

*Zayn*

*P.S.—enclosing a recent photo of the family. You will not find us on Google.*

Opshora reads the letter many times, like Zayn did with hers. She feels his words caressing her, unlocking her troubles, calming the sorrows that she held in her heart for so many years. She knows though she is in love with Antonio, her love for Zayn will always be there, an engulfing warmth of comfort. One part of her life, a portion of her heart, will always belong to him even if their paths never cross again.

She picks up the photograph. Christine looks surprisingly young, very much like the time she knew her. Silvery streaks in her jet-black hair stand out; the lines around her mouth expose gentle age marks. Zayn is slightly heavier than she remembers, with the hairline somewhat receding but the charm in his eyes and smile still so pleasant, heartwarming. The cowry necklace peeks out from beneath the shirt collar. He looks attractive in the casual bula shirt and sulu reminding her of the man she fell in love with at first sight. Lily takes after Salote. Malaika is stunning—a halo of dark, wavy hair cascades around her face. She doesn't take after anyone except she has her father's eyes laced with flashing vivacity. She could have been hers, and Zayn's—she could be the baby Opshora lost . . .

The phone rings. It's Antonio. He calls to remind her of the dinner he is cooking for her. He wants her to be with him while he cooks. "It is a special dish . . . I created exclusively for you, tesoro! I am almost ready to cook the best cauliflower steak for you . . . an alternative to beefsteak and I have eggplant manicotti with risotto to go with Brunello di Montalcino!" She smiles as she listens to Antonio's enthusiastic, cheerful tone. "I am waiting. All ingredients are prepared. You said you want to see me cook, righto?"

"Absolutely righto," Opshora agrees with equal eagerness.

"After dinner we can hang out at the dock . . . feed the sea gulls. Whatever you want." Antonio knows about her love for the water.

"What about your kitchen? Customers? They will miss you, signor!" Opshora teases.

"Marcelo can have them . . . this evening is only for you. I dedicate it to you, bellissima. Now hurry. My patience is running thin."

The clouds begin to move away further and further, pushed away by the sun beginning to emerge—shy at first, floating in a soft glow and then steady as Opshora sits on the terrace watching the waves and the skyline. The same waters must be touching the sapphire blue of the waves she rode in Fiji, steadied by Zayn's strong arms around her, tons and tons of waters away. The thought doesn't bring back the old aches anymore, just a hint of nostalgia. She decides to leave the house right away. She wants to tell Antonio about Zayn's letter—about her daughter who died before she lived!

A mile down the street, on a grassy mound close to the harbor stands Pasta Paradiso facing the bay. Antonio is waiting for her. Hurriedly she walks across the street, through the intersection, and under the lines of tall evergreen pines . . . the roads lead her to Antonio.

*The End*

Antonio's
Dream Dinner Recipes
for Opshora

## *Best Cauliflower Steak*

*Ingredients:*

2 heads of cauliflower, stem trimmed, cut vertically into four
    1½-inch planks
Salt
Freshly ground black pepper
¼ c. extra-virgin olive oil, plus more for brushing: 3 tsp.
Fresh lemon juice
½ tsp. garlic powder
1 c. pitted Castelvetrano olives
⅓ c. roughly chopped toasted almonds
1 stalk celery, finely diced
3 tbsp. minced red onion
1 tbsp. roughly chopped fresh parsley leaves
1 very thinly sliced roasted red pepper

*Directions for cooking:*

1.  Preheat a grill or grill pan over medium-high heat and
    lightly oil grate. Brush cauliflower steaks with olive oil.
    Season with salt and pepper (according to taste).

2.  Grill steaks, until tender and charred in places, about
    4 minutes per side.

3.  In a medium bowl, whisk together olive oil, lemon juice
    (add according to taste), and garlic powder. Tear olives
    into pieces and add into bowl along with almonds,
    celery, onion, parsley, and roasted pepper. Stir and then
    season with salt and pepper.

4.  Spoon olive mixture over cauliflower.

5.  Serve and enjoy!

# *Eggplant Manicotti*

*Ingredients:*

2 medium eggplants
Salt
2½ tbsp. extra-virgin olive oil
2 c. ricotta
½ c. sour cream
⅓ c. freshly grated Parmesan
¼ c. torn basil leaves
2 tbsp. freshly chopped parsley, plus more for garnish
Zest of ½ lemon
Freshly ground black pepper
Pinch crushed red pepper flakes
2 c. marinara
1 c. shredded mozzarella

*Directions for cooking:*

1.  Preheat oven to 400°. Lay eggplant slices on a paper towel-lined baking sheet. Sprinkle with salt (according to taste) and let sit for 15 minutes to draw out moisture.

2.  Pat eggplant slices dry with paper towels. Transfer eggplant to a large baking sheet. Drizzle eggplant with oil, bake until is pliable, 8 to10 minutes.

3.  In a medium bowl, combine ricotta, sour cream, Parmesan, basil, parsley, and lemon zest. Season with salt, pepper, and red pepper flakes (according to taste).

4.  While the eggplant is still warm, but cool enough to handle, spread about 1 tablespoon of filling onto each eggplant slice and roll up tightly.

5.  Add a thin layer of marinara to a 9 x 13-inch baking pan. Place rolled eggplants into pan, seam side down, fitting tightly as needed. Spoon remaining marinara over eggplant and sprinkle with mozzarella.

6.  Bake until eggplant is tender and cheese is melted–about 20 minutes.

7.  Garnish with more parsley

8.  Serve and relish!

## Risotto

*Ingredients:*

3½–4 c. vegetable broth (warmed on the stovetop, store-bought)
2 tbsp. water (or oil), divided
1 small bundle asparagus (ends trimmed or 1 small bundle broccolini, stalks trimmed or sliced button mushrooms
1 medium red bell pepper (seeds + stem removed, thinly sliced)
¼ tsp. each sea salt and black pepper
¾ c. thinly sliced shallot
1 c. Arborio rice
¼ c. dry white wine (or sub more vegetable broth)
½ c. Parmesan (plus more for serving)
Optional (for serving): Fresh chopped parsley

*Directions for cooking:*

1.  In a medium saucepan, heat vegetable broth over medium heat. Once simmering, reduce heat to low to keep warm.

2. Heat a large pan over medium heat. Once hot, add half of the water (or oil) and the asparagus (and/or broccolini or mushrooms) and the red bell pepper. Season with a pinch each salt and pepper and sauté until just tender and slightly browned (for 3–4 minutes), stirring frequently. Cover to steam and speed cooking time. Remove from pan, uncover, and set aside.

3. Heat another large rimmed pan over medium heat. Once hot, add remaining water (or oil) and shallot. Sauté for 1–2 minutes or until softened and very slightly browned.

4. Add Arborio rice and cook for 1 minute, stirring occasionally. Then add dry white wine (or more vegetable broth) and stir gently. Cook for 1–2 minutes or until the liquid is absorbed.

5. Using a ladle, add warmed vegetable broth ½ cup (120 ml) at a time, stirring almost constantly, giving the risotto little breaks to come back to a simmer. The heat should be medium, and there should always be a slight simmer. You want the mixture to be cooking but not boiling or it will get gummy and cook too fast.

6. Continue to add vegetable broth 1 ladle at a time, stirring constantly, until the rice is cooked through but not mushy. This whole process should take about 15–20 minutes (may take longer if making a larger batch).

7. Once the rice is cooked through, remove from heat and season with salt and pepper according to taste. Add Parmesan cheese and most of the cooked vegetables, reserving a few for serving. Stir to coat.

8. Taste and adjust flavor as needed, adding a pinch of salt and pepper to taste or more Parmesan to enhance the cheesiness.

9. To serve, divide between serving bowls and top with remaining vegetables, additional Parmesan cheese, and a sprinkle of parsley (optional).

10. Serve while warm and relish!

# Acknowledgments

As I was churning out the chapters, I shared the very first unedited drafts with my childhood best friend, Nasrin Murshed Ava. She read them diligently and her advice was to make a happy ending—I was unsure about it at the initial stages of crafting the book. I listened to her. I can't thank her enough for her undying encouragement and faith in me.

My special thanks to my niece, Rubayat Khan who was the next reviewer of my book and provided valuable feedback.

I had in-depth discussions with a number of immigrant-Americans from different cultures, upbringings, backgrounds and generations. I tried honestly to capture their views, feelings, struggles, and joys—of becoming Americans—by birth and through naturalization. They have made the book more meaningful and relevant.

From the core of my heart I thank Natasha Chisty, Nadiah Khan, Adrika Lazarus, Jenita Arshad, Syed Shabab Wahid, Tasmia Rahman, Tony Abato (late), Shailaja Maru, Gugan Ravi, Enna Zhang and many like them who allowed me to become a part of their stories. I am ever grateful to them for their courage and sincerity.

Jennifer Hager, my content editor has been a great source of inspiration. We constantly communicated on emails, long phone calls to discuss the book. We laughed, analyzed, shared stories, differed and agreed on many aspects of the various versions of the drafts. Her thorough guidance, understanding and care have given it an extra edge. My sincere thanks are to her.

I thank Sara DeHaan for her openness in letting me work with her on the cover design. I also thank her for the brilliant work she did in designing the book. She has special talents!

My thanks to my proofreader Varsana Tikovsky who worked on the draft with care.

Finally, I thank all well-wishers who encouraged me everyday in my literary pursuits, especially, Fatema Sultana Sharmin, Najma Hasib, Mansur Hasib, Sajjad Hossain Mozammel, Lazeena-Muna Mcquay, Shabnam Khan and Taslima Lazarus.

# About the Author

Nuzhat Shahzadi is a creative writer. She is a Bengalee American—grew up in East Bengal, initially a part of Pakistan that emerged as an independent sovereign nation, as Bangladesh in 1971 following a violent civil war. In her adolescence she got a first hand taste of living through a horrific genocide.

She authored and co-authored numerous entertainment-education materials and directed animation films on social issues honing the power of story telling to influence behavior. Her work with the United Nations took her to the heart of unchartered territories marred with armed conflicts in Asia and Africa—from the war torn landscape of Afghanistan, Sri Lanka, Nepal to the shores of Angola, Côte d'Ivoire...the slopes of Rwanda, Uganda and Mozambique that borne the scars of civil wars. She travelled extensively to many other regions that offered her the opportunity to work closely with the most marginalized grass roots communities.

In 2004–2005, Shahzadi took a break from the UN to head an HIV/AIDS project with the Johns Hopkins University/Center for Communication Programs, Baltimore. During this time she lived in "Little Italy" in downtown Baltimore and made friends with Italian-Americans. On rejoining the UN, she worked closely with Italian NGOs and the NATO contingent of Italian forces in Herat, Western Afghanistan on child protection issues. She got interested in the history of the Italians—and years later decided to write this book.

Shahzadi holds two post graduate degrees: a Masters in Public Health, and an MA in English literature. At present she lives in greater Washington D.C. area in the US.